The Woman in the Wood

LESLEY PEARSE

PENGUIN BOOKS

PENGUIN BOOKS

UK | USA | Canada | Ireland | Australia
India | New Zealand | South Africa

Penguin Books is part of the Penguin Random House group of companies
whose addresses can be found at global.penguinrandomhouse.com

First published by Michael Joseph 2017
Published in Penguin Books 2018

001

Set in 13.5/16 pt Garamond MT Std
Typeset by Jouve (UK), Milton Keynes
Printed in Great Britain by Clays Ltd, Elcograf S.p.A

A CIP catalogue record for this book is available from the British Library

ISBN: 978-1-405-95141-8

www.greenpenguin.co.uk

Penguin Random House is committed to a
sustainable future for our business, our readers
and our planet. This book is made from Forest
Stewardship Council® certified paper.

To my beautiful new granddaughter,
Alicia Rose McDonald, born 30 December 2016,
a little sister for Harley and Sienna.

I

West London, 1960

Maisy was woken by a piercing scream. Startled, she sat up in bed, assuming the sound was coming from the street. But then she heard the cry for a second time and realized it was coming from inside the house. It was her mother.

She rushed to her bedroom door and out on to the landing, then paused when she heard her father's voice travelling up from the floor below.

'Be quiet, Lily. You'll wake the twins and frighten them. I'm doing this for your own good.'

Maisy's twin brother Duncan came out of his room and joined her at the top of the stairs. 'What's going on?' he whispered.

Maisy put a finger to her lips to silence him and held his arm so he wouldn't run down the stairs. Their father, Alastair Mitcham, was a stern man who didn't take kindly to any interference.

'I don't want to go there! I'll get better here in my own home,' Lily Mitcham cried out. 'Don't make me go, Alastair!'

The pitiful pleading brought tears to both Maisy and Duncan's eyes, but they were only fifteen and a little afraid of their father, and they simply didn't know what to do.

'How many times have I tried to get professional help

for you? Each time you act the same way,' Alastair said, and the children heard the weariness and resignation in his voice and exchanged anxious looks. 'You aren't getting better; year by year you get worse. When did you last agree to go out of the house? I think that was two summers ago. You haven't even been downstairs for over a year.'

'But my back and legs . . .' she protested.

Alastair cut her short. 'There is nothing wrong with your back *or* legs, and well you know it. You can't hide behind a riding accident from some twelve years ago any longer. I'm sick of this, Lily. The only way I know to get you to face up to what really ails you is to take you to this place. Now, calm down, or I'll get the nurse who's waiting outside in the ambulance to come in and give you a shot of something.'

Maisy had heard enough. Despite her fear of her father and reluctance to drag her brother into trouble with her, she caught hold of his hand and pulled him to the stairs. Encouraged by her bravery, Duncan didn't try to pull back.

'Why are you sending Mother away?' Maisy asked when she was just a few steps above the first-floor landing.

Her father wheeled round. He was fully dressed in a suit and clearly hadn't heard them coming on their bare feet.

'This is nothing to do with you,' he snapped. 'Get back to bed, both of you.'

'She's our mother, so it has everything to do with us,' Maisy retorted. 'Where are you sending her? And why in the middle of the night? So the neighbours won't know? Or did you hope we wouldn't wake and you could make out she'd gone to stay with a relative for a holiday?'

It was the first time Maisy had ever stood up to her father. While he wasn't a violent man, he was so stern and forbidding that she and Duncan always did as he said. Her heart was racing and she was trembling, but even so she was determined to stick up for her mother.

'Don't let him send me away to an asylum,' their mother whimpered. 'It's cruel and horrible. I want to stay here.'

Shocked as she was to hear of her father's plans, when Maisy looked at her mother she realized why he was resorting to such drastic measures. Since she hadn't seen her mother's face clearly for many weeks, she hadn't been aware how much worse she had become. Her eyes were almost popping out of her head, and she was now so thin that the yellowish skin on her face appeared to be stretched over her cheekbones, with blue veins standing out on her forehead like thick crayon marks. Her brown hair was lank and greasy and her nightgown was very grubby. It was absolutely clear she needed help.

Right from when they were small children the twins had grown used to their mother being in bed most of the time. They had always been taken to school by someone else and she never took them for a day at the seaside, a picnic or even a visit to a park. It was all they knew and so they had accepted her claim that it was due to a riding accident.

'Father, don't do this,' Duncan said.

Still holding their mother's arm tightly, he turned to face them. 'I have to. She is ill. I never wanted you to know this, but she has been steadily getting worse and I'm afraid of what she will do. Just a few days ago she tried to drink some poison. Thankfully, Betty caught her just as she was about to swallow it and saved her life. But it doesn't bear thinking about what might have happened.'

Their mother tried to escape from her husband's grip, the expression on her face like a savage animal, teeth bared. Maisy instinctively took a step back, and Duncan took her hand.

'OK, Father,' he said, looking fearfully at his mother. 'But shall I go out and ask the nurse to come in to help?'

'Thank you, son, that would be best. Maisy, will you get your mother's dressing gown and slippers? She was struggling too much for me to hold them.'

A few minutes later the twins watched as the stout, middle-aged nurse, who had been waiting outside in the private ambulance, injected their mother with a sedative.

The effect was almost instantaneous. Lily stopped struggling and relaxed, and a vacant look came to her face. Alastair helped his wife into her dressing gown and put the slippers on her feet. 'That's better,' he said, kissing her cheek, a gesture that reassured the twins he really did have their mother's best interests at heart. 'Now, children, why don't you say goodbye to your mother and go back to bed? Whatever she may have said, she will be looked after properly, I assure you. It's a private home offering the best care available. Now I'm going to follow the ambulance in my car, and it will probably be a few hours before I get back. But don't worry, Betty will be in at breakfast time as usual.'

They watched from the sitting room window as the nurse helped their mother into the back of the ambulance. Their father started up his car and waited for the ambulance to move.

For a moment the twins said nothing, just stood at the window in the dark room like two statues.

Although no one had ever said openly that their mother was mentally ill, of late the twins had suspected there was something more to her mysterious illness than a riding accident from long ago. Everything about their home was different to other people's. Their parents slept in separate rooms, their mother had all her meals in hers, and sometimes they heard the sound of breaking plates and shouting. Betty the housekeeper always claimed their mother had dropped something, just as she always covered any strange noises by saying it was because she was in pain. Now it was all falling into place.

'That was horrible,' Duncan said eventually, his voice trembling. 'Not just for Mother, but for Father too. Still, I'm sure it's for the best. Shall we make some hot milk and then go back to bed? It's only half past two.'

'I never knew she was that bad,' Maisy said as they went down to the kitchen. 'I mean, I know she's always been poorly and a bit strange too, but I never thought she was . . .' She paused.

'Mad?' Duncan said. 'Neither did I, but then we've never known any different, have we? I'm sure they'll make her better; everything will be all right.'

Maisy poured some milk into a saucepan and lit the gas under it. Her brother was always the optimistic one, she thought to herself. She tended to be the opposite.

They looked alike, inasmuch as both had thick blond hair and deep blue eyes. But Duncan was taller than her, probably five feet six, while she was five three. He had a square face and a strong jaw, while Maisy's face was heart-shaped, with a dimple in her chin. She tanned easily to a golden brown while her brother was prone to freckles.

Their large, semi-detached home was in London's Holland Park. It had four floors, including the basement. It had last been decorated in Edwardian times, and though it must have been lovely then, it had grown very shabby over the years, and after the war decorating materials were hard to come by. Betty had told Maisy she'd overheard their father saying he wanted to sell it as it was too big and expensive to run. Betty thought it would be best converted into flats as so many other big houses in the area had been. The housekeeper had an opinion about everything, including that their mother was an attention seeker.

Because of the way things were at home, neither Duncan nor Maisy ever attempted to bring school friends back. They knew it would be embarrassing with a mother in bed all the time and a father who, when he was there, shut himself up in his study. Consequently they rarely got invited to anyone else's home. Their world was a very small one. A private school just the other side of the park, visits to the library and an occasional treat of the cinema. Fortunately they were close friends, and didn't think they needed anyone else.

They just had one close relative, Violet Mitcham, their paternal grandmother. She was a widow and lived in the New Forest, and she was as chilly as her only son. She only came to London to see them all once every couple of years. According to Betty she had never approved of Lily because she was so 'weak'.

The twins had very good memories of Grandmother Goldney, Lily's mother. They had been born in January

6

1945 in her house in Tenterden in Kent, where their mother had been living on and off for much of the war. Betty came from the town as well, and when they all returned to their London home Betty came with them as housekeeper. They went back to Tenterden for a month every August, but when they were eight Grandmother Goldie, as they had called her, died of pneumonia.

Their father had worked for the Foreign Office all his life. It was a reserved occupation during the war, so he didn't have to join up, but it took him away from home a great deal, which was why their mother spent so much time in Kent and the twins were born there. He never talked about what his job entailed, and though Duncan liked to pretend he was a spy, Betty pooh-poohed that notion and said he just did clerical work.

'What will happen now, do you suppose?' Duncan asked, bringing Maisy back to the present by pointing to the milk which was almost boiling. 'Do you think we'll just carry on the same?'

'Why would it be any different?' Maisy asked. She didn't want to be mean about their mother, but it wasn't as if she had ever done anything for them. 'For weeks now she's been asleep every time we went into her room. Looking back, I wonder if she was pretending to sleep because she didn't want to talk to us.'

'But why? And if it's true, how do you suppose she got like that?'

'I think if I was married to a man like Father I'd hide away,' Maisy said, semi-seriously. 'Let's face it, he's no fun. Have you ever heard him laugh? Whistle a tune, dance, crack a joke?'

'Now you mention it, I haven't. But let's go back to bed now. We've still got to go to school tomorrow.'

'Why don't we play truant for once?' Maisy suggested. 'We could go up to the West End and look in the shops, even go to the pictures in the afternoon to see something Father wouldn't approve of.'

'He said he was coming back here after taking Mother to that place. He might not go to work afterwards. I don't think we'd better.'

Maisy pouted. 'You're such a goody-goody. Watch out or you might end up like him.'

'So he actually took her to that place, then?' Betty said at breakfast later that morning. The twins hadn't needed to tell her; Father had left her a note explaining. 'I've been telling him for months that she needed real help, but he wouldn't listen until that business with the poison.'

The twins had mixed views on Betty. She was an attractive woman in her early forties with rich auburn hair and a voluptuous figure. She had a clear complexion and not even a trace of wrinkles around her eyes. As she'd been a big part of their lives since as far back as they could remember, they saw her like an aunt rather than a housekeeper, but in the last couple of years they had got the idea she saw herself as mistress of the house. She took liberties. They'd seen her wearing clothes that belonged to their mother, she ordered Maisy and Duncan about as if she were one of their parents, and she was far too familiar with their father. It crossed Maisy's mind she might have designs on him and that was why she seemed pleased he'd finally put their mother in this home, but she wasn't going to tell Duncan what she thought. It would upset him.

Still, she couldn't resist a sly dig at Betty. 'You'll have a lot less to do now, won't you? Though judging by the state Mother was in earlier today, maybe you haven't been checking on her much lately?'

'You cheeky little baggage,' Betty retorted. 'This is a big house to look after, and just cooking and doing the washing and ironing for you two kids and Mr Mitcham is a full-time job. I can't force your mother to eat or wash herself and change her nightdress. You have no idea how difficult she can be.'

'Then it's as well she's gone somewhere where the staff are used to such problems,' Maisy said airily. 'By the way, isn't that one of Mother's cardigans you're wearing?'

She left the kitchen without waiting for Betty's reply. She thought she would mention it to her father in the evening. He must have gone straight to his office that morning as he hadn't been home. But first she thought she'd just nip upstairs and have one more go at persuading Duncan to play truant today.

In the days that followed, everything seemed slightly off centre to the twins. There was a calmer atmosphere and Father was more attentive to them, inasmuch as he quizzed them daily about their schoolwork. Betty was more cheerful, making them special meals and not complaining about anything for a change. But it was worrying, as if something bad was expected any day.

On the Friday afternoon two weeks later, the twins arrived home from school to find their father already there, talking on the telephone in his study, two suitcases standing in the hall.

'Yes, they're here now. We'll leave just as soon as they've changed out of their school uniforms and had some tea. I should be there by eight at the latest,' they heard him say.

Next week was the start of the Easter holidays, and they looked at one another in surprise. It seemed their father was taking them away somewhere.

He put down the receiver and came out into the hall. 'I expect you heard what I was saying on the telephone. I'm taking you down to Nightingales and you need to get a move on. Go to it.'

The twins didn't rush. They weren't thrilled to be going to Nightingales, Grandmother Mitcham's home. Maisy and Duncan hadn't been there since they were five or six, and the only image of it which had stayed in their minds was of the grumpy old lady who didn't really want to see them.

'It might be better now we're older,' said Duncan, ever the optimist.

'Pigs might fly,' Maisy said. 'Why two suitcases, though, if we're only going for a short visit?'

'Perhaps it's forever,' Duncan said and grinned maliciously.

It wasn't until they were in the back of the car and out of London that their father spoke to them again.

'I have decided that you must stay with your grandmother on a semi-permanent basis. I'm not impressed with your school in Holland Park, so I plan to find somewhere better local to your grandmother. That will take a little time, so for now you'll be having a holiday. On top of the question of your education, I'm thinking of selling the house and buying something smaller. If I can find the right school with good teachers, you two will go on to university.'

The twins exchanged horrified glances. It sounded as if they were being shipped off in the same way as their mother.

'I'm aware my mother isn't used to children, and maybe you think this will be awful for you,' he added, his voice softer now, as if he'd picked up on their horror. 'But it won't be. You'll be in the care of Janice the housekeeper, who I assure you is a good, kind woman. Also, Nightingales is beautiful and you'll be able to explore the New Forest and meet other young people. I think you can be very much happier there than you have been in London.'

When the twins didn't respond, he spoke again. 'I know it was a nasty shock about your mother and now this is a second one. But I really am trying to do the best for you, so please give it a try.'

'Yes, Father,' the twins said dutifully in unison, without conviction.

It began to rain soon after that and the sky grew dark. The twins dozed a little and only woke up properly when the car bumped on uneven ground. It was too dark to see where they were.

'Are we there?' Duncan asked.

'Yes, this is the lane to your grandmother's house. It's high time it was asphalted. There's no street light either.'

The car headlights picked up the sign 'Nightingales' on a wooden gate set in a picket fence. Some twenty or thirty yards back from the gate was the house, but all they could see of it in the dark was a well-lit porch and the two windows on either side.

'Well, here we are,' Father said. 'Now don't mind your grandmother if she's a bit brusque. And be polite, please, and do as you're told.'

Maisy's first impression as they were ushered by her father into a large, comfortable sitting room was that her grandmother was very rude. There was no attempt to get out of her chair to greet them, or to give them a smile, or even request that they come nearer so she could see them better. Maisy knew from Betty she was only seventy, not a great age which might excuse her. She was well dressed in a dusky pink knitted two-piece with pearls at her neck.

'Well, Mother, I expect you'll find them very much grown up since you last saw them?' Father said.

Maisy looked at him, surprised by his almost fawning tone.

'Oh Alastair, children do grow, that's expected,' she said. 'I hope you've warned them that I will not stand for any insolence, mischief or noise. They will eat in the kitchen with Janice, and only come in here when I summon them.'

Maisy's heart sank. She glanced at Duncan and saw that he looked equally dismayed.

The old lady picked up a small handbell and rang it. Within seconds a brown-haired woman of about forty with a pleasant, open face came in and beamed at the children.

'Bring tea for myself and my son, Janice,' Grandmother

said. 'Take the children with you, give them some supper and show them to their rooms.'

Janice looked enquiringly at their father. 'Would you like a sandwich, soup or some cold cuts, Mr Mitcham? You've had a long drive and as I understand it you're going back tonight?'

'Yes, I am, Janice. A sandwich would be most appreciated, and a piece of your memorable fruit cake too, if there is any.'

'I made one just yesterday,' she smiled. 'A ham sandwich?'

He nodded, then moved towards the children, patting each of them awkwardly on the shoulder. 'I'll say goodbye now. Be good for Grandmother and write to me each week.'

Janice led the twins out across the wide, flagstoned hall, past a huge, ancient trunk carved of dark wood and a grandfather clock with a very loud tick.

'Wait till it chimes,' Janice said with a little chuckle. 'Enough to make you jump out of your skin.'

'Don't you remember the house?' she asked as they went into the kitchen at the back of the house. 'I know you were only about six when you last came, but children usually remember something.'

'I seem to remember a pond with goldfish,' Duncan said.

Janice smiled. 'Well, you're right about that. I expect you'll remember the garden when you see it again – on your last visit you were out there most of the time.'

The scrubbed wooden table in the middle of the room

was already laid for supper, the fruit cake on one plate, a Victoria sandwich on another. 'I whipped the sponge up when I heard you were coming,' Janice said. 'Not all children like fruit cake.'

'We eat anything,' Duncan said. 'Betty our housekeeper says we're human dustbins.'

Janice laughed and reached out to pat his cheek affectionately. 'I'm liking you both already. Now, I thought a bowl of vegetable soup first, so sit down, and while you eat it I'll make the tea for Mrs Mitcham and your father.'

They heard him leave about an hour later. He didn't come into the kitchen to say goodbye, and a few minutes later they heard Grandmother go up the front stairs to bed.

But Janice's warmth and jollity more than made up for being ignored. After delicious soup, ham sandwiches and cake, she took them up the back stairs just off the kitchen and showed them their rooms.

They were both a bit shabby. Janice said that during the war various officers had come to stay there, but the twins weren't bothered by that. They were just delighted to know that they were sleeping at the opposite end of the house to Grandmother, and that they had their own staircase so they never needed to go anywhere near the old lady.

Janice claimed she wasn't as fierce and cold as she liked to make out, and that she'd actually said, 'It might be nice to have children in the house to brighten it up.' However, Maisy suspected she'd made that bit up to be kind. But both she and Duncan really liked Janice. She had a gentle, motherly quality about her, she laughed easily and she seemed genuinely pleased to have them to take care of.

'I love to cook but it's not much fun for just one elderly lady who eats like a bird,' she said. 'When old Mr Mitcham was alive he was poorly and needed a great deal of help – sometimes I never got a moment to myself – but since then I've had too much time on my hands and it gets a bit boring.'

She told them there were a couple of bicycles in the shed and she would get Mr Pike the gardener to clean them up so they could use them. They could catch a bus to Lyndhurst, or further afield to Southampton or Bournemouth if they wanted to, and she was sure some of the young people in the village would want to make friends with them.

'We've even got a real live witch in the village,' she said. 'She's called Sybil Leek. She's really famous cos she writes books about witchcraft, and she's on the wireless too. You'll see her when you go into Burley – she walks about in a long black cloak with a jackdaw called Hotfoot Jackson on her shoulder.'

The twins stared open-mouthed in astonishment. Janice laughed. 'It's true. I'm not making it up, I promise. I think there's something about the forest that attracts odd people. Actually, there's another woman who there are dozens of stories about, much more fascinating than the ones about Sybil. She's called Grace Deville and she lives in a very remote spot in a little shack. You'll hear people refer to her as the "Woman in the Wood". She always wears men's trousers and she doesn't like visitors. When people stumble upon her place by accident, she sees them off with her shotgun. The things they say about her! Everything from being mad to killing her own baby and poisoning people. It's probably all rumour. But then people don't like Sybil much, either, because she attracts weird, witch-loving people to the village.'

'Oh my goodness,' Maisy gasped. 'To think we thought all the drama happened in London!'

'Tomorrow you can start checking it all out,' Janice said. 'Now, it's time you went to bed. I've put hot-water bottles in them.' She kissed them both on the cheeks. 'Sleep tight.'

2

Duncan braked so hard his bicycle spun on the dusty forest footpath. 'I think that might be it,' he yelled back to Maisy, pointing to a plume of smoke rising above the trees. 'Janice said she had a fire going constantly.'

They had been at Nightingales just over a week now, and despite their grandmother's obvious lack of interest in them, the twins were surprised to find that they were really quite happy to be there. They had already spied on the witch Sybil Leek, seeing her out walking with her pet jackdaw, and had peered through her windows to check if she had a cauldron and spell books. Now they wanted to see Grace Deville, the Woman in the Wood. As Mr Pike the gardener had only this morning finished fixing up the bikes, this was the first time they were able to come this far into the forest.

Maisy braked and jumped off her bike. 'It could just be a woodcutter's fire,' she said, looking at the smoke reflectively. 'But let's go and look anyway.'

They hesitated. The path towards the smoke was little more than an animal track. It certainly wouldn't be possible to ride down; it was so overgrown it would be difficult even to push their bikes along it. But, as Londoners, they were nervous about leaving their bikes on the path. Back home you didn't leave your belongings anywhere in case they were stolen.

'I think they'll be all right left here,' Duncan said. 'We

haven't seen one person since we left Burley, and who would come into a forest to look for something to steal?'

Maisy propped her bike against a tree and swished her plaits back over her shoulder. She felt good today. Janice had remarked on how pretty she was over breakfast. As no one had ever said this to her before, Maisy wasn't inclined to believe it. But it still felt nice to be told.

'What if this woman really is totally mad?' she asked her brother. 'Remember what Janice said – she might come charging at us with her shotgun. She must be tough if she's lived out here alone for years.'

Duncan bent over to examine his grazed knee. The previous day he'd fallen over and since then he'd been complaining bitterly that he was still expected to wear grey flannel shorts. Long trousers were only for wearing to church or other formal occasions.

'She can't be mad or even a witch if she wears men's trousers,' he said with an exasperated tone. 'Trousers are sensible out here. Besides, why would she attack us if we don't threaten her in any way?'

'Well, even our own parents don't like us much,' Maisy said. 'So maybe there really is something horrid about us.'

'Don't be ridiculous.' Duncan sniffed disdainfully. 'We weren't sent here because they didn't like us, as you very well know. It was only because Father . . .' He paused, not knowing how to explain the reason.

'Cos Father wants to sell the house, have a fling with Betty and doesn't want us around?' Maisy suggested.

'That wasn't what I was trying to say; you always have to be so dramatic. Anyway, I'm glad to be here. I like it.'

'I like it too, but I just wish Father and Grandmother

could talk to us properly about what's happened and why. We aren't babies. When I tried to explain that to Grandmother she said, "Children should be seen and not heard, but in my opinion it's preferable they aren't seen either." She also said that Father had informed her that this was the right place for us to be and the asylum was the right place for Mother, and that she wanted no further questions on either subject.'

Duncan seemed happy enough to be told what was what, with no explanation as to why, but Maisy wasn't. She wanted to know why her father didn't want to spend any time with his children, and why the only form of communication he seemed capable of was a question and answer system. What position did they hold in class? Which of the classics were they reading? Could they tell him the capital of Brazil/Albania/Venezuela, or some other, even more obscure country?

She wondered if he had a friend at work, someone he chatted normally to, perhaps had lunch or a drink with. But if he had it was never mentioned. For as long as she could remember, when he wasn't away on business he left home for his office in Whitehall at precisely eight thirty each morning, and walked up to Notting Hill Gate to catch the tube to Westminster. He always wore a pinstriped navy suit and bowler hat and carried a furled umbrella, just like thousands of other businessmen. When he'd gone away for his work he had never warned them he was going, or even told them where he'd been when he came home. The only way the twins had ever known he was going away was when he took a small suitcase with him.

It wasn't as if they could ever ask their mother about

anything – she was always too poorly, lying back on her pillows with that vacant look they'd become so used to. They had, until recent events, believed it was the after-effects of her long-ago riding accident, though they had speculated that maybe she had some disease too. They were puzzled as to why Betty or their father hardly ever called a doctor to her. Maisy had asked Father once and he'd said it wasn't a child's place to question adults.

At least now she knew what was wrong with her mother, and however bad that was, Maisy felt she and Duncan could cope with it. They had one another, after all, and they had Janice. The housekeeper's interest and loving care more than made up for their frosty, distant grandmother.

'I used to play board games with Alastair when we were young,' she told them one evening. 'When Mrs Mitcham told me you two were coming to stay, I was so excited about seeing you again. Now I'll have to rack my brains to try and remember some little stories about your dad.'

To Maisy the very best thing about coming here to live was walking out into the garden with Duncan on their first morning and seeing Nightingales in all its glory.

It was mellow red brick with triangular eaves at either end of the house, and all the upstairs windows were set into the roof. Not that they could see much of the brick, as the house was almost covered in a profusion of wisteria, honeysuckle and roses. Janice had told them that when they came into flower the scent wafted into all the bedrooms and it looked sensational.

The garden was vast by their London standard, and was mostly well-kept lawns and trees, but Janice had informed them that after the daffodils and tulips ended the borders would be a blaze of colour for the whole summer.

Nightingales was over two hundred years old, and Grandmother's family had lived there for half of that time. They had barely seen their grandmother since they arrived. They heard her playing the piano most days, and sometimes she hobbled around the garden when the sun was shining. But so far, she hadn't summoned them to her sitting room.

They liked having meals with Janice in the kitchen, and in the evenings they played cards with her, read or listened to the wireless. They did wonder how long it would be before they had to go to a local school, but they didn't ask Janice in case she spoke to Grandmother and she interpreted it as them wanting to go home. That was the last thing they wanted.

They felt guilty at admitting to feeling this way even to one another, but back in Holland Park there had always been a tense atmosphere, like something bad might happen at any minute. There had been no escape from it, since they hadn't been allowed to go anywhere after school, and the most they had been allowed at weekends had been an hour's walk.

Betty was mostly grumpy, and Rose the maid and Mrs Gait, who both came in daily to do cleaning and laundry respectively, were too nervous of getting on Betty's wrong side to chat. The freedom of Nightingales felt like paradise.

'What do we say to Grace Deville if she's in?' Maisy asked. 'Could we ask her why she lives out here alone?'

'Don't be silly. She's not going to tell us that.' Duncan

smirked. 'I know Janice said some people believe she's a witch, but even if she is, she's not going to be like the one in *Hansel and Gretel*, putting us in a cage and fattening us up to eat.'

'Yes, but what if she really did kill her baby?'

They had both asked Janice a great many questions about this woman, but disappointingly she either knew little or didn't think it was right to tell them.

'Janice said there was absolutely no proof of that, and it was in her opinion a nasty story spread by mean-spirited and cruel people who had nothing better to do than make things up,' Duncan said loftily. 'Anyway, let's stop talking and creep along silently so we can spy on her.'

It was further than they had expected, at least a mile from where they'd left their bikes. They walked in silence, Duncan in front of Maisy, but they were both flagging and Maisy was about to suggest turning back when suddenly the narrow path came out into a glade.

There in front of them was a shack. Surely it must be the one where Grace Deville lived.

'Whoa,' Duncan said, holding out one arm so his sister didn't blunder on past him. 'Let's hide and watch for a while.'

Maisy was happy to comply. She wasn't keen to go charging in to talk to a woman who by all accounts didn't like people.

The pair of them crawled under a thick bush, lay down on their stomachs and parted the leaves to see.

The shack was prettier than Maisy had expected. It reminded her of the games pavilion at her old school, with a couple of steps leading up to a wooden veranda. It was rather dilapidated – the roof was sagging in the middle, several of the banisters on the veranda were missing, and the paint was peeling off – but there was a big wicker chair with a red cushion and a small table with some books on it, and Maisy thought she'd rather like to live here herself.

Clearly there was no electricity, but there were water butts to catch rainwater, and there was also a little stream bubbling away just a few yards from the front door. Beyond the shack were a few small sheds; she assumed one of these was Grace's lavatory. Close to it was a hen house, the hens spilling out into an adjoining pen.

'It's really nice,' Maisy whispered. 'I feel like we're in a Famous Five book and any moment a man with a limp will come staggering along with a lumpy sack over his shoulder.'

Duncan gave an amused little grunt. 'It's all tidier than I expected,' he admitted. 'Look at those piles of logs in the shed, so neatly stacked. And that vegetable patch is thriving.'

Maisy looked towards the vegetable patch and saw Duncan was right: there were straight lines of vegetables pushing up through the soil, and the woman had even erected stick wigwams for runner beans. It looked as well cared for as their grandmother's kitchen garden, and she had Mr Pike to look after it for her.

Maisy and Duncan liked to help Mr Pike in the garden. In London they only had a tiny patch of grass which was always in the shade. There was nothing to it other than a mossy lawn and a few evergreen shrubs, so they'd never taken any interest in it. But Mr Pike was jolly and they liked the way he told them about different plants and trees; he'd even given them a little plot of their own to grow stuff. Maisy had planted some flowers, and Duncan had opted for lettuce and radishes. They couldn't wait for the seeds to sprout.

'Here she comes,' Duncan whispered. 'I hope her dog doesn't smell us and come charging to attack us. Yikes, she's got a dead rabbit over her arm!'

The way the animal flopped over the woman's arm reminded Maisy of a fox stole her mother had. Its glass eyes and paws had always disturbed her. 'Do you think she killed it herself?'

'Mr Pike told me he snares rabbits, but she can't have killed it that way or she wouldn't have the gun,' Duncan said knowledgeably.

As they watched, the woman placed the rabbit on a big tree stump, withdrew a knife from her belt and proceeded to skin it. Her dog, a black-and-white collie, sat back on his haunches watching her hungrily.

The twins also watched as she skinned the animal but in their case in horrified fascination. She put the rabbit to one side and sliced from its throat right down its belly, then withdrew the bloody innards with her bare hand.

'Yuck,' Maisy whispered.

There was no doubt that the woman had done this dozens of times before; every movement was sure and confident. She put the entrails into a bowl then took them over to a funny-looking contraption hanging in a tree, which looked like it was made of muslin, reinforced with a stiff board. She stowed the bowl of innards within.

'I think that's for the dog later,' Duncan whispered. 'Unless of course it's ingredients for a spell!'

Back at the tree stump she proceeded to cut the rabbit

into pieces before washing the blood off her hands in the stream.

'She isn't as old as I expected,' Maisy whispered. 'She looks about the same age as Mother.'

'Mother is only thirty-eight but she looks older,' Duncan whispered back. 'I think this woman must be late forties from what Janice said, but she certainly doesn't look it. Then again, she doesn't look like I expected either.'

Maisy guessed that her brother had held a similar mental picture in his head to the one she had: an old crone with a hooked nose, dirty, straggly hair and black teeth. But this woman wasn't like that at all.

Her hair was grey and long, but she had tied it back at the nape of her neck with a dark ribbon or cloth. She had a clear, unlined complexion and she was slender with the ease of movement of someone in their twenties. She was wearing a pair of dark men's trousers and a green plaid shirt, both very shabby, and on her feet she wore brown leather boots like the ones people wore for hiking.

While she was no beauty, she wasn't ugly either, and she certainly didn't look mad or like a witch. She had gone indoors now, taking the rabbit meat with her. Once again the dog had followed her.

'Shall we go and speak to her?' Maisy asked her brother.

'Let's wriggle back out of here on to the path and wait out of sight until she comes out again. We could start talking to each other so she can hear us, making out we're lost, and then go out into the clearing and look surprised to see anyone. Then we can try and strike up a conversation.'

Maisy looked admiringly at her brother. He always seemed to know how to handle any situation.

They waited about six minutes before the woman came out again. Duncan put his hand on his sister's shoulder, a warning to follow his lead. 'Listen, I can hear a stream,' he said in a loud voice. 'We can get a drink, and if we can't see a way back to Burley maybe we'd better retrace our steps.'

As her brother moved forward to walk out of the wood, Maisy took up the talking. 'We were supposed to be home for lunch, so don't even think of going off anywhere else or we'll be in trouble.'

They had both reached the clearing and they continued to talk, pretending they hadn't yet spotted the woman who was now hoeing her vegetable patch.

'Oh, hullo there,' Duncan called out to her a moment later. 'Sorry to interrupt you, is there a quick way back to Burley from here?'

The collie looked up at them and made a threatening growl.

'Go back the way you came,' the woman replied, the curtness of her instruction showing she expected to be obeyed.

'I'm so sorry,' Duncan said. 'We're new to the area and were just exploring, we didn't mean any harm. May we just get a drink from the stream? We're really thirsty.'

'Quickly then and be gone,' she said. She looked down at the dog who was poised to defend her. 'It's fine, Toby.'

The twins made their way to the stream somewhat hesitantly, knelt down and cupped their hands in the water to drink. Maisy wished they'd just gone back into the wood immediately as it was clear this strange woman wasn't ever going to be friendly.

Duncan clearly thought he could win her round. 'What

a lovely spot to live,' he said cheerily as he got back on his feet. 'Must be a bit harsh in the winter, though?'

'Are you half-witted?' the woman asked. 'I would've thought I made it quite clear I didn't wish to see anyone, much less talk to them. You've had your drink, now go.'

'We're sorry if we've offended you,' Duncan said, giving her his best wide-eyed smile, which usually resulted in people warming to him.

There was no response. The woman returned to her hoeing with her back to him. Duncan looked at his sister and shrugged, clearly defeated.

'At least we've seen her,' Maisy said once they were back on the forest track. 'I was a bit disappointed, really. I expected her to live in a hovel with feral cats and be really hideous.'

Duncan laughed; his sister had always had an over-active imagination. 'We can come and spy on her again,' he suggested. 'You never know, we might catch her burying an unwary traveller.'

3

'Sit down,' Grandmother ordered. 'On that sofa, so I can see you properly.' She pointed to the seat opposite her, facing the French windows.

Five weeks had passed and this was the first time Grandmother had asked to see them. They had occasionally run into her in the garden, or in the kitchen when she was giving Janice some instruction, but she was invariably curt with them, never even asking how they were or what they'd been doing with themselves.

This morning, when Janice had told them that she wanted to see them, they were scared it meant she was sending them home to London. They certainly didn't want to go, yet knew it would be pointless to plead with her, so they obediently sat as instructed. The sun was in their eyes and they couldn't see the old lady clearly – but perhaps that was how she wanted it.

They knew from Janice that she was only seventy, but the many lines on her face made her look older, as did the snow-white hair fixed up in a bun. Yet she wore attractive clothes – today a blue dress with a toning lacy cardigan. Her clothes matched her blue eyes which, although cold and forbidding, were rather lovely and hinted at her having been a beauty when she was young. But apart from attending church, she rarely went out, even though Janice had told them that she was still capable of walking for miles when she chose to.

'You know your mother has been committed to an asylum? Well, they don't like you to call it that any more, so I'll refer to it as a nursing home,' she stated, without any kind of preamble.

Both Duncan and Maisy nodded.

'I have to tell you now that she has been assessed and she is likely to have to stay there for the foreseeable future.'

The twins gasped. 'But why?' Duncan asked. 'We thought it would just be for a few weeks.'

'Your mother's problems are long-standing ones. She has never been happy,' Grandmother said with a sigh. 'I was against the marriage because I could see she was something of a broken reed, and over the years she has become further and further removed from reality. Your father had no choice but to place her somewhere she could be monitored around the clock after she'd tried to take poison. That task cannot be left to servants.'

'But Mother isn't mad,' Maisy burst out. She knew something was badly wrong with her, but she couldn't accept it was madness. 'I don't believe she tried to take poison. We've only got Betty's word for that.'

'You are just a child,' Grandmother responded. 'What can you possibly know about such things? I know nothing more about Betty than what my son tells me, but he trusts her.'

'I think she may have got worse because she's been taken from home and she knows we are here,' Duncan said stoutly.

The old lady pursed her lips. 'According to your father, she has hardly noticed she isn't at home and hasn't asked about you two at all. That is how far removed from reality she is.'

'I don't believe she hasn't asked about us,' Maisy said with some indignation, tears starting to roll down her cheeks.

'Tell me something, Maisy. How long is it since you spent more than a few minutes with her?' Grandmother asked, raising one eyebrow questioningly.

The twins looked at one another. Since Christmas their mother had been up in her bedroom almost constantly. They would go in to see her when they got home from school but mostly she was too sleepy to talk to them.

'Last summer she was fine,' Duncan said defensively. 'We went out to Hyde Park with her one afternoon.'

The old lady didn't respond immediately; she looked as if she was trying to find the right words.

'Any child should be able to cite more than one occasion in a year when they did something with their mother,' she said at length. 'You two had become so used to her "illness" that you no longer even questioned it. In my view your mother should have been hospitalized long ago, before she caused you two any damage or distress.'

'She wouldn't do anything to hurt us,' Maisy burst out. 'You don't know her, you've only visited once and that was years ago.'

'Don't take that tone with me, child,' Grandmother snapped back. 'You cannot possibly understand what goes on between adults; let's just say that your mother and I didn't get on. That is why I had such reservations when your father asked if you could come here. I said then, better to get her committed so you could stay in your home and continue with school. But your father insisted you'd benefit from being under Janice's care.'

Grandmother paused, looking hard at the pair of them.

'So far I'd say he was right. I've barely known you were in the house, the staff all tell me you are delightful, polite children, and I know Janice has become very fond of you both. Are you happy here?'

Duncan wondered how she could tell them that their mother had been put in an asylum one minute, then ask if they were happy the next.

'We were until you told us this about Mother,' he said, struggling to control his emotions. He could just about deal with knowing their mother was mentally ill, but now it seemed Grandmother was saying she'd never get better.

'I had to tell you the truth, however distressing,' she said, her tone softening. 'I will admit I am not maternal; your father was away at boarding school from an early age, so I didn't learn how to communicate with young people. But you two strike me as well balanced and intelligent, and I think it's time to make plans for your future. Schooling will be a part of this.'

'We could get jobs, and then we could pay our way,' Maisy suggested. 'We are fifteen now.'

Surprisingly their grandmother smiled at that. It softened her face and gave the twins the idea she wasn't always the cold, stern woman they'd taken her for.

'I want more for my grandchildren than working in a shop or on a farm,' she said. 'Your father would like you both to go to university, so I have engaged a teacher for you. Mr Dove was wounded in the war and is in a wheelchair, but he used to teach at one of the best schools in

England, and was highly thought of. You will go to his cottage in the village each morning, and return home for lunch. The afternoons will be free except when Mr Dove gives you homework. How does that sound?'

Being asked what they thought was so surprising that they just looked at one another helplessly.

Maisy recovered first. 'It sounds very good, Grand-mother, thank you.'

'Well, that's settled then,' she said. 'I shall telephone Mr Dove this evening and suggest you start on Monday. I hope you will work hard, pass your exams and ultimately attend university. Do you have any idea what careers you'd like?'

'I'd like to be a barrister,' Duncan said.

'And you, Maisy?' Grandmother looked at her intently.

Maisy had heard Duncan say before that he wanted to be a barrister, but she hadn't ever considered doing anything other than getting married and having children. She sensed her grandmother wouldn't be impressed by such a lack of ambition.

'A scientist,' she said. 'I'd like to find cures for terrible diseases.'

Grandmother dismissed them then without further comment or questions.

Once outside in the garden, Duncan rounded on his sister.

'A scientist?' he queried. 'Where did that come from?'

'I don't know.' She shrugged. 'But I had to say some-thing impressive, didn't I?'

They wandered down through the walled kitchen gar-den to the bench at the far end. The day was sunny but cold, yet with the wall shielding them from the wind it was pleasant to sit there.

'I don't believe Mother is truly mad,' Duncan burst out after a long silence. 'If she was we'd have known long ago. I bet Father wants to get shot of her so he can find another woman.'

'Maybe that is it, but we've never seen him do anything to support that idea. I have thought Betty might have designs on him, but he's always seemed devoted to Mother. I mean, he always goes straight in to see her when he comes home from work. '

'We've never known what goes on between them when they're alone,' Duncan argued. 'Maybe he made her so miserable moaning at her all the time that she went funny in the head. I think he wants a jollier life without kids and a wife.'

'Has he ever struck you as the kind of man who would want "jolly"?'

Duncan chuckled. Ever since they were ten or eleven they'd made jokes to each other about their father being such a serious, humourless man. 'No, I suppose not.'

'Who knows what caused it?' Maisy said. 'I'm sure I'd go mad if I was unappreciated, and had no one to make me laugh or have fun with.'

They lapsed into silence for some time. Then Duncan sighed deeply. 'It's just as well we've got one another. Imagine how awful this would be if you were an only child. But I still don't believe Mother is mad, and when I can figure out a way of proving it, I'll get her out of that place. However, it is great that we can stay here. What do you think of a teacher in a wheelchair?'

'We'll be able to outrun him.' Maisy giggled. 'Let's go and ask Janice about him; she's bound to know every last thing.'

Janice was in the kitchen preparing vegetables for lunch. She stopped working when the children came in and held out her arms to them, clearly expecting them to be upset to hear their mother wasn't on the mend as they'd hoped.

The twins ran to her, burying their faces in her soft, plump neck which smelled of vanilla. Being hugged made Maisy start crying again, and Duncan was trying very hard not to join in.

'I'm really sorry about your mum; it's tough for kids of your age to deal with stuff like that. But if it's any consolation I'm glad I can hold on to you both for a bit longer, until your mum gets better. And I do believe she will get better.'

She dried their eyes, made them a cup of tea and gave them a slice of fruit cake each. Duncan asked her then about Mr Dove.

'He's a good, kind man and they say he's a wonderful teacher,' she said. 'He's extremely grateful to your grandmother too as he thought he'd never get a teaching job again. He's only in his late thirties and his wife went off and left him when she knew he'd never walk again.'

Maisy's eyebrows shot up. 'Really? How awful! But how does he manage on his own?'

'He has a woman who comes in to help and I've heard he's very resourceful, managing to do quite a lot for himself. But having the job of teaching you two will boost his self-esteem. So mind you behave and listen to what he tells you.'

After the twins had gone off to run an errand in the village for Janice, she sat down at the kitchen table, thinking about them and how their mother's illness might affect their lives.

She had been speaking from the heart when she said she was glad she'd have them here for longer. They had brought sunshine into Nightingales and although their grandmother had avoided contact with them until today, even she had remarked begrudgingly that it was nice to hear chatter and laughter in the house.

Most people in the village considered Mrs Mitcham to be a cantankerous, mean old woman who could turn milk sour just by glancing at it. She was certainly very difficult – by all accounts even as a young woman she'd been a crashing snob and cold-hearted – but in the twenty-six years Janice had been in her service, first as a fourteen-year-old kitchen maid straight out of St Mary's orphanage in Southampton and gradually rising to become the housekeeper, she'd seen another side of her employer. She was fair, loyal, and every now and again she had moments of surprising tenderness and generosity, especially to anyone she perceived as vulnerable.

Janice had loved Nightingales at first sight. After the huge, spartan dormitory at St Mary's, where any little treasure she acquired was soon stolen by another orphan or confiscated by the nuns, a room of her own up in the attic was heavenly. Food was good and plentiful, and the work never as hard as it had been at St Mary's. Because she never wanted a day to dawn when she couldn't look out on to the beautiful garden, wake to birdsong, or have a full belly, she resolved right away to learn every aspect of running a house and make herself indispensable to Mrs Mitcham.

There had been a brief period in the summer of 1939 when she dared dream of her wedding, a home of her own and children, because she'd fallen in love with a young far-rier named William Gateshead. But Will joined up as soon as war was declared and he was killed in the retreat from Dunkirk just a year later.

That was the first time she saw Mrs Mitcham's tender side, as she held out her arms to Janice and let her cry. 'I am so sorry, my dear,' she said. 'Fate can be wickedly cruel sometimes, and there is nothing one can say that will take the sting from it. But you know you will have a home here at Nightingales for as long as you need it.'

People said she would find another young man, but Will had been her love and no one else she met ever matched up to him. When Mr Mitcham had a stroke just as the war ended, becoming paralysed down his right side, Janice found solace in being needed.

But after Mr Mitcham died, as Janice had told the twins, she felt that time hung on her hands. She even found herself thinking of moving on to another, more fulfill-ing job.

Just as she was despairing, the twins arrived, and sud-denly she was busy again. It was very satisfying to make rich desserts, hearty casseroles, cakes, apple pies and bis-cuits, and even to see a washing line full of drying clothes or a basket stuffed with clothes waiting for ironing. Yet it was even better to have the twins to talk to, to play board games with, to tuck into bed at night. She saw Alastair in their faces, sometimes heard his voice in theirs, but she was so very glad they hadn't inherited his insular character.

Alastair had been seventeen when she arrived at Nightingales. He was home from boarding school for the summer holiday, and looking back with acquired wisdom, Janice could see that they had both been brought up without any real care or affection, made to obey orders without question, and they knew nothing of the opposite sex. She couldn't claim they ever became friends – any conversation was stilted and forced – yet there was a little something between them, an attraction, a sense that they had things in common. He taught her some card games, the ones she'd taught the twins. They would play in the kitchen in the evenings, with old Mrs Bodbury, the housekeeper at that time, checking on them now and then to see they weren't doing anything more subversive.

Then the following year Alastair went off to Oxford, and each time he came home again he seemed to grow further away from her. She would ask about his studies, what friends he'd made and if any of them were girls. He somewhat ruefully told her that girls didn't like him.

He was nearly twenty, Janice sixteen, when he brought Lily home for the first time. Alastair was not handsome – he had too big a forehead, his eyes were too pale, and the skin on his face had an odd, stretched look – but even so Janice was astounded he would even look twice at a whey-faced, ratty-haired girl like Lily Goldney. More worrying was that while Alastair was looking adoringly at her, she looked afraid of her own shadow.

'She's a poor wee thing,' Mrs Bodbury proclaimed, making Janice glad that it wasn't just her who was not impressed.

Mrs Mitcham wasn't the kind to take anyone under her wing and try to bring out the best in them, and Janice got to hear from the maid that Lily barely said a word at meals, hardly ate anything and appeared terrified of Alastair's parents.

Alastair didn't bring her home again, and his parents thought he'd dropped her. Then to everyone's astonishment, in 1935, four years later, he informed his parents he'd married Lily in her Kent village.

Unsurprisingly, Mrs Mitcham was furious. 'He's thrown his life away,' she ranted to her husband, at such a volume that Janice could hear her from the kitchen. 'I've known potatoes with more personality. Mark my words, he'll regret this.'

But Alastair didn't appear to regret anything. He had what Janice believed to be an important job in the Foreign Office, and he must have been well paid even back when most people were struggling in the Depression, because he bought a house. Janice had never been to London at that time, but she was told Holland Park was a very smart address and that the houses were huge. Later on she was to learn from Mrs Mitcham that he'd bought it with a legacy from his grandfather, adding with a disapproving sniff that it would be wasted on Lily as she had no sense of style.

Lily must have been very relieved Alastair didn't have to join up in 1939, as soon after she found she was pregnant. She went back to her family in Kent because she was afraid London would be bombed, but sadly she lost that baby at four months. Maybe that was the real start of the trouble with her nerves. Alastair had a good petrol allowance, which enabled him to drive down to Kent often and to Burley sometimes to see his parents. In 1944 he announced Lily was pregnant again.

In late January of 1945 he arrived at Nightingales, as always bringing them butter, cheese, ham and other foodstuffs that were hard to get hold of. He was also brimming with joy about his news: he was the father of healthy twins, a boy and a girl. His face shining with happiness, he told them that the war would be over before long, and although he would be called on to go over to Europe on various missions, helping to sort out the problem of displaced people, Lily would be secure again and he hoped that together they could create a real family home in Holland Park.

Later that same day he came into the kitchen to talk to Janice alone. She guessed his mother had been scathing about Lily's ability to be a good wife and mother, and he needed to talk to someone who wasn't so negative.

'Mother seems to think Lily is shirking her duties as a wife and mother by staying in Kent,' he confided. 'But it would be madness to bring them home now when the V-2s are targeting London, wouldn't it? I also said she needs her mother to help her, anyway; twins are very tiring.'

Janice sensed his mother had been cruel, pouring scorn on Lily's abilities and making her son feel he would always be surplus to requirements in the twins' life as his mother-in-law would control everything.

By then Janice had got to know Alastair much better

and had come to see he wasn't the cold-hearted copy of his mother that she'd once thought, but a loyal and caring man.

His visit she would always remember best was in 1940, just after she got the news that her William had been killed as the troops retreated from Dunkirk. Alastair came into the kitchen to offer his condolences, and he hugged her and said he hoped she would find another good man in the fullness of time and have a whole parcel of children, because she deserved happiness.

Over the years Janice had found you could assess a person's true character by the way they reacted to serious situations and tragedies. He said and did just the right thing when William died, comforting her and proving he was capable of true compassion for others. She also remembered a time not so long after when he'd come down while the London Blitz was raging. He had a cup of tea with her in the kitchen and talked about the cruelty of war, separating people who should be together, destroying lovely old buildings and laying waste the very fabric of life as they had once known it.

Once the war was finally over, Lily did return to London with the twins. Yet despite all the efforts Alastair expended to make life easier for his wife, including bringing Betty, a woman Lily had known all her life, back with them to act as housekeeper, things were not good.

'I have to go away frequently,' Alastair told Janice on one visit. 'I can't help it, it's my job, but Lily either sulks or throws a tantrum every time. I don't understand why. I've got her more than adequate help, she has Betty for company, and her mother comes up when she can. Lily barely looks at Duncan and Maisy, and she takes herself off to bed, blaming a riding accident she had years ago for making her nerves bad.'

Janice knew that it must have been very hard for a proud man like Alastair to admit such things. She guessed, too, that every aspect of his marriage was affected, and she wouldn't have blamed him if he'd given up on Lily and got a divorce.

While not wanting to think of anyone in an asylum, especially as she'd grown so fond of the twins and knew how distressing they found it, Janice felt that Lily needed to be in that place. Over the years she'd gleaned a great deal about her, and, whether it was fair or not, she couldn't help but secretly despise the woman for being so weak and not appreciating how lucky she was to have a home, a husband and two children.

When William was killed, Janice had wanted to die too; there just didn't seem to be anything to live for. But she pushed the thought away, got on with her work and told herself that thousands of other women had lost their menfolk at Dunkirk, and tens of thousands more would die before victory was won.

Eventually the agony of loss turned to an ever-present ache, and after a few years it was reduced to a sadness that she could cope with. Nowadays the reminders of him were only occasional; sometimes she shed a few tears, but mostly she smiled at the good memories. Alastair had said she should be proud of William's bravery, and she was. Alastair's kindness to her, when she needed it most, meant a great deal. One day she would tell his children about it and try to explain to them that they must trust their father, for he was a good man. She had the feeling that right now they thought he was devious and uncaring.

When Janice went to collect Mrs Mitcham's dinner tray that evening, the old lady asked her to sit down for a moment.

'How did the children take the news of their mother staying in the asylum, or home as my son likes to call it?' she asked briskly. 'They were both like him, and didn't show their feelings to me.'

'They were upset and Maisy cried,' Janice admitted. 'But I think they were glad they are to stay here.'

'Because of you, of course!' The old lady lifted one eyebrow.

'I don't know about that. They like everything about being here,' Janice said hurriedly.

'I should've encouraged Alastair to court you. I knew he liked you.'

An unintentional giggle slipped out from Janice. 'You wouldn't have approved of him seeing a lowly scullery maid.'

'If I'd known how you would turn out, I would've given it my blessing,' Mrs Mitcham said. 'You are a good woman, Janice; you would have made a fine wife and mother, far better than I ever was. But that's all water under the bridge. We can't change the past, or our natures, but we can improve on the future. I wish the twins to be happy here. Have you got any suggestions as to what I could do to help that?'

Janice thought this was a day of surprises: first to be told she would've been a good wife to Alastair, and now that Mrs Mitcham was concerned for the twins' happiness.

'You need to have them in and talk to them, on a regular basis,' she said without any hesitation. 'Just for a few minutes, perhaps when I give you your afternoon tea. The three of you could have it together.'

'I never even did that with Alastair,' the old lady said, sounding alarmed.

'Quite so, maybe that's why he finds it so hard to talk about his feelings,' Janice said. 'I'm sure you don't wish the twins to have the same problem.'

Mrs Mitcham waved her hands in a dismissive gesture. 'People talk far too much about such things.'

'I wasn't suggesting you talk to the twins about *feelings*, but about their lessons with Mr Dove, or perhaps a bit of village gossip. Maybe you could tell them some stories about your own childhood here?'

'They wouldn't be interested in that, surely?'

'I bet they would be,' Janice said. 'And you could play a few card games with them. They like playing cards.'

'I don't know what to say about their mother,' her employer suddenly blurted out.

'You only have to say she was shy and you never got to know her well. That is, after all, the truth,' Janice said soothingly. 'Turn their questions around, ask them about her.'

'How is it that you always know the right thing to say?'

Janice shrugged. 'I suppose I try to put myself in other people's shoes. And if I can't think of anything nice to say, I say nothing.'

'I wish I had that gift,' the old lady said with a sigh.

'Even when I'm trying to be pleasant it never seems to come out right. But maybe I can learn from the children.'

'I think we can both learn from them,' Janice said. 'I'm really glad they'll be staying with us, and we must endeavour to become a proper family.'

4

'Duncan, this precis on *Jane Eyre* is appalling.' Mr Dove slammed Duncan's homework book down on the table. 'It appears you hadn't grasped even the most fundamental idea of what the story is about. Did you actually read it?'

The twins were sitting on either side of the table in their teacher's kitchen, and Mr Dove was at the head of the table in a wheelchair, his back to the window. He was an attractive man in his thirties with thick fair hair which touched his collar. He was very conscious of this and had said he had to wait for a hairdresser to come and cut it in his home, as he couldn't catch the bus to her. In Maisy's opinion his hair was just fine, as were his white teeth and wide, sunny smile, but she felt his grey-blue eyes had seen too much sadness.

'Yes, sir, well, at least most of it,' Duncan replied a little sheepishly. 'But it's a girls' book.'

The teacher looked from one twin to the other and half smiled. 'I gave Maisy *Kidnapped* to read, which some would consider more suitable for a boy. Yet she managed to write an excellent, well thought-out precis on it. A book becomes known as a classic because it is a good story and can be read by everyone, regardless of gender. So, Duncan, are you going to go through life ignoring everything you consider to be a touch feminine?'

Duncan blushed. 'No, sir.'

'I'm very glad to hear it. So I want you to read it again properly during your holiday and write a new precis, proving you've not only read it but understand the dilemmas Jane Eyre had to deal with. I shall expect to see it when your lessons start again in September.'

'Yes, sir,' Duncan said. 'Was my maths homework all right?'

Mr Dove nodded. 'Yes, it was excellent, but I'll get back to that later. I want to move on to history now, and see what, if anything, you both remember from last week's lesson about Henry the Eighth.'

It was now close to the end of July and the twins had been having lessons with Mr Dove for ten weeks. They liked him far more than any of their previous teachers in London. He was interesting, caring and often very funny. Duncan, who was bright but sometimes lazy, had in the past only ever done just enough work to keep out of trouble; now he often found himself going an extra mile because he liked the way Mr Dove challenged him.

Maisy was not as clever as her brother, but she'd always been a plodder, staying up late to finish homework which she presented neatly with no spelling mistakes. At her old school she'd been praised for this, but Mr Dove was more interested in his pupils getting carried away with the tasks he'd set them than caring about whether their handwriting was neat. Because of the way he presented English literature and history to her, Maisy was becoming passionate about both subjects.

After almost four months the twins were now entirely settled at their grandmother's. On Sunday afternoons she always asked them into her sitting room for afternoon tea, and they dreaded it because it was so strained. Yet they sensed she was really trying, so they tried too, and sometimes they found a bit of common ground to discuss, which pleased them all.

Their previous life in London was hardly ever mentioned now – not to her, to Janice or even to each other – and they certainly didn't want to go back.

Yet it did sadden them that there were no letters from their mother. Their father wrote once a week enclosing a postal order for their pocket money. His letters were all very similar: a question as to what they were studying with Mr Dove, comments on the weather, a reminder they were to do all they could to help their grandmother and Janice, and finally a brief comment about their mother.

'Your mother is quite comfortable . . . Your mother is eating better . . . Your mother enjoys sitting outside in the sun.' Never once was there a message from her to them. He didn't even add that he knew how she was because he'd visited her or whether these tiny newsflashes had just come from him telephoning the nursing home.

They dutifully replied each week, but it was a chore because they hardly knew what to say to him. Mostly they described what books they were reading, the meals Janice had cooked and what was coming up in the garden.

Mr Dove spoke to them about their parents after the second week of lessons with him. Duncan had remarked that he didn't know why their father always asked what they were learning as he clearly didn't care about his children at all.

'Asking what you are learning is the only way some adults can show they care,' Mr Dove responded.

'But that's weird. Why not ask if we're happy or if we've made new friends here?' Duncan retorted.

'Perhaps your father doesn't really understand the importance of happiness, or of having friends.'

Duncan pulled a bewildered face. 'Everyone knows that!'

Dove smiled. 'Not everyone. You, Duncan, are lucky to have a twin sister you are very close to. You two are ready-made friends and you make each other happy. But maybe your father never had a real friend, and no one ever concerned themselves about whether he was happy. It is forces such as these which shape our adult character and personality.'

'I don't understand,' Duncan said, shaking his head.

'Well, lucky children get loving and attentive parents, and in time they grow up, marry and have children of their own who they are loving and attentive to. But the unlucky ones who have cruel or neglectful parents are likely to treat their own children just the same. It is called "learned behaviour".'

'But our father isn't cruel and he hasn't neglected us,' Maisy spoke up indignantly.

'I wasn't suggesting he had,' Dove said. 'I was just trying to make you look at why your father is the way he is.'

'He's like our grandmother, you mean?' Duncan suggested.

Dove grimaced, neither confirming nor denying it.

'Can we change him?' Maisy asked.

'You could try writing to ask if he misses you, and say you miss him and hope he might come here to see you.'

'He'd probably just ignore that.' Duncan shrugged. 'He

stuck Mother in a home to get rid of her and shoved us down here for the same reason.'

'I don't for one moment believe that.' Dove wagged a disapproving finger at Duncan. 'I know I've never met your father, but I'm a hundred percent sure he just has difficulty in speaking about anything to do with emotions. He's not alone in this; all over England there are men who were damaged by the war. Some by sights they'd seen or things that had happened to them, but a great many more came home to find the baby they left at the start of war was now a five- or six-year-old who resented a stranger getting between it and its mother. That proved almost worse than the war to some men. Your father might not have been on active service, but he rarely saw you two as babies because he had to go to Europe to sort out the problems there soon after you were born. As I understand it, he couldn't be with you all for about three years in fact.'

'I don't think we were ever resentful. I remember getting excited when he was due home,' Duncan said thoughtfully. 'Anyway, surely it was up to him to try and make up for that separation?'

'He never cuddled or played with us,' Maisy joined in.

'That brings us right back to what I said about learned behaviour. Maybe your father cannot do those things because he has never experienced them himself? I was lucky; my parents were loving and demonstrative, which taught me to be the same with my younger siblings. I loved helping them to read, write and do sums, and I expect that's why I became a teacher.'

Maisy felt a little surge of love for this man who she saw as a tragic hero. Even though he was crippled and his wife had left him, he wasn't bitter and he had enough goodness in him to be kind to her and Duncan.

'So you think Grandmother made our father the way he is?' Duncan asked.

'I'm in no position to blame anyone for anything. I just want you to open your minds, consider possibilities and come to your own conclusions. In my opinion it was boarding school that achieved most of your father's stiff upper lip and coolness. I believe public schools tend to put a straitjacket on boys' emotions. Cloistered with just men and other boys, rampant bullying and no feminine influence, except maybe a dragon of a matron – it's a wonder any boy comes out unscathed. But I think your grandmother might just have learned a lesson there – she hasn't once suggested boarding schools for you two.'

'We used to wish we could go to boarding schools,' Maisy admitted. 'The only thing that put us off is that we'd be in separate places.'

'They aren't like the ones in children's fiction, except maybe *Tom Brown's Schooldays*.' Dove smiled. 'If I had my way all children would attend day schools. I shudder when I hear of boys going from one male-dominated institution into another such as the armed forces.'

'But you taught at one, then went into the army,' Duncan said.

Dove nodded sadly. 'Yes, and the funny thing was that I actually thought I could help some of those chaps who had been indoctrinated with cruelty and had such snobbish ideas about class and a lack of respect for women. But I very much doubt I managed to change anyone's outlook. Once those ideas are ingrained it's the Devil's own job to remove them.'

As the twins walked home to Nightingales for their lunch they chatted about what Dove had said.

'He's such a good man,' Duncan said. 'You'd think he'd feel sorry for himself, but he doesn't. Mother wasn't anywhere near as badly hurt in her riding accident, but she's let it ruin her life.'

'Maybe her accident has always been just an excuse to stay away from everyone,' Maisy said. 'Or perhaps her problems are caused by something else other than the accident, something that she can't talk about.'

'Like a bogeyman jumping on her in the woods.' Duncan laughed. 'Speaking of stuff in the woods, do you fancy coming down this afternoon to see if we can see the witch again?'

'No, thank you, it's creepy. You go if you want. Janice was going to show me how to crochet.'

Duncan stopped in his tracks, looking at her in shock and disbelief. 'I can't believe you'd prefer to do that rather than ride out in the forest and spy on Grace Deville! I can see I'll need to find a new chum for the holidays.'

Maisy laughed. She wished he would find a male friend, just so she could escape doing all the boyish things he always wanted to do. These days she'd rather read than play cricket with him, climbing trees didn't get her excited any more and fishing was so boring. She liked looking in shops, having picnics and dancing. Janice had told her there was a lady in Lyndhurst who gave ballroom dancing classes twice a week during the school holidays and Maisy really wanted to go. Duncan had sniggered at that; he said he'd rather stick his hand in a cow pat.

'I hope you do find a chum as I'm going to ballroom

dancing as soon as it starts,' she said after a couple of min-utes. 'Of course I hope you'll change your mind and come with me, because everyone needs to learn to dance or be a failure at balls and parties.'

'I shan't be going to anything so banal,' he said loftily. 'I've decided I'm going to become an explorer.'

Maisy raised her eyebrows. 'Oh really? Up the Amazon, investigating tribes of cannibals?'

'Maybe, or the polar regions. Don't scoff, I mean to do it. I shall get a degree in something useful like geography and maybe botany, then I'll be off.'

Maisy didn't think this worthy of a reply. Duncan had a new idea for a career every month, most of them straight out of the pages of *Boy's Own*.

They got back to Nightingales to find Janice laying the table in the garden for lunch. 'Your grandmother suggested it,' she said when she saw their surprised faces. 'She said we should make the most of this glorious weather.'

'Are you joining us too?' Maisy asked, seeing a fourth place.

'No, the extra place is for Mr Grainger. He's a friend of your grandmother's and he wanted to meet you. They're in the sitting room at the moment but they'll be out shortly, so go and wash your hands and faces. Duncan, put a clean shirt on, please, you've got your breakfast down your front. A short-sleeved open-necked one will do.'

'What does this man want to meet us for?' Maisy asked her brother as they went up the stairs.

Duncan shrugged. 'Just curious about us, I suppose, like lots of the local people are. Mrs Jackson at the bakery is the worst – she's always fishing for information from me about us, our parents and our grandmother.'

'I hate her,' Maisy said emphatically. 'She's got piggy eyes and that wart by her nose jiggles when she speaks.'

'You shouldn't use strong adjectives like "hate" when you only mean you dislike her; you should save it for a time when real hatred comes along.'

Maisy giggled. 'Hark at you! That's straight out of Mr Dove's phrase book.'

Duncan put his nose in the air, went into his bedroom and slammed the door behind him. Maisy smiled. He had been copying Mr Dove a lot recently, and it embarrassed him to have it pointed out.

'So is the New Forest very boring to you after London?' Mr Grainger asked Duncan over lunch.

'No, sir, we love it here,' Duncan replied. 'It's super to ride our bikes, explore the forest and see wild ponies and deer.'

Maisy smiled to herself. She could see by the animated expression on her brother's face that he really liked this man. She liked him too. He wasn't stiff or stuffy; in fact he had a similar easy manner to Mr Dove. But she wondered how he could be a friend of her grandmother's when he was, at Maisy's estimation, only in his late thirties or early forties. He was also nice-looking with very dark hair and periwinkle-blue eyes.

'They are very good at entertaining themselves,' Grandmother said, with a note of pride in her voice. 'Alastair at the same age used to just hang around looking miserable, but I suppose it's harder for an only child.'

'But Alastair had a great many interests – model-making, playing the piano, and I seem to remember that he liked bird-watching,' Mr Grainger said.

'Did you know our father when he was a boy?' Duncan asked, clearly surprised.

Grainger nodded. 'Yes, I did. I was a bit younger but I came to stay with an aunt nearby. When your dad was home in the school holidays he taught me to ride a bike and showed me how to build a camp in the forest.'

'As I recall he got you soaking wet and badly scratched by brambles,' Grandmother retorted. 'I had to take him to task for not taking care of you.'

Grainger looked at the twins and smiled. 'I didn't mind at all. My aunt didn't let me do anything that was fun, she tried to wrap me in cotton wool. But for your father I would've ended up a real drip.'

'What do you do for a job?' Duncan asked.

Grandmother glared at him; clearly she thought that was a rude question.

'I'm a solicitor,' Grainger said, smiling at Grandmother as if to reassure her that he didn't consider it impertinence.

'Do you defend robbers and murderers?' Maisy asked.

He laughed. 'No, I'm not a criminal lawyer. My work is mainly with property.'

'That's a shame,' Duncan said. 'I'd love to get some inside information on villains.'

'Enough of that,' Grandmother snapped. 'Now if you've finished your lunch you can leave the table.'

'We could meet up one day in Southampton and I could show you the courts and tell you a few stories I know about villains,' Mr Grainger offered.

'Enough, Donald!' Grandmother rebuked him, shoo-ing the twins away from the table. 'The boy doesn't need to know about ghastly people.'

'Alastair must be very proud of his children; they are bright and well-mannered,' Grainger said after the twins had gone out of earshot. 'Such a shame about their mother.'

'He should never have married her. She was never right, always like a trembling leaf, and she didn't even have a mind of her own. I can't imagine what Alastair saw in her.'

Donald Grainger felt he ought to be shocked by Mrs Mitcham's cruel description of her daughter-in-law, but in fact it amused him. For as long as he could remember she'd made caustic remarks about people. Besides, Mrs Mitcham was paying him to look after her affairs, so she could say what she liked.

She had known his Aunt Constance who, until her death seven years earlier, had lived just down the lane. His aunt had always told him that Violet Mitcham never pulled her punches, nor did she make allowances for anyone weaker than herself, yet underneath that formidable exter-ior there was a kind heart; you just had to know how to deal with her. Grainger was always on the lookout for that elusive side of her.

'I was quite shaken by how Lily was when I visited her on your behalf,' he said carefully. 'I know from what you told me that she was never what you'd call robust, and always shy, but I got the idea that she had been quite intelligent. Sadly she doesn't seem to have much grasp on reality any longer. She's so very thin and pale, and she didn't even ask about the twins.'

Grainger knew it was better not to elaborate, but the truth of the matter was that Alastair's wife was like a wraith, no light in her eyes, no desire to talk or ask questions. He'd been told by a nurse that if she wasn't made to get out of bed, to dress and sit in a chair, she'd spend every hour lying in bed staring at the ceiling.

The nurse had added that she answered questions briefly, she would say if she was too cold, too hot or hungry, but there was never anything that would pass as conversation. He knew that all Mrs Mitcham really wanted was a rough idea of her life expectancy, but none of the nurses or her doctor were prepared to tell him that.

Mrs Mitcham pursed her lips. 'Donald, I'm more concerned about how much it is costing Alastair to keep her in that place. She's still a young woman – unless you know otherwise she could live till she's ninety – and Alastair tells me the doctors are no closer to finding a cure for whatever it is that ails her. It might be wicked to say this, but I wish when she wanted to take the poison Betty had turned a blind eye.'

Grainger kept his expression neutral. 'I'm sure you don't really mean that,' he said. 'We all make bitter remarks when we are angry and distressed.'

She shrugged, giving the impression that she was definitely not distressed and resented anyone thinking she might be. She got up from the table. 'I think it best that we continue our conversation in my sitting room, since I do not wish to be overheard.'

Mrs Mitcham waited until Grainger was sitting in an armchair before sitting opposite him.

'What this business of Lily's failing mental health has

56

done,' she spoke slowly and firmly as if she'd rehearsed this, 'is to make me realize I must change my will. I cannot countenance the idea of Alastair inheriting this house and my money and then squandering it on keeping her in that place. So I want you to draw up a new will and make Duncan my heir. You, of course, will remain my executor.'

Grainger was flabbergasted. When she'd invited him here today he'd thought maybe she wanted to discuss starting a trust or something similar for her grandchildren. He could understand perfectly her desire to safeguard the home she loved and the money her husband had worked so hard for, but it was extreme to cut her only child out of her will. Alastair was, after all, only doing what a good husband should do. He was honouring his marriage vows and protecting his sick wife. When he got to hear about this he was going to feel even more undervalued than he did already.

But Donald Grainger was, if nothing else, a realist. He'd known Violet Mitcham right from a small child and he was aware of her reputation. Therefore he knew that nothing he could say or do would make her change her mind; she was incredibly stubborn and single-minded. Furthermore, if he tried to do so, she would just tell him to leave and she would get another solicitor.

'If Duncan is to be your heir then we must discuss what safeguards we can put in place,' he said warily. 'I'm sure you won't want the boy getting his legacy too young, before he learns to handle money wisely. But at the same time, if you should pass away while he is still at university, it might be advisable for your executors to be given the authority to give him a small allowance.'

Mrs Mitcham looked at him sternly for what seemed several minutes. He guessed she was considering whether she could trust him not to go running to Alastair to tell him about this.

'My plan was for Duncan to inherit at thirty. That's a good age; he'll probably be married and settled by then. But yes, in the unlikely event of me dying while he is still studying, I agree he should have a monthly allowance. Nonetheless, I plan to be around to see him graduate and beyond.'

'But should the worst happen and you die before Duncan's thirtieth, what do you want to do with Nightingales? It's never good to leave an old property like this empty.'

'I'm sure I can depend on you to keep an eye on things. But Janice will stay on, and Mr Pike my gardener. I want it in my will too that Janice has a home here for as long as she needs it. I also want her to have the sum of two hundred pounds. I want to leave Pike fifty pounds.'

'Alastair?'

She shook her head irritably. 'He already has a home in London, and a good income. But as a token I'll leave him two hundred.'

Grainger knew she was rich, but at the same time he had no idea of just how much money she had tucked away. He wondered what Alastair had done to make her react like this. Surely it couldn't just be the nursing home fees?

'It is usual to appoint a second heir, just in case the chosen first one should die,' he said cautiously, half expecting her to jump down his throat. 'In that unlikely event, if you haven't named someone else, it will revert to Alastair. Is that what you wish? Or should you name Maisy as the second in line?'

She frowned, turning the faint wrinkles on her forehead to deep furrows. 'I hadn't considered that. A healthy boy isn't likely to die young. But if you say I must appoint someone, then it had better be his sister. I did intend her to have my jewellery. But not this ring.' She lightly tapped the large sapphire she wore on her finger. 'It was my engagement ring, given to us by Harold's mother. I'd like Duncan to be able to give it to his fiancée when the time comes.'

'That is a nice touch,' Grainger said, hoping that for Maisy's sake the rest of her grandmother's jewellery was equally valuable. 'I'm sure whoever Duncan marries will be thrilled to receive such a beautiful ring.'

'I will of course want it noted that if Duncan's marriage should break down he must retrieve the ring,' she said through pursed lips.

They went through a few minor bequests of items of silver and a carriage clock, mostly to friends and neighbours. Grainger wondered that she had any friends at all as she made quite cruel comments about every one of the recipients. But he said nothing, just wrote down her wishes.

'If that is everything, I'll get it typed up and bring it back for you to sign,' he said, getting to his feet. He'd had enough of her for one day. It was hard work trying to be charming to someone so hard-headed. 'Meanwhile, if you think of anything else you want included, let me know.'

'Draw it up quickly,' she snapped. 'I want it signed, witnessed and tucked away for safety as soon as possible.'

Grainger looked down at the old lady before he left the room. He had written hundreds of wills over the years and most of his clients became emotional when they spoke of their loved ones. But the only time Violet Mitcham's voice had trembled was when she spoke about her engagement ring.

He felt it was hardly surprising that Alastair had fallen for a delicate, emotional, clinging woman; no doubt that felt like true love and adoration to a man starved of affection.

He just hoped the meanness of spirit and the flashes of cruelty and spite he'd witnessed today wouldn't be passed on to Duncan and Maisy. He wanted to see them on his way out, maybe suggest they come to his office one day, so he could get to know them better. He couldn't of course break the confidential nature of today's discussions, but at the very least he could tell them they had a friend in him if they needed it.

As luck would have it Maisy was sitting on a bench in the garden doing some crocheting. As Grainger approached she looked up and grinned at him.

'Are you off now?' she asked.

'Yes, I am,' he said. 'It was good to meet you and Duncan. Where is he?'

'Oh, he's gone out into the forest, he loves it there. Did you need him for something?'

'No, not really.' Grainger smiled warmly at her. 'I had thought we could've had a little chat, you know, man-to-man stuff. But do tell him if either of you ever have any worries or problems you want to talk over, pop in to see me, or ring me.' He handed her a card. 'I mean it now. I realize that it might be difficult to discuss some things with your grandmother. I can't boast I have much influence there, but I am a good listener and sometimes that's all we need.'

Maisy looked at his card thoughtfully for a moment or two. 'Thank you, Mr Grainger, it was a pleasure to meet you. I see you are in Southampton. That's a place Duncan and I would like to visit, especially to see the big ships in port, bound for exotic destinations.'

'I hope you will come to see me then, Maisy – maybe while you're on holiday this summer?'

Maisy watched him as he continued down the garden path to his car parked just outside the gate. She liked the lithe, smooth way he walked; it reminded her of a cat. She had observed that men wearing dark business suits always seemed to have a stiff gait, and until now she had assumed it was caused by their suits, but the way Mr Grainger walked made her think that his naked body might be lean and muscular.

Thinking such a thing startled her. Why would she consider what any man looked like without his clothes? But then she'd had a lot of strange thoughts recently – imagining dancing with a man's arms around her and wondering how it felt to kiss a man on the lips.

She smiled to herself, imagining walking into Mr Grainger's office and confessing that to him. After all, he had said it might be difficult to discuss some things with her grandmother.

'I don't think you can tell anyone such things,' she murmured to herself.

5

On the Saturday afternoon following Mr Grainger's visit to Nightingales, Maisy was lying on her bed reading when Duncan burst into her room, red-faced and sweaty-looking. 'Guess what? I actually spoke to Grace Deville today,' he blurted out. 'We had a real conversation!'

Maisy closed her book and sighed. 'About what?'

'Owls,' he said. 'She's got one as a pet.'

'You can't surely have one as a pet,' she said in disbelief, but she sat up, suddenly all ears. 'Does it sit on her shoulder?'

'No, of course not. When I say it's a pet, she's got it in a cage. She's reared it from a chick. It had fallen out of its nest. She feeds it on bits of raw meat.'

'So how did you get near enough to her to find out such a thing?' she asked. She was actually sorry she hadn't gone with him; doing crochet had proved quite boring.

'I was spying on her and she tripped over in her garden and banged her head. I went to help her up and she was really dizzy, so I got her some water and bathed her head for her.'

'Gosh, you got that close!' Maisy said in disbelief. 'What was she like to you?'

'Still frosty, but she was shaken up and so I think she was glad I'd come along when I did. I had to go into her house to get a bowl and a cloth; it's really cosy in there, but she cooks on a fire and she has an oil lamp for light.'

'Wish I'd seen it. I bet I could give it a better description than that! So what did you talk about to her?'

Duncan grimaced. 'Well, it was a bit one-sided. I told her about us coming to live with Grandmother, cos Mother was ill. I hoped she'd tell me stuff about herself.'

'But she sent you off with a flea in your ear?' Maisy laughed.

'Not exactly. We started talking after I'd cleaned her wound. She said I was a kind boy. Then she asked if I wanted to see her owl. I did, of course. She even gave me a bit of rabbit meat to feed him. He took it from my hand. She calls him Barney as he's a barn owl. But I got the feeling she wasn't that comfortable with me being there and I thought it best to leave before she told me to go. That way I can go back to see how she is.'

'So you didn't actually learn anything more about her?' Maisy grinned.

'I think I did well to get a foot in the door,' Duncan said indignantly. 'But when I go back I'm not taking you as I need to tread carefully.'

That irritated Maisy but she wasn't going to give him the satisfaction of knowing it. 'I can't think why you'd want to go back — she's obviously barmy. I'd rather meet up with people who want to know me.'

'She's *not* barmy.' Duncan's lip curled the way it always did when he felt belittled. 'I'd say she was highly intelligent; she told me quite a lot about owls. She paints too. When I went in her house I saw she was doing a watercolour of some wild flowers, and it was very good. So tell me about your afternoon doing crochet. Was it exciting?'

That question was pure sarcasm and it stung.

'Exciting isn't always what one wants,' she bit back. 'I enjoy being creative, it's so satisfying.'

The twins didn't speak to each other over their supper. Afterwards Janice asked if they wanted to play Scrabble with her. Duncan said he had a book he wanted to read, and Maisy thought that an excuse to get away from her. 'I think I'll do some more crochet,' she said. 'I'm really getting the hang of it now.'

Duncan left the kitchen first; Maisy stayed on to dry the dishes.

'Have you two had a falling-out?' Janice asked.

'Not exactly, we just don't seem to want to do the same things any longer.'

Janice raised her eyebrows. 'Well, I can't see Duncan wanting to crochet. What does he want to do?'

'Just career around the forest on his bike,' Maisy said. 'I can't see the point in that. I want to do girls' things, like dancing, looking in shops, reading fashion magazines.'

Janice smiled. 'You both need friends of your own sex. When I was still at the orphanage in Southampton us girls spent our spare time doing one another's hair. Of course when I came here to work I had no one young to talk to.'

'Were you lonely?' Maisy asked.

'Yes, I was. Sometimes I used to cry myself to sleep because of it. I did make friends a bit later on with another maid in the village. She was called Pauline, but she used to scare me because she was always after the boys.'

'Didn't you like boys?'

'I was terrified of them. One of the nuns at the convent used to go on and on about men only wanting one thing. I

64

didn't know then what the one thing was – I imagined them sucking your blood like a vampire!'

Maisy squealed with laughter and Janice joined in. 'In fact, I hadn't the first idea about babies, men or anything until I met Pauline,' she said as her laughter subsided. 'I was what you might call a late developer.'

'I think I am too, I don't know much about that sort of thing,' Maisy admitted shamefacedly. 'The girls at school used to whisper about things, but I never knew if they were making it up.'

'I'd tell you but I think I'd be too embarrassed, and maybe get it wrong,' Janice said. 'But I can get you a book about it from the library if you like?'

Maisy blushed scarlet. 'Umm, thank you, Janice, that would be kind. I'd better go now and make it up with Duncan.'

On the first Tuesday of what was to be their holiday from lessons with Mr Dove, Maisy caught the bus into Lynd-hurst alone to go to the ballroom dancing classes she'd seen advertised. She was nervous because she didn't often go to places by herself. Duncan had refused point-blank to come with her. He said he was going into the forest to make a camp with Colin, his new friend in the village.

Maisy hadn't met Colin yet and she didn't want to; he sounded very uncouth. Duncan was cross with her for saying that. He told her that she was a snob and it wasn't Colin's fault that his father was only a farm labourer and they lived in a council house.

As the bus trundled along through the more open, heath-like parts of the forest, Maisy looked out for the wild ponies, and thought how wonderful it was to live in a place where horses and other animals could just wander at will, foraging for food. After having to stay indoors in London, only going out under close supervision, it was so lovely to have freedom at last.

Grandmother had approved of ballroom dancing lessons; she said it was an essential skill for all young people. She even gave Maisy ten pounds to buy a suitable dress and shoes, and said it was a shame Duncan had to be so silly, thinking dancing was for sissies.

Maisy was carrying her new silver dancing shoes in a bag. They had three-inch heels with a T-bar strap which she was told was essential so they didn't slip off while she was dancing. Night after night Maisy had been practising walking and dancing in the shoes because she'd never had any high-heeled shoes before. She loved them so much that every morning when she woke up she tried them on and admired the way they made her legs look so slender.

The dress she'd bought wasn't as exciting as the shoes, only white with navy blue polka dots, but the skirt was a full circle, so when she twirled around it looked good. Janice said she would run her up a net petticoat to make the skirt look more bouncy. But for now, until she'd mastered a couple of dances, an ordinary petticoat was enough.

Arriving at the village hall, Maisy's palms were clammy with nerves and her heart was thumping. Once inside she saw there were only three boys, the rest were all girls, and that made her feel a little less nervous.

Mrs Crocket, the dancing teacher, was dressed in pale pink tulle, her red hair piled up on her head in extravagant curls. Maisy had heard she was a ballroom dancing

66

champion, and she looked it. Everyone was ordered to put on their shoes, and a record was put on a wind-up gramophone. The song was 'Lonely Ballerina' and Mrs Crocket said they would be learning to waltz to it.

She put everyone into couples, ignoring girls who said they wanted to dance with their friend. When she came to Maisy, she took her hand and led her to a tall, slender brunette. 'Linda, you will be the man for now, and this is your partner.' She waited for Maisy to say her name.

'Maisy and Linda,' she said. 'You will dance together until such time that I decide you need new partners.'

'Haven't seen you before,' Linda whispered. 'Hope I don't tread on your toes in those pretty shoes.'

'I haven't been around here long,' Maisy whispered back. 'I haven't a clue about ballroom dancing, so I hope I don't embarrass you.'

Mrs Crocket went through instructions of step back on your right, left foot to the side, then slide feet together to go forward on the right again. The boy partners had to do the same but going forward. Then, after showing them the correct hold for the dance, she put the music on.

Mrs Crocket called out her instructions and for those who were in difficulties she went up to them and demonstrated, dancing alongside them.

Linda and Maisy caught on really quickly and were soon doing the steps without having to chant the movements out loud. After about twenty minutes, when Mrs Crocket had got everyone taking the right steps, she moved on to show them how they should rise and fall.

By the end of the hour-long lesson, almost everyone could do the waltz, though some looked better doing it than others. Mrs Crocket singled out Maisy and Linda for praise, and told everyone to practise until they came again in two days' time.

They put their street shoes back on and as they left the hall Linda asked Maisy if she'd like to come to her house for a cup of tea and a chat.

By the time Maisy caught the 5.45 bus back to Burley, she had a new best friend, and couldn't wait to see her again.

Linda was the daughter of Dr Evans, the local GP. Her mother was his receptionist. The practice was at their home, a large, red-brick Victorian house, with most of the ground floor taken up by the surgery and waiting room.

Maisy didn't meet Linda's parents, as they had an ante-natal clinic that afternoon. Linda took Maisy through a side door and up a boxed-in staircase to the apartment above.

Maisy was impressed because it was very modern inside, especially the kitchen, which looked straight out of an American Doris Day film, all pretty pale blues and cream with flouncy checked curtains.

Linda went to a boarding school, and so she said she was in the same situation as Maisy, not having any real friends in the village.

'The local girls think I'm toffee-nosed,' she laughed, as she made them both a cup of tea. 'I joined the dancing class hoping to make some pals as I don't want to spend the whole summer on my own. I felt a bit sick when I got there and everyone was in pairs, except for those three drippy boys. I didn't want any one of them putting his arms around me!'

She told Maisy a little about her all-girls school, which she made sound really grim, and that her father had plans for her to become a doctor like him. Because of this, Maisy felt she had to be careful what she said about her mother, so she just said that she and Duncan had come to stay with their grandmother because their mother was ill.

Fortunately Linda was far more interested in hearing about Maisy's twin brother than about her mother, and having established family history they moved on to films and music they liked.

'I can't wait till Thursday for the next dance lesson to see you again. Can you meet up tomorrow?' Linda asked as she walked Maisy to the bus stop. 'We could meet half-way if you've got a bike.'

Maisy eagerly agreed, saying that she did have a bike and would love to meet up.

'Super!' Linda grinned. 'It's going to be fun riding around the forest. Let's both bring a picnic and we can share.'

Now as Maisy rode home on the bus she thought she'd never been so happy. She really liked Linda. She was more striking than pretty, with her almond-shaped dark eyes and high cheekbones, and so outgoing, genuine, along with being funny too. The whole of the summer was look-ing like it would be exciting now. She just hoped Duncan wouldn't feel left out.

When Maisy told Duncan about Linda he didn't look the least bothered about the possibility of being left alone. He muttered something about building a camp but didn't reveal if there were boys involved other than Colin, or even where it was. As far as Maisy was concerned, he was happy enough and she didn't have to concern herself with him.

The following day she and Linda rode their bikes in the forest. On Thursday there was another dancing class where they learned the rudiments of the quickstep. Friday it rained and Maisy stayed at home and made cakes with Janice. On Saturday she caught the bus to Southampton with Linda to look in the shops.

Sunday was always dull, as Grandmother insisted they went to church with her and Janice, and then the twins had to have afternoon tea with her.

They didn't mind the church service so much, but they hated the way local people peered at them. The vicar waited in the porch after the service to shake hands with his parishioners, and many of them lingered in the churchyard to chat. They often buttonholed Maisy or Duncan to tell them they were old friends of their father, or some similar connection. The twins hated it. They knew people suspected there was some juicy story to explain why they were here with their grandmother and they wanted to dig it out.

Grandmother didn't approve of them going off anywhere on Sundays other than for a brief walk after lunch, but on this occasion Maisy was quite glad of the quiet time up in her bedroom. She worked on different ways of doing her hair and tried on her clothes to see if any of them could be altered to seem more adult. She had blouses with prim little Peter Pan collars; she even had a dress with smocking across her chest that made her look like she was nine.

She was very relieved Linda favoured wearing shorts and a loose blouse. Maisy liked herself in them too as she knew her legs were good; she just wished her breasts would hurry up and grow so she looked as adult as Linda, who was already a respectable 34B.

Maisy hadn't needed to wait for Janice to get the book about reproduction from the library because it transpired over their picnic that Linda knew it all, and she explained it clearly after Maisy admitted she didn't know anything. She thought Dr and Mrs Evans must be very sophisticated, because it was they who had taught Linda. Linda even smoothed out a sandwich bag and sketched a woman's belly showing where the ovaries and the womb were, and explained how her egg could be fertilized by male sperm to make a baby.

Maisy giggled as Linda told her about the male part in making a baby. She didn't really believe their penis could grow to two or three times the size, to go into a woman. She wasn't even sure where Linda meant it would go. Perhaps Linda realized this, for she then told Maisy she should explore herself a bit.

'My mum said it's no good waiting until you get married and hope your husband knows everything, because he probably won't. She said all women should arm themselves with knowledge as they are the ones that stand to lose most if they have a baby before marriage. And it can be utter misery being married and not enjoying sex because you are ignorant about how it works.'

That was the most astounding thing Maisy had ever heard. She really couldn't believe someone of her own age could be so adult and sophisticated.

All through August Maisy met up with Linda as often as she could. Along with mastering the waltz and the quickstep they were now pretty good at the foxtrot too. On wet days they practised the dances in Linda's bedroom, shrieking with laughter as they tried to pose as profession-als, holding their heads high and wearing haughty expressions. But Maisy was getting quite worried about how she'd survive once Linda went back to boarding school in September. They'd become everything to one another and the prospect of missing her friend, cold Autumn weather, darkness falling before teatime and Sat-urdays with absolutely nothing to do but read or listen to the wireless was all too depressing. She would of course have Duncan, but he'd become so involved with the friends he'd made in Burley that she was worried he'd always be with them. After all, none of them went to boarding schools.

Linda was surprised their grandmother hadn't got a tele-vision, and even more surprised that Maisy and Duncan could survive without one. 'I love it, everything from *Rin Tin Tin*, *Lassie* and *Champion the Wonder Horse*, to *Emergency – Ward Ten*, *Wagon Train* and quiz programmes like *Take Your Pick!*' she said. 'We can only see an hour of TV after prep at school, but we all go mad if we aren't allowed to see *Wagon Train*. I always want to kiss the screen when Robert Horton, the man that plays Flint McCullough the scout, is on. He's so dreamy.'

'Duncan asked Grandmother if she'd like one, but she reacted like he'd asked her if she fancied eating human flesh,' Maisy said with a giggle.

Maisy was thinking about how she was going to cope without Linda on the last Sunday evening in August. She was sitting at the kitchen table trying to play patience. Sunday's usual programme of *Sing Something Simple* was on the wireless, Janice was polishing silver and Duncan was sorting his stamp collection.

Janice looked sharply from Maisy to Duncan. 'You two don't seem to have much to say to each other these days,' she said. 'I hope you haven't fallen out?'

'Not at all,' Duncan said. 'We're fine, aren't we, Maisy?'

Maisy smiled at Janice. 'You've got a silver polish smear on your cheek, Janice. I think we're just growing up now and finding new friends.'

'Well, that's how it should be,' Janice said. 'I've got some things to do in my room. I'll see you again before bedtime.'

Maisy didn't really know what Duncan had been up to recently because she was always with Linda, but now she felt a bit guilty. Once Janice had gone, she got up and went round the table to put her arm around her brother's shoulder. 'We are OK, aren't we? I'd hate it if you were hurt because of Linda.'

They had been so close for so long that she couldn't quite understand why she was willing to leave her brother out of things now. She wished she knew how to tell him how good it was to do girls' things with someone she really liked, or that she'd started to look at boys flirtatiously and loved it when they looked back at her admiringly. But she couldn't.

That didn't mean she didn't care about him.

'It's fine, Sis, I'm not hurt. If anything, I'm glad I can be free to go and lark about with boys. We've lived in each other's pockets too much really, haven't we?'

Maisy sighed with relief.

'Well, that's good then. Now shall we play Chinese Chequers if you've finished sorting your stamps?'

They played Chinese Chequers for a while, and Duncan said the boys in the village all thought he was a bit special because he came from London and lived with his stinking rich grandmother who had a housekeeper and a gardener. 'I quite like them all looking up to me,' he admitted. 'It's a lot better than the way boys treated me in London, calling me weird and sissy because I didn't play football in the street.'

'I know exactly what you mean,' Maisy told him. 'I had my share of name-calling too.'

'But I sometimes feel a bit guilty that we've almost forgotten Mother because we're enjoying being here,' he said, looking troubled. 'So I want to go and see her. I've saved up some pocket money so I might go just before we start lessons again.'

Maisy suddenly realized that the quiet, thoughtful state of mind she'd noticed he'd been in occasionally wasn't, as she had thought, because of her, but because of their mother. It made Maisy feel a little guilty herself that along with barely giving her brother a second thought for weeks, she almost never thought about her mother.

'But we don't know the address of where she is,' she pointed out. 'Don't you think it's odd that Father hasn't given it to us? For all we know he might not be taking our letters to her. He might have just shut her away and forgotten about her.'

'Funny you should say that. Grace Deville said something similar.'

'You've seen her again? You didn't say.'

'Well, I've got in the habit of saying nothing because I don't want the village boys going there. But I go to see her every week. She's not easy to like, Maisy – almost always grumpy and so suspicious of people. But I think life has dealt her a poor hand. She wanted to know about Mother and I told her the truth because I know she won't say anything to anyone. She went very quiet and when I asked her what was wrong she said, "Mind they don't just keep her there." I asked her what she meant, and she said her folks put her away because they said she was a danger to herself, and she was in the asylum for twelve years.'

Maisy gasped. 'What did she mean, she was a danger to herself?'

Duncan shook his head. 'She wouldn't say. Maybe she tried to kill herself, like our mother.'

'But she's so strong and fearless living out there all alone. I can't imagine her ever being so sad that she wanted to kill herself.'

'That's what I thought. I was dying to know more, and I wondered if she escaped from the asylum and had to hide in the woods so she wouldn't be found. I think you can probably learn to do almost anything if you really need to.'

'I'd die of starvation,' Maisy said with a grin. 'I might be able to light a fire, even make a rough shelter, but I couldn't kill animals, skin them and eat them.'

'I wanted her to tell me how she survived in the early days, if she built her little house herself and all that kind of thing, but she clammed up. I'll have to wait till she's ready to talk again.'

There was something about the way Duncan said 'ready to talk again' that made Maisy suspect he'd gone out there many more times than he was letting on. She guessed he didn't know much more about Grace than he'd already said, but it sounded as if he had definitely established a relationship with her. Maisy had noticed he had a way with older women; at home in London he used to talk to the lady next door, and he chatted easily with women in the village shops here.

'Why don't we write a joint letter to Father, saying we'd like to write directly to Mother and need her address?' she suggested. 'If he doesn't give it to us then we'll know he's got something to hide.'

'Good thinking.' Duncan grinned. 'And now I'm going to thrash you at this game because you aren't concentrating.'

The following morning Maisy awoke to find the sun was already very warm, with the promise of a hot day ahead.

Leaping out of bed, she pulled out her favourite pink gingham sundress which she hadn't had occasion to wear since the previous summer. But to her surprise it was too tight where it buttoned down the front of the bodice, along with being a little too short. In fact, it was so tight it gaped when she buttoned it. All at once she realized this was because her breasts had begun to grow at last. They were only very small as yet, but it was a start.

Tossing the sundress aside, she put on a pair of blue shorts and a blouse, then without even brushing her hair she rushed down to tell Janice her news.

'I can't remember being that pleased when mine started sprouting.' Janice laughed. 'But then I was in a convent and the nuns made us keep our vests on, even in the bath. They said you couldn't be naked in front of God. But I suppose you thought you were going to be flat-chested forever, so no wonder you look like a dog with three tails now.'

'Yes.' Maisy beamed. 'I thought I was a freak.'

'Well, you aren't, and I suppose I need to tackle your grandmother about getting you some new clothes that do fit you.'

Maisy got the nine o'clock bus to Lyndhurst that morning as it was too hot to ride her bike. When she arrived Mrs Evans told her she was driving into Bournemouth to visit an old friend who was there on holiday. 'You two can come with me and I'll drop you off at the beach, if you like,' she suggested.

Maisy really admired her friend's mother. She was tall and willowy, her dark hair swept back into a sleek chignon, and with a complexion like alabaster. She was wearing a simple blue shirt dress with silver heeled sandals, and to Maisy's mind she looked like a film star.

Both girls were delighted, doing a gleeful little waltz around the kitchen.

Mrs Evans laughed with them. 'Run along and get your stuff together, Linda. Can you lend Maisy a bathing costume?'

Maisy wasn't sure the red costume Linda picked out would fit her – it looked awfully small – but there was no time to try it on as Mrs Evans was sitting in the car waiting for them.

'It'll be fine,' Linda reassured her. 'You're tiny, I don't know why you think otherwise.'

'I'll pick you up at six o'clock outside Beales Department Store,' Mrs Evans said as they approached the already bustling promenade. She pulled up to let them out and handed them each a two shilling piece to buy some lunch. 'Please behave in a ladylike manner and take care in the sea,' she added.

Maisy thought Linda was so lucky to have such a wonderful mother. Even when she gave out a warning like that, she only sounded caring, not fierce.

As the older woman drove off, the two girls exchanged gleeful grins.

'What first?' Linda asked. 'The beach or a walk along the prom to see who's about?'

Maisy knew Linda meant boys; she was always saying the ones who lived in Lyndhurst were either gormless louts or prissy grammar school boys. Up to this moment Maisy had been scared of showing any interest in boys, but in view of discovering she was now about to sprout real breasts, she felt bolder.

'A walk along the prom,' she said. 'We could hand-pick some company.'

Linda giggled. 'I could've kissed Mummy this morning when she said she'd drop us here. A beautiful day, you for company and a selection of boys to flirt with – what could be better?'

The girls found so much to laugh about. First there were the two pimply-faced boys who followed them along the prom, then when they'd given them the slip by going into a shoe shop and nipping out the back way, they attracted the attention of two even uglier boys. They screamed with laughter at these two diligently following them, as if they believed the girls would turn and offer to kiss them.

'Why do they do it?' Maisy asked. 'Do they hope we might walk to some secluded place where they can leap on us?'

Linda giggled. 'They don't think,' she said. 'They're so uncertain about themselves all they can do is follow girls around. If we turned and spoke to them they'd probably run off in fright. We should really feel sorry for them.'

'Or we could walk really fast and wear them out.'

'That would wear us out too,' Linda said. 'So it's into another shop again to lose them.'

After losing their admirers, the girls decided to go on the beach and sunbathe. They changed into their bathing costumes in the toilets and to Maisy's delight her borrowed costume fitted perfectly.

'Looks better on you than it ever did on me,' Linda said, looking at her friend appraisingly. 'You must keep it, it's far too small for me now.'

It was heavenly to lie on the beach on their towels, with the smell of seaweed, the seagulls wheeling overhead and the sea pounding on the shore. Maisy found herself dozing off and when she saw Linda was already asleep she let herself follow suit.

The girls woke with a start at water dripping on to their faces. Leaping up they saw it was Alan Walker and Steven Carter, grinning like Cheshire Cats. Linda had introduced Maisy to these two boys in Lyndhurst after their first dancing lesson; she'd admitted later that they were the only two boys in the village that she liked. That particular evening Maisy had to go straight home, but Linda told her the following day that they had walked her back to her house.

Both boys had deep suntans. 'We hoped we might run

into you in the village,' Steven said. 'We went away camping just after we last saw you. If we hadn't, we might have sat on the doorstep of the dancing class till you came out, so we were really surprised to come across you here.'

'We do a great deal more than just go to dancing lessons,' Linda said and Maisy noticed she was striking a pose, stomach sucked in, one leg out in front of the other, and running her fingers through her hair.

'Such as?' Alan asked.

Maisy had thought on her first meeting with these two that they were nice-looking. Steven was tallest, probably six foot, with dark hair and wide blue eyes. Alan had light brown hair streaked blond by the sun, a dimple in his chin and a mischievous grin.

'We like the theatre, roller skating, cycling and netball, and Maisy plays the piano.'

Maisy had a job not to laugh. Her friend had plucked those interests out of the air. To her knowledge, Linda had never mentioned liking netball, and Maisy had always hated it. She did play the piano, but Linda had never heard her.

'We're very keen readers too,' Maisy threw in. 'What interests do you two have?'

Alan's eyes flickered over her body in her red bathing costume. 'We like swimming, we were just going in. Come with us?'

Both boys began stripping off; beneath their trousers they were wearing swimming trunks.

Linda had said earlier she didn't want to do more than paddle because she didn't want to get her hair wet, but that was now forgotten.

'Last one into the sea buys ice creams all round,' she said, and with that darted off down the beach.

Maisy ran after her, and as they dashed into the sea, it was so cold that she shrieked. The boys reached them just a few seconds later, and Alan took Maisy's hand and led her into deeper water.

She sensed that because she had squealed at the cold water Alan assumed she couldn't swim very well, if at all. Maybe he was leading her out into deep water in the hopes she would get scared and cling on to him. But Maisy was a strong swimmer, so she let go of his hand and struck out in a fast crawl.

About two hundred yards out, she turned and trod water to see if Alan was following her. He was but it looked as if he was struggling. She swam back to him.

'Gosh, you're good,' he panted out. 'You went off like a rocket.'

'I love swimming,' she said. 'But it looks to me that you've come far enough. We'd better go back.'

It occurred to her that maybe swimming hadn't been such a good idea. Her hair would be a mess now, and though she had never cared that much about what she looked like before, suddenly she did.

Back in the shallows they held hands and jumped waves like a couple of small children. Steven and Linda were sitting on the beach chatting, with their feet in the sea.

'Are you just here on holiday?' Alan asked her. 'Only I hadn't seen you before that night when you'd been dancing.'

They walked along in the shallow water chatting, and Maisy explained that she and her twin brother had come to stay with their grandmother in Burley and that they had a private tutor.

'My father hopes we'll both go to university,' she said with a grin. 'But I'm not sure I'd like that.'

'Steven and I are going to Bristol University in October,' Alan said. 'I want to be a vet, and that's the best place. Steve is doing law. We can't wait to get there.'

Maisy didn't know why she should suddenly feel sad. That was a stupid reaction when she'd only known him for five minutes.

'A vet, how wonderful,' she exclaimed. 'But doesn't it take years to qualify? Like being a doctor?'

'Yes, seven years,' he said. 'But there's nothing else I want to do. I've wanted it since I was about six. What about you? Have you got some grand plan?'

'I told my grandmother I wanted to be a scientist once, but I only said it to try and impress her. I haven't a clue about what I really want to do. My brother has a new scheme every week – an explorer, a test pilot, always something dramatic. But I don't know about me. I worry sometimes that I've got no ambition. Maybe I could teach.'

'You could be a model, you're very pretty,' he said.

Maisy glowed at the compliment. 'Thank you, kind sir,' she said with a giggle.

It was the very best of days. They ate fish and chips, swam some more and lounged on the beach, happy to just chat.

Both the boys had sisters. Perhaps that was why they were comfortable talking to girls; certainly the conversation never lagged. But suddenly it was five thirty and the girls had to go and meet Linda's mother.

'Why don't you join the dancing class?' Linda suggested to the boys. 'I know it's only on for another two weeks but it's good fun. I'm sure you could pick it up quickly.'

'As long as we can dance with you two,' Steven said. 'If you have to be at Beales for six o'clock, we'd better go now.'

Alan took Maisy's hand as they made their way to the big department store, but just before they reached it, he pulled her into a shop doorway to kiss her.

Maisy had always been scared that when eventually someone did kiss her, she'd freeze with fear because she didn't know what to do. But to her delight it felt very natural and lovely. His mouth was soft and warm, he held her face between his two hands and the tip of his tongue just teased her lips in a way that gave her the funniest tightening feeling inside her.

But they had to run then to catch up with Linda and Steven.

Mrs Evans was waiting in her car. It seemed she knew the boys and their parents and offered them a lift back too. Linda sat in the front, and Maisy in the back between the two boys. Alan continued to hold her hand, stroking it with his thumb in a way that made her heart beat a little faster.

'We'll come to dancing on Tuesday, shall we?' Steven asked. 'It's at six, isn't it?'

'Can't come soon enough for me,' Alan whispered in Maisy's ear.

Mrs Evans talked to the boys about their university places for the remainder of the journey home. It was quite obvious that she approved of them and would even

83

welcome Steven courting her daughter. But Maisy wondered what her grandmother's reaction would be. Somehow she didn't think she'd approve of her granddaughter having a boyfriend.

Alan walked Maisy to the bus stop once they got back to Lyndhurst. The High Street was crowded with holidaymakers, and although he put his arms around her as they waited in the queue and kissed her nose and forehead, it wasn't an appropriate place for anything more.

'Forty-eight hours till I see you again,' he whispered. 'That's going to seem forever.'

Maisy felt exactly the same. But she couldn't suggest meeting him somewhere tomorrow as Janice had mentioned she wanted to take the twins into Southampton to buy some new clothes.

'I wish,' she said, but the bus pulled up and everyone in the queue surged forward before she could finish what she wanted to say, which was that she wished she didn't have to go home. Alan kissed her cheeks and squeezed her hand, then stood back until she'd found a seat.

He ran alongside the bus for some distance, waving and blowing kisses. Maisy's face was pink from the sun, but her colour increased at the excitement of finally having a boyfriend.

All she could think about on the ride home was his kiss. She closed her eyes and relived it, again and again.

It felt as if she had suddenly stepped into adulthood today. First finding her breasts were at last growing and then meeting Alan.

She was still glowing when she got in. Janice was doing some ironing and she looked worried.

'What's up?' Maisy asked. 'I did tell you I wouldn't be in till after seven as I was coming back on the bus. You said that was OK and you'd keep some supper for me.'

'It's not that. Duncan hasn't come home,' Janice said. 'He said he'd be back by six at the latest.'

'It's a bit soon to be worried.' Maisy went over to the housekeeper and gave her a hug. 'It's been a beautiful day, I expect he's lost track of time.'

'Yes, you're right, but he's always so reliable,' Janice said. 'Now tell me about your day.'

At nine Duncan still hadn't come home and Janice went in to inform Mrs Mitcham. When she came back into the kitchen she wiped a tear from her eye. 'I might have known she wouldn't share my concern,' she said to Maisy, who was doing some crochet and listening to the wireless. 'She just said boys will be boys, and it's a fine dry evening so why was I getting worked up.'

'She has got a point, Janice,' Maisy said. 'He's fifteen, not a little boy. But if you like I'll ride down to Colin's house to see if he's there.'

Colin Fairly lived in a council house down in the village. It was a messy place with lots of junk piled up in the front garden. Duncan had shown her where Colin lived a few weeks earlier and he said it was even worse inside. He'd added that Mr Fairly got drunk most nights so his mother had a job to make ends meet.

Mrs Fairly came to the door when Maisy knocked. She was a harassed, tired-looking woman of about forty-five, wearing a shapeless dress, and her hair was straggly and greasy.

'Our Colin came in about five for his tea,' she said. 'I asked who he'd been with all day, but he weren't with Duncan.'

'Is he in now?' Maisy asked. 'He might know where my brother is.'

'No, he's out someplace. But I'll ask him about Duncan and if he knows anything I'll get him to come up to your gran's house and tell you.'

'Thank you, Mrs Fairly, that would be much appreciated,' Maisy said. 'Sorry to have disturbed you.'

'It's a pleasure helping out someone as polite and well mannered as you,' the woman said, smiling to reveal several missing teeth. 'Your Duncan's the same, a real little gent. I tell my Colin, you copy him, not the rough boys round here.'

Maisy smiled, but it was a forced one as she too was getting worried now. It really wasn't like Duncan to be this late coming home. They'd had punctuality instilled into them almost from birth. In London they had known being late would worry their mother and annoy their father, and here it was Janice cooking for them that made them punctual. Duncan was always hungry, so he wouldn't easily skip a meal.

She rode around for a while, going to a few places where she knew local boys hung out in the evenings, but he wasn't with any of them and no one had seen him. She didn't like cycling in the dark, so she decided to go home.

'I wonder if he went to see our mother,' she said to Janice when she got back in. 'He said he was thinking about going next week. But maybe he just felt today was the day and went.'

'But he doesn't know where the place is,' Janice said,

chewing her lower lip with anxiety. 'Besides, it's ten o'clock now. If he had found the address and gone there and had to stay the night somewhere, he would have phoned.'

'I'm going in to see Grandmother,' Maisy said. 'You're right; if something unexpected had happened he would've phoned.'

Grandmother was listening to a play on the wireless and looked none too pleased at being interrupted. 'Not you panicking too!' she exclaimed.

'Not panicking, but worried,' Maisy said firmly. 'None of the village boys have seen him. I wondered if he'd gone to see our mother, but as far as I know he doesn't have her address. Should we telephone Father?'

'Of course not,' the old lady sniffed. 'Boys of his age are always off on the rampage. He's probably made a camp in the forest and he'll be back in the morning wanting breakfast. Alastair was always doing that when he was a boy.'

'With all due respect, Grandmother, Duncan and I have been brought up to always be home on time. He wouldn't stay the night in the forest without any warning, but he could be lying there with a broken leg, so I think we should call the police.'

'Nonsense!' Grandmother waved her arm dismissively. 'I'll not phone anyone for something so trivial. Even if he has broken his leg, the police couldn't find him in the dark. Now off to bed with you and let's not hear any more of this foolishness.'

'At least let me phone Father,' Maisy pleaded.

'What good can he do? He's too far away. Besides, he's rarely at home these days. Off to bed with you.'

87

Maisy had no real choice but to obey. She told Janice what had been said and the pair of them agreed that Grandmother was right – even if Duncan was hurt and lying in the forest, no one could find him now in the dark.

'If we haven't heard from him by eight tomorrow morning, I'll call the police,' Janice said. 'At least it's a warm night. He won't freeze, wherever he is.'

Maisy went up to bed. She felt a flash of crossness that Duncan had spoiled her perfect day, and then guilt. She had wanted to close her eyes and think of Alan, but now she would have to try and fall asleep with the image of her twin lying on the ground in pain.

6

By ten o'clock the next morning, with still no word from Duncan, Maisy knew something was badly wrong. It wasn't just that he wouldn't have left them without saying where he was going; it was a feeling deep inside her: that the strong connection they'd always had was severed. She fervently hoped that this was just her overactive imagination, that he was alive and well and in time they would laugh about it.

Grandmother finally telephoned the police. She did say, however, that if Duncan walked up the garden path later she was going to take both Janice and Maisy to task for wasting her time. It was chilling that she didn't seem the least bit concerned at his disappearance.

The police said they couldn't put him on the missing persons list until he'd been gone twenty-four hours and recommended they contact all his friends, because if Duncan thought he was in trouble at home he might have gone to one of them.

'Well, I'm not going to sit on my hands and wait,' Maisy said. 'I'm going into the forest to find him.'

'Shall I telephone Alastair?' Janice asked Grandmother.

'There's no need to bother him with this,' Grandmother stated calmly. 'It's simply not necessary in my opinion.'

Maisy wanted to scream at her grandmother that she was hateful and callous, but she resolved to keep quiet for now and find him herself; that way she could make her grandmother feel ashamed. After a quick change into a pair of slacks to protect her legs from brambles and a hasty word to Janice, she leapt on to her bike and set off.

It was even hotter than the previous day, and just the gentle hill out of Burley had Maisy sweating profusely. But her anxiety for Duncan kept her going, and as she turned on to the narrow lane into the forest, her eyes swept over the ground on either side in the hopes of seeing something unusual. The whole area was busy with cars, cyclists and hikers because it was peak holiday season, and she realized that if Duncan had been lying hurt anywhere near a well-used track or lane, he would've been found by now, and if not, very soon would be.

'But not if he's near Grace Deville's house,' she murmured aloud. That was a really dense part of the forest and this far into the summer the undergrowth must be virtually impassable.

She had only been to Grace's shack once before and to her alarm she found it hard to recognize the way because everywhere was so overgrown. She left her bike and struggled along several small tracks which just petered out after a time. She was almost on the point of giving up the search when she saw a track where there was evidence of broken twigs and flattened weeds, as if someone had used it recently. It could of course just have been an animal, but she didn't think so.

She picked up a stout stick to beat back the brambles and stinging nettles, but there were sections when the track virtually disappeared, and she was worried she would get stuck. Even with the stick the brambles caught at her hair, and her arms were badly scratched. It was fearfully hot too, and she had nothing to drink.

Just as she was thinking she must turn back, she saw the bushes were thinner up ahead, so she pressed on, and finally to her relief she broke through into the glade where Grace lived. Seeing the woman weeding her vegetable plot, she ran the last hundred yards.

Grace looked up in alarm. 'Get out! This is private property!' she shouted.

'I know it is,' Maisy called back breathlessly, but still coming on. She was too upset to feel fear. 'I don't know if you remember me, but I'm Duncan's sister. He's missing, gone all night, and I'm frantic that he might be lying in the forest hurt. Have you seen him?'

The woman's hostile look vanished and she frowned with concern. 'Not for a few days,' she said.

Maisy was close to her now. 'Has he said anything to you that might suggest he was going to make a trip some-where?'

The older woman looked thoughtful. 'He did say he wanted to go and see his mother. He often talks about her. But you're his sister – surely he'd tell you if that was where he was going?'

'But neither of us know where Mother is,' Maisy said. 'We would've gone together if we knew. I'm sure if he managed to get our father to tell him the address he would've told me, so I don't believe that's where he's gone. But I do know he likes you, that's why I hoped he'd come here.'

All at once Maisy began to cry; she tried to stop it but she just couldn't. The heat, thirst, anxiety and her grandmother's reluctance to do anything all seemed to come together in one big wave of insurmountable difficulty.

'I like him too,' Grace said and put one hand tentatively on Maisy's shoulder. 'Now stop crying. He's a sensible boy, I'm sure he hasn't come to any harm. Sit down and have a drink of water. You're overheated.'

She brought Maisy some water in a tin cup and made her sit in the shade. 'Now let's put our heads together,' she said, sitting down on a log. 'He left your house when yesterday? And what was he wearing?'

'He was still at home when I left before nine. Janice – she's the housekeeper – said he went out about ten wearing shorts and a short-sleeved shirt. He took his bike.'

'Well, if he was going off to London I think he'd have been out the door much earlier. I also don't think he'd be wearing shorts. Not to catch a train and visit his mother. '

Maisy nodded. She hadn't thought of that. 'You're right. Not unless the shorts were a smokescreen for our grandmother and Janice, and he had some long trousers or even his suit outside somewhere to pick up before he cycled to the station.'

'Why would he hide his clothes? Is it because your grandmother wouldn't approve?'

Maisy nodded glumly. 'She's a bit of a dragon and she doesn't like our mother.'

'So if he did go to see her he must have got the address from your father. Have you spoken to him yet?'

Maisy didn't know why people made out Grace was mad. She certainly wasn't, and despite her scary manner on first meeting, she was kind too.

'No, I haven't, and Grandmother said there was no

point in telephoning him until we are sure something is wrong. She seems to think it's quite normal for boys to go off into the forest to sleep. I agree Duncan would probably love to do that, but only with a friend and all the right equipment. And he'd never do it without telling anyone.'

'No, he struck me as a very sensitive, conscientious boy. Do you know, he's the only person I've talked to properly in ten years or more. I frighten everyone else off.'

Maisy wasn't sure which was the biggest surprise: that a person could live ten years without speaking to anyone, or Grace admitting such a thing.

'Can you think of anything else he said to you that might give us a hint where he is, or did he mention anyone at all?' she asked.

'There was your teacher, Mr Dove; I felt he'd been a huge influence on him. He said they'd talked about all sorts of things, and he'd made him see his father in a different light.'

'Really? Duncan never said anything like that to me.'

'Maybe that was because he didn't wish you or his grandmother to see his sensitivity. People are fond of saying boys shouldn't cry, they have to be strong and keep the stiff upper lip. They aren't encouraged to talk about their feelings and certainly not to analyse anyone else's.'

'That's just the sort of thing Mr Dove says. He lost the use of his legs in the war but he's not bitter about it. He understands people. I think you do too.'

'I understand them so well that I hide from them,' Grace said, and gave a humourless laugh. 'I think maybe your Mr Dove and I come at things from opposite sides. I am still bitter about things I can't forgive. But I've talked to you for too long, Maisy. You must go home and see if there's any news of your brother.'

'May I come back?' Maisy asked. 'I promise I won't be a nuisance.'

'Come back and tell me when Duncan is found,' Grace said.

Maisy realized that was Grace's way of telling her she was welcome to come once more, but that was all. She stood up and held out her hand to the older woman.

'Thank you for being so kind,' she said. 'I see now why my brother liked to visit you.'

Grace took Maisy's hand between her two deeply tanned, rough-looking ones and her tawny eyes appeared to be seeing right down to Maisy's soul. 'It is good after all these years of people thinking the worst of me to meet two people with open minds,' she said. 'But go home now. I hope Duncan will soon be back.'

Maisy continued to look all around her as she rode back to Nightingales, but she felt a terrible sense of foreboding. She tried to tell herself she was making a drama about something that would turn out to be quite trivial and he'd be home again soon with a story to tell, but she didn't believe it.

Duncan wasn't home. Instead the local constable, PC Welby, was speaking to her grandmother in the garden. As Maisy leaned her bike against the shed, she heard her grandmother speak.

'This is an overreaction, he's just a boy out adventuring. He'll come back when he's hungry.'

Maisy saw red at that remark, furious that her grandmother was being so blind and stubborn. 'Why don't you tell the police that this isn't like him, then maybe they'll start looking for him?' she yelled out.

PC Welby wheeled round to look at Maisy. 'I take it you are Duncan's twin sister? And you don't agree with Mrs Mitcham?'

'Yes, I am Maisy Mitcham, and no, I don't agree with my grandmother. I know my brother far better than anyone else does. Grandmother hasn't said more than a few hundred words to him in his whole life. He wouldn't go off "adventuring" without telling someone or leaving a note. He's either out there somewhere too hurt or sick to get help, or someone has got him.' This idea had come to her as she'd been cycling home and to her it seemed logical.

'How dare you be so rude?' Grandmother said, taking a few warning steps towards Maisy as if she was going to box her ears. 'I have a lifetime of experience with people. You are still a child, and I would remind you that you are a guest in my home.'

Welby ignored the older woman and looked at Maisy. 'Why would you think someone has got him? To demand a ransom, do you mean?'

Maisy shrugged. 'Why not? Rumour has it Mrs Mitcham is a wealthy woman. If that is the case we'll hear from the kidnappers soon. But surely in the meantime there should be a thorough search in case he's lying out there hurt? You should be questioning people too.'

'Mrs Mitcham is right – you are rude. You don't need to tell me how to do my job,' Welby said, his plump face tightening with indignation. 'Now tell me who his friends are.'

Maisy was chastened; she needed people on her side, not to put their backs up.

'I'm sorry, sir. I didn't mean to be rude to either of you,' she said. 'I'm just scared and I want to see someone taking his disappearance seriously. I did go and see some of his friends last night, but I'm sure they'll be more honest with you than they might be with me.'

She told him all the names she knew, including Grace Deville, and that she'd been out to see her already. Welby wrote their names down in his pocket book. Grandmother asked Welby to step into the house with her. Maisy had no doubt she wanted to tell the policeman that her grand-daughter had an overactive imagination. She used the chance to jump on her bike again and ride down to see Mr Dove.

He, at least, was shocked, and truly concerned. 'I agree with you, Maisy, Duncan isn't the kind of lad to do something hare-brained or to go off to London without telling someone. In fact, I think if he had decided to go and see his mother he would've run it past me.'

'Has he talked about anything to you that might point to him going off?'

Dove sighed and rubbed his chin. 'He did ask me a while ago about "mad" people. I told him he must never use that term and that there are few people who are truly "mad" like a lunatic. There are of course a small minority who have something like schizophrenia where they can behave in an extraordinary manner, and even be violent, but I believe that the vast majority of people who become mentally ill do so because they can't cope with something in their life.'

'My mother too?'

'That's what Duncan asked, but I wasn't much help.

96

I've never met her and even you two don't know what, if any, her problems are, or much about her background. He asked me what treatments mental patients get, and again, I know very little. I have heard about electric shock treatment, but recently I read about a doctor in Switzerland who treated his patients with nothing more than a good balanced diet, plenty of exercise and letting them talk.'

'Diet?' Maisy raised an eyebrow. 'Surely that wouldn't make any difference?'

Dove shrugged. 'Well, to me it sounded like good sense. I got very low after I lost the use of my legs, and I know talking about how I felt, getting out in the fresh air and learning to get around in my wheelchair got me out of the doldrums. But you can't generalize; people are all different.'

'I don't believe Duncan has gone to see our mother anyway. I think he's been kidnapped,' Maisy said heatedly. 'It's the only thing that makes sense to me. People around here think Grandmother is sitting on a fortune and they know my father is in London doing something for the government, so they probably think he's stinking rich too. Anyone who has ever met Duncan would know he was hardly likely to fight his way out of a nasty situation. He's soft and gentle, an ideal target.'

Dove shook his head. 'You've seen too many American films. I can't think of one case of kidnapping here in England. But we'll soon know if that *is* what has happened when they demand money for him.'

'Do you think my grandmother would pay it?' Maisy said doubtfully.

Dove sighed deeply. 'Who knows, Maisy? Let's just wait until it happens.'

When Maisy got back to Nightingales she was called in to see her grandmother in her sitting room. She was sitting in her usual chair, her back to the window, her face like stone and her back as stiff as a tree trunk.

'I understand you are upset about your brother, but any more rudeness from you and I will lock you in your room,' she said. 'I have telephoned your father and he's coming down on the train. He said he wants you to stay in the house until he gets here.'

'You mean I can't go out in the forest and look for Duncan some more?'

'No, Maisy. If he was taken by someone, they might take you too. Not that I think he was; I still believe he simply went off adventuring. But that isn't all I need to take you to task over. You said earlier that you'd been out talking to that mad woman that lives in the forest. What on earth were you thinking of?'

'She's not mad,' Maisy said. 'She's just a bit different. Duncan liked her, he often went to see her. I only went to ask if she knew where he might have gone.'

'Well, by now the police will have taken her in for questioning.'

Maisy felt sickened. She hadn't intended to get Grace involved, and she could see now that people were likely to blame her because she was unconventional and different from them.

'She doesn't know anything and she'll be bullied,' she blurted out. 'It's not right.'

'How do you know that she doesn't know anything?

Why, she could've killed your brother and buried him out there in the forest.'

'She didn't, she wouldn't.' Maisy began to cry. 'Why would she?'

'You've got a lot to learn about human nature, my girl,' the old lady said scornfully. 'There are so many hair-raising stories about that woman. If only one percent of them were true, I'd have reason to worry. Now stop blubbering and go to your room. I've had quite enough of you for one day.'

'How can you be so callous?' Maisy asked, her anger overcoming her fear of the old lady. 'One minute you're saying my brother could've been murdered and buried in the forest, then when I get upset you order me to my room. Don't you have any feelings for your son or your grandchildren?'

'I do have feelings – mainly irritation. Now get out of here and tell Janice to bring me some tea.'

Maisy rushed into Janice's arms, sobbing wildly as she blurted out what her grandmother had said to her. 'She's so nasty,' she cried. 'She doesn't care about anyone but herself.'

'That's not strictly true. In the past I have found her to be quite surprising – one minute she seems completely uncaring, and then she suddenly rallies to a cause and becomes quite a firebrand. I bet you that's what will happen now, you wait and see. She was only sharp with you because she's frightened.'

Maisy wasn't convinced. Her stomach churning with fear, she turned down the offer of a sandwich and sloped off to her bedroom feeling completely alone in the world.

As she lay on her bed she reflected that just twenty-four hours ago she was having the happiest day of her life, laughing and chatting with Alan and believing that it was the start of a whole new wonderful era. Coming home on the bus she could think of nothing but his kiss, but now she felt it was wrong to give him even a passing thought. Her mind should be focussed only on Duncan.

It was six in the evening by the time her father arrived, but that proved to be another disappointment. Maisy went running down the stairs to meet him, expecting he would hug her and reassure her he would find Duncan. Instead he pushed her from him, holding her at arm's-length. 'There's no need for dramatics,' he said. 'Now where's my mother?'

He went into the sitting room and shut the door, leaving Maisy outside. She slunk off back to the kitchen trying very hard not to cry.

'They've always been like that,' Janice said, immediately picking up on Maisy's hurt. 'They just don't know how to behave like parents. I'll go in to see if they want anything just now and find out about supper, and whether you are to join them or not. I've made your father's favourite, toad-in-the-hole, but I doubt I'll get any appreciation either.'

Maisy wondered then why on earth Janice had stayed all these years. A woman with her housekeeping skills could attract a good salary and have proper status rather than be the general dogsbody as she was here.

It was after nine before her father came to speak to her in the kitchen. She hadn't been asked to join her father and grandmother for supper, so she had stayed with Janice.

She barely ate anything anyway; her stomach felt as if it was tied in knots.

He asked Janice to leave the room so he could speak to Maisy alone.

The moment the door had closed behind Janice, he rounded on Maisy. 'Why weren't you two together yesterday?' he asked, his voice very sharp.

Maisy went over to the window. 'I went out to Bournemouth for the day with Linda Evans, a girl I met at ballroom dancing classes. Duncan was seeing his friends.'

'You surely remember I have always said you must stick together?'

'Father, we are fifteen, not five. We have different interests now.'

'Be that as it may, if you'd planned to be together yesterday Duncan wouldn't be missing now.'

Maisy felt that such a stupid remark didn't warrant a reply, so she just stared at her father, hoping he could read her thoughts. Not for the first time she noticed what an odd-looking man he was. His forehead bulged, his hair was more ginger than blond, and his eyes were such a pale blue there was almost no colour in them. Added to this his skin looked too thin, like it had been stretched over the bones in his face. His nose was long and narrow and his mouth was too small.

Grandmother had said she and Duncan took after their grandfather, and from the photograph in her sitting room it appeared to be true. He had been a handsome man with thick blond hair like theirs and very blue eyes. Maisy hoped she hadn't inherited anything from either of her parents: their looks or their characters.

'So explain to me why Duncan was in the habit of visiting Grace Deville,' Father barked at her. 'I cannot imagine why a fifteen-year-old boy would want to visit a crazy old harridan.'

'When your own mother is in an asylum maybe it's a comfort to talk to other crazy people.'

The hard slap across her cheek seemed to come out of nowhere. She hadn't seen her father move to strike her, and it knocked her right back against the window. 'How dare you be so insolent?' he raged. 'You are a child, Maisy. You show me respect and obey me at all times. Is that understood?'

'It's difficult to respect someone who shows no interest in you,' she flung back at him, angry now and unafraid. 'You sent us here without any explanation about what was wrong with Mother. Why doesn't she write to us? When is she going to get better? Does she even know where we are? I was frightened for Duncan when he didn't come home last night, but Grandmother cares so little about both of us she wouldn't even telephone you. When I have children I will treasure them, and tell them I love them.'

'We don't do that sloppy stuff in our family,' he said angrily.

'You mean Grandmother never showed you an ounce of love so you feel you've got to bring us up the same way.'

'You are getting above yourself,' he said, taking a warning step towards her again. 'My mother has got nothing to do with this.'

'But she has, Father. She's stunted you, she's as cold as ice to us. If it wasn't for Janice we'd probably have run away by now. But Duncan hasn't run from Grandmother, however hateful she can be. He wouldn't leave me here alone. When are all you adults going to believe what I say? I know him better than anyone. He didn't run away, he's been taken. And if you don't make the police find whoever took him, and quickly, then they might kill him.'

'I really don't know what's come over you.' He shook his head as if in despair. 'All this blaming, all the melodrama. I don't understand.'

'What is there to understand?' Maisy almost felt sorry for him that he couldn't grasp this was serious. 'Your son, who has never been disobedient, rode off on his bike and he's been gone for more than twenty-four hours. I'm not being melodramatic, that is a fact. You should be at the police station making them start a search. You should be out searching yourself, not sitting with Grandmother having a cosy dinner, or slapping me for being what you call insolent.'

'I came to ask you what the connection with Grace Deville was all about.'

If Maisy hadn't been so distraught, she might have laughed. She could see he had no idea what to do about his son's disappearance and was astounded a fifteen-year-old was ahead of him.

'Duncan likes to talk to people and find out what they're all about,' she said, softening her tone because she was getting to feel a bit sorry for him. 'He heard lots of stories about the woman and went out of his way to befriend her so he could find out the truth. It was something he did on his own, and when I saw her earlier today I sensed she'd grown to like him. She was kind to me too. Grace Deville isn't mad, and if the police think it's her that's done away with him, then they've all got screws missing.'

'Suppose I take your word for that, then what do you think has happened to him?'

'Well, if he isn't lying in some secluded part of the forest with a broken leg or worse, I believe he was taken to make you and Grandmother pay out money to get him back. Everyone around here believes you're very rich.'

'But we aren't.'

'That's not how it looks to really poor people,' Maisy said. She moved closer to her father and put her hand on his arm. 'Some of the boys Duncan made friends with have the seats out of their trousers and holes in their shoes. Any one of them could have told someone else about Nightingales, that you live in London and that we have a private tutor. People get jealous about things like that.'

'Well, I can't help that,' he huffed.

'No, you can't, though Grandmother has actively offended almost everyone in the village at some time, so it's hardly surprising if someone wants to teach her a lesson. But you could act now, get back to the police. Organize a search party. Even offer a reward for information.'

He had turned away from her to look out of the window and she thought that he was taking on board what she'd said, maybe he was even going to agree with her. But when he turned back to face her, his expression told her the exact opposite.

'I think, young lady, that you've grown too big for your boots. I've never heard such impudence. How dare you criticize me or your grandmother? When all this business is over I can see I must take you in hand.'

All at once Maisy crumpled, tears streaming down her cheeks. She had tried to be adult and composed, saying what she thought clearly and honestly, and she'd actually hoped he would be impressed, but she was foolish to think such things. He had never cared about her and Duncan. He wasn't even here because he was frantic with worry about his son, but just because it was expected of him. She had no doubt that he was already wondering how soon he could get away, without everyone realizing he just didn't care.

'Stop those crocodile tears,' he snapped at her. 'I know how little they mean. Your mother was the expert on crying to order for attention.'

Maisy ran for the door and up the stairs to her room. Once the door was locked behind her, she threw herself on the bed and sobbed. She wished she could run away, if only to make things look really bad for her father and grandmother. But aside from having nowhere to go, and very little money either, she needed to be here for when they found Duncan.

'But I will go as soon as I'm sixteen,' she muttered into her pillow. 'I'll never come back here.'

She had a picture in her mind of cycling with Duncan through the forest, laughing when they bumped over holes or rocks, always in tune with one another, sharing everything. Had she been selfish to want to go to dancing classes? If she hadn't gone she'd never have met Linda and she wouldn't have been in Bournemouth yesterday.

It was all so terribly unfair. Why did she have to meet Alan and for just a few hours feel happier than she'd ever been before, but then have it snatched away?

Tomorrow she would have to telephone Linda and explain what had happened, but she couldn't hope that Alan would wait for her until all this was resolved. Even Linda would find another friend.

But the worst of it was that she sensed it was never going to be resolved. That Duncan wasn't going to be found, dead or alive.

7

November

'Please try to concentrate,' Mr Dove pleaded with Maisy. 'I do understand you find it difficult to get Duncan out of your mind, but you must try to put thoughts of him to one side in lesson time.'

Maisy lifted red-rimmed eyes to her teacher. She wished she could do as he asked, but she couldn't get her brother out of her mind, not at night, nor by day. Her eyes bore testament to lack of sleep and endless crying.

No one seemed able to understand just how much pain she was in. In the first weeks there were searches to take part in; everyone for miles around was involved and that was heartening.

The hope that the police might have found a new lead, even that Duncan would breeze back in with some wild story of joining a travelling fair or of just getting on a train, was enough to get up with a little optimism each morning. Every single moment of daylight was used, at least by Maisy, going up and down every path in the forest, searching, poking bushes, hunting for any tiny scrap of something that might offer up a clue to what had happened to him.

But after a few weeks the organized police searches stopped, reporters were losing interest and the local people shrugged, as if there was no hope of finding him alive.

Even Maisy felt she hadn't got anything left in her to search the same places again. Now she just felt desperately sad. She wasn't sleeping, could only pick at food and she had no energy for anything.

'I'll try, sir,' she said in a small voice. 'It's just that nothing in this world seems important except for Duncan.'

It was November now, a fierce wind blowing down the last remaining leaves on the trees, and so very cold. It was well over two months since Duncan had disappeared and although the police told them they were still actively following up leads, it didn't seem that way.

Maisy knew the police and local volunteers had covered every square mile of the forest because she had been with them every day. They had found one of Duncan's brown sandals amongst some bracken quite close to the Lyndhurst road. The buckle was missing, so it was possible it came off his foot while he was cycling and for some reason he didn't go back for it.

His bike still hadn't been found which, as the police quickly pointed out, meant he could've ridden into Southampton, Bournemouth or even further afield. But as Maisy pointed out in return, he wouldn't continue to ride far with only one shoe.

They held Grace Deville in custody for two days, and then released her without charge after the police had searched the ground in a mile radius of her shack and found nothing. She couldn't have managed to carry a body further than that.

It transpired she owned a van which she kept about half a mile from her shack next to a cottage owned by an old man called Enoch. He was an odd character too, who earned a living making charcoal and keeping pigs which he let loose in the forest. But he said Grace hadn't moved her van for nearly a week, so she certainly hadn't transported a body anywhere in it.

Janice heard all the gossip when she went to the grocer's in Burley. She told Maisy that many local people were still claiming Grace had killed and buried Duncan. But as Maisy told everyone who would listen, Grace had liked Duncan, he liked and respected her too, they'd become friends. What possible motive would she have for killing him?

When Linda, Alan and Steven read about Duncan in the newspaper they came out to Burley to see Maisy. Their sympathy was very welcome and comforting, especially Alan's. He had held her hand and said that although he understood she couldn't see him just now, he would keep in touch and be praying for her brother.

Alan and Steven had joined the search too. By all accounts they really pushed themselves, walking much further than some of Grandmother's neighbours who actually knew Duncan. Maisy could see for herself that Alan really cared; she longed to fall into his arms and, for just a few short moments, be able to think about something other than her brother.

But that wasn't possible. Grandmother wasn't letting her go anywhere alone, Janice seemed to have developed eyes in the back of her head, and her father had also insisted she stay at home. Besides, Maisy felt it wasn't appropriate to be seeing a boy at such a time.

Linda went back to her boarding school a week after Duncan disappeared, and in early October Maisy got a letter from Alan telling her he was now at Bristol University and hoped she'd write and tell him what was happening. She had written back, and to Linda at her school too, but there was nothing to tell them about Duncan.

Mr Grainger drove out to Nightingales to see Maisy and her grandmother after the initial shock waves had begun to dissipate.

True to form, Grandmother kept him in her sitting room with her for ages while Maisy paced the hall, wanting to speak to him, as she thought a solicitor might be able to pull strings others couldn't.

When he eventually emerged he pulled a little face and inclined his head towards the sitting room. 'Let's have a little chat on our own in the garden,' he said. 'That's really what I came for. I'm sorry of course for all of you, but it must come hardest for you.'

He was so kind, putting his arm around her and letting her cry. 'There are no words really for a situation like this. I wish I could tell you that I'm sure he'll be found, but I can't in all honesty. No one can predict that. But what I will say is Duncan struck me as a strong, brave boy, capable of reasoning with whoever has taken him, showing that he isn't easily intimidated. Those are traits that historically always serve people well if they are taken hostage or prisoner.'

'I never saw him as strong-willed or brave,' she sobbed. 'I even told the police he's a bit soft. He used to have nightmares when he was little and I used to be the one to make them go away. But I'm glad you saw him differently. I know he wanted to be a strong, brave man.'

'I saw a spark of defiance,' he said. 'I liked that. But tell me, Maisy, is there anything I can do to help?'

'Do you have any influence with the police? They don't seem to be doing much,' she said. 'It would be so good to have someone to push them harder. Could you do that?'

'I will certainly try,' he said. 'Now, chin up, flash that beautiful smile and trust the legal system, which, although slow sometimes, is usually thorough.'

Despite the confidence Mr Grainger appeared to have in the police, Maisy didn't share it, because they hadn't come up with one new lead since finding Duncan's sandal. She felt that everyone but her, Janice and Grandmother had given up on her brother. The newspapers made much of the story for just a few short days, comparing Duncan's disappearance almost in passing with those other young boys who had disappeared from towns along the south coast in the past year.

When Maisy read about these other boys, she urged her grandmother to call the police to investigate this further, or to at least tell her son he ought to be doing so. Her father did act then; he came down to Nightingales and went to see a senior police officer in Southampton. When he came back he looked even more troubled as he'd been told that two boys' bodies had been found in shallow graves on waste ground in the past two months, and there was another boy still missing.

In an attempt to embarrass the police into making a bigger effort to find whoever was responsible for these crimes, Alastair had gone to a national newspaper with the story. They did print a very sensational article suggesting that this could be the work of a psychopath. But to Alastair, Violet and Maisy's dismay, they concentrated on digging up dirt about the families of the two dead boys.

One had a father in prison, the other a neglectful mother, and both boys had problems at school. As if that wasn't enough, they then went on to reveal Duncan's mother was in an asylum, which was why he and his sister had been sent to their grandmother's. Their final piece of blatant slander was to report that Alastair Mitcham, although able-bodied, had held a desk job during the war.

Having told the general public that Duncan's mother was mad, the father a shirker and that in all probability the boy had run off to the bright lights of Brighton or London, the press then lost interest and suddenly cut off from the story.

As Janice said, 'They've besmirched us all, and they don't even care if Duncan is alive or dead.' As for the police, they claimed to still be on the case, but it didn't look to Maisy or Janice as though they were making much of an effort.

Maisy found she couldn't make much of an effort either, in her lessons or in writing to Linda and Alan. She wanted to keep in touch with them because she needed them, but she was all too aware that fun-loving, jolly people like them couldn't possibly understand how low her spirits were. It was just impossible for her to write the kind of bright and breezy letters they would want to receive. She hadn't written to either of them now since mid-October.

'I understand completely,' Dove said, wheeling his chair over to Maisy and putting his arm around her. 'But you must make something of your life, for Duncan's sake if nothing else. You know he wouldn't like to see you this crushed and miserable. Now would he?'

Maisy shook her head. She was able to reason with herself, insist she had to do well in exams and go to university because Duncan would have wanted that for her – but reason didn't help. It didn't wipe out the bleakness inside her, or the wish that she could wander into the forest, lie down and let death come to her too.

'So where were we?' Dove said. 'I wanted your thoughts on *A Tale of Two Cities*, whether or not you feel it is one of Dickens's best books, or inferior, to, say, *Great Expectations*?'

Maisy thought for a minute. 'I thought it was very different to his other books, but maybe that was just because so much of it is set in France. I really liked it. Dickens kept the excitement brewing for me. And Sydney Carlton giving his life to save his friend was very moving.'

Dove raised one eyebrow quizzically. 'So you are still able to immerse yourself in a story and feel for the characters?'

'Yes, I can. It helps take my mind off things,' she said. 'Crying for Sydney made me feel a bit better. But tell me, sir, do you think Duncan is still alive?'

Dove wished she hadn't asked him that. He knew only too well that if missing children aren't found within just a couple of days it usually means they've been murdered. Of course Duncan wasn't strictly a child, but then he hadn't got it in him to just disappear to live a different life. And if he'd been kidnapped the family would've been contacted by now with a demand for money.

'There is still the possibility that he met someone who persuaded him to go with him or her,' he said cautiously. In his opinion anyone luring a fifteen-year-old boy away from their home could only be doing it for one purpose, and that, for a sensitive boy like Duncan, was worse than death.

'You mean to work for them or something?' she asked.

Dove wished he hadn't brought this up. 'Maybe,' he said. 'Then Duncan was too afraid to come home because he knew he'd be in trouble. But that's a long shot, Maisy. I'm trying to find reasons, excuses, ideas, anything to hang a bit of hope on.'

'But you actually think there is none?'

Her stricken little face was enough to melt a heart of stone and James Dove didn't have one of those. 'There's always hope,' he lied. 'We have to think positive thoughts.'

Maisy clutched her coat round her more tightly as she walked back to Nightingales after her lessons. It was freezing, and she wished she'd worn her slacks, since short socks and bare legs in such weather was misery.

When she spotted a police car outside the gate of Nightingales she ran the rest of the way, bursting in through the kitchen door, her face alight with expectancy.

'Have they found him?' she asked Janice, who was ironing.

'I don't know,' Janice said, standing the iron up on its base and moving towards Maisy. 'But I don't think so or your grandmother would've rung the bell to tell me. Maybe they've just found a new piece of evidence.'

Maisy wasn't going to wait to be told of any new developments. She threw open the door into the hall, rushed across it and into the sitting room, still wearing her coat.

'What news is there?' she asked breathlessly.

'How dare you burst in here uninvited?' Grandmother asked, getting up out of her armchair indignantly.

'Because he's my twin brother and I love him,' Maisy

shot back, her voice rising in anger at the selfish old woman. She took a couple of steps towards Sergeant Fowler who she'd met several times in the past couple of months. He was probably close to retirement age with a heavily lined face like a bloodhound, but she'd found him to be quite kindly. 'Please tell me, have you found him?'

The sergeant looked down at his feet; it was quite obvious he didn't want to admit it.

'You've found his body?' she cried out. 'No, no, please tell me that's not true?'

'We have found *a* body, Miss Mitcham,' he said. 'He's the right age, height and weight, but until the pathologist can say when he died we can't confirm it is your brother.'

'Can't I identify him?' Maisy asked.

'Don't be so stupid, child,' her grandmother barked out. 'He isn't in a fit state now for anyone to identify him.'

Maisy looked from the policeman to her grandmother; she couldn't quite focus on either of their faces. Suddenly the room seemed to spin. She reached out for the back of the settee to steady herself but missed it and felt herself falling.

A strong smell brought her round. She was aware she was on the floor, and her grandmother was holding a bottle of smelling salts beneath her nose. Maisy rolled away from it and tried to get up.

'You fainted.' She recognized the sergeant's voice and it came back to her what had been said. 'Come on, now, let me help you up on to a chair. It's hardly surprising you passed out, shock can do that to you.'

Once Maisy was on the settee and she'd had some water, she observed her grandmother sitting opposite her was trembling, and very pale. It was a reminder that however hateful she could be, she too must be as frightened as Maisy was.

'I'm sorry, Grandmother, for barging in and for being a bit stupid. I'm just so frantic with worry,' she said.

'I know,' Grandmother said. 'And I wish I knew the right things to say to you to make it easier to bear. But I don't. We have to wait now until the pathologist has examined this boy they've found, so you've got to be brave and composed for a little longer.'

Sergeant Fowler crouched down by Maisy. 'All of the team that have been trying to find Duncan really hope this isn't him, miss. We'd rather find out he'd stowed away on a ship bound for Australia. And that has happened too. Two years ago we were searching for two boys and it turned out that's what they'd done.'

Maisy tried to smile because she recognized he was being kind. 'I wish Duncan had done that, but I know he would never do such a thing. The truth is, Duncan was always a goody-goody, and not terribly brave either. I just wish you policemen would realize that building a camp in the forest was as daring as he could get. He was a happy boy, he had no reason to run away.'

'I think we all appreciate that now.' Sergeant Fowler tweaked her cheek. 'Would anyone run away from such a devoted, loving sister? I have to go now, but I'll be in touch as soon as we have some results.'

The sergeant said he'd let himself out. After he'd closed the door behind him, Maisy and her grandmother stayed in their seats for some little while. Grandmother eventually broke the silence.

'I don't think it will be Duncan,' she said thoughtfully.

'Why?' Maisy asked.

'Well, for a start they found this boy near Portsmouth and he was wearing a jumper. Duncan didn't leave here wearing a jumper. Janice went through his clothes and the only things missing were those items he'd been wearing that morning when he left.'

'He could've bought a jumper.'

'What boy of fifteen buys a jumper in summer? I suspect this boy they've found either died before Duncan disappeared, or more recently.'

In Maisy's mind, as long as Duncan's death wasn't confirmed there was still hope he was alive. 'Did Sergeant Fowler tell you how this boy died?' she asked.

'No, he didn't. They don't give out information like that until they're sure of identity. Now calm down, Maisy, and go and have your lunch with Janice. As soon as I know anything I will tell you.'

As Maisy went back to the kitchen she thought on how her grandmother had softened after her faint. She wished she could be like that all the time, especially now when they all needed kindness. She hoped it also meant that her grandmother would start bullying and pestering the police for action. But perhaps it was too late for that now.

Janice was preparing a tray for her mistress's lunch. She looked up, wide-eyed and anxious. 'What was the news?'

Maisy told her. 'Grandmother said I must be calm until we know if it is Duncan, or not.'

Janice's eyes welled up and, abandoning the tray, she came to Maisy with open arms to hug her.

'I'm so glad I've got you,' Maisy murmured into her neck.

'And I'm glad I've got you too,' Janice replied. 'We will get through this, Maisy; especially if we cling together.'

After Maisy had helped clear away the lunch and the washing-up, she asked if she could go out on her bike for a while. 'Just a little spin to clear my head,' she said.

Janice frowned. 'It's bitterly cold and windy, but I suppose you have been cooped up a great deal lately. Don't be long, though. It gets dark by five.'

Maisy put on her warm slacks and another jumper, then with a woolly hat pulled down over her ears, a thick scarf and her coat, she felt ready for the chill outside.

She knew exactly where she was going, and that it wouldn't be approved of. But that didn't matter to her.

There were no tourists in cars, no dog walkers or hikers now in the forest. She had it all to herself, and the trees, stripped of their leaves, looked gaunt and skeletal. She found the little track to Grace's shack easily this time, left her bike and pushed through, panting with the exertion of the fast ride.

Grace's garden looked very bare compared with how it had been on her last visit. But it was tidy, as if still looked after, and smoke was coming from her chimney. Maisy just had to hope she didn't blame her for all she'd been put through.

She was hesitant walking down through the garden and up the couple of steps on to the worn-looking veranda, half expecting Grace to rush out in anger and order her away.

Moving from foot to foot to keep warm as she knocked, she was now doubting the wisdom of coming here. The door opened and Toby came charging out barking, but Grace stared at Maisy for a moment or two without speaking. She looked drawn and tired, wearing a grey woolly hat and an olive-green thick sweater which was so big it almost reached her knees.

'Stop that noise, Toby,' she said eventually. 'It's just Maisy.'

'They've found a boy's body, they think it may be Duncan. Although you have every reason not to care any more after all the police have done to you, I felt you probably still did care,' Maisy blurted out in almost one breath.

Grace opened the door wider and then her arms.

'Oh, you poor child,' she said, rocking Maisy gently. 'And of course I care about him, and you.'

She brought Maisy in and led her to a chair. The fire was blazing but the room wasn't very warm. 'Now tell me where they found this body.'

'Near Portsmouth.'

'Two other boys' bodies have been found in the last few months, one near Littlehampton and the other near Southampton,' Grace said. 'Four other boys from the south coast area have disappeared in the last year. That's not including Duncan.'

Maisy was shocked that there were three she didn't know about, and yet touched that Grace, who clearly never normally kept abreast with local news, had been following it.

'You think one person has taken all of them?' she asked.

Grace frowned. 'It seems to me very likely. The boys are all a similar age. I have my own theory about what he wants with them, and unless he's hidden the other bodies very well, perhaps he only kills the boys who won't do what he wants of them.'

'Like what?' Maisy asked. 'How do you know about these other boys anyway?'

'I overheard a policeman talking about two other missing boys when they kept me at the police station, so when I got out I went to the reading room at the library in Southampton and looked through local newspapers to find out about each of them. Since then I've been going once a week and reading everything.'

Maisy was really impressed that Grace would do her own investigation, and she felt bad that neither she nor her father had been so active. 'But you didn't say what you think he wants of these boys.'

'No, I didn't, and I'm not going to as it's only a theory and I'm not going to put ideas into your head. Tell me, Maisy, how have you been bearing up?'

'Struggling a lot of the time,' she admitted. 'If it wasn't for Janice and my teacher Mr Dove I think I'd be a complete wreck. I fainted when the police came today to tell us about this body. I seem to be on a knife's edge all the time now. But you had a bad time at the hands of the police; it was so wrong of them to come and arrest you.'

'Maisy, don't feel badly that you aren't coping very well. Duncan is your brother, you were so very close, it would be understandable if you collapsed altogether. Especially now when they have a body but can't confirm if it's Duncan or not. As for me, I quite understand why the police arrested me.' She shrugged. 'I know local people think I'm a witch, mad or a criminal because I'm hidden away out here. There would've been a public outcry if the police hadn't searched my home and taken me in for questioning. But they didn't hurt me, Maisy, and I think many of the policemen felt bad that I was accused once they'd spoken to me and found I was rational.'

'Don't you get tired of people thinking badly of you?' Maisy asked.

'I don't care about what people think. That's why I live out here and I try to keep away from them all.'

'I bet you wish now that you never got to know Duncan and me.'

Grace looked at Maisy for a moment, the ghost of a smile on her lips. 'No, you two are an exception to my rule. Like your brother, you have a good heart, and deep down I don't think this body belongs to him.'

'Don't you?' Maisy so much wanted to believe that.

'No, I don't; he was found too far away from here. But whoever he is he will have family who will grieve for him. Anyway, Maisy, you must go home now. You shouldn't be out in the forest alone. I bet your grandmother doesn't know you've come here?'

Maisy admitted she would be angry if she knew.

'Don't make her angry, child,' Grace said, her tone chiding but gentle. 'She may give you the impression she is heartless, but I expect she's much like me and has been hurt so badly in the past she doesn't know how to show her true feelings. Now off with you.'

'May I come back to tell you who the dead boy is?'

'No, my dear, stay away. It will be in the newspapers. When I walk to the shop for milk, I'll pick one up.'

'You don't want to see me again, then?' Maisy asked, her eyes filling up with tears.

'It isn't that.' Grace made a brushing gesture with her hands. 'I just feel it's dangerous for you to be out here alone. Now go.'

*

It had been a Monday when Sergeant Fowler informed them a boy's body had been found. Five days later he returned to Nightingales to tell them it wasn't Duncan but a boy called John Seeward from Portsmouth.

Maisy was at her lessons with Mr Dove when he called, but Grandmother informed her when she got home.

'He was murdered and buried in a shallow grave a month before Duncan disappeared,' she said. 'They had some difficulty at first in establishing the approximate date of his death because of the hot weather back in July and August, but his dental records proved his identity.'

Maisy was so relieved she nearly fainted again, but her grandmother caught hold of her arms, led her to a chair and made her put her head between her legs.

'If you get the vapours every time we get a bit of news, then I'll tie some smelling salts around your neck,' she said.

Maisy almost giggled at her grandmother trying to be funny. 'Sorry about that. Gosh, it's wonderful it isn't Duncan, but the parents of the dead boy must be devastated. How had he been killed?'

'Strangled.' Grandmother winced as she said it. 'I wouldn't normally tell you that, but it will be in the newspapers tomorrow for all to read. I've no doubt they will sensationalize it even more.'

8

The plan to get a job and leave Nightingales came to Maisy at Christmas because she was so unhappy.

It had been four long months and there had been no more news of what had happened to Duncan to cheer or finalize it for her, and with Linda being away at school and no other friends to talk to, she was desperately lonely.

No one, not Grandmother, Mr Dove or even Janice seemed to fully understand how she felt. It was as if part of her had been torn out leaving a gaping wound.

Right from birth, she and Duncan had been together, learning to walk, playing, eating and sleeping together. Even when they started school they clung together. They didn't have real friends, just acquaintances; they didn't need them. They had each other. Maybe in the month or so before Duncan disappeared they'd begun to have separate interests and new friends, but they'd still spent their evenings and Sundays together.

Maisy couldn't imagine how anyone else could ever fill the place Duncan once occupied. She could feel no joy without him to share it, nothing was funny any more, even food didn't seem to taste the same, and the forest looked sombre and sinister without him at her side.

There had been a brief, very welcome respite when Linda came home for the Christmas holidays. She telephoned immediately because there was a dance at Lyndhurst village hall a few days before Christmas. She wanted Maisy to come and stay overnight at her house. She also said she was sure Alan and Steven would be at the dance too as they were both home from university.

Surprisingly, Grandmother and Janice were happy to let her go; perhaps they hoped it would take her mind off Duncan. Grandmother even gave her twenty pounds for a new dress and she went into Southampton with Linda to buy it.

That day it was almost as though nothing bad had ever happened. Maisy managed to put aside all thoughts of Duncan and just enjoy herself with her friend. The dress she bought was midnight-blue crêpe, with a scoop neck, elbow-length sleeves and a full skirt. She also bought a net cancan petticoat to go under it. With her silver dancing shoes, she felt she looked sophisticated and glamorous.

Yet that evening as she rode home on the bus, grief came down on her like a thick, cold fog. She felt guilty that for a few hours she'd forgotten Duncan, and even worse she'd been telling Linda how much she wanted to see Alan again, as if that was all she'd had on her mind since he left for university.

When she got home she tried to tell Janice how she felt. The older woman was sympathetic but she insisted there was nothing wrong with putting aside her anxiety about Duncan and being excited about the dance. Or to look forward to seeing a boy she liked. She insisted this was normal and what Duncan would want for her.

*

Getting changed for the dance at Linda's home, giggling as they did their hair and put on a little mascara, face powder and a hint of lipstick, all they were allowed, was a new experience for Maisy. When Dr and Mrs Evans told them both how lovely they looked, Maisy felt like she was stepping through a doorway into a better place, where nothing but good things could happen.

Arriving at the village hall, she was stunned at how it had been transformed into a Christmas grotto with a big, beautifully decorated tree, hundreds of sparkly garlands and lights.

Alan and Steven came over to claim them the minute they stepped inside and Alan hugged Maisy, admired her dress and said she was the prettiest girl in the hall. Maisy didn't think it could get any better than that.

As it was the first dance she had been to, she had nothing to compare it with. Linda scathingly said it was very much a village dance, with so many older people, but acknowledged the band was good. They mostly played ballroom dance music, but they did slip in a few rock and roll numbers for the younger people there.

Maisy was in heaven because Alan danced almost every dance with her. She was surprised that he knew the steps, even if he was a bit stiff. He said he and Steven had gone to some lessons at university.

Dr Evans butted in a few times and insisted on partnering Maisy for a waltz or a foxtrot. But Alan – very gamely, she thought – asked Mrs Evans to dance and pulled faces at Maisy over the doctor's wife's shoulder.

It seemed to Maisy that Alan had thought about her a great deal during his first term away, showing concern about what she'd been through and acknowledging how painful it must be to still not know what had happened to her brother. When he took her outside for a few kisses she was transported back to that special day in Bournemouth, before everything went dark and frightening. But it was bitterly cold outside so they had to go back in or run the risk of frostbite.

To see Alan looking so handsome in a smart dark suit, the music, the lights and the heady Christmas atmosphere was almost enough on its own, but the tender look on his face made Maisy believe it was possible to be happy again.

He and Steven walked the girls home after the dance, and when Alan kissed her goodnight it was like fireworks going off inside her. Maisy was still awake long after Linda had fallen asleep in the bed next to her. She felt she could still taste Alan on her lips. She stroked her cheek where he had caressed it, and her stomach seemed to contract deliciously as she relived his kisses.

The following morning Alan met her for a walk as they'd arranged, before she had to catch the bus home. Yet even before she approached him, waiting outside the post office, Maisy sensed something had changed. He had his hands in his overcoat pocket, the collar turned up and his chin tucked down into a scarf. It was very cold, but he was hunched and even at a distance of thirty yards he looked ill at ease.

'Is something wrong?' she asked when he greeted her, but his smile didn't quite reach his eyes and there was no attempt at kissing her.

'Er, no, it's just that people gossip in this village. Let's 'get out of it,' he said, turning into a side road and away from the main street.

'I don't suppose we'll be able to meet up again until after Christmas,' Maisy said. She thought maybe he was a bit shy and afraid he'd run into some old friends who might tease him for being with a girl. 'It's only two more days till Christmas Eve and our housekeeper expects me to help get things ready,' she went on.

She had hoped to look in all the High Street shop windows with him, as they were all beautifully decorated, but Alan was walking really fast as if to get away. 'But I expect your parents will want some help too, so maybe we could meet up the day after Boxing Day?'

When he didn't respond straight away Maisy knew something definitely *was* wrong. 'What is it?' she asked.

'Nothing,' he said, not even looking at her. He just buried his chin further into his scarf.

'I can see there's something wrong,' she said. 'Please tell me, Alan.'

He did turn his head to look at her then, but his eyes dropped from hers immediately. 'It's my folks,' he said gloomily. 'They laid into me this morning about us meeting up.'

'Do you mean because they wanted you to do something with them?' she asked.

'No, I mean they were cross because I wanted to meet you.'

'Why? They didn't mind us being at the dance together last night.'

He looked embarrassed. 'They didn't know I was meeting you there, but someone told them and I suppose they said we danced every dance together. You see, they told me before I went to university that I was to forget you.'

'But why?' Maisy stopped in her tracks, unable to understand.

Alan hung his head and he fiddled with a button on his coat. 'This is so hard to say, and it's unfair too. But they got themselves in a state because of what was said about your family in the newspapers. You know, your mother in that place and stuff. Also that you're only fifteen. My father actually said, "We think a friendship with this girl is detrimental to your future." I can't really believe he'd say such a thing. You can't help that your brother has disappeared, or that your mum is a bit doolally. But there it is, I've told you now.'

Maisy felt as though someone had flung open a trapdoor beneath her and she was being plunged into a dark hole. She wanted to scream that this wasn't fair, and to cry too, but she stifled the scream and bit back the tears, because she had to keep her dignity at all costs.

'And you are so spineless you're going along with it?' she retorted. 'So where are you supposed to be this morning? At a Bible meeting?'

He had the grace to look ashamed. 'I told them I had to explain face-to-face,' he said. 'If I really was spineless I wouldn't have turned up.'

That at least had to be true, but it made no difference to how much he had hurt her.

'How can any of this be my fault? Did I drive my mother mad or force my brother to disappear? Maybe you think I'm also responsible for my father having a desk job during the war?' she asked, trying not to raise her voice in anger.

'And why on earth should they think any of this would reflect badly on you? Intelligent people would assume that facing such difficult things at my age would make me a stronger, more compassionate character. At least that's what my teacher says. But then I doubt your stuffy parents would approve of him because he's lost the use of his legs.'

'Don't be like that, Maisy,' he begged her, catching hold of her arm. 'You sound so bitter.'

'I think I'm entitled to be bitter,' she snapped, brushing his hand away. 'How would you feel if you'd lost your twin brother and then people implied it made you a lesser person? By the way, I'll be sixteen in January, above the age of consent. But then I assume they think because my mother's "doolally", as you put it, that I'll get myself in the family way and then you'll have to marry me.'

She knew immediately that something like that had been said because Alan blanched.

'This is horrible,' he said. 'I really like you, Maisy, I couldn't wait to see you again and I'm ashamed my parents are being so small-minded, judging you without ever having met you. I really wanted you to be my girl, but I can't oppose my parents as I need their help while I'm at university.'

'So it comes down to money, does it?' she said sarcastically. 'Well, enjoy their help, become a vet and make them very proud of you. I expect they'll pick a wife for you too – they obviously don't think you're capable of thinking for yourself. Sounds like a fun life.'

With that she wheeled round and fled back to Linda's house to pick up her things. Somehow she managed to hold back her tears until she was safely in her friend's home.

'I don't believe it!' Linda gasped when Maisy finally was

able to tell her what had been said through her tears. 'The cheek of his parents! They aren't anything to write home about. His father is only an insurance man. His mum is as common as muck. I bet they had to get married themselves.'

'Did Steven say anything about it to you?' Maisy asked.

'No, not a word. But you mustn't be upset by this, Maisy. They're stupid, mean-spirited people, that's all, and Alan is pathetic if he allows them to run his life.'

Maisy had to go home on the next bus; she couldn't bear to talk about it any more. She felt humiliated, and couldn't help but wonder who else thought those things about her.

On Christmas Eve Janice cooked them a special dinner because Alastair was coming down from London for Christmas. At eight, when he still hadn't arrived, Grandmother said they must go ahead without him. It was such a shame as Janice had made his favourite steak and mushroom pie, with golden puff pastry. She'd even laid the dining table with the best silver and glass and lit candles.

Maisy didn't much care whether her father came or not. It wasn't as if he ever appeared pleased to see her, and she was still terribly hurt by Alan. Janice did her best to create a little jollity at the table, but it didn't really work. Grandmother was seething because her son was late, and Maisy, trapped in her sadness, didn't speak at all.

She excused herself by saying she had a headache just as soon as she'd helped wash up. About five minutes after she got into bed, she heard her father arrive, and Grandmother asking Janice to warm his dinner up for him. It struck

Maisy that he hadn't wanted to come here or he'd have been on time for dinner. To her that meant he had no interest or love for his remaining child either.

Christmas was painful. Forced cheer as they opened presents before going to church for the Christmas service. Janice served the lunch at one, and they went through the motions of pulling crackers and reading jokes out aloud, but there were more silences than laughs or even spontaneous conversation.

There was a point during the meal when Maisy looked at her father and wondered if he had ever cared about his wife and children. From the expression on his bony face, he was trying to hide the fact that he found the taste of the food repellent. But she knew it wasn't the food, he just hated being in that room, with what remained of his family. Surely if he was grieving for Duncan he would want to be with his daughter, and his mother? Maisy was certain that most people who had lost one child would try even harder with the remaining one.

Maisy insisted on doing the washing-up because she could see Janice was exhausted. She'd been up till late the previous evening, then up at five this morning to get everything organized for Christmas lunch. After the washing-up, Maisy went out for a brief walk, and it was then she first thought of leaving.

She hadn't given up on Duncan being found, but she couldn't stay here waiting any longer in this crippling state of sadness. She didn't want to let Mr Dove and Janice down, but she felt they would understand. As for her father and grandmother, she didn't much care what they thought.

Once she was sixteen they couldn't stop her leaving anyway. Janice always bought *The Lady* magazine and she'd once showed Maisy all the jobs advertised in the back of it, everything from cooks and housekeepers to butlers and valets.

She would apply for something in there.

On the first day back at lessons in January, Maisy told Mr Dove she was leaving Nightingales.

'I can't stand this terrible sadness and waiting any more,' she said. 'I've applied for a mother's help job in Brighton.'

Perhaps he realized she was dead set on this, because he didn't come up with the kind of arguments she'd expected.

'You do know that a great many women treat a mother's help like a slave?' was all he said.

'If they do I'll leave and get another job,' she said. 'But I'll be far happier with children to look after. It might be hard work, but at least there will be joy and laughter, all the things I don't get with Grandmother.'

'And what is your grandmother or your father going to say about this?' Dove looked at her sternly. 'You know your father wanted you to go to university?'

'I don't care what he wants. Do you know what he bought me for Christmas?'

Dove shook his head.

'A box of lace-trimmed hankies and a stationery set. That's what you give your ageing aunt, not a girl of nearly sixteen. He bought Grandmother a fluffy shawl to put round her shoulders in the evenings; that at least was appropriate and she liked it. But hankies for me!'

'Rather Victorian,' he said. 'But in his defence, Maisy, most men are useless at buying presents.'

'That's what Janice said.' Maisy sighed. 'She also said to think of poor little orphans that don't get anything at Christmas, but I'm not going to listen to anyone who tries to turn it around to make me look ungrateful and rude. It really isn't about the present, that's not important, but it did show me my father doesn't care about me. Grandmother is like an iceberg, so why should I waste another two years doing what they want me to do?'

'I'd be a poor teacher if I didn't try to make you see the value of a good education,' Dove said gently. 'Stay, pass your exams and get to university. With a degree behind you, the world is your oyster. I certainly want more for you than being a skivvy for parents who are too tight-fisted to pay for a qualified nanny for their children. In fact, I don't hold with anyone paying someone else to look after their children.'

'Janice has been like a mother to me, and she's just Grandmother's skivvy. So maybe I can be a mother to some kids that don't get any love from their own,' Maisy argued.

Mr Dove just looked at her for what seemed minutes. Maisy could see anxiety and sorrow in his eyes and it almost made her change her mind, because she knew how much his job teaching her meant to him. They were in the same boat, really: she'd lost her brother, and he'd lost the use of his legs. They were both very lonely. But finally he spoke. 'If you are dead set on this plan, will you make me a promise that you'll leave your grandmother's on good terms so you can return if you need to?'

'I doubt that's possible.' Maisy shrugged.

'Do you remember how we once discussed how we are all products of our upbringing?'

Maisy nodded.

'Good. Well, I am quite sure that both your father and grandmother care a great deal more about you than they are capable of showing. They've lost Duncan, and they won't want to lose you too. So don't be tempted to rush off without telling them where you're going. They may be pig-headed about it, but you must stay calm and tell them you find it hard to live there without your brother.'

'I haven't got the job yet,' Maisy said. 'Maybe they won't want me.'

'I bet they will,' Dove half smiled. 'Who could resist those wide blue eyes, the dimple and a smile that lights up a room? I'll give you a reference if you need one. But promise me you'll tell your grandmother about the job before you go for the interview.'

The reply to her application for the mother's help job came the day after her sixteenth birthday on January the 24th. There were two children, Paul aged four, and Annabel aged two. Mrs Ripley explained that both she and her husband were physiotherapists with a practice on the ground floor of their house on Brighton's seafront. Mrs Ripley wanted to go back to working full-time, and she needed someone to take care of the children.

Maisy really liked the tone of the letter, which was warm and inviting. Mrs Ripley said she had cleaning staff and Maisy's only duties would be to entertain the children and give them their lunch. She would have her own bedroom and bathroom, and Saturday afternoons and all day Sunday off.

Mrs Ripley suggested that when Maisy came to meet

the children she should stay the night so she had extra time to get to know the whole family.

Maisy really liked that Mrs Ripley didn't use the word 'interview', but only wrote about 'meeting the children'. It sounded kind, thoughtful and welcoming. Three pounds a week wasn't much of a wage, but then that would be all for her, and about average for such jobs.

She bit the bullet and went straight to her grandmother to inform her.

It was a bitterly cold day and Grandmother had pulled her chair right up to the fire. She had the fluffy pink shawl her son had given her for Christmas around her shoulders.

'Yes?' she asked in her usual frosty manner as Maisy came into the room.

'Sorry to intrude,' Maisy said nervously. 'I've got something to tell you . . . I'm going for an interview for a job.'

She blurted out the last part, and not in the gentle, measured way she'd practised up in her room.

'What sort of job?' Grandmother turned to look at Maisy, frowning as if 'job' was a dirty word.

Maisy explained, as quickly and concisely as she could.

'You applied for a job without consulting me first?' Grandmother roared at her. 'How dare you?'

'Grandmother, I am sixteen now, I'm able to look after myself and I don't want to stay here now that Duncan has gone. I'm terribly lonely.'

'You have that friend in Lyndhurst.'

'Yes, but she's gone back to school now. I want to be somewhere with life, noise and laughter. I just feel miserable all the time.'

'Your father will not let you do this; he wants you to go to university.'

'He only wants me to go there so he can feel he's done a good job as a parent,' Maisy responded, feeling bolder now as she sensed her grandmother had a tiny amount of sympathy with her. 'He hasn't done a good job; he's never had any interest in either of us. Look at him at Christmas! He barely spoke to me and he couldn't wait to get away. Besides, he can't stop me getting a job.'

'He can.'

'No, he can't. Maybe he'd have a case if I was doing something immoral or illegal, and the place I lived in was dangerous, but I'll be living with a respectable family, looking after their children.'

'Then I'd better telephone my son this evening and tell him your plans. On your head be it.'

'I'm going for the interview next Thursday and staying the night,' Maisy said. 'Mrs Ripley said she'd send me a return train ticket.'

'You'll be back in no time with your tail between your legs.' Grandmother sniffed. 'I've heard stories about how people treat mother's helps and au pairs. They'll work you to death.'

'I'd like to think I could come back if it's awful,' Maisy said, remembering what Mr Dove had suggested.

'I shall expect you to give it a fair trial,' Grandmother responded, her face like granite. 'Now clear off and help Janice.'

Maisy wasn't sure what to make of her grandmother's last remark. Did she realize Maisy wasn't frightened of her any more? Was there even a little bit of admiration? But she was beyond analysing other people's feelings; they didn't seem to care about hers.

Maisy had just got off the train from Brighton after going to her interview with the Ripleys, and was walking to the bus stop in Southampton to get back to Burley, when Mr Grainger pulled up beside her.

He leaned across to the passenger seat and opened the door, grinning charmingly at her. 'Hop in if you're going home. I'm going that way.'

Maisy was only too glad to have a lift, as the bus was slow and usually crowded. 'I'd love a lift,' she said and jumped in.

'You're looking glowing,' he told her. 'It must be the bracing winter air. You're lucky to have that complexion – not freckled like your brother.'

Maisy blushed at the compliment. He began to drive, and she told him that she'd been for a job interview as an au pair and stayed with the Ripleys in Brighton overnight. 'The Ripleys are super – young, enthusiastic, and their home is very modern. Their children are little poppets too – Annabel is two, Paul's four – and I think it's going to be a dream job. My room there is great, looking out on the promenade and sea. I can't wait to go.'

'So what does your grandmother think of this job? I believe the plan was that you were going to university?'

'It was her and Father's plan, never mine,' Maisy said. 'I'm so lonely there without Duncan. I need to be doing something, seeing people, getting out. Sometimes I feel I'm in a cage.'

Just admitting this made her start to cry. Despite having

found a job she wanted to do, on the train journey back to Southampton she'd felt alone as never before. She hadn't got parents like Linda's who she could telephone immediately and hear their congratulations and excitement. She knew Grandmother would be chilly with her, probably totally disapproving, and even Janice would be sad, rather than glad for her.

'Don't cry, sweetheart,' he said, putting his hand on her knee comfortingly, and he pulled over to the side of the road and put his arms around her. Maisy fell into his embrace willingly, she needed to be hugged. But to her dismay he caught hold of her face to kiss her on the lips and at the same time his hand moved up her skirt.

'Don't,' she said, pushing him away indignantly. 'What on earth do you think you're doing?'

She was so shocked. He was attractive, he'd been kind too, but she hadn't expected or wanted that.

'Oh Maisy, don't be silly. What's a kiss? I was only trying to make you feel better.'

'By pushing me into something completely inappropriate?' she retorted. 'I'll get the bus home.' She moved to open the door.

'No, you won't, I'll take you home. Look, Maisy, I'm sorry if I offended you.'

It did seem churlish to refuse a lift home, especially as she wasn't even sure where the nearest bus stop was. 'OK, but straight back to Burley,' she said, and sat there in silence for the rest of the way.

Later that evening, up in her bedroom, Maisy looked back on what had happened and found herself crying again.

Mr Grainger hadn't done anything further, but it had spoiled what should've been the best day since Duncan disappeared. She couldn't wait to leave now. Grandmother was scathing about her job, Janice was trying not to cry and even Mr Dove when she popped in to see him seemed lukewarm in his enthusiasm.

She doubted she'd ever come back here again.

9

He stood outside the red-brick school watching the boys thronging out into the playground and jostling towards the gate. It was very cold, giving him the opportunity to separate the tough, hardy boys from the softer, weaker ones.

The first group just had blazers over their grey school jumpers, school caps perched precariously on the back of their heads; if they had a coat too it was always unbuttoned and thrown on.

After these came the more fragile boys. They were always buttoned up, scarves carefully tucked in, gloves on hands, socks pulled up if they still wore short trousers. Caps were on straight, and still in good condition. And then there was invariably a sub-section, a tiny group of special boys. These often walked alone, whether because they were shy or misfits, he couldn't know at first glance. A few of them might be Mummy's boys, one or two a little slow at their lessons, and then, that precious commodity, the neglected boy. He was always the easiest to identify, a scruffy uniform, worn-out shoes, hair needing cutting, thin and pale. These were the boys who would interest him.

The neglected boy was easy to work on. He craved attention and he could be bought with food. But the best thing of all was that alarm bells didn't start to ring straight off when he didn't get home on time.

Today he saw a boy in the first group that he wished he

could poach. Thirteen or fourteen with peachy skin and golden hair left a little too long. A living dream with his long limbs, and a soft, full mouth. But he was a leader, the boys around him were all looking and listening, waiting for his decision on where to go now. If he was going straight home, so would his acolytes; if he said it was football in the park, they would follow, even if they'd been told not to by their parents.

Boys like that one were too hard to subjugate. They fought every inch of the way, were clever enough to try and outwit him. Once he'd seen that as a challenge, but not any more; he was getting too old for such games.

There was one likely boy today, trailing behind the others as if loath to go home. Grey socks falling down, his donkey jacket far too big for him. But a pretty boy nonetheless, a small, turned up nose and very dark hair. He would follow him to see where he lived and the family set-up. That would be enough for one day; it didn't do to rush these things. Besides, he hadn't got room for any more boys just now. Four was enough to deal with.

10

Brighton, 1962

'Maisy, I really think you should visit your grandmother, if only for a couple of days,' Mrs Ripley said. 'She's getting old, and if she should suddenly have a stroke or a heart attack and die, you'd feel terrible that you hadn't made it up with her.'

They were in the playroom on the first floor. Paul was at school and Maisy was helping Annabel do a wooden jigsaw. Mrs Ripley often popped into the playroom between clients and had a cup of tea with Maisy.

'I doubt I'd feel terrible.' Maisy grinned. 'But I *would* like to see Janice and Mr Dove, and my friend Linda.'

She showed Annabel how to put in a jigsaw piece the right way round. She was a sweet child; plump, with rosy cheeks and big dark eyes very much like her father's.

Coming to work for the Ripleys in Brighton had turned out to be the very best thing Maisy could've done. It hadn't stopped her thinking about Duncan, or hoping that he might turn up again one day, but she had learned to put her sorrow to one side and embrace the good things in her new life.

She had loved Paul and Annabel on sight, and they loved her. Her pretty, warm room up on the top floor, which had a wonderful view of the sea, gave her great pleasure, and the job was never arduous or boring. In fact, the weeks had sped by so fast she could hardly believe she'd now turned seventeen and had been here a whole year.

'Sometimes it falls on the wronged one to take the initiative to put things right,' Mrs Ripley said, raising one eyebrow.

She was in her late thirties, a buxom redhead, prone to freckles, which she hated, but in fact suited her. 'I had it with my mother,' she went on. 'She was a holy terror and horrible to Harold because she believed he persuaded me to leave home to go and train as a physiotherapist. She wouldn't believe that it was what I wanted. Anyway, I went away regardless of what she said and we didn't speak for two years. But Harold made me go home to ask her to come to our wedding. He was already in practice here in Brighton, and he had just bought this house. He knew when Mother saw how successful he was she would change her tune.'

'It worked, then?' Maisy asked.

'Yes, Mother is such a snob, now she tells people what a brilliant son-in-law she has.' Mrs Ripley laughed. 'To be honest, Maisy, I will never really like her. But she is my mother so I put up with her. I think it might be like that too for you and your grandmother.'

'And my father.' Maisy sighed. 'I haven't heard a word from him since he sent that nasty letter telling me what a fool I was giving up going to university. But Janice writes, telling me the news, or lack of it. She said the police have stopped trying to find Duncan. She was told that there are so many young people going missing every year, they can't keep on wasting police resources on those who may not want to be found. I think that means they see Duncan as one of those doesn't-want-to-be-founds.'

'But you still don't believe that?'

'No, I don't,' Maisy said. 'Even if he was angry with our father and grandmother, even if he met someone he wanted to live with and have fun with, he would've somehow let me know he was safe. So I have to face it that he must have been killed.'

'I suppose each time they find another of those young boys, you must think it could be Duncan this time?' Mrs Ripley asked. There had been six boys' bodies found now, all from towns along the south coast. The last two had been since Maisy came to work in Brighton. The police believed they were all killed by the same person. There was also a seventh boy, Peter Reilly from Seaford, who, like Duncan, was still missing.

Maisy nodded. She had talked through the whole Duncan story with Mrs Ripley soon after coming to work here, and it had helped enormously. She could see why Mabel Ripley was a renowned physiotherapist in Brighton, because she was such an understanding woman. Maisy knew very little about her patients or how she treated them, but she guessed the woman's ability to really listen, and to feel others' pain, whether this was mental or physical, must make her excellent at her job.

'So how about going home for Easter?' Mrs Ripley suggested. 'Harold and I are shutting up shop for a full two weeks, so we won't need your help. Not that I'm pushing you out the door, Maisy. You're welcome to stay here too if you want to. But I think you know it's time to make up with your grandmother.'

Maisy had been thinking recently that maybe she should try and hold out an olive branch. She was reluctant to do it because she felt she had been in the right. But Mrs Ripley was right too in saying that if her grandmother was to die without them making it up, Maisy would feel bad.

'I suppose I could write to her and ask if I can come,' she said, but she grimaced. The idea didn't appeal to her much because she couldn't imagine Grandmother would come down off her perch and be nice. She hadn't even kissed Maisy goodbye when she left Nightingales, no letters since, not a birthday or Christmas card. 'You know I loved it at Nightingales when Duncan was there, the house, the garden and the forest. But going back is bound to stir up all the feelings about Duncan again, and I don't know if I can cope with that.'

'I thought something similar about my home, but in fact going back was a healing experience,' Mrs Ripley said. 'Besides, you can see your friend, maybe thumb your nose at that boy Alan you were sweet on. Let's face it, you're looking very lovely these days. A figure like a beauty queen and your hair is enviable. He'll be left with egg on his face!'

That was one of the things Maisy really liked about her employer. She had made Maisy far more confident, encouraging her to be bolder in her clothes, enthusing about how pretty she was, and even taking her to the hairdresser's. Maisy had never had a haircut; her blond hair had just been left to grow and the ends were wispy, dry and flyaway. The hairdresser cut it to her shoulders, and now it was sleek and shiny and trouble-free, yet long enough to put up when she wanted to look more sophisticated.

'OK, you've talked me into it,' she laughed. 'I'll write tonight after typing classes.'

She had started going to night school to learn short-hand and typing back in September and she was doing very well. She knew that when Annabel started school next autumn Mrs Ripley wouldn't need her any more, and her long-term plan was to go to London then and get an office job.

'Won't you be popping into that coffee bar to see that young man of yours?' Mrs Ripley said teasingly.

Maisy had met Rupert, an art student, last summer. He worked in the Cadena Coffee Bar three evenings a week.

'He wasn't for me and it's been over for weeks,' Maisy informed her. 'He's a beatnik. I thought he was fascinating at first because he was so revolutionary, what with Ban the Bomb and all that, but it got pretty tiresome after a bit. When he suggested going to the pictures it was always something foreign with subtitles and mostly I had to pay as he never had any money. Do you remember when he took me dancing? I never told you, but it was in a horrible smoky cellar club and the jazz band played so loudly you couldn't hear anyone speak. I knew then I wanted to go to a proper dance on the pier with a normal man in a smart suit.'

'You've got the right idea, Maisy,' Mrs Ripley said, then glanced at her watch. 'Oh gosh, is that the time? Mr Pettigrew will be here any moment for his treatment. I must go.' She stood up, bent to kiss her little daughter, then hurried out.

'As for us, little one,' Maisy said, picking Annabel up in

her arms, 'we'll go out for a walk along the promenade, then go and pick your brother up from school.'

As Maisy pushed Annabel in her pushchair along Marine Parade, towards the pier, a squally cold wind off the sea threatened to sweep her off her feet. But she liked the wind and the rough sea; it was invigorating and made her feel alive.

Her life had changed so much since she came to work for the Ripleys. They treated her more like an older daughter than a paid help, and Maisy knew she stood taller now, comfortable in her own skin because she was appreciated. She'd made a few friends with other au pairs at Paul's school gates, who she could have a coffee or go to the pictures with. Jacky was one of these, and they often went dancing on the pier on Saturday nights. She was really good fun, but inclined to run off with blokes she'd met without even telling Maisy she was going.

Some of the mothers she talked to at the school, ones who like Mrs Ripley lived in big houses and had a busy social life, asked her to help serve dinner or drinks for them, and paid her well. Through these evenings she'd made two male friends as well. The first one was Ralph, who sometimes worked as a waiter at private functions, but by day he worked as a hairdresser and now always trimmed Maisy's hair. He was just a pal, not a proper boyfriend; he was fun, loved going shopping and to see weepy films, as she did.

Martin, however, had been a guest at one of the more recent parties Maisy had helped at, and he had become a real boyfriend. He wasn't as much fun as Ralph, he didn't do roaring with laughter or encouraging her to try on totally unsuitable dresses. He worked in a bank, dressed very smartly, and he was very good-looking with dark hair and smouldering eyes to match. She really fancied him. He was a wonderful kisser, and was always trying to have his way with her.

But Maisy was far too scared of having a baby, and anyway they had nowhere to go, as he still lived with his parents. She felt he was getting tired of trying to persuade her and that before long he'd call it a day. She knew it wouldn't upset her that much – she hadn't fallen for him, and besides, he could be very boring, going on and on about his work at the bank.

Maisy often stopped to think how much better life was for everyone in England now. Businesses were booming, most of the old bomb sites from the war were being built on at last, new houses were going up everywhere and there was plenty of work for everyone. When she was small, her father was one of the few people she knew with a car; now loads of people had them. As for television, that too was a normal thing in anyone's house, just as refrigerators and washing machines were. She had gone to London a couple of times last year with Jacky and she'd been astounded how much rebuilding had taken place, how smart the shops were, and by the luxury hotels and restaurants springing up everywhere.

Yet for all the good things in her life, Duncan was still a sore place inside her. It was a wound that she could ignore most of the time, but she knew would never completely heal. Mrs Ripley had been right: when two more boys' bodies had been found it had brought it all back.

Maisy just wished the police could find the monster who was doing it and get him to confess to the other boys' deaths so she would finally know what had happened to her brother. It was seventeen months now since he had disappeared and every single day of every month she'd offered up a prayer for him, even though the likelihood of his still being alive was only about one in a million.

But painful as it was, Maisy had learned to deal with it. She didn't look for reminders, she rarely told people about him any more. As long as she just held his memory close to her heart, she could live, outwardly at least, like any other carefree seventeen-year-old.

Paul's school was at the top of Regency Square, off King's Road. Because the wind was so strong, she bent over the pushchair to tuck Annabel's blanket in more securely.

She just happened to glance up ahead, and to her surprise she saw her father paying off a taxi in front of the Royal Hotel. Her first thought was that he'd come to Brighton to see her, and she was just opening her mouth to call out when she saw he wasn't alone. A woman had got out of the taxi too. They had just one suitcase, which the hotel doorman came forward to carry in.

Maisy remained bent over the pushchair so she could watch them, her heart pounding with a mixture of shock and anger. She thought of her father as callous, cold and mean-spirited, but she'd never, ever thought of him as a ladies' man.

The woman was smartly dressed in a camel coat with a fur collar, a fur hat and very high-heeled shoes. She was slender, possibly about forty, with the kind of poise

Maisy associated only with models or film stars. Maisy was too far away to be able to see her features clearly, but she somehow knew this was a strikingly attractive woman.

The taxi paid off, the woman put her hand through Alastair's arm. She was two or three inches shorter than he, and as they moved off to go into the hotel, she inclined her head towards his shoulder, the way a secretary or business colleague would never do.

Maisy straightened up from the pushchair as they disappeared into the hotel. She was so dumbstruck for a moment or two that her mind went completely blank.

As her father hadn't contacted her since his scathing letter about how she was destroying her chances in life by not going to university, she had no idea what was happening in his world. Any news she'd had of her mother had come via Janice, picked up from Grandmother. It seemed there was little improvement, but Mother was calm and comfortable.

So her father had another woman while his wife was incarcerated in an institution.

Maisy checked the time and found she had ten minutes before she had to meet Paul. Without stopping to think, she marched up to the hotel, pushing the pushchair. The door was opened for her by the liveried doorman and she went straight over to the reception desk.

'May I help you?' an older woman in a navy blue suit asked.

'Yes, I was wondering if you could tell me if Mr and Mrs Mitcham have checked in yet?'

The woman looked at a register. 'Yes, they have, just a

short while ago. Would you like me to ring their room for you?'

Maisy forced a smile. 'No, I'll surprise them later. Don't tell them I was asking, will you?'

She turned and left, anger bubbling up inside her. No wonder he wanted her mother in that place. Was this woman the reason he'd had her committed?

As Maisy sat on the bus from Southampton to Burley, she was feeling very emotional. It was two years and two weeks ago that she and Duncan first arrived in the village to stay with their grandmother. That year Easter Sunday was the first Sunday in the month, and she remembered then, as now, daffodils being in full flower, very new acid-green leaves sprouting out on trees and shrubs, pretty blossom too. There had been that clean country smell, with just a tinge of horse droppings, so different to London. She and Duncan had been scared at first, yet in a day or two they'd decided they never wanted to leave. She remembered the day Janice took them out to show them the old bicycles the gardener had oiled and cleaned up for them.

They had whooped and shrieked as they took their first ride into the forest. She remembered too the sun had been warm that day and they came home with pink faces from it.

Now she was going back. Her grandmother had replied – the first letter in a whole year – and not only had she agreed to let Maisy come and stay for a few days, she even sounded a tiny bit pleased at the prospect.

So much had changed for Maisy in these last two years.

Duncan disappearing was of course the biggest, worst and most difficult event to live with. But she'd grown up, sprouted breasts, had first love go wrong, learned to dance and started work, taking responsibility for two children. She'd also conquered shorthand and typing, could cook many different dishes and she'd sampled alcohol. She didn't think it was as great as other people claimed, but maybe she needed to try more. She also believed she thought like an adult now, not as a child.

Yet right now she was quaking in her smart patent leather shoes at the thought of meeting her grandmother.

Janice opened the door to her with a broad smile and arms flung wide to hug her. 'It's been far too long,' she exclaimed. After the longest hug she took Maisy's arms and pushed her back slightly, reaching out for her hair and running her fingers through it. 'Let me feast my eyes on you. So grown up and beautiful. It does my old heart good.'

'Your heart isn't old and it never will be,' Maisy said and they went inside and closed the door behind them.

'Mrs Mitcham is having a little nap now,' Janice said. 'She said she'd ring for tea later and you can take it in.'

Maisy pulled a face. They both knew the old lady was wide awake but wanted this visit entirely on her terms. 'So much the better, we can have a catch-up first,' she said. 'Now I want all the village gossip!'

Over a cup of tea at the kitchen table, Janice launched into who had done what, and who had upset someone else. Maisy liked to hear it, even if they were people she had never got to know well.

'What about Mr Dove?' she asked.

'Oh, he has another couple of private pupils, and he seems well. He always asks after you when I see him.'

'I'll pop down there tomorrow,' Maisy said. 'I miss him, and you of course, but not much else. But tell me, is there any news of Grace?'

Janice's face stiffened. 'She was taken in for questioning again after another boy went missing. There's plenty round here are convinced she's a killer. They'd form a lynch party if they could.'

'Surely you aren't starting to believe that too?' Maisy asked, shaking her head in disbelief that Janice of all people would get sucked into such madness. 'They use her as a scapegoat. Just because she's a bit odd doesn't make her a murderer. I don't hear anyone claiming Sybil Leek kills people and she's a self-confessed witch.'

She and Duncan had often crept after this odd woman in her long black clothes with her jackdaw on her shoulder, hoping to catch her casting some dastardly spell.

'Well, no, I'm not jumping on the band wagon, but I understand why she worries other people. Anyway, Sybil has left the village now, she became too famous for her own good,' Janice said. 'She was on radio and television, and she's written books on witchcraft. So many reporters came to the village to interview her, it all got quite out of hand. They say she's gone to America.'

Maisy's eyes opened wide in astonishment. 'Yet people don't blame *her* for anything! I always thought she was a lot weirder than Grace.'

'The thing is, Sybil always talked to people, so folk felt they knew all about her. I find when people don't know about someone, that's when they start to make things up. You're about the only person who has ever talked to Grace – to everyone else she's a mystery, and they hate that. Anyway, enough of witches and strange women. Tell me about you, your job and those little children.'

'Annabel and Paul are lovely,' Maisy said. 'How lucky am I to get paid just for playing with a couple of children?'

'You do more than play with them. You make most of their meals and do their washing, and besides, looking after little children is tiring.'

Maisy grinned. 'I don't find it tiring. And I'm so lucky that Mrs Ripley gives me free rein to do what I want with them. In the summer we went on the beach practically every day. The hardest thing will be leaving them when they don't need me any more. But my shorthand and typing are good now, so I'll be able to find a decent job.'

They chatted for some ten minutes about Brighton until the tinkling of Grandmother's bell rang out.

'That's your summons,' Janice said. 'Lovely to have you back for a few days, sweetheart. I've missed you so much.' She poured the boiling water into the silver teapot, slipped the red knitted cosy over the top and placed it on the previously laid tray.

'Mmm, chocolate cake,' Maisy said. 'I've missed that so much. I've made a few cakes at the Ripleys' but they weren't a patch on yours.'

Janice smiled. 'I made that yesterday especially for you. Now go on in and don't let her scare you.'

Maisy *was* scared but she was determined not to show it. Grandmother looked thinner, her eyes watery and her face

154

more lined, yet she was still dressed elegantly in a mauve dress and matching lacy cardigan.

'Thank you for letting me come to see you,' Maisy said, putting the tray down on a side table. 'I know I disappointed you and my father, but I needed to get away from all the sad memories here.'

'I couldn't imagine why you wanted to look after another woman's brats,' Grandmother responded with a disdainful sniff.

'I needed to be in a happy place,' Maisy said. 'And it turned out to be the perfect job for me. I love Paul and Annabel, they're delightful children, and Mr and Mrs Ripley are very kind to me. It would have been much better, of course, if I'd had your and Father's blessing.'

'Your father thinks that you have thrown away the chance of university. He's still angry with you.'

'I don't think he thinks about me often enough to be angry. Not now he's got a mistress,' Maisy retorted, her temper getting the better of her already.

She had intended to work her way round to that once she'd sounded out her grandmother, not just drop it in like a big clanger.

Her grandmother sat up straighter, her face showing complete surprise.

Maisy got up to pour the tea and put a cup and a slice of cake on the small table beside her grandmother's armchair.

'You are mistaken,' Grandmother said, her voice a little shaky. 'Of course he hasn't got a mistress – whatever made you say that?'

'I'm not mistaken. I saw them together in Brighton,

they had a room in the Royal Hotel. They checked in as Mr and Mrs Mitcham.'

'No, Alastair wouldn't do that,' Grandmother insisted.

'I saw him clearly. I was walking along the promenade with the pushchair and saw them getting out of a taxi. Father didn't see me, he was too wrapped up in the woman. I went into the hotel later and enquired if Mr and Mrs Mitcham had checked in, and the receptionist said they had and even offered to ring their room. Is this why he packed Mother off to that asylum?'

Maisy had never seen her grandmother look uncertain before. She had her hands clasped together in agitation and she was looking at Maisy as if waiting to be told she'd made it all up.

'That is what I saw, Grandmother. I think it's time there was more honesty in this family. I want to know the name and address of the place Mother is in. I have a right to this information. I'm afraid if you won't give it to me then I may have to contact a lawyer about it.'

'What on earth makes you threaten such a thing?' Grandmother said a little heatedly. 'Everything your father has done is to protect you.'

'That's rubbish,' Maisy said, feeler braver now. 'He put Mother in that place to get her out of the way. Maybe she is as mad as a hatter but he still has no right to prevent me from seeing her or knowing exactly what was wrong with her. He wanted me to go to university to make himself look good, but he doesn't care about me – not one letter in a whole year! I don't think he even pestered the police about Duncan, either. A good father would have come down here and moved heaven and earth to help find his son.'

'You are right to criticize him about that,' Grandmother said, somewhat reluctantly. 'I felt he should have stayed here during the search.'

'I think he was with this woman all along. No wonder he wanted Duncan and me shipped down here,' Maisy said. 'What a hypocrite he is.'

'Do not slander your father!'

'Is it slander if it's true? I could go up to London and check with the neighbours. They'd tell me if they'd seen her at our old house.'

'Maisy, that's enough!' The old lady looked hurt. 'I understand you are annoyed with your father, but men find it difficult to get through life without a woman. Two years alone is a long time.'

'Two years for a mother to be deprived of her children and home is a long time too. Especially as one of those children is probably dead. How can you justify that, Grandmother?'

'From what I understand, she doesn't even know what year it is, let alone what month and day.'

'But we only have his word for that. Give me the name of the home and I'll go to visit her and speak to her doctor there. If it is as Father says, I'll say no more on the subject.'

'You've got very lippy,' Grandmother replied, and there was a hint of admiration in her voice. 'You didn't used to say boo to a goose.'

'I grew up when my brother disappeared, and I'll tell you something else, Grandmother, I'm going to push the police harder too. If we had his body to bury we could grieve and then get on with our lives. Until that day it's always going to be unfinished business.'

*

157

When Maisy went back into the kitchen later she found Janice looking anxious.

'You can stop looking like that,' Maisy teased. 'It was OK. We had a few things to sort out, but she came round. I think if people had stood up to her more often in the past, she wouldn't be such a grumpy old toad now.' She took a piece of paper from her pocket and brandished it. 'Mother's address,' she said.

When she told Janice about seeing her father with the glamorous woman, Janice nodded, as if not entirely surprised. 'It never actually occurred to me that he might have someone else,' she said. 'I always thought he was a bit too upright to do that. But strangely he's called in here at least every three weeks for some months now, never staying the night. He told his mother he was on business down here but that didn't quite ring true. If he had business in Southampton he would surely have taken the train, but he was always in his car. So maybe she's down this way, maybe not far from here.'

'I don't really think it's my place to take him to task for having someone on the side,' Maisy said thoughtfully. 'But it is my place to find out how my mother is. So that's what I'll do.'

That night Maisy found she was unable to sleep. It felt strange to be back in her old bedroom – it was too quiet, and too dark. She'd grown used to traffic noise, and the glow of street lights. The darkness here was so thick it felt like a heavy curtain and the only sound was the occasional hoot of an owl. She also had so much to think about: going to see her mother, wondering what her father was up to, and then when she would see Linda, Mr Dove and Grace.

She wasn't sure why she felt she needed to see Grace, but some gut instinct told her she must. It would be fun to see Linda. They had written to one another three or four times, but that wasn't the same as seeing a friend face-to-face.

Might she run into Alan? She hoped so, and planned to put her hair up in a beehive, and wear her new white pencil skirt and navy and white candy-striped blazer that Martin said made her look like a beauty queen. She really hoped Alan would look at her and wish he'd been brave enough to defy his parents. Not that she cared about him any more, but it would be good for her ego.

Her first call of the morning was to see Mr Dove, and his face broke into the broadest of smiles when he opened his front door to her. 'Well, you look like you've stepped out of *Vogue*. Come on in, it's so very good to see you.' He wheeled his chair back into his living room, still smiling, and offered her a cup of tea.

Maisy made the tea for them both in his kitchen and then they sat down to talk. He was delighted her new life had turned out to be a happy one, and was impressed she'd been attending night school to learn secretarial skills.

Their conversation eventually turned back to Duncan after Dove mentioned the other bodies that had been found.

'I hope you won't find this offensive,' he said, pulling out a large sketchbook from his desk. 'But I've been doing a little sleuthing myself.'

He'd made a map of the south coast, and at each of the places where a body had been found he'd put a small red sticker with their name. The home of each boy was marked with a blue sticker, and finally there was a green sticker for the area where each of them was last seen.

'Does anything jump out at you about the placing of the stickers?' he asked.

Maisy studied them for a few moments. 'Well, they all seem to have about the same distance between where they lived, where they were last seen and where their bodies were found,' she said. 'Or is that just the way you drew the map?'

'No, I traced the map, so it's the correct scale. In each case the body was found around twenty miles from where the boy was last spotted; in four of the cases that was close to their school. Those four all disappeared in term time. With the other three, the distance was a little greater and they disappeared in the school holidays.'

'As Duncan did,' Maisy said.

Dove nodded.

'So the killer prefers to pick the boys up from school?' Maisy winced.

'It looks very likely that is his hunting ground. I think he follows them from school, learns a bit about them and maybe engages them in conversation somehow. No one witnessed any of the boys in distress or being bundled into a vehicle, so perhaps he lures them away with something they're interested in. I think the person the police should be looking for would be attractive. People, especially young people, usually respond better to strangers if they're attractive. He'd probably be physically fit and well dressed.'

'How did you get this detail?' Maisy asked. 'I don't recall so much in the newspapers.'

'Well, the last part is purely my theory, but I have a pal in the police where I got the rest.' Dove smiled. 'We were called up for the army on the same day and that's why we became friends. We were put in the same regiment, and he helped save me when I was wounded. He was the main reason I came this way to live when my marriage ended, because he lived here. He talks to me about the case because of Duncan having been my pupil.'

'I thought the police had stopped investigating?' Maisy said.

Dove shook his head. 'Oh no, they might like that to be put about to lure the killer into complacency, but nothing could be further from the truth. They're still hunting for further clues and possible witnesses. Harry, my friend, is a sergeant. He only joined the investigation team after you went off to Brighton, Maisy, which is why you didn't meet him. Because of me, he's like a dog with a bone on this.'

Maisy looked thoughtfully at the map and the stickers. 'Duncan is the odd one out. He's not from a seaside town like the others. His body hasn't been found. We've got Andrew Coates in Littlehampton, John Seeward in Portsmouth, Eric Jones in Southampton, Michael Redwood in Eastbourne, James Buckle in Newhaven and Ian Standing in Brighton. The other missing boy, Peter Reilly, was from Seaford. So why change to the New Forest for Duncan? But if he did kill my brother, and he acted in the same way as the other murders, Duncan's body would be within a twenty-mile radius of Nightingales. I assume the police covered that?'

'Yes, they did, Maisy. In fact, they covered much further than that.'

'Then there's his missing bike. As the police didn't find it, maybe the man put it in the vehicle with Duncan.'

'Yes, that makes sense,' Dove said. 'But another oddity is that all these boys whose bodies have been found were held somewhere for at least a month before being killed, some much longer, and then buried on waste ground. That was proved in the autopsies. Harry thinks, and I tend to agree with him, that the killer captures these boys for a purpose, and if they don't shape up for whatever it is he wants of them, he kills them.'

'What could he want them for? They're only fourteen or fifteen.'

When Dove didn't answer her question, she immediately guessed it was something too horrible to discuss with a girl of her age.

'Something . . .' She couldn't say the word 'sexual', and she blushed with embarrassment.

'Yes, that's what we both think,' Dove agreed, clearly understanding what she meant. 'But let's not dwell on that, Maisy.'

'If it's something like that, why are the police harassing Grace Deville?'

'I think they felt compelled to take her in for questioning because people were so convinced she was involved. But it was, is, ridiculous for anyone to suspect her. She has no motive, she liked Duncan and he liked her. She rarely leaves her home in the forest, and even if she had gone to each of the places the boys were taken, they wouldn't have stopped to talk to her. Besides, there would've been witnesses who had noticed her – by all accounts, she's hardly an ordinary-looking woman. On top of that, the police checked the mileage on her van and she does an average of less than ten miles a week in it. '

'I'm going to see her later,' Maisy said, giving her old tutor a defiant look that dared him to tell her that was unwise. 'I need to ask her if Duncan talked about anyone else to her, someone I don't know, maybe someone he met through the boys in the village. Also, last time I saw her she said something about the boys being taken for a purpose, sort of like you've just said. She knew all their names too; she'd been following the news reports, in much the same detail as you.'

'Really? She clearly did care about your brother, then?'

'Yes, very much so. I don't believe that Duncan would ordinarily accept a lift from a stranger, but if he'd had a flat tyre or some sort of accident and this person stopped to help him, then he might have agreed to be driven home.'

'Well now, clever Maisy, you might have come up with how this killer got Duncan. He could even have caused the accident.'

'The man might have a local connection. He could have recognized Duncan because he'd seen him around the village,' Maisy said. 'I mean, if he said to Duncan, "I know your grandmother," Duncan would be inclined to think that made the person safe. Anyway, I wanted to talk this idea over with Grace, and to see if she's come up with anything new.'

'I won't try and deter you from going to see her, but

please don't linger in the forest, Maisy. And please let me know if there are any further developments, won't you?'

Maisy smiled at him and stood up. 'I'll be back to see you again before I go back to Brighton, Mr Dove. You are one of the few people around here I care about.'

11

Maisy left Mr Dove's cottage and rode her bike out into the forest. After the hustle and bustle of Brighton it was so good to be on virtually empty roads, to see nothing more than the odd couple out on a dog walk.

There was something special about April, the vivid greenness of new growth on trees and bushes, wood anemones and celandines carpeting the ground, and the strappy leaves of the bluebells to come in May. The birds were in full chorus, and as she pedalled slowly, enjoying the sounds and sights, she observed nest building, and indeed birds flitting about as if they already had fledgling chicks that needed feeding.

The path through to Grace's shack was more clearly defined now – perhaps due to the police tramping out to see her – so much so that Maisy was able to wheel her bike almost the whole way. As she came out of the bushes into Grace's clearing, she saw her bent over her vegetable plot, weeding. Toby barked frantically.

Maisy waved when Grace looked up. 'OK to come and say hullo?' she called out.

Grace told Toby she was a friend and beckoned her over. 'I didn't think I'd see you again,' she said. 'I heard a whisper that your grandmother wasn't too happy about you leaving your lessons and going to work in Brighton.'

'She seems to have got over that now,' Maisy said as she

came closer, wondering who might have given Grace this information. 'But she hasn't written to me once since I left.'

'And how is the job?' Grace asked, rubbing her back as if it ached.

Maisy grinned. 'Great. I'm very happy there, but there are a couple of things I wanted to talk over with you. I know the police have been hounding you, and I'm so sorry about that. I'll understand if you want me to clear off.'

'The police weren't too bad,' Grace said. 'I think they were just going through the motions because people in the village think I'm dangerous. Come and sit down with me for a while.'

They sat on a bench, and Maisy told Grace the gist of what Mr Dove had said about the other murdered boys and why he thought Duncan and the other boy Peter Reilly still hadn't been found dead. She added the idea about Duncan having an accident on his bike.

'I wanted you to try and think back about whether he mentioned anyone, like a casual meeting with someone. If he did, it might be something the police could follow up. Mr Dove seems to think his police sergeant friend is really getting his teeth into the case.'

'I don't recall Duncan mentioning anyone other than some of the village boys that he made friends with. He was very quick to say he hadn't told them he sometimes visited me so they wouldn't come out here. But they're just boys, it couldn't be one of them. However, I don't think it would hurt for the police to look a little closer at their fathers or other older male relatives, any of whom could've met Duncan.'

She paused for a moment as if thinking something

through. 'I agree with your Mr Dove about why all the boys have been found except for Duncan and the other boy Peter. Perverted, evil men who prey on young people, be that girls or boys, will quickly lose interest in their victims if they turn out to be a disappointment.'

'In what way do you mean?' Maisy asked.

'Too compliant, not compliant enough. Someone who fights them, or doesn't fight at all. It's all about extremes.'

'You sound as if you know something about this kind of thing,' Maisy said cautiously.

'What makes you think that? It's just common sense,' Grace retorted brusquely.

'I'm sorry, I suppose it is,' Maisy said. But she didn't think it was; to her what Grace had said sounded like the voice of experience.

They talked a little more, mostly about Maisy's life in Brighton. She also told Grace that she now had the address of the place her mother was in. 'It's in Tenterden, Kent, so I thought I'd go there when I leave here.'

'Make sure you get to speak to the psychiatrist she's under,' Grace said. 'Might be a good idea to ring first and pin him down for an appointment. Ask him for full details of your mother's condition, the medication she is given, and what likelihood there is of her going back to a normal life. Make notes of the medication and any technical words he uses. That way you can speak to another psychiatrist and get a second opinion.'

'Is it possible she could've been sent there by my father just to get her out of the way, so he could have another woman, for instance?' Maisy asked. She wasn't going to admit she'd seen her father with someone.

'Years ago such incarcerations were quite common, for all kinds of often ridiculous reasons,' Grace said. 'As I know to my cost. But I would imagine they are very rare now. Divorce doesn't have the same stigma it used to have, so if this was just about your father wanting to be free, he could achieve that easily without getting your mother committed. You must of course consider that she might really not be capable of looking after herself and is possibly a danger to others. But you will find that out when you visit.'

'Why can't adults explain properly to their children about problems such as these?' Maisy asked. 'Here I am asking Mr Dove and you about it. My father could have stopped all that worry and mistrust by just explaining.'

Grace half smiled. 'Your father is the same generation as me. We were brought up in the dark about family problems, and warned it was bad form to ask leading questions. I had a cousin who was a bigamist; it didn't come out until he died, when two wives came forward to take the responsibility of burying him. He had four children with the first wife and two with the second. It turned out the wives and his brothers had always sensed something odd was going on, but no one wanted to be the one to ask questions.'

'How on earth did he get away with it?'

Grace shrugged. 'He was a salesman for a pharmaceutical company and he had a wide area to cover; both wives thought he was in lodgings on the nights he wasn't with them. But now I must get back to my weeding and it's time you went back home before it starts to get dark. It was good to see you again.'

Maisy was disappointed to be dismissed just when she felt they'd struck up a friendship, but then Grace wasn't used to company. 'Is there any way of contacting you, like an address you pick mail up from? Only I don't know when I'll be back here again and I'd like to tell you what happened about Mother.'

'I have a post office number and pick up any mail once a week,' Grace said. 'Not that I get much, but I'll write it down for you. You give me yours too, just in case something comes to me.'

The following morning Maisy went into Lyndhurst on the bus to see Linda. They greeted each other with whoops of delight and barely drew breath for a couple of hours, there was so much to say. Linda thought her friend's new look – the beehive, the pencil skirt and blazer – was great. But she had to go out with her mother to visit an aunt in hospital, so they arranged that Maisy would come back one day after Easter and stay the night.

'That way we can see if we can arrange to run into Alan and Steven,' Linda said. She said she had gone out with Steven a couple more times last year, but once she'd gone back to school she'd thought there was no point in carrying on writing to him as he was a bit of a Mummy's boy. 'That doesn't mean I'm not into flirting with him again now, though,' she added.

Maisy was on her way to catch the bus back to Nightingales when she saw a bus going the other way to Southampton, and on the spur of the moment thought she'd visit Donald Grainger in his office, to ask his advice on going to see her mother.

She had been shocked and embarrassed by the incident

when he'd made a pass at her, but looking back, now that she was a bit more experienced with men, it didn't seem quite so bad and she even wondered if she might have inadvertently encouraged it. She had after all quite fancied him – anyone would – and maybe he'd picked up on that.

She still had his card tucked into her handbag; it had been there so long she barely noticed it any more.

The woman sitting next to her on the bus knew the street where his office was. She said it was just around the corner from the big new C&A, which Maisy had been in several times before.

Maisy liked Southampton, though people in Burley were always complaining that the modern buildings which had replaced those bombed during the war were ugly. To Maisy, the main shopping street was almost as good as Oxford Street, but she wasn't interested in shopping for now. It didn't take her long to find 'Grainger, Moore and Edwards, Solicitors' above a bookshop.

It was an old building but it had been modernized with a plate-glass door at street level and a smart grey-and-black striped carpet on the stairs to the first floor and the reception desk.

'I wondered if I could see Mr Grainger?' Maisy asked the dumpy middle-aged receptionist banging away at a typewriter. The reception area had two corridors running off it, one to the back and the other, shorter one to the front. Maisy saw at least four doors in the longer one.

'Have you an appointment?' the receptionist asked, peering over her glasses at Maisy.

'No, I'm sorry. But maybe you could tell him it's Maisy Mitcham.'

The woman frowned at her as if it was unthinkable to expect to see the senior partner without an appointment, but she picked up the telephone and spoke to someone.

'His secretary said he's with a client at the moment, but if you'd like to sit and wait she'll speak to Mr Grainger when he becomes free.'

In twenty minutes Maisy saw three people come out of different rooms and go on down the stairs. Finally, a woman of about twenty-five in a tight black skirt, white blouse and high-heeled shoes came out from the door at the front of the building.

'Miss Mitcham?' she asked. 'Mr Grainger can see you now.'

Maisy followed the secretary, who led her through the outer office where she worked and then opened another door and beckoned Maisy to go in.

'Maisy Mitcham, what a pleasant surprise,' Grainger said, getting up from his desk and coming round to shake her hand. 'You always were a pretty girl, but now you are simply stunning.'

Maisy blushed. 'Thank you, Mr Grainger.' She wondered if Linda had ever met him, because she was sure her friend would be most impressed. He could pass for an Italian with his dark hair and olive skin. His pale grey suit was very sharp too – the new Italian styling with a short, boxy jacket.

'Are you staying with your grandmother?' he asked, after asking her to sit down and going back behind his desk to take his seat. 'I was with her a few weeks ago but she was rather vague about you.'

'Well, she would be. She was cross when I went off to

work in Brighton. She didn't write to me once after I left, but then I'm sure you know how she can be. Anyway, I asked if I could come back for a visit – someone had to be the first to make it up.'

'Yes, she's not the kind of granny we read about in books,' he said with a smile. 'She did tell me when you left that you'd gone to work as a mother's help. She was sure that was modern-day slavery.'

'She was wrong; the people I work for are lovely, as are their two children.'

'That is good news, especially after all the sadness you have had. I also never got a chance to apologize for my behaviour last time we met. I hope you forgave me, Maisy, but really it was unforgivable.'

'It's forgotten,' Maisy said airily.

'That is kind of you. My only excuse is that you are so very lovely.'

'Let's just forget about that and make certain it never happens again,' she said crisply. 'Now, I didn't come about Duncan, though the police are still investigating, I believe. I just hope that they'll find him soon, or at least his body, so we can grieve and bury him. It's living in limbo which is the worst thing.' She paused, then continued: 'Actually, I came because I finally managed to get the address of the home our mother was put into. I wanted your advice about how to proceed.'

'You certainly have had more than your fair share of troubles,' he said sympathetically. 'But as far as your mother is concerned, just telephone the home and ask if you can come. They cannot reasonably refuse to let you see her.'

'How much do you know about her condition?' Maisy asked.

He made a kind of shrugging gesture with his hands. 'Nothing much. You must remember I am your grandmother's solicitor, not your father's. Mrs Mitcham has often mentioned her daughter-in-law, but what she tells me is only her opinion, not necessarily fact. However, she did get me to call at the home once to report back to her how your mother was.'

'I'm surprised she cared; she's never approved of her,' Maisy said. 'But how was Mother when you went?'

'Frail, poorly. She ignored me completely, and I was told she doesn't know anyone any more. But that's all I can tell you.'

'Are you trying to say there's no point in me going?'

'Not at all, Maisy. If you feel you want to go, then you should. It's possible that the sound of your voice and sight of your face will stimulate her. Just don't expect too much.'

Maisy didn't know what to say in reply. She realized she'd have to think on what he'd said before she rushed to the home.

'I can see I've confused you,' Grainger said. 'It's late in the afternoon now. If you aren't on your way anywhere else, could I give you a ride home? We could stop and have a cup of tea somewhere if you'd like to talk some more, and you can tell me all about Brighton and your boyfriends. I promise faithfully I will behave impeccably.'

She thought it over for a moment or two. The bus would be crowded at this time of day, and, as always, very slow. Besides, he had apologized and promised there would be no repetition of his behaviour the last time he gave her a lift.

'That would be lovely, but I wouldn't want to put you out.'

'It won't, Burley is on the way to my home. I'd like to buy you tea.'

They stopped at the Forest Tea Shop, and by then Maisy was really enjoying being with Mr Grainger. She realized from a couple of things he said that he was probably older than she'd first thought, maybe even mid-forties. But he was fit; when he took his suit jacket off in the car she could see he was muscular. She asked if he played any sport and he said he liked tennis and swimming. 'I'm not really a team player at anything,' he said with a little chuckle. 'I play singles in tennis, and in swimming I just aim to beat my own fastest speed. I never compete. What about you, Maisy?'

'I love swimming, but that's about it,' she admitted. 'I'm not competitive at all. I used to hate netball and hockey at school – to me it seemed pointless charging around after a ball.'

He laughed. 'I was always afraid of getting hurt in rugby, but I didn't admit it or someone would've kicked my head in just to teach me not to be a drip.'

At the tea shop, they had a pot of tea and a toasted teacake. It was a pretty little place with polished brasses and copper pans hanging from the dark wood beams. Maisy guessed in high summer it would be packed out all day.

She told him about her job, and how she intended to go to London to find secretarial work the following year.

'You might aim to be a legal secretary,' he said. 'It's usually much better paid because of the accuracy needed. I could recommend you to some lawyers I know when the time comes.'

'That would be very kind,' she said. 'I'm going to miss Paul and Annabel, though. I'm not really sure right now that I'm cut out for office work.'

'To enjoy working with children is just a natural maternal instinct,' he said with a smile. 'I'm sure there will be many compensations working in an office. Making new friends – you might even end up marrying a lawyer and have children of your own.'

'That would be lovely.' She grinned. 'I'd like a house like Nightingales, three or four children and an interesting, kind husband, please. Do you have children?'

'No, my wife Deirdre and I weren't blessed with any, I'm afraid. A great sadness.'

'Yes, it must be, I'm sorry.'

'Don't be. We always tell one another how lucky we were to never have sleepless nights, or the mess and expense of children.'

Maisy smiled. She thought that was a sweet thing to say, but she didn't believe a word of it.

'Right! Time to get you home,' he said, indicating to the waitress he wanted the bill. 'I'd rather you didn't tell your grandmother I drove you home or she'll want to know why I didn't come in to see her. Is that all right with you?'

'Perfectly,' Maisy said. 'I wasn't going to own up that I'd called on you to ask about contacting my mother, anyway. She'll only pour cold water on the idea.'

They both grinned conspiratorially.

'Keep in touch, won't you, Maisy,' he said. 'Like I said, I'd like to help you get a good job in London.'

'Thank you so much, Mr Grainger. You've been so nice to me.'

'The pleasure was all mine, and it's Donald in future – at least, away from your grandmother!'

On the remainder of the drive home they spoke about films they'd seen recently. Maisy said she'd found *Pyscho* terrifying and never wanted to see a horror film again. Grainger laughed and said he thought it was a very clever film. 'But I prefer whodunnit films and books. I find it absorbing trying to pit my brain against the detective.'

He stopped the car at the end of the lane, but as Maisy went to get out she found her handbag had tipped over; the entire contents had spilled out into the footwell and some items had rolled right under the passenger seat.

'So sorry about that,' she said, bending back into the car to pick them all up. 'Now don't look at what's fallen out, it might embarrass me.'

'Women and their handbags amuse me,' he said as she began scooping up lipstick, a bottle of nail varnish, scissors and loose change. 'Do you really need all that equipment?'

Maisy laughed. 'Probably not. Handbags are a kind of dumping ground, I suppose.' She slid her fingers right under the seat to check she'd got everything and pulled out several coins and a biro. Further back there was what seemed to be more coins, so she gathered them up and put them in her bag without looking at them.

'That's it,' she said, smiling at Grainger. 'In future I'll make sure my bag is fastened so I don't expose any of my secrets.'

Maisy was still smiling as she got to the gate at Nightingales. It had been a great day all round, and tonight she would sit with Janice and chat. She was so glad she'd come to visit.

She headed straight for the kitchen. 'I hope you had a good day today,' Janice greeted her.

'It's been super,' Maisy said.

'Then I'm sorry to put a damper on it.' Janice grimaced. 'Your grandmother has suggested we all eat together this evening. To be fair to her, she is trying to be nice. I think it has begun to occur to her that her usual attitude doesn't do a lot for her popularity.'

Maisy laughed. 'Is there anything I can do?'

'I should change out of that tight skirt,' Janice said, looking her up and down. 'You look lovely but I should think it's a bit uncomfortable to sit in.'

Maisy went upstairs, took a pink wool dress out of the wardrobe and changed into it. Janice was right – a tight pencil skirt wasn't good for sitting and eating. She brushed out her beehive too, fixing it up at the sides with two pink hairslides, then rummaged in her handbag for her lipstick.

When she couldn't immediately find it, she turned the contents of her bag on to her bed, smiling at what Grainger had said about women's handbags. He was right, there was stuff in there she didn't need and lots of scraps of paper and other rubbish.

She sat down and began to sort through it, when suddenly she saw a shoe buckle. Silver, about three quarters of an inch square, still with a little bit of brown cotton attached.

With just one glance she knew what it was: the missing one from Duncan's sandal. It was too chunky to have come off anything she owned. And more importantly, she knew exactly where it had come from.

Mr Grainger's car.

12

Maisy's first reaction was to run down the stairs screaming that she'd found a vital clue. But reason prevailed when she remembered that by taking the buckle from Grainger's car, she had actually destroyed evidence.

His fingerprints, if they were ever on it, would be gone now. He could even claim it was never in his car, and no one could prove otherwise.

She sat down on her bed, trying to think. It was inconceivable that someone like Mr Grainger could be a killer. He was a solicitor for a start, and a really nice man.

But how did that buckle get in his car?

It was true he could have given Duncan a lift at any time, and Duncan could have got a new buckle sewn on to his sandal. But Maisy was pretty certain if he'd come in with a buckle-less sandal flapping on his foot, Duncan would have mentioned it, as well as getting a lift.

In the unlikely event that he had said nothing, got a brand-new buckle sewn on, and then that one came off too when he was cycling, then Grainger was in the clear. But she didn't believe that was what had happened.

What was much more likely was that Duncan would have greeted Grainger with delight if he'd come along just as he was trying to find a way of securing his sandal to his foot.

Grainger had told Maisy he always drove home through Burley, so he also had opportunity.

But why dump the sandal for the police to find later? And if he did that, why hold on to the buckle? Unless of course Duncan had the buckle in his hand, intending to get it sewn back on, but had dropped it in the car.

Maisy remembered in a book she'd read, the detective said two things were vital in finding a culprit. They needed opportunity and motive. Grainger had opportunity all right, but what possible motive could he have?

He was an attractive, intelligent, successful married man. Why would he snatch a young lad? Maisy would have understood it better if it was a girl – even her.

Suddenly the things both Grace and Mr Dove had alluded to came back to her. She hadn't really understood then, but she was beginning to do so now. Boys could be used in that way too.

The thought made her feel queasy. Surely Donald Grainger wasn't like that, though? It seemed so very unlikely that a man with his looks and standing could possibly do such things, or kill boys. But then some of the most famous murderers in the past were said to be handsome and personable. So his looks didn't rule him out.

What if it was him?

One thing stood out in all this. Duncan was in Grainger's car at some time to lose the buckle in it. So why, if the man had nothing to hide, didn't he come forward and tell the police? Duncan was the grandson of one of his clients, so no one would find it the least bit odd that he'd given him a lift.

If she was to run down to Mr Dove now and show him the buckle, no doubt he'd get his friend Harry on the case straight away. But Grainger knew the law and was also very smart. He could argue that the buckle had fallen out of Maisy's bag.

Besides, it was fairly certain he wouldn't have taken Duncan, or any of those other boys, to his own home, so even with a search warrant the police weren't going to find anything there. And even if they wanted to hold him in custody, the police wouldn't be able to do so without strong evidence to back it up. So he'd leave and make certain he'd left no proof of his guilt anywhere. Should Duncan and Peter Reilly still be alive, he was bound to kill them so that they couldn't talk.

Maisy felt sick. She sat down and put her head between her legs, waiting for the feeling to pass. She so much wanted and needed to talk this over with someone, but how could she? Grandmother would never believe it of Grainger. Janice might, but she'd insist the police had to be called, as would Mr Dove. Linda and her parents would probably think Maisy was being hysterical, and their only suggestion would be the police too.

That left only Grace. It was nearly seven, and dusk already. Maisy knew she couldn't cycle out into the forest now. But how was she going to get through a whole night with this on her mind?

'Is there something wrong with your dinner?' Grandmother asked, observing that Maisy wasn't really eating her lamb cutlets.

'No, not at all,' Maisy said. 'But I had some cake while I was in Lyndhurst this afternoon. I'm not really hungry.'

'Pity they stopped the sugar rationing in 'fifty-three,' Grandmother said. 'Young people seem to stuff themselves with sweets and cakes now.'

'I think we all did when rationing ended,' Janice said with a smile. 'You too, Mrs Mitcham.'

'Yes, I suppose I did,' she sighed. 'Well, if you can't eat it maybe Janice can warm it up for tomorrow. A shame to waste it. Now tell me, Maisy, when do you finish this night school course? Will you get a proper diploma?'

'I take the final exam next month,' Maisy replied. 'And yes, I will get a diploma.'

'So what then?'

Maisy had been wondering if there was any way she could get her grandmother to tell her anything about Grainger, and suddenly she saw an opportunity.

'On the bus today I was thinking that maybe I could become a solicitor,' she said. She hadn't thought that, of course, but a white lie wouldn't hurt. 'How did Mr Grainger get into it, Grandmother?'

'He was always a clever boy, though Alastair was jealous and used to claim he was just sneaky. He didn't go to university, just got himself articled to a solicitor in South-ampton. He rather distinguished himself during the war – he was in the RAF, which stood him in good stead.'

'What made Father claim he was sneaky?'

Grandmother pursed her lips. 'As I said, jealousy. Don-ald had so much charm and good looks, and although it pains me to say it, poor Alastair is an odd-looking man, and was even odder as a boy.'

'Oh, Mrs Mitcham,' Janice exclaimed. 'That's an awful thing to say!'

Grandmother smirked. 'You always did take his part, Janice. Anyway, let's just say Alastair was no heart-throb. But he claimed Donald told a lot of lies, listened at keyholes and smarmed his way into people's affections. Later on, Alastair was also very suspicious about how Donald got to be made a partner in the solicitors' firm he's still with. We knew he'd sold his aunt's cottage when she died, but it was in such a bad state it didn't fetch much. Even so, Alastair claimed the cottage should have gone to his aunt's two daughters, and he'd got it by being underhand. Absolute rubbish born out of jealousy, I think. I've always found Donald to be straightforward, honest and very kindly.'

'He seemed like that to me when he came to lunch,' Maisy said. 'Where does he live, Grandmother? In Southampton?'

'No, in Ringwood. I thought he would come to live in Burley as he'd been so happy here as a boy, but he said Ringwood had good road links and he needed that.'

'What's his wife like? He's very good-looking so I expect she's lovely.' Maisy was rather enjoying this little interrogation, though she realized if she kept it up too long her grandmother might find it suspicious.

'She's an attractive, glamorous woman, if rather vacuous. But then I don't think Donald likes clever women. Before he married Deirdre he always had a ravishing beauty on his arm at social functions. So many women set their caps at him back then, but they would, he was a good catch. Still, I've never heard any whispers about him straying from the fold since he got married. Why are you asking me about him?'

'Only because I got this idea of being a solicitor, and he's the only one I've ever met,' Maisy said. 'Do you think he'd give me some advice on it?'

'I'm sure he would, but I'm not sure your father would approve. It would be more tactful to ask his advice instead – he does after all know a great deal about law. Aside from being a very clever man, Maisy, your father's work in the Foreign Office is very important and he knows all the right people.'

Maisy opened her mouth to add 'and the right women', but she thought better of it. Her grandmother had been nice to her this evening, at least as nice as she was capable of being. She didn't want to spoil that.

Later, after Grandmother had gone up to bed and Maisy was helping Janice clear up in the kitchen, Janice asked what her game was.

'What game?' Maisy said.

Janice grimaced. 'Asking all those questions about Mr Grainger. Have you run into him today? I know he's an attractive man but he's far too old for you, Maisy.'

For a second Maisy was tempted to tell Janice about the buckle. But like Mr Dove, she'd insist on taking this to the police. So she laughed. 'Don't be daft, Janice. I want someone young enough to enjoy rock and roll. I was only interested in the solicitor thing. Why do you think my father claimed he was sneaky? I thought they were good friends.'

'No, they were never that, as far as I remember. Donald Grainger used to get sent round here by his aunt, and poor Alastair was expected to entertain him. It must have been a trial for Alastair, as he was about six years older than Donald. To be honest, but don't tell your grandmother this, I don't like Donald much either. He was a lovely looking young boy, but he *was* creepy, always under your feet or watching you. Yet somehow he sweet-talked your grand-mother into becoming her solicitor after your grandfather died. I can tell you your father wasn't best pleased, they had quite a row about it. Alastair said she was a vain old woman taken in by a handsome face, but she insisted she knew he was the right man for the job. So that was that.'

Maisy so much wanted to ask if Janice had ever heard any rumours about him liking young boys, but she didn't dare. She knew it would alert Janice to the fact that she had some information.

She went off to bed then, resigned to having to wait to consult Grace the next day. That was going to be difficult as it was Good Friday, and Grandmother would probably want Maisy to go to church with her. The thought of the gloomy three-hour service was totally depressing, and no doubt Grandmother would think going out on a bike or taking a walk on the day they crucified Christ was bad form.

By an astounding stroke of luck after breakfast the next day, Janice asked Maisy if she would mind taking some marmalade she'd made to a friend of hers who lived about a mile out of Burley.

'I promised to let her have it for the church bring-and-buy sale on Easter Sunday, but it's a bit of a hike for me to go to Enid's cottage, and anyway she'll want me to stay and chat. But you can drop it with her and scarper.'

'I don't mind at all.' Maisy grinned. It was a beautiful sunny morning. 'But won't Grandmother expect me to go to church with her?'

'No, she has no time for that long vigil any more. The

last time she went was two years ago when you and Duncan went with her. She admitted afterwards it was an ordeal for you both, and her knees hurt from all the kneeling. Years ago she used to expect me to go with her; I can tell you it was a great relief when she let me off.'

Maisy beamed. 'A bike ride is just what I fancy. I might even go on to Lyndhurst. Anything else you need?'

Janice said there wasn't, and handed Maisy four pots of marmalade packed around with newspaper. 'They should go in the bike's basket,' she said and gave Maisy a peck on the cheek. 'Lunch at one sharp! As always on Good Friday, it's fish.'

Maisy rode as fast as she could, dropping the marmalade off first at Enid's cottage, making the excuse she couldn't stop as she had arranged to meet someone in ten minutes' time. Then she set off for Grace's shack.

'Sorry to intrude again so quickly,' she said as she came through into the clearing and found Grace hanging some washing on a line. 'But I've got something.'

Toby came over to greet her, his tail wagging furiously. Maisy bent to pet him, and then she and Grace sat on the bench in the sunshine and Maisy immediately blurted out about the buckle and her suspicions about Donald Grainger.

Grace listened carefully. 'I do know who he is but I don't know him. All I know is what other people have said about him. I came to live here in the forest in 1945 when he'd just been demobbed and there was talk about him then. I heard stuff while I was getting my rations. Back then all the local girls were after him. They said he was a hero and that sort of rubbish.'

'Was he?'

'How could he be? He was ground staff, and there isn't a lot of chance for heroics there. I think he spread a few yarns himself, and what with his good looks, people believed it all.

'But what really got people talking was when his aunt died. She was called Constance, and she lived just down the lane from your grandmother. She died around the time of the Coronation in 1953 and left the cottage to him. It was nothing much, rough as they come, but her two daughters were apparently savage about it.'

'Yes, Janice told me that. But he still got the cottage.'

'Your grandmother was the person who stuck up for him, and she'd always had a lot of clout in the area. By all accounts she said he'd been like a son to Constance, visiting her every week, whereas her daughters never came near.'

'So he was left looking like the good guy?'

'Exactly,' Grace agreed. 'But Maisy, this is all repeated gossip, stuff I've overheard in the village shop, and it may not be completely true. Anyway, what he got from his aunt wouldn't have been much – the cottage was run-down with no modern conveniences. There are many people who also say he purposely pursues and charms older women, and that includes your grandmother, into handling their affairs. It is definitely true that a woman in Brockenhurst left him everything, just three or four years ago. Her family con-tested it, but they lost. Apparently, like Constance's daughters, they hadn't been anywhere near her for years, while he had popped in to see her all the time.'

'How do most people react to him now? Grandmother thinks he's perfect,' Maisy said. She was inclined to believe the gossip, but then until she'd found that buckle she'd thought he was a lovely man.

Grace shrugged. 'There are two camps. One camp, to which your grandmother clearly belongs, believes he's a saint. The other the exact opposite – they say he preys on the old and weak. I don't have any view. I've never spoken to him, I only know him by sight. And I suspect from what I've heard about your grandmother that she'd be a match for Lucifer himself.'

Maisy laughed at that. 'Have you ever heard any gossip about his . . .' She stopped short because she was embarrassed and didn't know how to say it.

'Sexuality?' Grace prompted.

Maisy nodded.

'No, I've never heard gossip about that. As I understand it, most ladies around here swoon about him. But let me tell you a bit of background information. In 1939 when the war started I was discharged from the institution I was in. It was suggested I join the Land Army and I was sent down here.'

Grace waved her arm in the direction of Burley. 'I was sent to a small farm the other side of the village owned by an elderly couple called Brady. I was the only help they got, but it suited me just fine because after what I'd been through I couldn't have coped with a whole parcel of other girls. I knew nothing about farming, but Bert Brady was a patient man and taught me everything.'

Maisy was wondering where this was going. It didn't appear to have anything to do with Grainger.

'I needed to explain to you how it was for me, so you can judge if there's anything in what I'm going to tell you,' Grace said.

'As you probably know, locals can graze animals in the

forest, and the Bradys were no exception,' she went on. 'Soon after I arrived they asked me to come over here to check on their pigs. Well, I wasn't too sure about that. I didn't know where to go, or what to look for when I got here. I was a bit frightened too. Anyway, Mr Brady laughed at me and said there was nothing to hurt me in the forest, because I was the wrong sex. I was so unworldly then I had no idea what he meant by that. Mrs Brady told me later that there had been reports of men lurking there, looking for other men.'

'Really?' Maisy was shocked. She'd been told that in Brighton there were clubs like that, but she couldn't really believe such things went on in a forest.

'I know it sounds bizarre, but apparently it was true. Men who were that way would meet up there, close to where that Forest Tea Shop is now. Whether Grainger was ever involved I couldn't say. But he did come back here frequently during the war.'

Maisy thought on this for a few moments. 'What can we do, Grace?' she asked eventually. 'Should I take that buckle to the police and put my trust in them to investigate Grainger? Or should I try to find something more in case they just think I'm a crank? But how *can* I find something more? I'll have to go back to Brighton next weekend. I can't let it go, though. Duncan might still be alive and even if he isn't, I need to know.'

Grace put her strong hand on Maisy's arm. 'I know exactly how you feel and I really sympathize. I've never admitted this to anyone before, but I feel I need to tell you. I was raped by a family member, not once, but time and time again, for many years. The reason I got put into an asylum was because I tried to get help; they said I was mad and got me locked away.'

Maisy's jaw dropped. She had thought something bad had caused Grace to be put away, but she hadn't suspected anything like this.

'I'm so sorry, Grace,' she gasped. 'That is awful.'

Grace shrugged, a gesture that said the word 'awful' didn't come close to describing it. 'Since I finally got out of that place I've trusted no one. Even though Mr and Mrs Brady treated me well, I was still wary. And the longer I've lived out here alone, rumoured to be barmy, or a witch, the less I've been inclined to talk to anyone.

'Then your Duncan came here. He braved my nastiness, and in his little way he made me less suspicious of people, enough for me to think of him as a friend. Then you came, Maisy, and I see you are from the same mould. You've touched me because you don't appear to believe I'm mad, and you value my opinion. So *I am* going to help you find out what's happened to Duncan.'

'But how? What do we do?'

'Nothing for today. It's Good Friday, after all, and your grandmother wouldn't approve of you gadding about, especially with me. Come here tomorrow morning. I'll have had time to think about it and plan what to do next.'

'I've just thought of something,' Maisy said. 'Mr Grainger gave me a lift home one afternoon, before I went to Brighton. He said something a bit odd. I didn't think anything of it at the time, but now it looks to me as if he knew Duncan much better than he should.'

'What did he say?'

'Nothing much really, just a reference to Duncan's

freckles. But Grace, back then he'd only met Duncan once at lunch with Grandmother. Why would he remember his freckles? They've never seemed obvious to anyone else at first meeting.'

'I suspect you've got something else on your mind that's worrying you. What is it, Maisy?'

Maisy blushed, embarrassed that Grace was so intuitive. 'Yes, there is something else. When he gave me the lift, he also tried to kiss me. I found it creepy, but then I was very naïve back then.'

'I see,' Grace said thoughtfully. 'Trying to kiss a young and pretty girl doesn't make a man a sex maniac or a murderer. But it does show a lack of restraint when that girl is his client's granddaughter. Let me think on that one and we'll talk some more tomorrow.'

13

Grace watched Maisy's retreating figure going up the bank into the bushes and a lump came up in her throat. She felt for her; the poor girl had the worries of the world on her slender shoulders.

She was such a pretty girl. The combination of bright blue eyes, long blond hair in one fat, sleek plait and a peaches-and-cream complexion was enough on its own. But she had something more than just good looks; she was kind, giving and extraordinarily understanding for someone so young. At seventeen she should be out having fun, not trying to find a missing twin brother, or concerning herself with her mother being in an institution and her father seeing another woman.

How good it would be to have a daughter like her!

Funny she should even think such a thing, when she'd never wanted children of her own.

When she was sent to the asylum in North London after telling her father that her uncle, his brother, had been raping her and terrorizing her constantly for several years, her first thought was that at last she'd be safe. She assumed that the asylum was a temporary measure while she was examined and her uncle was tried and convicted.

But no one believed her claim. Her father and stepmother, the doctors and even the police, were all impervious to her entreaties. Every time she pleaded with them to listen, even showed them old scars from a razor blade on her stomach and legs, they shook their heads and said it was a sick, strange fantasy and she'd inflicted the scars on herself, but that she was in the right place now where she'd be looked after.

She became hoarse with desperately trying to convince people, anyone, that what she said was true. Then to make matters even worse, the ward sister, a big brute of a woman, informed her that she was in fact four months pregnant.

Her father and stepmother claimed her allegation of abuse at the hands of her uncle was purely a smokescreen to hide the truth, which was that she was a dirty little hussy and had been having sex with someone she knew they would never approve of.

They didn't even tell her they were going to abort the baby. They just gave her a drug which started the contractions. After twenty-four hours of pain they operated on her, without any anaesthetic, to remove the now dead foetus. The ward sister enjoyed telling her that she would never be able to bear another child. She said it served her right as she wasn't fit to be a mother.

Back then in those endless, dark, lonely months and years of incarceration, it was the cruelty with which she'd been treated in her own home that changed her, far more than the casual indifference she suffered at the asylum .

She had always known her stepmother didn't want her around, but it was difficult to believe that a grown woman, however irritated by her stepchild, would turn a blind eye to her brother-in-law raping her husband's daughter on a regular basis. At fourteen Grace had begged her to persuade her father to let her go into service. She had said, 'Into service? Why, Grace, you are our servant here.'

She was just seventeen, the same age Maisy was now, when they put her in that terrible place, and if war hadn't broken out, maybe she'd still be there.

But the war rescued her. A more enlightened doctor said she was sane, and so twelve years later, aged twenty-nine, she was recommended for work with the Land Army and they sent her to the Brady's farm in the New Forest.

It was only there on the farm, when she saw lambs and calves born, that she felt a crushing sorrow at the thought of never holding her own baby in her arms. Occasionally she watched courting couples walking hand in hand through the forest, and she was reminded she'd never experienced love either. All she knew of the human sexual act was degradation, domination, fear and pain. Her body still bore the physical scars her uncle had inflicted on her with a razor blade, but the scars inside her hurt far more.

She found peace and a measure of happiness with the Bradys because they were kind to her, they never pried and they allowed her solitude when she wanted it. She loved farm work. The animals gave her such joy, and she embraced each season with delight, whether they were ploughing, seeding or harvesting. Nature gave her back some dignity and she was appreciated.

In late 1944 when people at last began to talk about how life would be once the war was over, and the Bradys spoke excitedly of how wonderful it would be when their two soldier sons came home to run the farm, Grace panicked. She knew that even if the Bradys could afford to keep her on, she would never be able to cope with sharing the same house as two young and vigorous unmarried men, and it would be hard to get any other job when so many returning servicemen were given first priority.

Even though the Bradys had never told anyone about her past, her inability to communicate with people singled her out as being strange. There were many nights back at the farm in the first couple of years there when she'd wake from a nightmare that her uncle was cutting her and raping her again. Mrs Brady used to come into her room and hold her until the nightmares went.

Just as they'd understood her fears back then, they sensed her present anxiety about her future too. Mr Brady knew how much she loved the forest, and he came up with a solution for her. He had built a shack in the forest when he was single, and he said she could have it if she wished. He took her out to see it on New Year's Day of '45. It had snowed and they had to fight through undergrowth and brambles to reach it, but the moment she saw the shack, looking like something out of a fairy tale with its heavy coating of snow, she knew she could be happy there.

There was no real security – the shack had been built on common land, and someone in authority could order her out and pull it down if they felt like it – but that didn't worry Grace. She was tough, she had learned simple carpentry on the farm, and she relished the mending, cleaning and making of it into a little home.

Grace had stopped believing in God at the age of nine, which was when Uncle Max had come to stay and had begun to come to her room at night, terrorizing her into not telling anyone. Her constant prayers for help in the early days had gone unnoticed. But perhaps there was a

God after all. Just a few days after seeing the shack, she was notified by a solicitor that on 25 November her father, uncle and stepmother had all been killed in a V-2 rocket blast while they were shopping in Woolworths in London's New Cross. The explosion had killed 123 people, and countless more were injured. Grace felt sorrow for the 120, and for their loved ones, but for the other three she could only feel delight at their deaths. Finally she had been given a kind of restitution.

The solicitor, presumably appointed by a government body as he was entirely unknown to Grace, had tracked her down to inform her of the deaths and to tell her that, as the only surviving member of the family, she would inherit everything. It amounted to the house in Lewisham where she'd grown up, and a sum of approximately three thousand pounds.

She instructed the solicitor to sell the house; she never wanted to see it again. She put all the money into a post office savings account in Burley.

When spring arrived, birdsong woke her at first light. The days were long and hard, clearing ground to plant vegetables and soft fruits, building a pen for chickens, and chopping wood for her fire, but at twilight, sitting sleepily on her porch, she would watch rabbits, foxes and deer going about their business. She felt joyous.

Grace got her first dog, a collie cross she called Billy, soon after she moved in, and she spent hours training him to keep her safe and to be her perfect companion. He had died five years ago and she buried him close to the shack. Now she had Toby, a very similar looking black-and-white collie, who had a gentler and more biddable nature.

She hoped that one day soon Maisy would feel the kind of peace she had now.

Maisy went home and ate her lunch with Janice. Apparently Grandmother wasn't feeling too well and Janice had given her some lunch on a tray in her bedroom.

'Not too sick to eat, though.' Janice laughed. 'I'm going to put my feet up and read this afternoon. What about you?'

'I don't know,' Maisy said. She had an idea but she didn't want to tell Janice. 'Maybe I'll just go for a bike ride and see if there're any new lambs in the fields.'

She dried up the dishes for Janice, then as soon as the older woman had gone through to her room, Maisy got out the telephone book.

To her delight there was only one D. Grainger listed in Ringwood, at Cherry Trees, Southampton Road.

While she had no real idea what she hoped to gain by checking out where he lived, especially on a holiday weekend when he would most likely be there, she wanted to see what his house was like.

It was only about five miles or so to Ringwood and a pleasant ride on a sunny spring day. Within twenty minutes she was at the start of Southampton Road and as she could see some cherry trees in full blossom further along, she guessed that was Grainger's house.

She had borrowed a brown waterproof jacket belonging to Janice because it had a hood. Rain wasn't expected, but it was all she could think of as a spur-of-the-moment disguise. Hardly adequate, but she had thought if Grainger should catch sight of her and recognize her, she could pretend great surprise and say she was just exploring.

The houses were a mixture of styles and ages. Some were very old cottages – mostly a bit run-down, perhaps owned by older people – and there were quite a few semi-detached houses built in the thirties. Then there were a few post-war buildings, and she saw one brand-new bungalow looking entirely out of place.

Cherry Trees was one of the older properties – not a cottage as she'd expected, but a sturdy-looking, rather plain villa with bay windows. The front garden was attractive, with four cherry trees, two close to the gate and two further back flanking the sides of the house. There were innumerable bushes around a very well-kept lawn, masses of daffodils and primroses were in full flower, and there were tulips yet to come. It was a beautiful garden already and she guessed that in another month's time when the flowering bushes blossomed it would look stunning. She wondered if it was his work; she couldn't imagine someone so smart gardening.

On the right side of the house there was a garage, and she could see his maroon Jaguar sitting there through the open door of the garage. She wondered if this meant he had just come in, or whether he was going out.

She couldn't linger, of course, but the style of the house and its neat garden didn't sit quite right with her idea of the swanky RAF man turned solicitor who charmed old ladies. She had imagined something older, a bit posh.

It was the kind of house a very sedate middle-aged couple would live in; the snowy white nets at the windows would traditionally hide the wife while she monitored her neighbours. But then maybe his wife was like that.

Maisy rode right along to the end of the road to where

there were some shops, and she went into a newsagent's to buy a Mars bar. As she bit into it a clear picture of Duncan came into her mind, and tears filled her eyes.

Mars bars were his favourite. He had always raved about them, claiming they were so big that they made you feel a bit sick if you ate one all at once. That had always sounded illogical to Maisy, but as she sat on the wall outside the shop and finished it she thought that he was right: she didn't think she'd want to eat anything for the rest of the day.

As she sat there she saw Grainger drive by in his Jaguar. She didn't think he'd seen her since his head was turned towards his wife in the passenger seat.

Maisy got back on her bike and rode slowly down the road again. To her surprise they had left the garage doors open. This could of course mean they would return very quickly, but she felt it was an open invitation to use the opportunity to take a quick peep.

She went up to the front door and rang the bell first, just in case anyone was watching. No one answered, as she half expected, so she walked in a hesitant manner into the garage, calling out his name.

Like the garden, the garage was kept very neat, a hose, lawnmower and garden tools all hanging on hooks on the wall to one side. Old paint tins were stored above. On the other side, screws, nails and other assorted ironmongery were in jars on shelves and beneath these hung hammers and other hand tools. Even the concrete garage floor had been painted dark red, and recently swept. At the back of the garage was a door through to the garden. She tried it but it was locked.

Aware she couldn't linger in here without raising the neighbours' suspicions, she began to walk away, but a crate on the floor, holding all manner of odd things, as if being collected to give to a jumble sale, caught her eye and she couldn't resist a look.

Amongst the things she spotted a black bicycle pump.

Without even touching it she just knew it was Duncan's. Mr Pike had given them both pumps and told them not to lose them, and because Duncan claimed his sister lost everything not screwed down, he had stuck a tiny gold star on his.

There it was, in the box. The old star was worn away in part now, but it was his pump.

Maisy went straight to her bike then without touching the pump. Jumped on and rode off at speed. Maybe the buckle didn't prove anything, but with the pump in his possession too, Grainger had to have taken Duncan. Her brother had always made certain his pump was clipped on to his bike. The only way they would be separated was if the bike was involved in an accident or put in the back of a car and it fell off.

She rode like fury back to see Grace, her mind like a whirlpool of facts, ideas and images.

'What on earth!' Grace exclaimed as Maisy came haring across her garden. 'I thought we were going to meet tomorrow?'

Maisy was so excited and breathless from the fast ride she had difficulty in speaking, but eventually she managed to explain properly.

'Well, it looks as if he is really our man,' Grace agreed when she'd finished. 'But what to do?'

'We go to the police together, now?'

Grace looked at the girl's eager, trusting face and wished it was that simple. 'The chances are they won't believe us,' she said with a despairing shrug. 'They might go round there and ask him about the pump, but he could say he drove Duncan and his bike home one afternoon and the pump must have fallen off the bike. There's no one but Duncan who can say that isn't true.'

'But we can't do nothing,' Maisy said.

'We need to watch his house, and follow him,' Grace said. 'Not you, but me, because he doesn't know me. It's too late now, but I'll go there in the morning and watch and wait.'

'I want to come,' Maisy said.

'No one notices a middle-aged woman; it's well known we're invisible,' Grace said. 'But a glimpse of your pretty hair and face and he'll be off like a race horse. If I see anything at all that's suspicious I'll either come for you, telephone you or get the police.'

Grace knew Maisy was disappointed to be sent home, but she also knew she was right to do this watching and waiting alone. The chances were Grainger would be home all day with his wife tomorrow, so the likelihood of catching him at anything suspicious enough to call the police was negligible. But hanging around the neighbourhood asking a few questions might bring something new to the surface.

She was up early the next morning, and decided that for today she would be the Grace that she might have been if her life hadn't been blighted.

No moleskin trousers, heavily darned, shapeless jumper

and sturdy boots for her today. She put on stockings – not nylon ones, she'd never had a pair of those, but brown lisle, and a petticoat. Then for the navy blue wool dress with a lace collar, a navy coat, and a pair of brown lace-up shoes. She brushed out her hair, then twisted it up on top of her head in a topknot, fixing it firmly.

Finally, the hat. The coat, dress and shoes were the clothes she'd been given when she left the asylum, surprisingly good quality, no doubt donated by some kind-hearted, wealthy woman. But she hated the old lady brown straw cloche hat they'd given her then, and had bought one of her own choice a couple of weeks later when she and Mrs Brady went into Lyndhurst. It was emerald green felt with a narrow brim, pinned up on one side with a cluster of dark blue flowers. It made her feel feminine yet also powerful.

She put it on in front of the small, cracked mirror by her bed. With a touch of lipstick and some powder on her nose, she knew no one would recognize her as the 'Woman in the Wood'. She looked like any other respectable, middle-aged housewife going about her business.

Pausing to look at herself just a little longer, she smiled. Looking as she did now, she knew she'd be able to speak to anyone when she needed to. And she intended to find out something today. Maisy was depending on her.

She locked the door of the shack, called Toby to her side and set off for Enoch's cottage. It was a good arrangement they had: he allowed her to keep her van on his land in return for doing a few little jobs for him as needed.

Enoch was the strong, silent type, a typical countryman. About seventy, she thought, and she suspected he couldn't read much more than his own name. She certainly couldn't claim they were friends – they'd never said more than a few words of greeting to each other. If he wanted anything doing, usually some clothing to be mended, or for her to hold one of his animals while he gave it some medicine, he pointed and maybe used three or four words. But it was a relationship that suited them both.

She'd learned to drive and do basic mechanical repairs while with the Bradys, first just the tractor and then their truck when they took livestock to market. She hadn't ever thought of owning a car or van of her own; she liked to walk or ride a bike, and prided herself on being as strong as a horse. But age crept up on her. When she found herself struggling to carry bags of chicken feed, oil for her lamp and other heavy items, she bought the somewhat battered old Morris van. She didn't cut a track from Enoch's cottage to her home, but left it overgrown so as not to encourage walkers that way. If she had anything heavy to carry from the van, she borrowed his wheelbarrow.

The other advantage of owning a van was that if she was ever evicted from the shack, she would at least be able to transport all her belongings, maybe even sleep in it till she found somewhere else. She started it up every few days, even if she wasn't going anywhere, just to be sure the battery didn't get flat.

'So it's off to Ringwood,' she said to Toby as they made their way through the forest. He gave her that look which told her that he didn't mind where they went, as long as he was with her.

Grace knew Southampton Road because she'd bought some hens the previous year from someone who lived there. She parked up her van and walked along the street, looking at each of the houses. They were very ordinary, with nothing flashy or unusual that might show that the owner wanted their house to stand out. But there was also nothing so mucky or run-down that the neighbours would wince as they passed that house. It made it even more inexplicable that a murderer with a taste for young boys lived amongst them.

But then, as Grace knew only too well, perverted men who had hideous plans for children didn't advertise themselves. Outwardly they appeared normal: in her uncle's case, he was considered shy, quietly spoken, meticulous in his dress and to have an artistic flair. Not someone who would score lines on a young girl with a razor blade to ensure she did as she was told.

After walking about eight hundred yards along the road she realized there was nothing about Cherry Trees that would help her tell whether the Graingers were in or out, as the net curtains did a first-class job of concealment. The garage door was closed too, so she walked back to the van and got in.

Expecting that she would have to wait for a long time, she balanced an old book on the steering wheel as if she was reading, and settled down to watch Grainger's house.

She saw his next-door neighbours come out, neatly dressed as if they were going to an early church service. Further along the road, she spotted a young mother coming out with a pram, accompanied by a boy of five or six with a scooter. The boy sped off in front of his mother.

The time passed very slowly, but then, as Grace reminded herself, she wasn't used to sitting around. It was eight thirty when she arrived, and by twelve thirty she was not only hungry but her bottom ached because the seat wasn't comfortable. She'd only seen about eight people pass the van, and it occurred to her that someone in one of the houses might find it suspicious that she was sitting there for so long. After all, if she saw someone sitting for that long in the forest, she'd be concerned.

But then, just as she thought she ought to at least drive round the block, Grainger came out of his house.

He was wearing dark grey slacks and a grey-green tweed jacket, and he was carrying an oilcloth shopping bag – big enough to hold medicine, water or even provisions, Grace thought. He opened his garage door and got into his car, then reversed out along the drive and drove off towards Southampton.

Grace waited just long enough before she drove off to make sure he wouldn't realize he was being followed.

He turned off the main road to Southampton on to a road Grace didn't know. She saw a signpost pointing to Wellow and remembered she'd read somewhere that was the village where Florence Nightingale's old family home was located.

This was no longer forest or moorland, but arable land with few houses. She was driving on very narrow, winding lanes and she had to stay well back from Grainger or risk his becoming aware he was being followed. But hanging back on such lanes meant he could turn off anywhere and she could drive on past him. So each time she came to a drive, a lane branching off or any other place he could go, she had to stop and look.

By pure chance, she glanced up a hill and saw his Jaguar

on a lane crossing it. She had missed where he had turned off and she had to reverse to find it. Her heart was thumping now, sure she was on the point of discovering, if not Duncan, some evidence about him.

She almost missed the place again; it was just a farm track and clearly rarely used as a thick bush half concealed it.

To drive up the track was a recipe for disaster. Not only was there the possibility of getting stuck in mud, but she might run into Grainger. Once he'd seen her van somewhere so remote, he was going to remember it, and her – especially her hat. So the only thing to do was change, and walk with Toby, hoping he hadn't gone miles.

She had an old pair of boots in the back of the van, another old coat and a knitted hat, so she parked her van up in a gateway to a field and changed. The irony of coming out dressed up, and then having to put her more normal attire back on didn't escape her.

Grace walked and walked, looking over hedges and across fields with Toby padding along beside her, but the Jaguar was nowhere to be seen. She was on the point of turning back when she heard a car engine, and because of the narrowness of the lane, she grabbed Toby and stepped right back against the hedge for safety.

It was Grainger in his Jaguar, and he drove so fast that if she had hesitated before moving out of the way he would have mown her down.

She stood still for a minute or so, weighing up whether to walk on to where he'd been, or to go back and get the van. She decided to walk on, mostly because she felt he'd come from somewhere close by or she would have heard his car well before she did.

About a mile further on there was a track off to the right, and in the mud were recent damp tyre prints. It led down a slight incline towards a copse, and tucked behind the copse she could just see a small cottage. In summer with the trees in full leaf, the cottage would be invisible from the point where she was standing. Beyond it she saw it was all woodland. The land around the cottage was stony, not good for growing crops or for grazing, but she thought in the past it might have been used for sheep, and maybe a shepherd had lived in the cottage.

As there was no smoke coming from the chimney, Grace didn't think anyone was in, but she would walk down and knock. If someone did answer she would pretend she was lost.

She looked down at Toby, who was watching her expectantly. 'Come on then, Toby, let's go and see what we can find.'

It was clear no one lived there. It was just a single-storey stone-built cottage. She went right round it, checking each of the four boarded-up windows, but they were all secure. Yet she could see weeds and grass had been trampled recently by the sturdy back door, so even if not Grainger, someone had been in there in the past few days.

She called out loudly and listened carefully, but she could hear nothing. Walking round the cottage again she noted that it was built on sloping ground, so the stone wall beneath the windows at the front was much higher than the one at the back. This could mean there was a cellar, good for storing vegetables during the winter. But she could see no old door or even a small window on ground level and she went round twice checking to see if there were signs of one being bricked up.

She could see nothing unusual; it all looked as if it had remained the way it was built back in the last century. She banged loudly on the stone with a metal rod lying on the grass. It sounded to her like gunshot, so loud the people a mile away could probably hear it. No reply. She banged again, but this time she thought she heard something from inside. Faint, but it was a response.

A bubble of excitement ran through her. She banged again, harder still, and once again, there was a feeble answer, either coming from very far down or the person was weak. Either way she needed to get into the cottage now.

But how? She had no tools, and the boarded-up windows were very secure, the front and back doors strong. Short of having a jemmy or crowbar she couldn't think of any way of getting in.

Walking backwards away from the cottage, Grace studied it as a whole. While all the walls and windows looked virtually impenetrable, the roof tiles didn't look so good. In theory it should be possible to lift some tiles and get in through the ceiling. But she knew she couldn't climb up there. Ten years ago she would have managed it easily, but she was stiffer now, afraid of falling, the penalty of ageing.

There was a straight choice between calling the police and getting Maisy.

She stood for a moment weighing it up. The police were unlikely to believe a well-known solicitor could be snatching boys, using them and then killing them. She wasn't entirely sure she believed it herself.

Maybe she had imagined that answering rap on stone. It could've been an echo. Yet she had a gut feeling someone was in that house and they were in a bad way.

She looked down at Toby. 'We get Maisy,' she said.

That too was problematic. Would she be allowed out? That grandmother of hers was likely to get one glimpse of Grace and throw a fit that Maisy was consorting with her.

Grace decided she'd cross all bridges as she came to them and walked back to the van as fast as she could. She was very tired now – she'd walked miles and her legs were trembling – but she took off the old clothes and put her smarter things back on. She really hoped she could get Maisy's attention without having to knock on the front door. But maybe the smarter clothes might mollify the old lady if she caught a glimpse of her.

It took less than half an hour to get back to Burley, and Grace left the van at the bottom of the lane and walked up to Nightingales, her heart thumping with nerves.

During the war, she had once brought some eggs and a chicken to the house, a present from Mrs Brady when she heard the old lady was ill. Mrs Mitcham was so rude, snatching the parcel out of Grace's hands and slamming the door in her face. She did send a thank-you letter to Mrs Brady later and apologized for being what she called 'offhand', her excuse being that she was very poorly, so that was something. She couldn't have known, of course, that it was the first time Grace had ever plucked up enough courage to deliver anything, and that reception set her back months.

It was nearly five now. With luck Mrs Mitcham might be dozing by the fire and the housekeeper preparing the evening meal in the kitchen. From what Maisy had said about Janice, she sounded a kindly soul, but one thing Grace didn't want was her interfering and calling the police.

The gate at Nightingales was set at an angle to the front downstairs windows, which was fortunate. Grace ordered Toby to wait in the lane and then slipped in through the gate, holding it so it wouldn't bang, and tiptoed along the path. It forked at the side of the house, right fork to the front door, left around the back.

Grace went left. She bent right over as she went past windows, just in case anyone was looking.

As she approached the kitchen door she heard a bell tinkle, and she stopped dead.

'Oh, what does she want now?' she heard someone say, presumably the housekeeper.

'More tea, I expect. She said the soup at lunch was very salty. Shall I go?' The voice was Maisy's and Grace thought her luck was in.

'No, I'd better. She's bound to have some instructions for supper,' the older woman said wearily.

Grace waited till her footsteps had passed the door and then she opened it. 'Maisy,' she whispered. 'Come out here.'

Grace slunk back against the wall. Her heart was hammering.

'Grace!' Maisy exclaimed as she came out. Her face was a picture of astonishment. 'What is it? Why are you all dressed up?'

'Long story, no time. Meet me at the end of the lane as soon as you can, wear clothes for climbing. Don't ask! Just do it.'

Grace took in the girl's puzzled expression, but she didn't want to risk waiting there any longer. She turned away and slunk back past the back windows.

She didn't chance going out through the front gate as the housekeeper might see her. Instead she went straight down the side garden and wriggled through a small hole under a bush that she'd noticed on her way up the lane. She whistled to Toby, who bounded down to join her, then hurried to the van.

It seemed forever before Maisy came out. She'd put on a dark jacket, slacks and plimsolls.

Grace started the van, turned it round swiftly, then beckoned at the girl furiously to get in.

'What on earth is this?' Maisy gasped. 'Grandmother and Janice will kill me when they find I've gone missing.'

As Grace drove she told Maisy what she'd found. 'Don't get your hopes up,' she said firmly. 'He might not be in there, but I'm sure someone is. I'll take the blame for involving you when I get back.'

Maisy was excited to think they might be set to rescue Duncan, but also terrified. This had all happened too quickly and she wasn't totally convinced that Grace knew what she was doing. 'I left a note on my bed saying I had to pop out to see someone,' she said. 'But Janice will panic if I'm not back for supper.'

'Supper! How can you even think of that when your brother might be in that house, sick and in pain?' Grace pulled up outside a small cottage in the forest which Maisy had cycled past dozens of times.

Maisy looked to the cottage and back at Grace, eyes wide in disbelief. 'Surely this isn't it?'

'No, of course not. It belongs to old Enoch. I leave my van here with him, and I'm just going to ask him to lend me some tools. You stay here.'

Grace disappeared into the cottage and within a few minutes she was back, holding a cloth bag.

'That's the most he's ever said to me at one time,' Grace said, as calmly as if she was talking about what he needed from the shops. 'He wanted me to tell him what I was doing. But I said I couldn't explain as it was an emergency and I didn't have time to go and get my own tools.'

The light was just beginning to fade by the time they got to the remote cottage and to Maisy it all looked very spooky as she got out of the van. 'You really want me to climb up on that roof and pull tiles off?'

'Yes, I do.' Grace nodded, then told Toby he had to stay in the van. 'There's nothing to it, tiles just lift off. It's what's underneath which is more of a problem.'

'Umm, how am I going to get up there?'

Grace caught hold of Maisy's arm and led her down the slope towards the cottage. 'Look up at that corner,' she said, pointing to the back of the house. 'It's not as high as at the front and there's that drainpipe to hold on to. If you get on my shoulders you should be able to pull yourself up from there.'

Grace had obviously thought it all through. She put the bag of tools over Maisy's head and diagonally across her chest, then clasped her hands together to form a foot-hold so that Maisy could jump up and climb on to her shoulders.

That part was easy enough with the support of the drainpipe, but as Maisy straightened up she found she was still a couple of feet short of the guttering around the roof.

'Hold the top of the drainpipe rather than the guttering,'

Grace called out. 'It's usually stronger. Think of rescuing Duncan and you'll do it.'

Maisy managed to throw the bag of tools on to the roof, and clinging to the pipe and digging her toes into the stone walls of the cottage she hauled herself up to the top and over on to the roof.

'Well done,' Grace called out. 'Best to stay at the back of the house. Start lifting tiles as close to the gutter as possible. Mind you don't slip.'

As Grace had said, it was easy to lift the tiles – they came off like jigsaw pieces one after the other. Once the hole was big enough she shone the torch which she'd found in the toolbag down through it to see what lay below. There was some dark brown stuff that looked and felt like thick felt. She took the knife from the bag and poked it through: it was relatively easy to slice open.

'There's an attic,' she called back down to Grace. 'Not much headroom, but I'll climb in and look around.'

'Be careful you stand on the rafters or you'll fall through the ceiling,' Grace called back.

There was still some light in the sky, and holding the torch Maisy lowered herself through the hole, feeling around with her feet until she found something reassuringly solid enough to stand on. At the point when she found a beam, the top half of her body was still sticking out of the roof, so she had to lower herself down to a crouch to see the attic better.

It was empty, very dusty, and only high enough to stand upright under the apex of the roof. Maisy shuffled along to that point, and saw there was a trapdoor in the centre. Using the knife, she prised it up enough to get her fingers in, then pulled it right back.

Beneath her was thick darkness because of the boarded-up windows, but shining the torch around she saw a sink on one wall, an old table, a couple of chairs and in the corner of the room a mattress. It was very dirty and it smelled horribly of mould and festering rubbish. The next problem was going to be getting down there.

Maisie hadn't admitted to Grace that she wasn't much good at climbing, and she certainly wasn't brave enough to lower herself into that filthy room and just drop. But she knew she had to, there was no other way, and if Duncan was in there somewhere it would be worth breaking her leg.

So she tied the bag of tools around her neck again, held the torch in her mouth and sat on the side of the trap, putting her hands on the front edge. She got a good grip, then taking a deep breath she swung down then dropped the last three feet or so.

The first thing she did was go towards the back door to open it. But there were two locks, both locked from the outside. She found that the front door was the same.

This was a major setback and panic washed over her. To be locked into a pitch-dark room which stunk of something horrible, was too awful. But she controlled her panic enough to bang on the back door to alert Grace.

'It's locked from the outside,' she called out. 'So is the front door.'

There was a moment's silence, Grace clearly digesting this news and how to deal with it. 'Stay calm,' she said, her voice muffled by the door. 'There's a jemmy thing in the bag, try to force the door with that. If you can't, break a window then try and jemmy out the board over it.'

'I'm going to look and see if there's a cellar here first,' Maisy called back.

She shone the torch around. It was clear someone had been holed up in here quite recently: there were empty food cans, dirty crockery, lots of cigarette ends on the floor, and on a shelf by the window there was a one-ring camping stove with a camping kettle.

There was another room with a mattress, but she couldn't see a door to a cellar.

It was while she was in this room that Maisy heard a cry. It was very faint, almost like a child's. 'Is that you, Duncan?' she called out. 'Or is it Peter Reilly? It's Maisy. Answer me if you can hear.'

She waited, hardly breathing with the effort of listening.

'We're both here, Maisy,' the voice came back and she knew it was Duncan speaking.

Tears of joy ran down her cheeks unchecked. She and Grace had done it.

14

Maisy concentrated the torch beam on to the floor, going round the whole room looking at the floorboards. Just beneath the bedroom window at the front of the house she saw a piece of old carpet. She pulled it back and there was a trapdoor, secured with two bolts.

She drew back the bolts and pulled on the metal ring attached to the heavy door. As it opened the evil smell which rose up nearly made her drop the door to cover her nose. It was a vile mixture of excrement, mould and blood, a smell that said something hellish was down below.

She fixed the trapdoor back against the wall and shone the torch down. There she saw two white faces staring up at the light. They were lying down beside one another and even without being able to see clearly Maisy knew they were badly hurt. Close to the boys she saw three, no, four pairs of eyes glinting in the torchlight. Rats!

She shuddered. How could she go down there?

'Grace is here with me, Duncan,' she said, trying to keep her voice calm and measured. 'But she's outside and the doors are locked. I came in through the roof. I'm going to try and open a window up here so she can get in and help me, but I may have to send her off to get the police and an ambulance. Just bear with me for a few moments.'

There were no steps down to where the boys were, but she had seen a wooden ladder lying on its side across the room.

First she needed air. Trying to suppress the urge to vomit at the smell she went over to the window. The glass was broken already, and she knocked the rest out with the jemmy.

Grace was there immediately, wanting to know what she'd seen. Through the cracks in the boards Maisy reported about the boys, the terrible smell and the rats. She was sucking the fresh air from the window into her lungs as she spoke, and trying very hard not to cry.

'You must go for help,' she said. 'We won't be able to get them out of that cellar on our own. But I'll see if I can get the boards off the window while you're gone.'

'Will you be scared in there without me?' Grace said, her voice the softest Maisy had ever heard it.

'Yes, I will be,' Maisy said, 'but the sooner we get help, the sooner we can be away from here. You could knock on anyone's door where they've got a phone line. It's an emergency.'

'OK. You're right, it's the best thing to do, but I don't like to leave you.'

'Oh Grace,' Maisy sighed. 'I thought you were supposed to be the witch of the forest with no kind feelings.'

'So did I until I met you and your brother,' Grace replied, her voice trembling with emotion. 'Bye. Be brave, little one.'

She must have run to the van because Maisy heard the sound of the engine starting up just a few seconds later, and then the van pulling away fast.

Knowing she was now alone in the dark and filth with two seriously injured boys in terrible conditions was terrifying, so much so that she had to force herself to breathe deeply in order to think.

The ladder was so old and heavy Maisy could barely drag it towards the trapdoor. She had to put the torch down to do it, and then the room became so dark she almost lost her bearings. But little by little she inched it towards the trapdoor, and then manoeuvred it into place so she could lower it down.

She shone the light down first to make sure she wasn't going to drop it on the boys, then, warning them what she was going to do, she gradually fed it down. Her arms felt as though they were being pulled from their sockets with the weight of it, but finally it reached the cellar floor and she wedged it tightly at the top so it couldn't fall over.

She didn't want to go down there. Her whole being was silently pleading for her to wait for the police and ambulance men to do it. But he was her brother and he must have been through hell. She wasn't going to leave him to strangers.

Climbing down that ladder was the most frightening thing she'd ever experienced. She could hear the rats she'd seen earlier scuttling about. Adding that to the smell, and the darkness, plus the knowledge that both boys might have appalling injuries, it was as if she was descending into hell.

'I'm nearly there now,' she said at the halfway point of the ladder, more to encourage herself than to help them. 'Another half hour and you'll be out of here safe and on the way to hospital.'

'You're being very brave, sis,' Duncan said. 'I told Peter the other day that you wouldn't give up looking for me. I kept sensing you were thinking about me.'

She could hear how poorly he was by the effort it was

taking him to speak. He attempted to sit up but flopped back. She reached the bottom of the ladder and went over to kneel beside him, and stroked back his hair.

'Don't try to move or talk any more,' she said, trying hard not to cry. 'You can tell me all about it when you're better.'

His face seemed ravaged, gaunt, with hollow cheeks. In the poor light she couldn't tell if it was blood or dirt on his face and all down his shirt. The clothes he had on, long trousers and long-sleeved shirt, weren't his and his feet were bare.

Down here the smell was even worse. In one way it was good she couldn't see beyond the beam of light because she felt if she saw it all she'd have to run away.

She reached over him to comfort Peter then. He didn't speak and appeared even weaker than Duncan, but she thought he was aware rescue was at hand.

'I must go back up and try to get that window clear,' she said. 'Hold on just a bit longer.'

Such was her relief to get out of the cellar that she attacked the window far more forcefully, prising at the boards. Whoever had put them on had meant them to stay put: the timber was new and strong and they'd been screwed into place.

As she pushed and wrestled with the wood she asked herself what kind of beast would prepare such a prison for young boys. The picture in her mind of someone capable of this didn't fit suave, charming Donald Grainger. This was the stuff of horror films. He had to be a split personality like Jekyll and Hyde.

She got one board off and began on the next one. She was making a great deal of noise, but that didn't matter any more. She hoped someone would appear soon and offer to help, or just be there with her.

Hearing a vehicle coming she called out to the boys that rescue was here, and continued to bang harder on the window boards, partly so they'd know where to come.

Suddenly there was bright light: the beam of a powerful torch. She blinked, trying to see the person behind it, wondering if it was a policeman or ambulance man.

'Thank God you've come,' she exclaimed. 'The boys are in the cellar.'

But all at once it came to her that this person had come through the door, which meant they had a key. She hadn't heard that over the noise she was making.

It wasn't a rescue party at all. It was him.

'Why did you have to snoop, Maisy?' he said, confirming it was indeed Grainger. 'Now I'll have to kill you as well.'

Maisy felt her knees buckle under her with terror, but all the same she lunged at him, brandishing the jemmy. Unable to see him behind the beam of the torch, she just ran into the wall.

'Silly, silly girl,' he said, grabbing her two arms up behind her back, forcing her to drop her weapon. He was strong, holding her with just one hand, the torch in the other. She fought for her life, kicking out and struggling. Yet she couldn't escape his grip. He put the torch away – perhaps in his pocket – as the light went dimmer. Then she felt him tying her wrists tightly. She kicked out at him again, but he punched her face hard, knocking her back against the wall, then kicked her legs out from under her so she fell to the floor.

In just a few moments he had tied her ankles too.

'There now,' he said. 'You can't do any more damage.'

'The police are coming, they'll be here any minute,' she screamed at him. 'My friend drove to phone them. You go and get away while you still can.'

'You're lying,' he said, holding the torch so it shone in her face. 'You came here alone.'

White-hot anger made her braver. 'Don't be ridiculous, it's too far to walk from Burley,' she roared at him. 'My friend followed you from your house to here earlier in the day, then she came to get me. How else would I find this place? You don't advertise you've got a torture chamber right out in the middle of nowhere. And how would I get on the roof without help?'

She wished she could see his face because by his silence she knew he realized she was speaking the truth. 'Go now, while you still can,' she shouted at him. 'The police will be here any minute. It will take you ages to get Duncan and Peter out of the cellar, you haven't got time for that.'

Again a few moments' silence, then he reached down, caught hold of one of her arms and jerked her up on to her feet. 'I might not have got time to get them out, but I can take you,' he snarled at her. 'You'll be my hostage.'

He half carried, half dragged her out to his Jaguar, opened the boot and pushed her into it. He hesitated for just a second, then, picking up something – a rag, sock or glove – he thrust it into her mouth.

'You're going to bitterly regret your interference,' he snarled at her before slamming the boot down. A few seconds later he started up the car.

A little later as the car sped on its way, Maisy heard an ambulance bell clanging in the distance. Although it was a relief in that she knew Duncan and Peter would be taken care of now, she was terrified at what her own fate would be.

Grainger was desperate. As he drove towards Southampton he realized that he was in the kind of predicament he'd made no advance plans for.

As soon as the police and ambulance arrived at the cottage and saw the state of the two boys, he would become the most dangerous, wanted man in the country, and every policeman in a fifty-mile radius would be out looking for him.

He couldn't go back to his house for clothes, his passport or money, and he had no other place to go and hide up in. There would be road blocks too. As soon as the news broke to the press that the psychopath killing young boys was in fact Donald Grainger, the well-known solicitor with an office in Southampton, the game would be up.

But he had Maisy Mitcham. Since he had nothing to lose now, he intended to kill her – and before he did he would inflict as much pain on her as possible.

Grace had to go right into the village of Wellow to find a phone. It was too dark to make out telephone wires so she plumped for a rather grand house which was certain to have one. The man who answered the door was equally grand, but intelligent enough to grasp immediately that this was a real emergency, and he directed her to his phone in the hall.

She managed to get hold of the emergency service operator and swiftly explained the situation. Asked the name of the lane she'd driven up to get to the cottage, she said she didn't know, but she described it as best she could and stressed that both boys were extremely badly hurt. She gave the operator the address she was phoning from and they asked if she would stay there in case they needed her to guide the ambulance. She agreed she would.

As she put the phone down, the man – a big, burly chap with a high colour, wearing a maroon cardigan – had been joined by his wife. She was younger, around the same age as Grace and wearing a lovely dark blue wool dress as if she was expecting guests.

Their eyes were as big as millstones at what they'd overheard. Grace asked if she might make another call, and could she borrow their telephone directory.

They obliged, and Grace found Mrs Mitcham's number and rang her. When the old lady heard who she was she barked at her in a very unpleasant manner, so Grace put her in her place.

'If I could just get a word in edgeways! It is important,' she barked back. 'Maisy and I have found your grandson, but he's very badly hurt. The other missing boy is there too. Maisy is still in the place with him waiting for the ambulance and police to arrive. I dare say we'll both have to go to the police station with them, so I cannot tell you when Maisy will be home. But I'm sure if you telephone the local police they'll keep you posted. By the way, your precious solicitor Grainger is the man who did this – but don't go warning him, as the police will be on their way to arrest him.'

She put the receiver down and half smiled at her hosts. 'Sorry about that. People do take good news the wrong way sometimes.'

'Did you say Grainger the solicitor is responsible for this crime?' the gentleman asked in his plummy accent.

'Yes, I did. I hope he doesn't handle any affairs for you?'

'No, but we do know him socially.' He looked at his wife in horror. 'He always seemed such a nice chap!'

'Appearances can be deceptive,' Grace said.

It was only a few minutes later that a police car called at the house to collect Grace so she could guide them and the ambulance to the cottage. They wanted her to leave her van in Wellow and take her with them, but because Toby was in the van she said she'd drive it and lead the way.

Grace was very concerned at the scale of the injuries Maisy had said the boys had sustained, but she couldn't help but be excited as she led the emergency services back up the narrow lanes. She and Maisy had done well: they'd found Duncan and Peter and proved Grainger was responsible. She didn't think it would be hard for the police to prove he killed the other six boys too.

She drove right up to the cottage and leapt out to call to Maisy that she was back with help, but as she skirted round to the back door she found it wide open.

'Oh no,' she gasped, feeling as if her blood was draining away. 'Oh dear God, please don't let him have taken Maisy!'

She ran back to the police car just pulling in behind her van. 'I think Grainger has come back here,' she yelled out. 'The door was locked, and it's open now.'

Armed with powerful torches, the police went in, and Grace slunk in behind them feeling sick with fright.

Two policemen went down to the cellar and one came up again to report.

'It is Duncan Mitcham and Peter Reilly. They're in a bad way. Duncan said Grainger turned up a little while ago; he heard him hit his sister and say he was taking her hostage.'

'Right!' The senior officer took control, telling his men this was now a crime scene. Once the boys had been taken to hospital they would examine the cellar for evidence that the dead boys had also been kept here.

'I think they must've been,' the policeman who had already been down there offered. 'There's enough shit and blood for an army down there.'

Grace broke down then. She felt she was responsible for Maisy becoming that evil man's captive, and there was absolutely no reason why he wouldn't kill her.

'What can I do?' she implored the more senior policeman. 'I rang Maisy's grandmother while I was waiting for you to come. I thought then both of us would have to go to the police station to be questioned, so I told the old lady Maisy would be late getting home. But she won't be going home, will she? He'll kill her.'

'Not if we can help it.' The policeman put a hand on her shoulder to comfort her. 'I just wish you'd rung us when you found this place. We could've staked it out until Grainger came back. Why didn't you?'

'Because we couldn't trust you to act,' Grace said, tears running in streams down her cheeks. 'And don't tell me you would have. You'd have been more inclined to come and arrest me.'

He at least had the grace to look ashamed and led her

out to the police car so she could tell him everything she knew.

It wasn't much, just what Maisy had told her about finding Duncan's buckle in Grainger's car and seeing Duncan's bicycle pump in his garage, then how Grace had stayed outside his house and followed him here.

'You know the rest,' she said. 'The door was locked, so Maisy climbed up on the roof and got in that way. You can bet she put up a fight with that monster, she's a plucky wee thing.'

As they sat there in the car she watched the ambulance men bring out the first boy on a stretcher and put him in an ambulance. A short while later the second one was brought out.

'Can I speak to Duncan?' Grace asked.

'I think it better you don't,' the policeman said, his voice soft with sympathy. 'Both boys are in a bad way, and if Duncan sees your troubled face he's going to worry more about his sister. You take your dog home now. We know where you are if we need you.'

'Will you tell Mrs Mitcham what's happened?'

'Yes, I promise you that. And we'll leave no stone unturned to find Grainger and Maisy. This time you must trust us.'

15

Janice braced herself before entering the hospital side ward where the two boys were. She had been beside herself with fear for Maisy ever since Mrs Mitcham got the call from the police late on Saturday night to say Grainger had got her. She hadn't slept, she hadn't eaten anything, all she'd done was pace up and down willing the phone to ring with news that Grainger had been caught.

But now, seeing a policeman standing guard outside the ward was just another reminder that Grainger was still on the loose. He may even have killed Maisy by now, and the boys who had already been through such hell might still be in danger.

It was Tuesday, the day after Easter Monday. The boys had been in such a terrible state they hadn't been allowed any visitors until now. Both Peter's legs and several of his ribs were broken, he also had a severe chest infection. Duncan's injuries were untreated, infected cigarette burns and broken ribs, and bruises and lacerations covered almost his entire body.

The doctor who examined them on admission to the hospital had reported they were victims of systematic beatings and sexual abuse, along with being half starved. One of the policemen who had been first on the scene in that cellar said the conditions there defied description or belief. Duncan had told him that both boys wished they could die to end the torment.

It seemed Duncan had told the police that before Grainger had taken him and Peter to that cottage and literally pushed them into the cellar, they had been kept in a boarded-up house with other boys. There they had use of a bathroom, they were brought food, and there was furniture too. Duncan said he knew Grainger had killed two of the boys, but he hadn't known what he did with their bodies.

While Duncan had tried very hard to tell the police all he could, the medical staff had called a halt on questioning as he was so weak. Peter was far too sick to be questioned at all.

One visitor was all they were allowed today. Janice had volunteered to come rather than Mrs Mitcham, as the old lady was so severely shaken by what had happened that her doctor feared any more distress might prompt a stroke or heart attack. Tomorrow Alastair would be seeing Duncan, and Peter's parents would visit their son.

Janice had never seen Mrs Mitcham cry until Easter Sunday, when the full force of what had happened to Duncan hit her along with the shock of Maisy being taken. For Janice this emotional reaction of her employer proved both astonishing and distressing. The old lady was truly devastated, full of guilt that she had introduced Grainger to her grandchildren, and shocked that she'd been unable to see through his charming facade.

'I let both of them down,' she wept. 'Just as I let Alastair down. I was an unnatural mother and I'm an even worse grandmother. I've always been selfish and proud, and this is where it has led to.'

Janice hardly knew what to say. Had she been cruel she would have agreed – after all, Mrs Mitcham was telling the truth. But Janice wasn't cruel, so she just put her arms round the old lady and said she couldn't hold herself responsible for other people's sins.

Janice's stomach turned over as she went into the little ward. The other boy, Peter, was in traction for his broken legs, and the pulleys and weights over his bed looked terrifying. He was asleep and all she could really see of him was a shock of strawberry-blond hair. She'd been told that he was utterly traumatized by what had happened to him and that it was feared the mental scars would never fade.

The doctors might say that Duncan had come off a great deal lighter but it didn't look that way. He had so many bruises, some fresh, some fading, that he was unrecognizable as the fresh-faced, prone-to-freckles boy who had disappeared over a year before. He was so thin his eyes seemed sunken back into his head. His blond hair had grown so long it almost touched his shoulders, and although a nurse had said they'd tried to wash it as best they could, it still looked very dirty and unkempt.

His left arm was in a sling because his wrist was sprained and his right arm had a drip in it, but Janice knew that his hospital gown was hiding bruises, cuts and burn marks that would make her want to cry. As for the sexual abuse he'd suffered – she wondered whether he would ever return to being the joyful, generous and happy-go-lucky boy he used to be.

He smiled at her in welcome, but the smile didn't reach his eyes.

'I'm so pleased to see you,' he said, and even his voice sounded weak.

'Oh Duncan,' she exclaimed, her eyes filling with tears. 'There were times when we thought we'd never see you again. I'm so very happy to see you, but not looking so poorly.'

'I'm on the mend now. Well, I'm not sure if that's true. I doubt I'll get better until they find Maisy,' he said, then looked at the bag she was carrying. 'I hope there's cake and other goodies made by you in that bag?'

She sensed this was a ruse to stop her talking about how he looked, so she unpacked it on to his locker: chocolate cake, Easter biscuits, a chicken and mushroom pie, chocolate, and one of her special trifles made in a glass jar. 'I'll ask the nurse to dole this out to you gradually. You'll be sick if you eat it all now when you've been starved, but I wanted you to have lots to choose from when you're up to it,' she said, bending over to kiss his forehead. 'When you get home I shall give you so much food you won't be able to move.'

She placed a pair of pyjamas in his locker along with a toothbrush, comb and face flannel.

'Is there any news of Maisy?' he asked, and his quavering voice told Janice that he would rather have stayed in the cellar than his sister be with Grainger.

'The police are working their way through the files in his office to see if they can find evidence of another property where he might be keeping her.'

'I've told them about the one the other side of Southampton,' he said. 'I was there with some other boys for a long while.' His face clouded over then and he reached out for an Easter biscuit from the locker. 'These are marvellous,' he said as he bit into it. 'Will you ask Peter if he wants one?'

'He's asleep.'

'He isn't, he just acts like he is. But offer him food and he responds.'

Janice did as he asked. The other boy looked at her blankly as if his mind had gone.

'It's an Easter biscuit, Peter,' she said, holding it out to him. 'I made them for you both.'

She took his hand and put the biscuit in it. Gingerly, he lifted it to his nose and sniffed it, then ate it so fast she was afraid he'd choke.

'Food is the only way to get through to him,' Duncan whispered as Janice returned to his bed. 'We didn't know if it was night or day in that cellar, and never knew when we'd get something to eat. Sometimes it was days on end before he brought food. I don't know how long we were in there, whether it was just weeks or longer. At first Peter used to talk to me – we'd make up stories, talk about our families, we even chanted the times tables. But then he just shut down.' He paused, his eyes full of despair as if he was reliving it again.

'Tell me about Grace,' he went on after a few seconds. 'The police said it was she who found out where we were.'

'So it seems. I wish I could tell you lots about her – goodness knows, it seems we owe her everything – but I don't know anything much.' Janice sighed. 'She and Maisy went to rescue you, but your grandmother and I had no idea Maisy had even left the house, let alone how they found you, or what that entailed. Would you like me to ask Grace to come and see you?'

'Yes, I would like that. I thought about her a lot while we were in that place. I even dreamt about her one night. But tell me, what are the police doing to find Maisy?'

'I only know what I've already told you,' Janice said sadly. 'Grainger's picture is in all the papers now. The story was on the news yesterday, and there's been more today. Someone is bound to come forward to say they've seen him.'

'I can't believe I once thought he was a good man,' Duncan said and his bruised eyes filled with tears.

'Try not to dwell on that,' Janice said. Though she thought saying that was about as stupid as asking the tide not to come in, or the wind not to blow. 'Your father is coming to see you tomorrow.'

'I don't know that he'll be able to even look at me,' Duncan said brokenly.

Janice sensed he meant because of the sexual abuse. 'Don't be ridiculous,' she said fiercely. 'The dreadful man who did this to you is the only one to blame. Don't you dare feel you are to blame in any way.'

'But both Peter and I managed to escape being killed by doing what he wanted,' Duncan admitted, putting his unhurt arm across his eyes to shield himself. 'Doesn't that make us as bad as him?'

'No, it doesn't,' she said firmly, taking his arm away from his eyes. 'You had to do whatever you could to survive. No one would blame you for that.'

'I don't think Father will see it that way.'

'Then you are going to be surprised. I spoke to him on the telephone, the day after Maisy and Grace found you. He was overjoyed you were alive and all his anger and disgust is directed at Grainger. That's how we all feel, Duncan, your grandmother included. The only reason she isn't here now is because we were told only one visitor, and

I said I thought it would be better if that was me today. She cried, Duncan. The first time I ever saw her do that. She's an old lady with limited experience of worldly things, and this has shaken her to the core.'

'I can't bear the thought of what Grainger might do to Maisy,' Duncan suddenly blurted out. 'He does it with girls as well as boys, he told us that once and boasted that he was married. But Maisy won't be able to get round him. He enjoys fear more than anything, and inflicting pain.'

Janice shuddered. She could easily imagine what terrible things a man could do to a pretty girl like Maisy. In a way she was glad her imagination hadn't worked so well with Duncan, because if she'd known what he was going through she wouldn't have been able to function.

'Your sister isn't easily intimidated,' Janice said, hoping that Duncan would believe that. 'I'm sure she'll find some way of protecting herself. Besides, the police will soon find him.'

'They never found me, and anyway, Maisy may very well be dead by the time they stir themselves,' Duncan said, his eyes so full of despair that Janice felt his heart was already breaking. 'You tell me what possible reason Grainger will have for keeping her alive.'

Janice couldn't think of one. Alone, Grainger might be able to charm someone to help him get out of the country. Maisy was just a hindrance.

'I didn't think you'd be able to,' Duncan said, and grimaced.

'Maisy never gave up on you,' Janice said firmly. 'So don't you take that attitude. You must rack your brain to think of anything, however small, that might tell the police where he's taken her. Think over anything he said to you, or to one of the other boys.'

'I've re-run every word I heard him say already and I can tell you they make me feel sick to my stomach,' Duncan said, his face darkening with anger. 'I can't even begin to tell anyone, least of all you, the sadistic, perverted and horrible things he did to us. I'll never feel clean again. I wish he had killed me.'

At that statement Janice knew she was completely out of her depth. She was still a virgin; her experiences with men amounted to nothing more than kisses. Before her sweetheart was killed in the war she was always dreaming of making love with him. In those dreams it was gentle and beautiful, just thinking about it made her feel excited. She had always hoped that both Duncan and Maisy would find their true love, and enjoy that bliss which she had never experienced.

'I'm so very glad he didn't kill you,' she whispered, leaning forward to kiss his cheek. 'I wish I had the right words to make you feel better, but I don't. All I can say is that to me, Maisy and you were the children I'd have most liked to be mine. I hurt for both of you. I'm going to pray for a miracle to save your sister.'

Janice left the hospital in tears. It was all so much worse than she'd expected and she felt so impotent. Last night she'd had to telephone Mr and Mrs Ripley in Brighton to tell them what had happened to Maisy. That was bad enough; their shock and horror was evident by the way their voices shook. Today they must have seen the national newspapers and no doubt they were as distraught as she was.

She supposed that the publicity was a good thing, though – someone might come forward who knew something. But it would also mean packs of reporters in the village, just as there were when Sybil Leek went on television to say she was a witch. Janice shuddered when she remembered what people had said to journalists when Duncan first went missing. How they had loved relating how cold-hearted Mrs Mitcham was and describing how she had never shown any love or affection to her only son, saying she made him so icy and distant that he ignored his own children and drove his wife mad.

But the news now had some real meat at the core of it. Donald Grainger wasn't just a murderer; he snatched young boys away from their schools and imprisoned them for his own perverted desires. Once they were of no further use to him, he killed them and dumped them in shallow graves. This was going to be a horror story like that of John Reginald Christie, who killed eight women in the forties and fifties and buried them at Rillington Place: a story that would never die.

Maisy shivered, her arm throbbing with pain from where he had twisted it up behind her back in the cottage. She feared he'd broken it.

She didn't know where she was as it was dark when he hauled her out of the boot of his car. She'd been in there since he caught her at the cottage, but she had no idea how long that was.

He'd been driving some of the time, but for long periods he had parked the car up. She heard him slam the door and lock it, leaving her there. She couldn't hear a sound from outside, so maybe he'd pulled off the road into a wood or field. But each time he went she thought he wasn't coming back and she'd die in there.

Finally he brought her here and threw her down on the bare concrete floor like she was a worthless piece of rubbish. She felt like it too, as she'd wet herself in the boot of his car, and she knew she stunk.

But between the car boot and here she had smelled sea and seaweed and felt shingle under her feet as he dragged her, still gagged, with something pulled over her head from his car. She had got the idea that this wasn't another cottage, but something like a concrete bunker or sea defence from the war, because sound echoed in it.

Once he'd thrown her on the floor, he took the hood off her, grinning as he kicked her legs, arms, back and stomach, ranting at her all the while. She couldn't even scream for fear of the gag going further down her throat and choking her.

'Why couldn't you keep your nose out, you filthy, stinking bitch? Your fucking grandmother said you two were soft and not very bright, but what did she know? I think you are sneaky, devious and a real troublemaker, but you aren't going to live to make any more trouble for me.'

So he went on, repeating the same thing over and over, blaming her for 'spoiling his plans', and kicking her as though he was adding punctuation to the rant. She found it hard to believe that this demented, cruel man was the same charming and sophisticated solicitor who had taken her into a café for tea and cake, and driven her home. What could make a man switch like that?

For ages after he'd gone she just lay there, her whole

body on fire with pain. Somehow she managed to eject the gag from her mouth, and then she lay there sobbing at the hopelessness of her situation. She felt he was bound to return to kill her; in fact, if he hadn't been so rattled by the police being on his tail she felt sure he would have killed her already.

But gradually her mind cleared, and despite how hurt and scared she was, she knew she had to try and escape. First she needed to find some way to untie her ankles and wrists and look for a way out. In books and films there was always something sharp close to hand that the prisoner could wriggle up to and use to cut the ropes, but she doubted she'd be that lucky.

However, she was determined to try, so by turning on to her less damaged side, she wriggled like a caterpillar towards the wall, intending to go right round to assess the layout of her prison. Pain shot through her arm as she tried to sweep her tied hands in a fan shape behind her, but she ignored it, as she had to search for anything that might help her.

It crossed her mind that she was moving like a seal on dry land, and despite the seriousness of her predicament, it made her smile and gave her the will to keep on going.

It took forever to work her way around the pitch-dark space, but even if she hadn't found anything to use to cut her bonds, she had learned that it was an oblong shape, about ten feet wide and perhaps sixteen or eighteen feet long. No one else had been in here for a very long time. It smelled musty but not foul, and there was no litter, only a few empty sacks in one corner. That suggested he couldn't have used this place to keep anyone else, which could be because it wasn't secure enough, or it was somewhere people passed by.

The door to the place was metal, and there was a strong draught coming under it, so as soon as it was daylight she would turn herself so she could kick her bound feet on it. Hopefully someone might hear her.

She wriggled around again to the door, and feeling the bottom edge she found it was quite sharp, but there wasn't enough space beneath it to get her bound hands under and rub at the rope. She worked her way to the end of the door, and to her surprise and delight, there was a loose flap of metal on the corner.

It was very difficult to get herself into a position where she could rub her bound wrists against the metal. Her arms hurt when she tried to lift them, and she cut her hand on the metal flap at her first attempt. But after many attempts, with rests in between, she finally managed to make a little progress and cut a few strands of the rope.

Hungry, thirsty, scared and in pain, it was hard to keep at it. The draught coming under the door was icy, making it hard to move her fingers.

'Keep scraping for twenty seconds,' she said aloud, and then tried hard to exceed that time. It was so tempting to crawl back to the sacks and burrow into them. But she knew she mustn't do that in case he came tonight. She wanted to be ready to fight him off.

The plan was formed as she lay scrunched up scraping at the rope. She intended to be standing up when he opened the door, ready to spring at him and claw his eyes. She'd read in a magazine that was a good move, and also kicking a man hard in the groin disabled him for long enough to run away. Just the thought of blinding him with her fingernails made her feel stronger – she fully intended to make him suffer grievously for hurting Duncan.

Grace put her best clothes on again to go and visit Duncan; she thought it would cheer him to see her looking smarter. When she got to the ward and saw how badly the boy had been hurt, she knew immediately what Janice had meant by feeling entirely impotent. No words would ever make him feel better, no gift, holiday or new friend would ever take away the memory of what that beast of a man had done to him. Somehow Duncan had to find something inside himself to get over what had been done to him. She had no advice to give him to help in that search.

But his smile at seeing her was at least warm. 'I wasn't sure if Janice could find you,' he said.

'She's a resourceful woman,' Grace replied. 'But I'd have come even if she hadn't braved the forest to find me. How are you now?'

'Feeling much better,' he said, but the smile and cheery tone didn't fool her. She knew it was an act to spare her. 'Lots of aches and pains, but I'm not hungry and thirsty any more, I'm warm, and I know there's not going to be any more beatings. Now will you explain how you and Maisy came to find me?'

It wasn't in Grace's nature to be boastful and anyway it gave her pleasure to let Maisy be the heroine of the rescue. She even exaggerated a little for dramatic effect.

'I wish you could've seen her up on that roof, chucking the tiles off. She was so brave. It isn't an easy thing to go into an unknown place in the dark. She must've been so scared when she found she couldn't get out the back door.'

'I hope she managed to stay brave once Grainger got her,' Duncan's voice trembled. 'I wasn't brave at all. The first place he took me to there were four other boys, including Peter.' He nodded towards the other bed. 'A boy called Ian died soon after I got there, and his body was left in the room we had to sleep in for three days. I screamed and screamed when I realized.'

'I think anyone would scream at that,' Grace said. She pulled a chair up beside his bed, sat down and gently took the fingers of the arm that was in a sling. 'I've read so many books about people in prison and concentration camps during the war – all of them expressed horror and outrage at the first dead person they saw, even if later on they became almost blasé about death. Being horrified and distressed doesn't make you weak, Duncan. Grainger probably thinks he's a big man, but it's he that's the weak one because he hasn't got the strength to turn away from perversion and cruelty.'

'Does what he did to me make me a homosexual?' Duncan whispered.

'No, it doesn't. In fact after what you've been through I suspect you might want to live the rest of your life with only women. But if you should by some chance turn out to be that way, that's the way you were designed, not because anyone made you go that way.'

'Are you sure?'

Grace smiled. 'Yes, my dear boy, though why you think I know these things I can't imagine. Everything I know comes out of books, not life experience.'

'What will I do when they let me out of here?' he said. 'Even if they do find Maisy quickly and she's not been hurt, I don't think I could bear to be in London with Father. Or with Grandmother, for that matter, however nice Janice is. I'll be afraid people will be looking at me and thinking things.'

Grace nodded. 'That's what I was like when I left the asylum. In fact, I was like that until I met you, Duncan, my boy.' She smiled at him and made him smile too. 'You could come and live in the forest with me for the summer. Just until you feel able to face folk again.'

'I'd like that,' he said, a dreamy, far-away look in his eyes. 'But I guess everything hinges on whether they find Maisy. I won't want to live at all if they don't find her, or she's been killed.'

'You mustn't think like that,' Grace said firmly. 'I have every faith that the determined little minx will escape him.'

Duncan tried to smile. 'I had a dream last night about her. She was in a kind of shelter, maybe a shed; it seemed to be on a beach. But it was just a dream. She's probably not in anywhere like that.' He paused for a moment, looking pensive.

'We used to be able to pick up on stuff about one another when we were younger. Things like her feeling ill in the night – I'd go into her room and it would be for real. Once she was home from school with German measles and she got the feeling someone was hurting me. She made our housekeeper go to meet me, and she found me being bullied by an older boy. We used to try reading each other's minds.'

'Did it work?'

'Kind of, well, sometimes.' He smirked. 'Usually when we thought about food because both of us were hungry. But we do kind of know stuff about each other without being told.'

'So what are you feeling about her now?'

'I feel she's still alive, but cold and hungry,' he said. He shrugged and pulled a glum face. 'But let's be realistic, Grace – I would think that, wouldn't I? It's the way I've been.'

'Yes, but it *is* possible you are picking up on Maisy too. It's said that most twins have almost telepathic powers about one another.'

She could see he really wanted to believe that he might be able to tune in to Maisy, only his head was telling him it wasn't possible. But Grace believed his dream meant something. When she was in the asylum feeling at her most hopeless she'd had a series of dreams about a house in a wood or forest. She had found it a comforting dream, something to make her believe her future might one day be brighter than the way things were now.

She couldn't believe her eyes when Mr Brady took her out to the forest and showed her his place. It was the same place she'd dreamt about, all those years before. She didn't tell him that; he might have thought she really was mad. But she took it as a sign that it was the place she was meant to be. Where she belonged.

So if Duncan was feeling his sister was in something that looked like a shelter near the sea, she and Toby were going to find it. Starting the minute she got out of this hospital.

She opened up her bag and brought out a bacon and egg tart she'd bought in a fancy grocer's in Brockenhurst, and a jar of preserved raspberries from her garden. 'The lady in the grocer's called that tart something posh and French,' she said. 'But I asked what was in it and she said bacon and egg, so that's what I'd call it. You need building up, and so does your friend, so give him some.'

'I will if the nurse lets me, but I don't think he's going to recover,' Duncan whispered. 'His parents came not long before you and he didn't seem to know them. I overheard them talking to the doctor and he was suggesting he should be moved to a mental hospital as soon as possible. His mother was crying, I felt so sorry for them.'

'Sometimes the brain shuts down because a memory is too painful to bear,' Grace said. 'But time is a great healer, I can vouch for that. It's time I went, Duncan – I've got important things to do, and Toby is waiting for me.'

'Can I really come and stay with you when they let me out of here?' he asked.

'Yes, you can, if you still want to. I never thought I'd see the day when I'd welcome a guest, but it seems that day is about to come.'

Outside the hospital, sitting in her van with Toby beside her, Grace studied her map of the south coast and particularly the locations where the other boys had been found, which she had marked with crosses.

The first had been Littlehampton, the second in Southampton, the third in Portsmouth and then on to Newhaven and Eastbourne. Then he came back west again to Seaford and Brighton.

Apart from Duncan, who appeared to be an anomaly, there was a pattern to the abductions. They were always on a Friday afternoon. Then a gap of eight to twelve weeks before the next one. Grace thought perhaps he had business in the areas. For some reason she didn't think the abductions were completely premeditated; she doubted he'd been watching any of the boys for a great length of time. It seemed to her that the desire for a new boy overwhelmed him and he felt safer going to a school where he'd never been before. Once he saw the kind of boy he was looking for, he felt compelled to take him.

She had read widely about all the dead boys. Their parents claimed they were quiet, shy boys, and that description fitted Duncan too. But there had been other things said, by neighbours and teachers; suggestions their home lives were not so good. She felt each boy was isolated, by personality, poverty or neglect.

It would be simple for a man such as Grainger to be able to identify these characteristics; he'd spent many hours in court watching the flotsam and jetsam of life.

As all the boys aside from Duncan were from seaside towns, it stood to reason Grainger was familiar with the coastline. Grace wasn't, unfortunately. But as each of the bodies were found about twenty miles from where they had been abducted, that suggested to her that he had some kind of compulsion to put them back on home ground.

Duncan had said he and the other boys were in a house somewhere beyond Southampton, so maybe that compulsion Grainger had extended to himself too. He couldn't go too far from his home territory.

He favoured seaside places, and he wouldn't have dared drive Maisy very far because he knew the police would be looking for his car.

She looked sideways at Toby curled up on the passenger seat.

'Well, Toby, let's check out how good you are at finding.'

Right since she first got Toby as a puppy she'd played retrieval games with him in the forest, taking something of hers and hiding it, then sending him off to find it. He was very good at it, and she hoped he'd be just as good with Maisy's scent.

She had found Maisy's scarf in the van and she took it from the glove compartment to let Toby sniff it. 'I'm going to keep letting you sniff it when we get to the seaside, and you, my boy, will help me find Maisy.'

He looked at her, dark brown eyes bright and intelligent, his ears cocked. He was raring to go.

'Maybe I'll change your name to Watson,' she said, ruffling his ears. 'Seeing as I'm going to be Sherlock.'

She started up the van and drove out of Southampton towards Lyndhurst, with the intention of going on to Christchurch to start searching. She had some blankets in the back of the van. Once it got dark she'd get in there and sleep, so she could continue her search at first light tomorrow.

16

For the first time in his life Donald Grainger didn't know what to do.

After dumping the girl he'd had to abandon his car because he knew the police would be looking for it. He had less than ten pounds on him, no change of clothes or shaving gear. He couldn't get on a bus as his face was on the front of every newspaper this morning. So he trudged back towards the coast, the collar of his raincoat turned up and the tweed cap he kept in the car in case of heavy rain pulled down low over his forehead.

As he walked he trawled through all his friends in his mind, wondering if any of them would help him now. He knew people with boats all along the Solent, many of whom he'd done favours for in the past, but he doubted that would help him once they'd read about what he'd done.

Some of them were bloody hypocrites – several of them liked underage boys and girls too. So many times these same men had promised they'd always have his back if there was trouble, just as he would have theirs. But he knew that he couldn't trust any of them. As soon as they put the phone down on him they'd be ringing the police.

So he had to think of someone he could blackmail into helping him.

Plenty of his clients had been involved in dodgy deals;

he'd even perjured himself in court to help a couple of them. But he needed someone who stood to lose everything they had if he squealed on them.

Then it came to him. Hugo Fairbanks.

Grainger smirked at the very thought of him: a public schoolboy who not only had a taste for young boys, but had destroyed his late wife's will, and maybe even hastened her death. Mildred Fairbanks had found out about his little peccadillo when she was dying of cancer and, never guessing that her solicitor had the same interests as her husband, came to see him to change her will.

Mildred came from 'old money'. Her grandfather and father had made fortunes in steel, and without any sons to leave their wealth to, she got it all. She was no beauty even when young, but now as the cancer spread she was painfully thin, flesh hanging off her big frame. The day she came to see Grainger she wanted Hugo's blood.

'I don't want him getting a penny, because he disgusts me,' she said, grimacing with distaste. 'I want him homeless and miserable, and if he tries to contest my will I want you to tell the court that he buggers young boys, and that was why I didn't want him getting my family's hard-earned fortune. You will do that, won't you?'

Of course Grainger promised he would. He drew up the will, in which she left everything to her nephew, got her to sign it, and one of his employees to witness it, then put it in his safe.

It was only about a month later that Mildred died – incredibly quickly for a woman who had told him she still had a year to live. Her doctor thought she had overdosed on her medication.

Hugo was still in the marital home because Mildred didn't want to give him any advance warning of her plans. Grainger felt it was very likely he gave her the overdose because he couldn't bear another year with her. Meanwhile Mildred would have been savouring the thought of him being out on the street after her death. Perhaps she even hoped he'd give her an overdose and welcomed it, anticipating he might be convicted of murder too.

The speed with which Hugo rushed to see Grainger so soon after Mildred's death was unseemly, even by Grainger's standards. He got the will out of the safe and handed it to him to read, then watched the colour drain from the man's face as it slowly dawned on him that Mildred was punishing him in possibly the only way she could really hurt him.

It said a great deal about the man's lack of any moral code when his first question was to ask who knew about this new will. Then, without any preamble, he suggested Grainger destroy it in return for a share of the fortune.

Grainger remembered pretending to be outraged. But then a few weeks later, having left Hugo to stew for long enough, he pretended to feel sorry for him and said he couldn't do anything even if he wanted to, as the witness knew a new will had been made.

In point of fact a witness doesn't ever get to read a will, and that same witness isn't likely to be there when it's being read, either, so it was quite feasible to destroy the new and read the old. Mildred had told Grainger she had no intention of telling anyone she'd changed her will, not even the nephew who stood to gain from it. She relished the shock value of the new one, and of course she trusted Grainger to do as she asked.

But Mildred was dead, she'd had her fun anticipating Hugo's distress, and Grainger had never liked her much anyway. He'd also had his fun watching the bombastic oaf fall apart. To make himself look like Hugo's true friend, he finally agreed to do it, salving his conscience by only asking for a mere two thousand pounds. The truth was he wanted Hugo in his pocket, just in case one day he needed something from him.

That day had come.

Hugo had a boat moored down in Lymington, small enough to slip under the radar. He would telephone him, get him to meet him, bringing money and food, then take him across to France.

What to do about that girl, though? He couldn't let her go; the police would be on to him the moment she was free.

'Kill her,' he murmured to himself. 'Maybe take her with us and sling her body in the sea.'

While Grainger was making his way towards Lymington, Linda had joined a search party to look for Maisy back in Lyndhurst.

As she waited amongst the crowd getting instructions from the police, to her surprise she saw Steven and Alan were there as well.

She was so distraught about Maisy being snatched and maybe already dead, she needed to be with someone who also knew her. She ran up to them. 'I'm so glad to see you. No one here really knows Maisy – well, not like we do,' she said, her eyes filling with tears again. 'It means a lot to me that you've joined the search.'

'I felt bad enough about her brother going missing,' Alan said, 'and I didn't even know him. But now Maisy, it's just awful. I liked her so much, and I was a real prat to lose her. But this was my only way of trying to show I cared, and Steve agreed to come too.'

Linda nodded. She knew why he had broken it off with Maisy and how that had made her friend feel. But that was in the past. Right now they needed all the eyes they could get on this search.

'Well, I'm really glad you two are joining the search. I didn't think you'd come back for the Easter hols as I hadn't seen you around.'

'We've been stuck into revision,' Steven said. 'We can't gad about any more if we want to get firsts. But let's forget our lives at uni. That's not important. This is. We can't really believe that Donald Grainger is the man who took Duncan and all those other boys. How could he have hidden what he was up to for so long? Do you think his wife knew?'

'My parents were often at the same parties and dinners as Grainger,' Alan admitted, hanging his head as if ashamed. 'I was very quick to point out what bad judges of character they are, consorting with a man like him, yet insisting I gave up seeing Maisy because her family "weren't quite the ticket", as my dad said at the time. Then I overhead Mum talking on the phone this morning; she was actually squeezing out tears as she told some friend I used to go out with Maisy. Such hypocrisy!'

Linda had experienced similar reactions from people

she knew too, and it sickened her. 'Well, I just hope you never go along with what your parents want again. You lost out on someone really special, Alan. I'm proud to say she's still my friend. I can't believe how brave she was the whole time Duncan was missing, and in the end it was purely her determination that saved him.' Her lips began to quiver and her eyes filled with tears. 'I keep praying that man won't kill her.'

Alan reached out and put a hand on her shoulder in comfort. 'We're all praying for that, Linda. But it looks like the search is starting, so eyes peeled for anything that might help.'

Linda was glad the police made everyone walk at least four feet apart from one another. It was intended so they could cover a big area thoroughly, but it also discouraged talking and possibly missing things. Linda was far too upset about what Maisy might be going through right now to hold a conversation with anyone.

One of her father's friends was the doctor who had examined the boys when they were first brought in to the hospital, and Linda had overheard her father telling her mother what he had told him. It sounded absolutely barbaric, so shocking that Linda had put her hands over her ears.

She'd heard enough to be deeply disturbed by it, and she couldn't get the images out of her mind. Without telling her father what she'd overheard, later she asked him if Duncan could recover from what he'd been through.

'It's hard to say, darling,' he sighed, looking very troubled. 'After the war I treated some men who had been prisoners of the Japanese. They'd been tortured, beaten and starved. Some bounced back; once they were well again you'd never know they'd been through anything that terrible. But others, however brave they'd been in the camps, couldn't get over it. They remained tortured by their memories; it was impossible for them to be the husband or father they'd been before the war. Some even committed suicide to release themselves from their torment.'

'Oh!' Linda exclaimed. 'That is awful.'

Her father hugged her. 'Duncan is young, and there is so much resilience in youth,' he said. 'He could be one of the lucky ones who can recover. Let's hope so.'

Linda had been studying art at Southampton Art College for over a year now, with a view to teaching art once she got her degree. Thinking back to her reunion with Maisy the other day, she realized that she had been rather self-satisfied and smug. She'd thought her friend being an au pair was somewhat demeaning; she couldn't imagine anything worse than teaching someone else's child to wipe its own bottom or cut up its food. Maisy hardly earned any money, she worked long hours and Linda doubted she was appreciated, either.

She was terribly ashamed of thinking that now. She asked herself what was so good about getting a degree in art. It would never help anyone, or change the world, whereas Maisy had not only spent a year loving another woman's children but she'd risked her life to save her brother.

But then she wasn't the only person who had got things wrong. Alan's parents had too, and her own to a certain extent. She remembered them saying Duncan had probably made some bad friends and gone off with them, and that the chances were Maisy knew where he was and would join him as soon as she could get away from her grandmother. But at least they had the grace to admit they were very wrong.

Then there were all those who blamed Grace Deville when Duncan first disappeared. It was the talk of the town, with some hotheads wanting to go into the forest and string her up. But since she'd outsmarted the police in detection work and made it perfectly clear she was neither bad nor mad, many of those same people were now saying she ought to be given a medal and a council house. How stupid they were – didn't they understand she had chosen to live in the forest because she didn't want to live close to small-minded people like them? As for a medal, from what Linda knew of the woman it would mean nothing to her. She'd probably think it was insulting.

Linda vowed to herself that if Maisy should be found unhurt, she was going to make sure she never again made rash assumptions or accusations about people, and that she'd be kinder to people less fortunate than herself.

Alastair Mitcham was nervous as he approached the hospital ward. He hated having to deal with emotionally charged incidents, whether they were his own or someone else's. He usually closed down and walked away if it was possible. But with his son rescued from the jaws of death by his own daughter, and her now being missing, he knew he couldn't hide from his emotions any more.

Even his mother, who he had always believed incapable of any human feelings, had sobbed when she related what Janice had told her about Duncan's condition.

'Son, you are going to have to show him that you love him,' she said brokenly. 'I know you're a cold fish because I made you that way, and I am ashamed of that now. But it's not too late for you and Duncan. You must tell him that the terrible things he's been through are not in any way his fault. The only way he can recover fully is by knowing he is loved, and that we are all prepared to listen to him and help him in any way we can.'

Alastair had sat beside his mother on the couch and held her in his arms as she cried. He cried too: for his missing daughter, his poor son, and for himself and his mother who had to have something as bad as this happen before they could speak of their feelings. He knew that the time was coming for him to reveal the truth about his wife. And maybe the other things he'd kept secret from them all.

He braced himself at the ward door, offering up a silent prayer for help and guidance.

As he walked into the small ward and saw Duncan looking so thin, battered and bruised in the hospital bed, he didn't have to think about showing emotion because it erupted inside him. Instinctively he bent to kiss his son's forehead and he felt tears welling in his eyes.

'Steady on, Dad. I might look rough but I am going to survive,' Duncan joked, a little weakly.

'I know, and I thank God for that,' Alastair replied, his voice quavering. 'But I've told myself that from now on I must prove to you, and to Maisy when we get her back, how much you both mean to me.'

'Do you think we will get her back?' Duncan asked.

'I'm counting on it,' Alastair said and tried to smile. 'I'm also counting on getting to be alone with that bastard Grainger just long enough to knock his teeth out. I never liked the little weasel when he was a boy. I caught him torturing a cat once and I should've flattened him then. But you are always inclined to believe boys will grow out of cruelty. He clearly didn't.'

Duncan could hardly believe his father was showing a whole new side of himself and he wanted to encourage more of it.

'It's so good to see you,' he said. 'I've been so afraid.'

Alastair took hold of his son's hand between his two and squeezed it, looking into his eyes. 'Janice told me you were worried about my reaction to what's been done to you. But let me tell you, son, you mustn't feel shame. None of this was your fault.'

Hearing his father saying such unexpected and tender things after a lifetime of coolness was too much for Duncan and he began to cry. But his father leaned over him in the bed and scooped him into his arms.

'My poor boy,' he said, rocking him comfortingly. 'You've been through a terrible time, and nothing I or anyone else says can make the memories of it go away. But I'm going to try and get help for you, and maybe you can even bring yourself to tell me some of it, just so you don't keep it all locked inside you.'

'I don't know the words to use,' Duncan whispered. 'I mean, I haven't even kissed a girl yet, so I don't know anything about the normal way of it. And now I'm so scared for Maisy, because I know he likes it with girls as well.'

'From what I remember of him he was always seriously weird,' Alastair said. 'Don't you go making the mistake of thinking he is a homosexual. I know that is illegal still, and some people see it as a crime, but I've had friends that are that way, and they are kind, loving, good men. They would never force anyone, let alone a child.

'Let's be clear about this: Grainger is what is known as a paedophile. He may have had many sexual relations with women, but his prime interest is in children, in his case mostly boys. Even more dangerous, he is also a psychopath. He likes to inflict pain on his victims and he gets pleasure from killing them.

'But you aren't quite the same as the sort of boys he usually goes for, which is probably why he didn't kill you. It was very bad luck that you ran into him at a time he was looking for a new victim. If I'd only known he'd cosied up to your grandmother and become her solicitor, I would have moved heaven and earth to prevent him even speaking to her.'

'You seem to know a lot about him,' Duncan said. 'Did he do something to you?'

Alastair looked horrified. 'Certainly not! I was older and stronger and he knew I didn't like or trust him. But there was always something distasteful at the core of him. No, I learned about such men after the war when I was over on the continent trying to sort out displaced people, refugees and suchlike. There was chaos everywhere, cities razed to the ground, terrible food shortages, and some people were like animals seeking revenge for what had been done to them or their families. Amongst the more understandable crimes – and many of these were barbaric enough – we also found perverts and psychopaths who were raping, maiming and killing for pleasure. All nationalities, Duncan, don't run away with the idea that these were all German. The Russians were the worst – they were supposed to be liberating, and were raping and plundering as they went. But there were Polish, French, Romanian, and English too. I learned things in that time that I wish I could erase forever from my mind.'

'Did the war make them like that?' Duncan asked.

Alastair pulled up a chair, sat down and leaned his arms on the bed.

'Was it the war?' He sounded like he was thinking aloud. 'No, son, I don't think it was just that. I think that many people have the potential to be depraved, but I've also observed there are certain things which seem to trigger such impulses. Cruelty to them as children, perhaps being belittled by their peers for some reason. But certainly during that time after the war, it appeared to be a major trigger for hitherto normal people to go off the rails. They found themselves in a world gone mad in the aftermath, with no semblance of law and order any more, and perhaps they had a deep anger, hatred or desire for revenge inside them. There were so many vulnerable people about, especially children everywhere, most of whom could be enticed with a loaf of bread, and suddenly all moral barriers broke down. These people might have come across to their victims as strong, but in fact they were weak, letting themselves be led by base desires.'

Duncan realized this was the most his father had ever said to him at one time. He also felt a degree of comfort knowing he understood what his son had been subjected to without his needing to spell it out.

'Have you got any idea what triggered such things in Grainger?' he asked.

'There was something hidden about his real family,' Alastair said. 'He was sent to live with his Aunt Constance in Burley and I remember when I asked him about his parents he never gave me a straight answer. My parents knew nothing, and my father was the kind of man who didn't approve of people poking their noses into other people's business. Janice told me once that she saw Donald's back one time on a hot day when he was playing with the garden hose. She said it was a mass of scars, as if he'd been badly beaten.'

'But surely if you'd been badly beaten as a child you wouldn't want to inflict pain on anyone?'

Alastair pursed his lips. 'Just the opposite, I'm afraid, Duncan. The beaten often become beaters.'

'Did you know that they had to take Peter to a mental hospital?' Duncan said, looking across to the empty bed. 'Somehow I don't think things will ever come right for him.'

Alastair shook his head. He didn't know what to say. He thought when he returned to England from Europe in 1948 he'd seen the last of the terrible things men could inflict on each other. Now he was here with his own son, reliving it again. His daughter was in the hands of the psychopath, and another young lad taken away to a mental hospital, his wits gone.

'What will happen next, Dad?' Duncan asked, interrupting his father's train of thought.

'I take you home, that's the next thing,' Alastair said. 'The ward sister told me she thought you'd be ready in about two or three days. But don't fret about Peter – there's every chance he'll get better.'

'Our mother hasn't,' Duncan said.

Alastair had known for a very long time that he ought to explain to the twins about their mother, but he'd kept putting it off, hoping that the problem would solve itself, one way or another. But now that he had decided to be more open and loving, he knew it was time to start talking.

'I'm afraid she is never going to get better. You will remember that she claimed her problem was through a riding accident – well, in a way that was true. She was taken to hospital after the fall from her horse and it was there they found something else, a small brain tumour.

'They weren't able to safely remove it, and back then I don't think they really knew much about such things. The surgeon seemed to think it might just disappear. It didn't, of course. Back during the war and immediately after, her only problem was bad headaches. When you twins were three, soon after I came back from Europe, I took her to see a specialist. He was convinced he could remove the tumour safely, but it didn't work out that way, and the part of her brain it was connected to was damaged. The headaches got worse and she became irrational, developing a fear of leaving her room.'

'Why didn't you ever explain?' Duncan asked.

'I couldn't find the words,' Alastair said. He took his son's hand in his and lifted it to his lips to kiss it. 'Being unable to speak about important things has always been my failing. I can write a report so clearly and concisely anyone could understand it, but I flounder with the spoken word, especially anything to do with emotions. How do you explain to children that something in their mother's brain is making her nasty and difficult and that eventually she'll need to be somewhere secure so she can't hurt herself or anyone else?'

Duncan nodded. Put like that, he did understand. 'Yes, it must have been hard. But I wish you had tried to tell us, because we got the idea you sent her away because you were tired of her being ill.'

Alastair shook his head. 'No, that wasn't the case. Well, at least, not until she became violent and abusive; then I had no choice but to act. So I did what I thought was the best thing for you and Maisy, and sent you to my mother's. I thought you'd be distracted from thinking about your mother and home by being in such a wonderful place and having so much freedom.

'But when your mother went to the private hospital she deteriorated. There is no possibility of a cure or of ever bringing her home again, and I had to agree for her to be moved to a secure hospital because she became a danger to others. She set fire to her bed one night; she threatened another patient with a knife out in the grounds. I didn't stop you from seeing her because I was being mean or secretive. She doesn't even know me any more, Duncan. She wouldn't know you either, and it would be far too upsetting for you.'

Duncan shuddered, remembering Bertha Rochester, the mad woman locked away in *Jane Eyre*. 'But what will become of her?' he asked.

'She is always getting bad chest infections, and the chances are that before long she'll get pneumonia and slip away. That would be the kindest thing, Duncan. Nothing can be done for her, apart from feeding her and keeping her warm and clean. There is no miracle cure.'

Duncan nodded. He could see anguish in his father's eyes and knew he had told him the whole truth. 'It would've been better if you'd explained properly before. We weren't babies to be protected,' he said reprovingly. 'But never mind us, it must've been hell for you all these years. Especially shielding us from how it was. When we get Maisy back we must try to pull together like a proper family.'

'I'm going in to see the police now and find out if there have been any developments,' Alastair said. 'I know they found Grainger's car abandoned today and there's been a full-scale search around Lyndhurst. Tomorrow they intend to expand the search area down towards the coast, and I'll join in with it. I also intend to go and speak to Grace Deville – that is, if I can find her. I owe her a great deal.'

They chatted for a little while. Duncan was eating the chocolate Alastair had brought him, breaking bits off now and then and offering them to his father. Alastair noticed that despite everything, including his sister being in great danger, Duncan seemed to have a self-assurance now which he'd never had back in London.

Perhaps he had developed it with Mr Dove. On his last trip down here, Alastair had talked with the teacher and sensed how fond the man was of the twins; he actually said they were his favourite pupils, and a bright man like him must have brought out a lot of good stuff in them. But then maybe Duncan was always self-assured and Alastair wasn't aware of it because he never got close enough to his son to notice such things.

'I'd better go now and talk to the police.' Alastair got up and reached out to ruffle his son's hair. 'You concentrate on getting your strength back. You'll need it when you see how emotional your grandmother's become.'

'Really?' Duncan's eyes widened.

'Yes, really. I think the Mitchams are in danger of becoming soppy.'

Duncan gave a half-smile. 'If they find Maisy.'

'Yes. Only if they find Maisy. But we have to believe they will.'

17

Hugo picked Grainger up at the appointed place on the Southampton Road at eight in the evening and drove him into some woods and then on to a muddy lane where they wouldn't be seen. He stopped the car and turned to Grainger.

'Look, matey, I feel for you, but aside from giving you a change of clothes and some cash, I can't help. You've murdered six boys, two more are seriously ill. And now you've got the girl. That's far too much for me.'

Grainger didn't reply for a moment or two, so that when he did it would have more impact. He had always despised Hugo, his public school banter, big florid face and wet, fleshy lips. He was overweight, he hee-hawed like a donkey at his own jokes, and had a problem with body odour. On top of all those disadvantages he was thick.

'You ought to know me well enough by now to realize I wouldn't have asked you to meet me without expecting something from you,' Grainger said eventually, with a wolfish smile. 'And I don't mean a clean shirt and some fresh socks. Thanks to me, you inherited a million or more. I know you finished Mildred off too, and you've been at some of the parties we've had in the past and shared the guests I brought. So you *will* help, Hugo, by taking me across the Channel, or I spill the beans.'

'My boat isn't strong enough to cross the Channel at

this time of year.' Hugo's voice had taken on a whining note. 'The waves are too big, we might capsize. And the police would know it was me who helped you.'

'I have every faith in your sailing skills,' Grainger said. 'Let's face it, you've done little else over the last ten years but perfect them. And why should the police connect you with me?'

'Because you are my solicitor!' Hugo whined fearfully.

'I have hundreds of clients.' Grainger's voice was silky, but still managed to convey a little menace. 'They are all in the Hampshire/Dorset area, at least half have boats and many have outbuildings where I could hide. In the time it would take for the police to check them all out, you could have sailed all the way to Australia and back.'

'Please don't ask me to do this,' Hugo begged. 'It's madness! I don't think you realize just how dangerous it is to take a small boat through one of the busiest shipping lanes in the world.'

'You get me to the French coast and you'll never see or hear from me again,' Grainger said. 'The police aren't checking boats yet; they still think I've got a little hideaway somewhere. If anyone asks, you've just been fishing. Everyone knows how much you like fishing.'

Grainger knew that Hugo had no choice but to agree, but he also knew he would be looking for some plan to turn hero. He was a similar size to him, though he didn't keep himself as fit, but no doubt he would think along the lines of pushing Grainger overboard, in one stroke ridding himself of his blackmailer and the need to go to France. Perhaps he'd even tell the police Grainger got him to take out the boat at gunpoint. He would of course claim to have knocked the gun out of Grainger's hand and into the sea.

'OK then,' Hugo said, the sudden calmness of his voice revealing that Grainger was right to distrust him. 'So what time do you want to leave?'

'At first light – it will be less suspicious than night-time. There's a little old wooden jetty about half a mile out of Lymington on the salt flats. Do you know it?'

Hugo nodded. 'We used to dive off it as kids,' he said.

'Bring the boat there then, at six. I've got a bit of business to attend to first.' He glanced sideways at Hugo and saw a glimpse of excitement on his face. The man believed he was soon to solve all his problems.

'You're not thinking of running to the police, are you now, Hugo? You do realize that if the coppers nab me tomorrow morning I will tell them everything about you? OK, I'll swing for murder, but you'll spend the rest of your life in gaol. They say old lags hate kiddy fiddlers.'

He saw Hugo gulp. 'Course I won't, old bean. Telling tales is not my thing. I'm a trifle nervous about the sailing – it's going to be tough – but I won't let you down.'

Grainger got Hugo to drop him a mile out of Lymington. He knew of a tiny cottage belonging to a client of one of his partners who had just recently passed away. It was tucked away so no one would hear him break the glass in the back door to get in. He needed to get a good sleep, as tomorrow he would have to keep his wits about him. He hadn't told Hugo they were going to take Maisy with them because he felt that might have been a step too far for the man. But she'd be very weak by now with no food or drink, so she wouldn't put up much of a struggle.

It was starting to rain. He'd heard on the weather forecast it was set for all day tomorrow which was ideal for him; it would keep dog walkers away.

He had a good feeling. Everything was going to be fine.

It wasn't fine for Maisy. She was sick and cold, and she had lost all track of time because despite what she'd hoped for, no daylight came into her prison and she had failed to find any way of getting herself untied.

Kicking on the door had achieved nothing, but as she couldn't see daylight around the opening, she thought perhaps there was another door beyond. She hurt all over, she had wet herself again, and as she kept going hot and cold she was fairly certain she had a high temperature.

The hunger wasn't so terrible now she was growing weaker, but the thirst was growing worse and worse. She had resigned herself to Grainger not coming back for her; why would he? He'd have to kill her to silence her, so it was easier to just leave her and let nature take its course.

She seemed to remember being told you could last a couple of weeks without any food, but it took just three or four days without a drink. At first she'd tortured herself thinking about that. She didn't know how many days she'd been in this place as she had no idea if the sleep she drifted in and out of was for just minutes or hours. The other thing she thought about was everything that had happened after Grace left the cottage to call the police. She so much wished she'd climbed out of the roof the way she'd got in and hidden up in the bushes until help arrived.

But now she couldn't even seem to think straight. At times she thought maybe she'd imagined Duncan and the other boy in the cellar, that the pain she was in, the hunger and thirst, was all part of a vivid nightmare. But then she'd get cramp in her leg or arm, she'd feel the wetness of her slacks and the hardness of the concrete beneath her, the biting cold, and she knew it was real. She just hoped her death would come quickly.

The one thing that seemed worse than dying was that she would never find out if Duncan and the other boy had recovered. Nor would she know whether Grace was in trouble for not going to the police with her suspicions about Grainger. Would her grandmother and father mourn her death? She knew Duncan would, Janice and Mr Dove too, maybe even Linda, but so few mourners made her life seem pretty meaningless.

Grace was in a very reflective mood that evening. She had parked up the van and fed Toby, and now she was eating fish and chips, with him sitting beside her in the passenger seat. So far in three days of searching she'd hadn't found anywhere along the coast she thought Grainger could have hidden Maisy. And Toby hadn't picked up on any scent.

He went off full of enthusiasm, sniffing away at neglected old houses, sheds, stables and newer, smarter places too, but each time he came back to her with a look that said 'She's not here.'

She was wary of drawing attention to herself by asking people questions. Besides, all the newspapers had pictures of Grainger on the front cover; there was even a picture of

Maisy. She'd overheard people in cafés discussing what a monster he was; if any of them had seen anything, they would've gone to the police.

Now she was growing very weary. She'd tramped so many miles, and she wasn't sleeping very well in the van. She wanted to be home, to have a good wash and to sit by her fire. Perhaps it had been a little arrogant of her to think she and Toby could find Maisy when the police couldn't.

She let Toby finish her chips; she'd lost her appetite through worrying about Maisy. How was Duncan going to recover without her? He could probably overcome all the hideous things done to him, but he was always going to think he was responsible for putting his sister in harm's way.

Watching the sun slide down into the sea, she told herself that she'd get up really early tomorrow and search the shoreline on the other side of Lymington. She had read somewhere that it was wild and marshy there, a haven for birds, so she doubted there would be anything Maisy could be held in. Just a three or four hours' search and then she'd go home to the forest.

The first slivers of light were coming into the sky when Grace woke the next morning, and she saw it was raining. She was stiff and cold, she had difficulty getting out of the back of the van and felt grumpy as she pulled on her oil-skin coat and hat. She stood for a few moments watching Toby rush about sniffing furiously and cocking his leg as if his life depended on it, and she considered driving home straight away. She was just too tired to go on.

But that seemed like betrayal; another three or four

hours wouldn't hurt her. So she changed out of the soft shoes she'd worn in the van and into her old boots. Then, picking up her stick and Maisy's scarf, she locked the van, called Toby and set off.

Her stick looked like any ordinary walking stick, but she'd bought it in a shop that sold specialist hiking and mountaineering gear. It was very strong metal and had a spike on the end, intended to give more stability on uneven ground, but she had found many other uses for it: grubbing out plants, prising open stiff gates and scraping away soil when she wanted to know what lay below. She had even hung dead rabbits or pheasants on it that she'd shot, to carry them home.

There was no one around and she went through the pretty little town of Lymington without seeing a soul. It was clearly too early yet for the Isle of Wight ferry.

Both the left and right coastal parts of Lymington were wild and marshy. There were a few shabby beach huts where there was sand, but they'd be so easy for anyone to get out of, it was hardly worth looking at them. She gave Toby the scarf to smell. He ran off to sniff round the huts, but he came back from them immediately, looking up at her as if waiting for new instructions.

She walked about another mile, then in the distance, half set into a sand dune, she could see something that might fit Duncan's description of 'a kind of shelter or shed'. She remembered seeing pictures of these things at the start of the war. They were gun emplacements in case of invasion.

Beyond that was a small, almost broken-down jetty, the kind that someone who lived close to the sea would erect themselves to moor their boat. She could see no house now, though, just windswept grasses and a few straggly bushes growing out of sand and shingle. The whole area looked very forlorn in the rain – even the seabirds appeared to have taken cover – but she guessed on a warm, sunny day it was a lovely place to walk.

She carried on, and once she was within a few hundred yards of the 'shelter' she gave Toby the scarf to sniff again and sent him off. At first he was criss-crossing the beach, continually looking back at her, but then suddenly he took off, straight for the shelter.

Grace's heart leapt; all at once her tiredness left her. Toby had definitely got wind of something; he was pawing at the door and barking. She speeded up and called him back before she got there to have him under her control.

'What is it, Toby?' she asked. He jumped up at her, clearly excited that he'd found something.

Then he barked again, this time turning towards a man walking along the beach towards them. He was a good six or eight hundred yards away, much too far away to make out his face. But as a precaution Grace shushed Toby, put him on his lead, then turned and walked away, over a sand dune.

Once there she lay down to watch the man, holding Toby tightly because she sensed the dog didn't like something about him. Could it be Grainger?

It was odd for anyone but dog walkers or keep-fit enthusiasts to be on a beach at this time of the morning. He surely wasn't exercising – not wearing a black waterproof coat and a sou'wester – and besides, he was carrying a small holdall. He was also looking out to sea, as if he was expecting a boat.

It was frustrating not to be able to see the man's face, but then she didn't know if she would recognize Grainger anyway, as she'd only seen him fleetingly while driving, and from the pictures in the press. But whoever this man was, why was he waiting here for a boat? There was a marina in Lymington.

Toby had definitely got the scent of something. He hadn't reacted like that anywhere else. But of course it might not be Maisy. It could simply be smelly rubbish.

Just then, she saw a small cabin cruiser out at sea but coming in to shore, and the waiting man stiffened and moved in the way people did when the expected lift was in sight.

Grace decided she would go round the back of the dunes and then hide behind the shelter to watch what was going on. As she approached the shelter, out of sight of both the man on the beach and the small boat, Toby got excited again, straining to get to it.

This made her feel it probably was Maisy in the shelter, but she held on tight to Toby, making him lie down and be quiet. She knew she had to watch the man on the beach to see what he was up to. If it was Grainger, she had to think things through before acting, or she might be hurt and then she wouldn't be able to get help.

When she peeped round the edge of the shelter again she saw the boat owner was mooring it to the small jetty. He disembarked from the boat to speak to the other man, and she saw that he was also in a black oilskin coat and sou'wester.

The men's voices were raised as if angry, but they weren't clear enough for her to hear what they were saying.

She slunk back behind the shelter. She could tell they were coming up the beach now towards her because their voices were growing louder and clearer.

'I am not taking her,' she heard one say.

'You are, you don't have any choice,' the other one responded. 'We can weigh her down and chuck her overboard. Problem solved.'

Grace felt a chill run down her spine. There was no doubt now. They were talking about Maisy. But what could she do? She didn't even know which of the men was Grainger now. She assumed it had to be the one first on the beach, but when she risked a quick peep around the wall again and saw the two men together, coming towards her, she didn't know which was which in their identical oilskins. She strained to hear what they were saying, hoping that would make it clear which was Grainger.

'I'll open the door and you be ready to grab her in case she's untied herself.'

'I can't, I won't,' the other man said, his tone pleading.

'You'll do it or else. Getting away in that boat is all that matters. Now stop being so pathetic.'

Grace's heart was thumping so loudly she thought they'd be able to hear it. She heard a key scrunching in a lock, the door being hauled back over stones, then a sharp intake of breath from one of the men.

It was that horrified gasp that made her forget her fear and move. She let go of Toby's collar and, holding her stick firmly in both hands, she leapt out from behind the wall to face the men.

Toby clearly saw them as a threat to her. He sprang at one of them, knocking him to the ground and pinning him there. The other man just froze, and Grace went for that one, bringing her stick down with all the force she could muster on to his head. Then, pulling back, she whipped it round, hitting first one side of his head and then the other.

Although he reeled back from the blows, the stick wasn't heavy enough to do serious damage, and all at once he ran for it, right down the beach and on to the boat.

To Grace it was a relief that the boatman had gone. Toby had bitten Grainger's face, which looked like a piece of steak now, and although he was trying to fight the dog off, Toby wasn't going to let him go.

That was when she saw Maisy.

She was curled up on her side, her hands and feet bound, filthy dirty, and clearly no longer conscious. There was no time now to check her pulse or even try to speak to her. She reached down, picked the girl up in her arms and took her outside the shelter, laying her down on the ground. Then quickly she returned to the man, dragging him further back into the shelter with Toby standing by growling as if he wanted to tear his throat out.

'You're going to get a taste of your own medicine now,' Grace snarled at him. She glanced around the place, saw the patch of wet where Maisy had been lying, felt how cold it was, and the lack of food or water. 'Let's see how you like it in here. Come, Toby!'

She was out of there in a second, praying that Grainger had left the key in the lock. Thankfully, he had, and she locked the heavy door behind her. The small boat was sailing away now, and finally she could breathe.

She dropped on to her knees beside Maisy. Rain on her face had brought her round, but it was clear by her vacant expression she didn't know where she was. 'It's me, Grace,' she said. 'I'm going to cut these ropes off you now, and get you away from here. You're safe now. I've got you.'

'Grace?'

The barely audible question made a lump come up in Grace's throat. 'Yes, it's me. Hold on, I've got a knife somewhere.'

She rummaged in her coat pocket and pulled out her penknife. 'I wish I had a drink for you too, but it's not far to go to the town.' She cut through the ropes on Maisy's wrists and chafed them between her hands to bring the circulation back, then turned her attention to the ones on her ankles.

'That's better,' she said as she finished. 'You're like a block of ice, but do you think, if I stand you up, that you could walk?'

Maisy didn't answer. Grace lifted her up, and with her arm around her supporting her, she tried to get her to walk, but Maisy seemed unable to even try. So Grace hauled her up in her arms and began walking with her.

Grace was strong, but by the time she'd gone five hundred yards she couldn't carry Maisy any longer and she laid her down on the ground again. She didn't know what to do. She was afraid to leave her to get help, and besides, Maisy needed urgent medical assistance.

After a brief rest, she stood Maisy up again and this time lifted her on to her shoulder, like a sack of potatoes. It was hard going over shingle and sand, but she staggered on until she came to the path leading into Lymington Town. There, to her relief, she saw a young woman coming towards her with a dog.

'Please go and call an ambulance and the police for me,' she begged the girl. 'This is Maisy Mitcham – she was taken by Donald Grainger, the murderer. I've just found her.'

The astonishment on the young woman's face would have been funny if the situation wasn't so serious. 'Of course,' she said and immediately turned and began running back to the town.

Grace carefully let Maisy down to lean against her chest, and with one arm holding her tight, she wriggled out of her own coat and then wrapped it around the girl to try and warm her.

'Am I safe now?' she heard Maisy whisper.

Tears sprang into Grace's eyes. 'Yes, you are, my little love. No one is ever going to hurt you again.'

18

Smiling broadly, Alastair Mitcham strode across the hospital waiting room to the dishevelled middle-aged woman sitting there and took her rough-looking hands in his.

'How on earth can I ever thank you enough for saving both my children?' he said, his voice shaking with emotion.

'No thanks are necessary,' Grace said. His gratitude was a little unnerving and she couldn't quite meet his eyes. 'I'm just waiting to hear that Maisy is all right and then I'm going home with Toby. It's been a long, tiring three days.'

'Please come home to Nightingales with me afterwards?' Alastair begged. 'Duncan and my mother would be so thrilled to see you and you can stay the night, have a hot bath, a good meal and be looked after. We'll welcome Toby too, of course. I'm told he was the one who actually found Maisy.'

Grace appreciated his offer and she would've liked to see Duncan, but she knew she'd feel awkward with his snobbish grandmother. 'Yes, it was Toby. I gave him Maisy's scarf for her scent, and he held Grainger down while I got her out of that place. Thank you for your kind offer, but as soon as we know about Maisy, I'd rather go home. I'm not one for company.'

Alastair was ashamed, remembering when Grace was a

suspect in Duncan's disappearance. She went through hell, her garden dug up, her home searched, and was vilified by people in the village just because she was a recluse and different from other people. He would always feel indebted to her for finding both his children, and he wished he could do something for her now to show her how he felt.

Before he could say anything more a doctor came into the room. 'Mr Mitcham?' he asked, looking at Alastair.

'Yes. How is Maisy?'

The doctor smiled reassuringly. 'We are rehydrating her and treating the many cuts and contusions on her body. Her forearm is cracked so we've put that in plaster. But she's going to be fine. A good long sleep, a hot meal and seeing her family again will soon put her to rights.'

'Had she been—?' Alastair couldn't bring himself to say the word 'raped'.

'No, she wasn't. We think her attacker beat her purely because she put the police on his trail. She told me that once he'd shut her in that place he didn't come back at all.'

'She would've died if Miss Deville hadn't found her, wouldn't she?'

The doctor looked at Grace and smiled.

'Yes, you were a real live heroine by all accounts. I don't think she could've survived another day without water. But all Maisy's questions have been about her brother. The staff who took care of Duncan, and now Maisy, are so very relieved they are both safe. I'll take you in to see her now, but only for a few minutes, please, as she needs to rest.'

Alastair gestured that Grace was to go first. 'No, you go,' she said. 'She'll only want her family.'

'I believe you are more important to Maisy than family, so you'll come in with me and no arguments.' Alastair put his hand on the small of her back and nudged her forward.

Maisy was in a side ward as Duncan had been, in her case mainly to protect her from unwanted attention from other patients, their visitors and journalists. With her right arm in plaster, a drip in her left arm, a bad bruise on her cheek and her face as white as the pillow, she looked frail. But she managed a bright smile for Grace.

'I thought I was dreaming that you'd come with Toby,' she said. 'What happened to Grainger?'

'I locked him in there once I'd got you out,' Grace said, a little smile playing on her lips. 'Toby mauled his handsome face too. Now you rest up, eat everything they give you and get better. Duncan will be wanting you home.'

'As I am,' Alastair butted in. 'I was so relieved and happy when the police rang me at Nightingales to tell us Miss Deville had found you. I do hope you aren't in too much pain, Maisy?'

'Just aches, really,' she said. 'But shouldn't you be getting back to your lady friend, Father? She'll be missing you.'

Grace cringed and backed towards the door to leave. She hated family confrontations; they unnerved her.

'Yes, I saw you together at the hotel in Brighton,' Maisy went on, two angry red spots coming up on her cheeks. 'You must have known I was working just further along that same road, but you couldn't spare the time to come and see me.'

'I'm going now, Maisy,' Grace said. 'I'll see you when you get home.'

She hurried out of the ward and down the corridor to get to the car park where she'd left her van with Toby in it. She wasn't altogether surprised to hear that Alastair had a mistress; it explained why Maisy was so down on him. The girl had certainly come to the point quickly today – but then Maisy was feisty, she'd want to deal with that head on.

As she stepped out of the hospital doors into the forecourt, cameras flashed and three or four journalists pounced on her.

'Miss Deville, can you tell us how you came to find Maisy Mitcham? Is it true you'd searched all the way along the coast from Bournemouth? What made you search for her? What is your relationship with her and her twin brother?'

Grace was frightened by these people shouting at her, and putting one hand over her face, she pushed through them and fled to her van. They followed her so she started it up and pulled out, waving her arms to warn them to get out of the way.

She had been so happy she'd found Maisy. It seemed like the biggest achievement in her life, and as she had waited for the ambulance with the girl folded into her arms, she'd felt something akin to a mother's love for her. A wonderful, warm feeling she doubted she'd ever experience again.

But now those newspaper people would spoil everything, she knew. They'd hound her, question her motives, and if she didn't give the answers they wanted, they'd brand her as mad.

It seemed ironic that Duncan and Maisy, with their sweet, innocent interest and friendship, had led Grace to joining the outside world, but now as a result of what had happened to them, the peace and seclusion she once had and treasured so much was going to be shattered.

She didn't think she could bear that.

Maisy looked angrily at her father. She had remained silent while he explained to her as he had to Duncan the truth about their mother's condition. She could accept that, and how hard it must have been for him, but still the thought of him having a mistress made her blood boil. She couldn't let it go.

'You marry for better or worse, in sickness and in health,' she snapped at him. 'You were a lousy father and a lousy husband who has betrayed our mother.'

'I agree I wasn't a great father to you, but in my defence I would say that I was working long hours and away from you a lot of the time. In normal marriages the parents do things together with their children – go to fairs and museums, trips to the seaside. Because of the way your mother was, we didn't do that. I so much wish I'd made an effort to do it alone with you, but you and Duncan didn't appear to need anyone but each other.'

Maisy pursed her lips. That last bit was probably true.

'That still doesn't excuse you being unfaithful.'

'Maybe not, but we all need someone, Maisy. Can you imagine what it's like to never be told you are loved, never a kiss or a pat on the back? I had no one to laugh with, no partner to share things with, take out to dinner or to the pictures. I was so very lonely, and then Jenny became my secretary and she understood how things were for me.'

'I bet she did,' Maisy retorted.

'She did, Maisy. Her husband had been very badly wounded in the war, and he was never the same man again. We didn't start the affair until two years ago, when he died. By then we'd become so close we just couldn't help it. You might not understand that now, but you will one day.'

Maisy sat for a little while picking at the fingernails of her right hand, which still had dirt beneath them from scrabbling at her prison door. The way he'd explained it, she could understand, she even felt sorry for him. But all those years of not talking to him about anything made it hard to know what to say now.

'Can we try and rebuild our lives together as a real family?' he asked.

His voice was so soft and tender it made tears come into her eyes.

All at once she didn't mind what he'd done or hadn't done. Thinking she was going to die had clarified what was important and what wasn't. 'Yes, Daddy,' she said, for the first time in over ten years dropping the title 'Father'. 'I think we should try that.'

Alastair had only just got back to Nightingales and was in the sitting room with his mother, Janice and Duncan, telling them about Maisy, when they saw a police car draw up outside.

'Not more questions?' Violet Mitcham said grumpily. 'They know more about this family now than I do!'

'A case like this will take some time to investigate and bring the guilty to trial,' Alastair reproved her.

Janice grinned at Alastair and jumped up to answer the door.

When she came back in, she was accompanied by a thickset, red-faced policeman who introduced himself as Sergeant Williams. It seemed that he had taken over from the kindly Sergeant Fowler, who had recently retired. After asking Duncan how he was feeling now and saying how glad he was that Maisy was safe, Sergeant Williams turned to Alastair and shook his hand.

'I'm sorry after all you've been through to give you something further to concern you, but the man Miss Deville locked into that gun emplacement was not Donald Grainger.'

'What?' Alastair exclaimed. 'So who was he?'

'Hugo Fairbanks. He lives in Bucklers Hard. We understand he is one of Grainger's clients, and the owner of the boat which Grainger presumably escaped in.'

'But I don't understand. How did that happen?' Alastair asked.

Sergeant Williams shrugged his shoulders. 'I haven't yet spoken to Miss Deville, but from what she told the police at the hospital, both men were wearing similar black oilskins and sou'westers because of the heavy rain, so she didn't see their faces clearly. She had only ever seen Grainger fleetingly anyway. We know she was in hiding until they opened the locked door and she told us that while she attacked one man with her stick, her dog got the other man. All she cared about then was getting Maisy out of there to safety. She assumed the man being attacked by her dog was Grainger, and the one who fled to the boat was the owner of it.'

'So where is Grainger now?' Duncan asked.

They all turned to look at him and saw that he'd

turned ashen. Janice sat down beside him and put her arms around him.

'We don't know, son,' the sergeant said. 'We are assuming in France. As soon as we knew we hadn't got Grainger, we alerted the French police. Hopefully we will hear from them soon, telling us they have him. But you mustn't concern yourself with this, Duncan. He won't dare come back to England, and even if he didn't sail to France he wouldn't come anywhere near here.'

'What are you doing with this man Fairbanks?' Alastair asked.

'We have him in custody, of course. A doctor was called to stitch up his face where Miss Deville's dog attacked him, and he'll be appearing in court tomorrow charged for the moment with aiding and abetting a serious crime. We will make sure he is held in custody until his trial. He is claiming he was being blackmailed by Grainger, but is reluctant to tell us why. Once we've investigated that, there may be further charges to be added.'

'So far the real detective work has all been done by amateurs.' Alastair's voiced dripped with sarcasm. 'Can we hope that we could have a few professionals on the case now?'

The sergeant's ruddy face became even redder. 'I'm told that Sussex, Hampshire and Dorset police are all joining forces on this now,' he said. 'Grainger's office is being searched meticulously as we speak. But I must be off now, as I have to find Miss Deville.'

'Can't you leave her alone today?' Duncan spoke up indignantly. 'She must be exhausted. It isn't fair to plague her when she's already done so much.'

'I'm afraid I'm just following orders,' Williams said. 'Thank you for your time.'

'It isn't right to keep pestering Grace,' Duncan exploded when the sergeant had left. 'Her little home in the woods has been her sanctuary, she'll hate people charging in there. It was almost like that sergeant was blaming her for getting the wrong man! Surely anyone with any sense could understand what it took for a woman of her age to take on two big men alone. If she'd stopped to check which one was being chewed by Toby, she might never have got Maisy out.'

'You are quite right,' his grandmother said. 'She was brave and clever, and it isn't right for her to be pestered now, after all she's done. I can't bear police and newspaper people coming here either, and I don't even claim to be a—' She stopped short, uttering a warning yell and pointing to a couple of men with cameras on the garden path. 'Look, there they are now!'

Alastair got up and drew the curtains shut. He ignored the banging on the door and continued walking around the house closing all the curtains.

'They should take the hint at that,' he said when he came back into the sitting room. 'At least it's late afternoon now and it will soon be dark. I'll write a warning note saying we have nothing to say to journalists and put it on the gate for tomorrow.'

'And I'll go and get supper ready,' Janice said.

'Let's have it in the kitchen tonight, it's cosier,' Violet said. 'And less work for you, Janice.'

Alastair caught Janice's eye and raised an eyebrow. She

stifled a giggle. She couldn't remember the last time her employer had been so thoughtful.

As Janice went out into the kitchen she felt like doing a dance of joy that Duncan was home and soon Maisy would be too. She had had a long chat with Duncan last night, and his only concern had been his sister; he passed off what had happened to him with a shrug.

Clearly he wasn't really over it – no one could go through such a long and terrible ordeal and not be scarred by it – but this morning, when they heard Maisy had been found, he'd been so happy. He had wanted to go to the hospital to visit her himself, but he was still too poorly.

Mrs Mitcham had been so much nicer too – so very different to how she'd been when Maisy had been taken. Then she'd shut herself up in her bedroom and wouldn't come out. It was obvious that she felt a huge burden of guilt at bringing Grainger into the house. She admitted that Alastair had warned her several years ago that Grainger wasn't to be trusted, but she'd put that down to jealousy and ignored him. But whether the solicitor was trustworthy or not, no one could have predicted he was a murderer and a pervert. What on earth must his wife be feeling now, knowing that she was married to such a man?

The only person Janice could discuss her fears with was Mr Dove. He'd been her rock, just as he had been to both her and Maisy when Duncan disappeared. It never ceased to amaze her that he wasn't bitter about his disability, or that his wife had left him. He was a good man with a big heart.

Janice just hoped this bad news that Grainger was still at large wasn't going to set Duncan and Maisy's recoveries back.

'So it wasn't Grainger that Toby attacked?' Grace asked Williams. She had been nodding off in front of the fire she'd just lit when the policeman came crashing through the bushes, setting Toby off in a frenzy of barking. 'Well, I thought it was, and my thoughts were all for Maisy. Anyway, I'm glad that man got his face chewed by Toby. He was obviously up to his neck in it too, or he wouldn't have brought his boat.'

She didn't ask the policeman to sit; she wanted him gone as soon as possible. 'Well, I've already told you everything I can, so please can you go now and leave me in peace.'

'I want to take you down to the station,' he said. 'We need a written statement.'

'You can whistle for that today,' she snapped at him. 'I am tired and hungry and I'm not going anywhere. I haven't forgotten all that nastiness when you came out here practically accusing me of killing Duncan and burying him in the woods. So forgive me if I'm not rushing to make statements or help you further.'

'I can arrest you for obstruction,' he warned her.

She turned to him, her eyes sparking fire. 'Just try it, sonny! I'm not scared of you. I'll make a statement when I feel like it and not before. Now scram!'

If she hadn't been so tired, Grace might have laughed to see the overweight sergeant floundering across her garden. He slipped in mud at one point and wobbled around until he got his footing again. As he disappeared into the bushes he glanced back fearfully.

'You ought to be afraid,' she said aloud. 'If the children in the village are to be believed I could turn you into a toad.'

19

Deirdre Grainger lay on her bed sobbing. She'd taken the phone off the hook and disconnected the front doorbell, but still people kept coming to the front door and banging on it.

People had always said that she looked like a model with her long, glossy auburn hair, perfect 36, 24, 36 figure, and such a pretty face, but she didn't think she'd ever dare show that face anywhere ever again.

At twenty-two, fifteen years ago, she had been swept away by Donald's charm and looks. He was perfect husband material, she thought: ambitious, hard-working, generous and kind, and when he proposed she accepted joyfully. They lived in two rooms in Southampton at first; he was still doing his articles then. But as soon as he became a qualified solicitor they moved to their first house. It was only a two-up two-down terrace, but Donald promised it was only temporary, and he kept his word, buying the house they lived in now within a year and having work done on it to make it a modern, beautiful home.

She didn't have to work, but she had a little part-time job in the mornings as a secretary at the local primary school. Donald liked her to have dinner nearly ready when he got home.

With expensive clothes and shoes, and a generous allowance for hairdressers and manicures, Deirdre had nothing to complain about in her marriage. Well, except that he did have some odd ideas about lovemaking. He was always asking her to put on a schoolgirl's gymslip and plait her hair. She didn't mind doing it now and again, but it gave her the creeps that he pretended she was just twelve. She also hated that he made her kneel down and take his penis in her mouth. He did that a lot, and it always seemed to her that he wasn't thinking about her at all, but had some strange fantasy going on.

But she had never considered there was anything seriously weird about him – not the kind of stuff the newspapers were saying he'd done. Most of her girlfriends had admitted their husbands had some little quirks, though they didn't actually reveal them. As one of them once remarked, 'As long as they want to do it with you, you don't have to worry about other women.'

But now it seemed other women weren't his thing, however much he flirted and charmed clients, his friends' wives at the golf club, and in fact almost any woman of any age with a pulse. Though now that she'd really had time to reflect on the past and the women he took a particular interest in she would change that last statement from 'with a pulse', to 'with a healthy bank balance'.

Still, charming women to leave him money or property was one thing; abducting, raping and killing young boys was in a different league. A woman could stand by a bounder – there was even a bit of a thrill knowing he was bringing back the spoils to you. But what he'd done was beyond understanding; it was vile, cruel and perverted.

'You must have known,' was what one detective said when she was taken in for questioning. But she didn't. She had had no idea.

She would admit he sometimes went out at odd times of the evening and night without a good explanation. She would admit too that sometimes he seemed very distant or distracted. But wouldn't any wife say that about her husband?

Everything they owned was in his name, and Deirdre suspected that once he was caught and tried, his estate would be seized. So she'd have nothing – no home and nothing to live on. She'd already had a phone call to ask her not to come back to work, and she wouldn't even be able to stay in the area. That was so unfair when she'd done nothing. Not one friend had contacted her to say they would stand by her, but then on reflection the only friends she had were wives of his friends and colleagues. Donald had long ago encouraged her to ditch the friends she'd had from her single days, saying they were all small-minded and boring.

She got up off the bed and opened the drawer in her dressing table where she kept her jewellery. Donald had bought her some lovely pieces, but then, as she could see now, it wasn't out of love for her, but merely to show off to other people.

Catching a train to London seemed a good idea. She could sell this lot there and maybe find a cheap place to live and a job where no one knew anything about her. She certainly had no intention of standing by him. He could rot in hell as far as she was concerned.

While his wife was planning to sell her jewellery, Donald Grainger was looking back, wishing he'd had the presence of mind to grab that stick from the old witch who'd attacked him, knock her and her dog out with it, then go through Hugo's pockets to find the money he'd promised him.

But he'd fled down the beach to the boat without thinking. When he looked back, the old girl was hauling Maisy out and locking Hugo in. It was once he'd started up the boat and chugged out into the Channel that he realized he was in deep trouble. He could handle a boat along the coast on a warm summer's day, but crossing the Channel in choppy seas required far more experience. He had found a small stash of French francs in a drawer in the cabin, presumably left from the last time Hugo went to France, and about ten pounds in change. There was some food in the cupboard too, and some clothes. But he wasn't stupid enough to think you just pointed a boat towards France and eventually arrived there. Strong currents could take him up the Channel towards Belgium or down towards the Bay of Biscay. Either way, he couldn't even be sure there was enough fuel to get him to shore.

In view of all this he felt the only thing to do was hug the English coastline and go down to Cornwall. His French was dismal anyway; at least in England he had a slim chance of being able to talk someone into helping him hide until he could get out of England safely.

On the way down the coast he had what he thought was a brilliant idea: to abandon the boat to make it look as if he'd been washed overboard. In fact he could easily have been washed overboard several times because the waves were so high, but he wished he knew more about currents to have some idea where the police would look for a washed up body.

Abandoning the oilskin coat and sou'wester, he put the raincoat he'd worn beneath it, his other clothes and shoes into a plastic bag, along with his money, blew some air into it and then sealed it tightly. All he needed now was to find a suitable place to swim ashore and wait for darkness before jumping in, leaving the engine running.

The sea was icy cold, and he certainly wasn't looking forward to jumping in wearing only his underpants. It didn't help that he didn't know exactly where he was. He'd been to Cornwall hundreds of times, but aside from one day trip out of Falmouth to fish, he'd never seen the rugged coastline from the sea.

Looking towards the shore he couldn't even see anything like a church steeple or other landmark, and the tiny villages he went past didn't look familiar from the sea. He also hadn't realized how many little coves there were. He was afraid if he struck out for one of them at night the waves might dash him on to the rocks, which looked lethal enough to tear him to ribbons.

He carried on sailing, all the time looking to his right for a suitable, accessible cove or beach. He thought again about that mad old witch from the woods. This was all her fault. If she'd kept her nose out, no one would ever have suspected him. He wouldn't have had to take Maisy, and Hugo wouldn't have become involved either.

'Damn you,' he muttered. The police would go through his office with a fine toothcomb now, assisted by his partners, and if they were to dig deeply enough they were going to find many irregularities, and links to men who shared the same interest in children.

He wondered how Deirdre would cope with the flak.

She had been the perfect wife for him: stunningly attractive, warm and sociable, but dim, so dim she never realized he thought of her as little more than a household appliance. He wasn't sure what being in love actually meant, but he certainly didn't love her. He'd chosen her for her looks, the perfect smokescreen for his real sexual interests. She could be a good hostess, a reasonable cook, she didn't ask too many questions and as long as he kept her in spending money she never grumbled.

Finally he saw a small sandy cove that looked promising. Nobody on the beach and no houses overlooking it. He went right past it slowly, checking for rocks under the water and scanning the entire cove to be absolutely certain there was no one around. He then turned around and went back.

The third pass was to be his last. On reflection he had decided jumping in after dark was a very bad idea, and he took the boat further out so it wouldn't crash on to the rocks of this cove. He slipped off Hugo's jacket which he'd put on when he'd taken his own clothes off, then shoved it into the cabin. The wind was very cold, and the thought of plunging into the sea was frightening, but he had no choice. Leaving the engine still running, he picked up his plastic bag, leapt up on to the seat at the stern and jumped.

The sea was so cold he felt his heart might stop, but he struck out in a fast crawl, pushing his bag in front of him. He glanced back to see the boat had already disappeared from view. Now he had to concentrate all his energy on reaching the shore.

It was further than it looked, and once his feet finally touched ground, he had difficulty in wading out on to the beach because he was shivering so badly. Getting out of the wind under the shelter of some rocks, he opened up his bag and fished out a small towel, removed his wet pants and dried himself quickly.

He was dressed in less than two minutes. It felt so good to have warm clothes and shoes on again, but the hard part was coming – finding somewhere to stay where he wouldn't be seen.

It was nearly seven and it would be dark soon. He took a narrow path up through the rocks and as he climbed he wondered where he was and how far it would be to the nearest town. Ideally he wanted to find a caravan site. Easter had passed and some people towed their caravans down to Cornwall to park them up for the summer season. He could break into one and hole up there while he planned what to do next.

'Oh for heaven's sake, there's that wretched policeman again!' Violet Mitcham exclaimed as she looked out of her bedroom window.

Janice, who was helping her sort out some old clothes to send to a jumble sale, joined her employer at the window. 'Duncan and Maisy don't need any more questions, or any further talk about Grainger,' she said. 'Thank goodness they've gone to see Grace.'

It was a week since Maisy had been found, and she had come out of hospital three days ago. Being back with her brother had made both of them feel better, and as it had been raining almost constantly during that time they were happy to stay indoors and avoid the nosy parkers and journalists. Many village people had come to the house with cake, biscuits or a casserole, and though it appeared kindly, all they really wanted was to see the twins and hopefully get some juicy gossip to take back.

Janice had reported yesterday that she hadn't seen any journalists in the village, so they were all hoping the story was losing its interest.

Alastair had had to drive back to London for work last night, but as he'd hugged his children goodbye he'd said he didn't want to leave them. That meant more to the twins than anything else. Finally they felt they had a real father, one who talked to them, showed them affection and wanted to understand them. They both told him they understood about Jenny, the woman he was seeing, and at some stage they'd even like to meet her, though Duncan admitted to Maisy he still felt that was a bit wrong while their mother was alive.

When the new day began with blue sky and sunshine the twins had begged to go and see Grace, and somewhat reluctantly Grandmother had agreed. As Duncan's wrist was still tender and Maisy had her arm in plaster, they couldn't ride their bikes, but if they walked they could take a short cut through some fields into the forest and not through the village.

'I suppose we'd better go down and see what the policeman wants,' Violet said grudgingly. 'He'll only come back again.'

Sergeant Williams realized he wasn't welcome when he wasn't invited in. His face grew a darker red and he seemed almost tongue-tied.

'What is it?' Violet said in irritation. 'Spit it out for goodness' sake.'

'It's Peter, the boy with Duncan – he died early this morning.'

'Oh dear, no! How awful for his parents,' Janice said. 'Do come in, you can't stand on the doorstep to tell us such a sad thing. What exactly did he die of?'

Williams took off his helmet and came in. 'Pneumonia, they think, he'll be having a post-mortem. The poor lad wasn't very robust to start with, according to his parents. But keeping someone in a damp cellar when they already have a weak chest is a recipe for disaster.'

Violet merely waved her hand towards the sitting room for him to go in. 'You surely weren't going to blab this out to my grandson?' she asked indignantly. 'Don't you think he's been through enough?'

The policeman shrugged. 'He'll find out soon anyway – better that it came from me.'

'I don't agree, so it's just as well he and Maisy are out. I will tell him at an appropriate moment. Now if that's all, we have things to do.'

'There is something more.'

'Yes? What now?'

'We think Grainger is in Cornwall, not France.'

'And it's taken a week to work that out?'

Janice turned away slightly, dying to laugh at how sharp Violet was being. The poor policeman was squirming.

'The boat belonging to Hugo Fairbanks was found smashed on rocks at first light this morning. The investigation team are checking it over, but the initial opinion was that he was either washed overboard or jumped, and the boat kept going.'

'So you don't know if he's alive or dead?'

'No, Mrs Mitcham. But we think it's more likely he's alive and hiding up somewhere.'

'Oh my goodness,' Violet exclaimed. 'You don't think he's coming back here, do you? Are you keeping an eye on his wife?'

'I can't see any reason he'd come back here; no one is going to help him. As for his wife, she's in shock over what he's done. People say she must have known, but in her case I really don't think she did.'

'She is a bit thick,' Violet sniffed. 'He brought her here to tea once and she didn't understand what a pastry fork was for. She looked at it as if it was an exhibit from Mars. But I sympathize with her not realizing what her husband was – he took me in completely. I thought he was kind, honest and an exemplary solicitor. However, if Deirdre loves him, as I'm sure she does, she is likely to help him regardless of what he's done.'

'I don't think so. Detective Inspector Froggatt, who interviewed her at length, said she was beside herself with anger and disgust. But we are monitoring her phone calls just in case it transpires she's as cunning as him. The DI asked me to remind you all to be cautious. He doesn't think for one moment Grainger is stupid enough to come to your house, but it's as well to be prepared.'

Janice was listening to this with horror, wishing they hadn't let the twins go out today. She wished too that Alastair hadn't gone back to London last night. They would all feel more secure with him in the house.

'Well, if you've no further horror stories for us, then we'll let you go,' Violet said. 'Please pass on our heartfelt condolences to Peter's parents. I would be grateful for their address; Duncan should write to them.'

*

When Williams had gone, Violet followed Janice into the kitchen. To the housekeeper's surprise, the old woman began to cry.

'I can't help it,' she said, dabbing at her eyes with a lace-trimmed handkerchief. 'Just imagine that was Duncan. Whatever would we do?'

20

'So how has Duncan really been?' Grace asked Maisy when her brother went outside to throw a ball for Toby.

The twins had been with Grace for nearly an hour, and although Duncan had been jovial, acting like nothing bad had ever happened to him, Grace wasn't fooled.

'He's been having terrible nightmares. Janice told me she stayed with him all night on one occasion; she said he was too scared to close his eyes. He won't talk about what he went through. Mr Dove said that until he does the memories won't start to fade. He suggested that if Duncan finds it hard to actually say it aloud, he could try writing it all down – not necessarily for anyone to read, but to help himself.'

Grace nodded. 'That sounds like good advice, and Mr Dove understands about horror. He was wounded in the jungle and lay there for two days before his comrades could come back to get him. What hell he must have gone through.'

Maisy shuddered, imagining snakes and the like slithering past while she was in agony. 'What my brother really wants is to come out here and stay with you. He's got the idea that chopping wood, digging and doing other jobs for you will make him better. He really doesn't want to talk, or see people.'

'How well I understand that,' Grace sighed in agreement. 'But I suppose your grandmother won't allow it?'

'I think she might if I ask her,' Maisy said. 'But what about you? Are you sure you would like that?'

Grace smiled. 'There was a time I would've buried myself alive rather than have anyone here with me. But you two are special. And I'd like a crack at getting him to tell me what happened. Physical hard work is good for troubled souls as well – it brings back the appetite and helps you to sleep well. It's also the busiest time of year for gardens – weeds springing up overnight, seeds to be planted, new beds to be prepared.'

'Then I'll ask Grandmother when I get back.'

'But what about you, Maisy? Your bruises are fading, but probably not the fear of what you expected to happen to you.'

'I'm fine, really fine. I didn't go through anything nearly as bad as Duncan did. The trouble is, I don't quite know what to do with myself now. Should I go back to Brighton or stay here with Duncan? I don't mean right away, but in a few weeks.'

'Until the plaster on your arm comes off, you won't be much use looking after small children. I think Duncan will need you close for a while too.' Grace smiled. 'But for all I know there might be a young man in Brighton?'

'There is, well, there was, but he hasn't tried to get in touch with me. Although I didn't give him the telephone number at Nightingales, when he read about Duncan being found and me being snatched, you would've thought he'd have gone to see Mr and Mrs Ripley to ask after me.'

'Yes, you would,' Grace agreed. 'Young men, and young women for that matter, are fickle creatures. Was he special?'

Maisy shook her head. 'No, he was nice, but not the man of my dreams.'

'What's the dream man like?' Grace asked.

'I haven't given him that much thought, really. It's how someone makes you feel that counts. I did meet a boy ages ago before I went to Brighton – he made me feel weak at the knees, and I so much liked being with him – but his parents didn't like what they knew about my family. Besides, he was going off to university.'

'He doesn't sound as if he had a mind of his own,' Grace pointed out.

'Maybe he was too easily swayed by his parents then, but my friend in Lyndhurst rang me when I got out of hospital, and she told me he joined in the search for me, and told her how much he regretted listening to his folks. He also rang her again to say how relieved he was to hear I'd been found. He asked if she thought he should ring the house and speak to me, but Linda said she wasn't sure, better that he waited till she'd spoken to me.'

'Ah ha.' Grace smiled. 'Could this be why you say you feel fine now?'

'It helped,' Maisy admitted. 'He'll have gone back to university now. But you never know, in the summer holidays I might run into him. Speaking of running, we ought to go now. We were told not to be too long as they worry.'

Maisy called to Duncan to ask him to come and say goodbye.

He was silent on the way home, and Maisy guessed he was brooding about Grainger again. 'I told Grace I was going to ask Grandmother tonight about you coming to stay out here,' she said. 'I think it will be good for you.'

Duncan stopped walking for a moment and turned to her. 'Yes, I do too. I really understand now why Grace wanted to live in the forest. There's something cleansing about it. The quiet and the smell of damp soil, and looking up at the sky between the trees, makes you feel very small, but protected.'

Maisy looked up and she could see what he meant. No one looking at you or judging you, the wild flowers, trees, weeds, insects, birds and animals all living together in harmony. The silence was good too; it let you think and kept your brain safe from being bombarded with advertisements, small talk and gossip.

She wouldn't want to live in the forest herself, it would be too creepy at night, but she could understand its appeal for her brother. Every now and then she would recall his face when she'd shone her torch down into that cellar. The look in his eyes had told a story of immeasurable pain and humiliation. It was no surprise he wanted to be away from people, and maybe the forest would help him, if not to forget, at least to push it down into a place he didn't have to visit.

They talked a little on the way home about their father and his lady friend. Apparently her name was Jennifer Dottridge, she was thirty-nine, and she'd married her childhood sweetheart Kenneth when she was eighteen, in 1941, when he'd had leave from the army before going out to Singapore.

She didn't see him again until Christmas of 1945 because he was captured by the Japanese when Singapore fell and put in a prisoner of war camp. He weighed only five stone when the camp was liberated, with infected ulcers on his legs and malaria. The doctor who saw him at the time of liberation was astounded he had survived. But he never really got well again; the malaria kept coming back and he had many digestive problems.

Alastair had explained to the twins that Jenny had had a brief honeymoon with her strong, healthy sweetheart, and then he was gone, only to return five years later a mere shadow of the man she married. She was the breadwinner, housekeeper, nurse, organizer, counsellor and every-thing else, while he had sat in a chair wrapped in his own thoughts, sometimes not even aware of who she was.

'I can see the parallels now to our parents' marriage,' Duncan said thoughtfully. 'It was a good job really that Jenny didn't have a child, or she might have done what Father and everyone else did to us, not letting on how bad Mother was. He was only trying to protect us, and we thought the worst of him.'

'Yes, I'm sorry that I was so nasty to him about Jenny, he didn't deserve that.'

'Or Jenny either. I believe a lot of men came home from the war really messed up. Awful for their families. By the way, what did you and Grace talk about while I was outside?'

'A bit about you; and I told her about Alan, the boy I met in Bournemouth on the day you disappeared. He's at Bristol University now.'

'Speaking of which, I suppose I ought to start thinking about a career.'

'Get completely fit before you do that,' she said. 'I had planned to go to London to work once I'd passed my Pit-man's night-school course. Maybe we should both go?

Anyway, what do you want to do? And don't tell me you still want to be an explorer!'

Duncan laughed. 'Yes, that was the plan, wasn't it? It feels as if that was ten years ago. I think I'd like to be a doctor, but I'll have so much catching up to do with O and A levels.'

'It would be worth it, though. I think you'd make a great doctor, and Dad and Grandmother will be thrilled!'

'Gran doesn't actually do thrilled,' he pointed out, grinning wickedly. 'She's more likely to say, "You think you've got the brains for that?"'

Maisy laughed. 'She told me when I first came home that I should aim higher than being a secretary. But now she knows about Jenny being Dad's secretary she'll probably suggest I work for a rich and clever married man and hope his wife dies.'

'She's so much more human now,' Duncan said. 'I can't say I love her, or possibly even like her, but I respect her for being herself. She's even started to own up to her failings.'

As they walked through the garden gate, Janice opened the front door. She looked anxious. 'Thank goodness you're back. I was getting worried. You must go straight in to see your grandmother.'

The twins looked at each other in puzzlement. Something had obviously happened while they'd been out.

'I thought you were never coming back!' Grandmother exclaimed. 'They've found the boat Donald Grainger got away in, all smashed up on rocks in Cornwall.'

'Was he drowned?' Duncan asked, trying to smile as if the news pleased him, but he knew that couldn't be the case or his grandmother wouldn't look so worried.

'He could've been, but they haven't found his body yet. He might have jumped off, hoping everyone would think he was dead.'

'Well, he won't come back here, will he?' Maisy said. She wished her grandmother had been a bit more tactful. Duncan had gone very pale.

'His wife lives here; she might get him money, arrange for him to get out of the country.'

'I would've expected her to turn him in to the police after what he's done,' Maisy said. 'Surely she wouldn't help him?'

'You never know how people will react at times like this. But you two must stay in until we know he isn't around here.'

Maisy knew that there was no point in asking if Duncan could go and stay with Grace now. She'd seen that stern look of her grandmother's before, and she knew it meant no compromise.

Grainger woke to the sound of people's voices outside the caravan he had broken into late last night. He had prised off the lock on the door, and it was held closed now only by a flimsy bolt on the inside.

He peeped out round a curtain and saw a little weed of a middle-aged man wearing a trilby hat and a cream raincoat; his wife was huge, with bleached blond hair. They looked like the couple on the saucy seaside posters.

She was telling her husband to use some muscle to get the door open.

'No, we can't do that, the police will want to check for fingerprints. We'd better go over to the clubhouse and phone them,' the man said.

'You mean you're scared he's still in there,' she retorted. 'Well, get going then, it's cold standing here.'

Grainger pulled his clothes and shoes on quickly. He was angry. He had thought he'd be safe in here for a couple of weeks. He'd chosen this one out of twenty or more without any lights on last night, because it was close to the fence with the woods beyond.

He peered out again: the man had gone and she had lit up a cigarette and walked a little way away, perhaps to talk to someone. Their two suitcases were sitting on the grass.

Pulling the bolt back gingerly so it made no noise, he opened the door then leapt out. Running full tilt towards the fence around the wood, he vaulted over it and ran into the trees.

He heard the woman scream but he didn't turn to look at her and carried on running for as long as he could manage.

A stitch in his side made him stop, and when he turned to look back, the caravan site was no longer visible.

He doubled over until the stitch went, but he was still panting. He knew that if the boat had been found smashed on the rocks, the Cornish police would be searching for him, or his dead body. Unless the men who came to investigate the caravan were complete fools, they would immediately know it was him who had been there. He needed to get out of Cornwall immediately, before they set up a road block and a full man hunt.

He did know how to hot-wire a car – he'd learned that back in the air force – but that would mean going into a town to pick one and he might be spotted. Maybe there would be a car on a remote farm.

The wood seemed to be getting denser, and he was beginning to think he'd never get out when he heard the sound of a tractor up ahead.

Through the trees he saw a field with a man ploughing on the far side. He climbed over the fence and walked as fast as he could, keeping to a narrow strip of grass along the edge of the field. It seemed like miles, but to his relief he eventually came to a hedge with a lane behind it. Once on the lane he hesitated over which way to go. But if the sun was on his back he'd be going east. At least that way he wouldn't end up in Penzance.

He walked for about ten minutes up the narrow lane, which was flanked by thick, tall hedges. Hearing a car coming up behind him, he glanced round to see it was a green Rover 90, driven by a little old lady so small she could barely see over the steering wheel. On an impulse he stuck out his thumb to hitch-hike.

She stopped, wound her window down and asked in a rich Cornish accent where he was going to. That threw him; he didn't know where he was and where this road led to.

'Dorchester, eventually,' he said with his widest smile – that usually floored old dears. 'But I'd settle for the main road so I can phone a mechanic to retrieve my car. It broke down a couple of miles back.'

'You poor thing,' she said. 'Hop in. You can use the phone at my house, it's only about a mile further on.'

In an instant Grainger knew what he must do. He didn't want to do it, he liked old ladies with cheeks like rosy apples and sparkling eyes. But she might have family at her house, a housekeeper or a nosy neighbour, and aside from that he wanted her car.

He opened the back door of the car to put his jacket on the seat, then, moving as if to go round the bonnet, he quickly opened her door and grabbed her by the throat before she even got a chance to call out, let alone attempt to fight him off.

She stopped breathing in just seconds. Her eyes seemed to almost pop out of her head; her hands came up to try and ward him off as she bucked involuntarily. Then she was still.

Grainger bundled her over into the passenger seat and then drove. Less than a hundred yards further on there was a passing place by another wooded area. He pulled in, picked her up and carried her through a broken bit of fence and right into the wood.

She weighed no more than seven stone, but after a hundred yards or so, even such a light body was becoming heavy. He laid her down in a hollow, scooped up some leaves to cover her, then went back to the car.

The danger period would be someone recognizing her car when he came to some houses. But there was nothing he could do about that, just hope for the best.

Grainger kept driving until he came to a crossroads. Ahead was Truro, to the left Trelisick and the ferry across to St Mawes. He knew roughly where he was now.

The car had an almost full tank of petrol, and when he pulled over to see what was in the shopping bag in the footwell, he found her purse containing just over fifteen pounds. There was also a photograph of the old lady with three small blond children, presumably her grandchildren, and a tin with some angel cakes. She must have just collected them from whoever she'd been visiting.

For a split second he felt a pang of guilt. His aunt in

Burley had always made angel cakes for him, and he had a momentary vision of her wagging a disapproving finger at him. Though she had only wagged the finger at very minor misdemeanours, he could almost hearing her saying, 'He ought to be hung up by his feet and a bit cut off him every day.' That was what she'd said when John Christie was found guilty of murdering several women. She'd added to it: 'And after two weeks he should be taken down and hanged.'

He ate one of the angel cakes, savouring the sweetness. He would be hanged when he was caught, a terrifying thought, especially as he was certain that he had no chance of wriggling out of it. But as he now knew what the end would be, he thought he might as well settle a few old scores before then.

Grace Deville was someone he had in his sights. If it hadn't been for her snooping he would never have been caught. He'd like to get Duncan too, because that boy was so proud. He'd never snivelled. He'd fought back, never pretending he liked it the way the other boys did, hoping that would mean he'd go easier on them.

He was like his father. Alastair was always true to himself, held himself aloof, and refused to be party to any of the little schemes Grainger tried to involve him in. He also didn't tell tales. If he had, maybe the young Donald Grainger would have been carted off to an approved school. He'd like to do something to teach Alastair a lesson about looking down his nose at other people. But then if he got his boy, that would hurt him far more than anything else.

21

'I can't understand why on earth you would want to go and stay in the forest. It doesn't make any sense to me when you have such a comfortable home here,' Grandmother said. She was sitting by the window, the sun streaming in behind her. She always seemed to position herself so that sunshine prevented whoever she was talking to from seeing her face.

Duncan squirmed. He might not be able to see her expression, but he knew that tone. She hadn't said he couldn't go, but she'd be angry if he did.

'I want silence, to dig and plant, feed chickens and not to have to talk to anyone,' he said. 'I know that sounds like I'm being weird, but for me it's the only way to deal with what happened.'

'You think that staying with that crazy old coot in the forest can do what the top psychiatrist your father wants you to see can't do?' she roared at him, forgetting the measured and calm stance she had intended to keep. 'Have you seen the newspapers today? They call her the "Woman in the Wood" and point out once again that she spent years in a lunatic asylum, which is perhaps why she doesn't care about running water and electricity. That says it all about her. Yes, I'm grateful to her for finding both you and Maisy – God knows she was miraculous – but she's peculiar, and I'm not happy at you deciding you prefer peculiarity to normality here.'

'Normality?' Duncan questioned, riled at her being so

bigoted. 'Tell me, Grandmother, what is normal about you? With your total lack of maternal instinct you made my father as chilly as you are. When Maisy and I first came here, you did nothing to comfort or reassure us. Janice did that, a saint of a woman who for some ridiculous reason stays working for you when she'd be valued elsewhere. So how do you expect me to value your opinion that Grace is barmy and I should avoid her?'

'Why is living with her more attractive than living here?' his grandmother blurted out, her voice shaking with emotion.

'Because she understands what I've been through, because she can see that I became an adult while I was imprisoned,' he shouted at her. 'You don't see that, you think I'm just a boy who needs protecting. Well, that ship has sailed, Grandmother. There was no one to protect me, and I survived. I learned things while I was there that no one would ever want to learn or see. I hadn't even kissed a girl when I was captured; I was robbed of all the thrill and excitement there should be in a first sexual encounter. I'm seventeen now and I'm scared I'll never be able to behave like a normal man. Somehow I have to find a way to stop being scared of that. And I think I'll be able to find it with Grace.'

'I agree with that.'

Both Duncan and his grandmother turned at the sound of Maisy's voice behind them in the doorway.

She had fire in her eyes and her mouth set in a straight, resolute line.

'Let him go, Grandmother. Grace is a good woman, she knows things that I doubt even your expensive psychiatrist knows. If he's just as troubled in three months from now, then you can gloat that you were right. But I'd put money on him being more like our old Duncan again by then.'

The old lady seemed to deflate before their eyes. She turned in her seat towards the window and looked as though she was going to cry. 'For goodness' sake, go,' she said, making a shooing gesture with her hand. 'You'll be freezing cold and bitten alive by midges, but don't come back grizzling to me about it. And you, Maisy, if you've recovered, perhaps it's time you went back to work in Brighton and finished that typing course.'

The twins exchanged glances. Struggling not to look pleased they'd won that battle, they turned and went out into the garden without saying anything further.

The garden was looking beautiful. Warm May sunshine had brought so many flowers into bloom and the cherry trees were heavy with pink blossom. They sat on a bench on the lawn.

'Thanks, sis,' Duncan said. 'I shouldn't have said such nasty things to her, but she makes me so angry!'

Maisy nodded in agreement. 'I know, she can be so unreasonable and such a snob. But in her own way she does care about us; she's just a product of her upbringing. That and having a stubborn streak like a piece of steel running through her.'

'Will you go back to Brighton?' Duncan asked.

'Yes,' Maisy sighed. 'But not immediately, as much as I want to see the kids. I'll have to wait till they take this plaster off my arm anyway, and however annoying Grandmother is, I think she and Janice need to have one of us here for a bit longer.'

'Because they still haven't found Grainger?'

Maisy didn't answer straight away. It had been a horrible shock to read that the police in Cornwall had found an old lady's body in some woods. A good friend of hers had said he'd seen a man driving her car through Truro and his description of the male driver, although vague, had matched Grainger, and the timing of it fitted in with the estimated time of the old lady's death. Also, the previous sighting of Grainger at the caravan park was just a few hours before and a mere three miles away from the body.

That was nearly a fortnight ago, and if the police had had sightings of him since, or had recovered the Rover 90, they hadn't released the news to the press. Janice had heard that Grainger's home was being watched around the clock, although the gossips claimed that Deirdre, his wife, had told the vicar when he called on her that she would never help him or give him shelter.

'He really is a monster, isn't he?' Maisy said eventually. 'Killing an old lady for her car. Her poor husband is in a wheelchair; he'll have to go into a home now.'

'What makes a person like that?' Duncan asked. 'Have we all got the potential in us, or could it be a special little bug thing placed in the brain of just a few people? Or is it caused by something in our childhood?'

'If it was caused by something in our childhood there would be a lot more maniacs,' Maisy said. 'Look at the stuff that happened to kids during the war – us included, and we aren't evil. I think it must be the little bug thing. I wonder where Grainger is now, though.'

'I think he must've got out of the country,' Duncan said reflectively. 'That fellow who the boat belonged to said that was what he intended.'

'But he turned out to be a crook too,' Maisy said. 'According to Sergeant Williams he confessed to destroying his wife's will, and Williams told Janice they believe he may even have given her an overdose of painkillers. Then there are all those other clients of Grainger's the police have had in for questioning.'

'Yes, two of them were men that came to the first place Grainger took me to. I was so glad I could identify them by their pictures.'

Sometimes Duncan thought this whole business would never end. It seemed that every few days a policeman turned up wanting him to look at pictures, ask about someone, or get him to repeat details he'd given them in his original statement.

'It's quite a little rat's nest they seem to have uncovered,' Maisy said. 'But it's funny that nothing further has been reported about them since.'

'Probably they got a lawyer to put a gag on the press until Grainger is arrested and charged. I don't think he's stupid enough to come back around here, though. If I was him I'd go out into the wilds of Wales or Scotland where people don't read the newspapers much, and hole up there.'

They sat in silence for a while enjoying the sunshine.

'So when are you going to Grace's?' Maisy asked.

'This afternoon.' Duncan grinned. 'Before Grandmother finds some new reason to stop me going. Will you pop out to see me sometimes, though? Especially before you go back to Brighton.'

'I'll leave you for at least a week,' Maisy said with a smile. 'You may be desperate for my company by then.'

*

Duncan insisted he wanted to go to Grace's alone that afternoon. He packed a few old clothes and a pair of boots suitable for working outside in an old kitbag and slung it over his shoulder. Janice had made a large fruit cake and some jam for him to take with him, and he tied that bag to his handlebars.

'Please don't worry about me, I'll be fine.' He kissed Janice. Grandmother was making a show of not coming out to see him off.

Maisy stood watching him as he rode down the lane to the village. She really hoped Grace could reach those places in his mind that he was keeping locked. Maisy felt she couldn't go back to Brighton, or to London, until she knew he'd faced his demons and vanquished them.

She decided to visit Mr Dove, and called out to Janice where she was going.

He was sitting in his wheelchair at the front of his cottage in the sunshine, reading a book. As usual he had a rug over his missing legs. He'd told her once he put it there to help others deal with his disability, otherwise they tended to look at where his legs should be, rather than at him.

'What a lovely surprise,' he said, beaming a warm welcome. 'I had started to think you had either decided you didn't like me, or you'd gone back to Brighton.'

She laughed. 'Of course I still like you. I can't go anywhere – not Brighton, London or anywhere else – until the plaster comes off my arm. Duncan's just left to stay with Grace for a while.'

'I think that will do him good,' Dove said. 'But it will be lonely for you.'

'I'll be fine,' Maisy said. 'People seem to think twins share a brain and a heart. We can work quite well separately.'

'I think by that you mean that you're prepared to be lonely if he comes back happier?'

'Yes, I suppose so, clever clogs. Now can I make us a cup of tea or something?'

'Tea would be good, but the kitchen is a bit of a mess,' he admitted. 'It's on my list of things to do this evening.'

He was right, the kitchen was a mess, and as Maisy waited for the kettle to boil she stacked up the dirty dishes next to the sink. She would have done more but it was hard to do much with an arm in plaster.

'There we are,' she said, putting Dove's tea down on the little table beside him. 'I'll just nip back and get mine.'

At first they only talked about books and programmes on the wireless, but then the teacher looked at her sternly. 'What is it, Maisy? I can see something is troubling you. Is it just Duncan going?'

'No, I really am fine about that,' she said. 'It's Grainger. I know it's silly, but I keep getting the feeling he's around here somewhere, watching me.'

Dove's eyes widened. 'I have to say, I think such a thing is utterly implausible. He's better known round here than anywhere – someone would be bound to spot him. But tell me why you think he might want to watch you.'

'Because I was instrumental in getting the police on his tail, both at the cottage where he was holding Duncan, and later on at the place on the beach. Perhaps he wants to teach me a lesson about sticking my nose into things.'

Dove laughed. 'I don't think so, Maisy. He's definitely a psychopath, but that doesn't make him stupid. He's not going to risk his freedom by coming to see you. If I may say so, sweetheart, you are being a little paranoid.'

'Perhaps I am.' She laughed, but without humour. 'So let's change the subject. Have you got any new pupils?'

'I have indeed. Two boys, who both need bringing up to scratch for their exams. I'm also coaching a twelve-year-old girl who needs general help to catch up with her peers. She was in hospital for over a year.'

'Poor kid! I hope she's better now?'

'Like many kids who've had some adversity, she's very determined not just to catch up, but surpass. Anyway, tell me your plans for when the arm is better.'

'I really don't know. I'd like to be with the children in Brighton, and I need to go back there at least to finish my typing course. But I don't want to leave Duncan, and anyway, the Ripleys won't need me for much longer. I've thought of going to London to find a secretarial job, but lately I've become unsure of everything.'

Mr Dove smiled at her, his eyes full of understanding. 'Then abandon all plans for the time being. Just see what turns up. I'm glad you seem to have made a real connection with your father at last. He came to see me when you were missing and I really liked him.'

'You did?'

'Yes, Maisy. He's an interesting man. Like me, he loves books and history. He told me a bit about the turmoil in Europe after the war, with all the refugees and displaced people, some so full of hatred towards the Nazis or the Russians, they were taking brutal revenge. He was one of the top men sorting it out over there – I don't think you knew that?'

'No, I didn't,' she admitted. 'We used to ask him what he'd been doing when he'd been away, but he was always vague, and to be honest, both Duncan and I thought he just shuffled papers around.'

'He was vague because he witnessed things you can't tell children about. And he was in the front line, Maisy, he was no paper shuffler. He's a father to be proud of.'

Maisy's eyes welled up. 'We thought he stayed away because he didn't like us, or Mother,' she said in a small, shaky voice.

'Heroes don't always carry guns or wear uniforms. Sometimes, too, they are so intent on putting things right for other people – getting them shelter, medical help and food to eat – they overlook their own family. Alastair Mitcham is never going to be a man who does small talk, or readily shows his emotions, but what I saw in him when you were missing, and Duncan was in hospital, was the sort of quiet courage that meant he would give his life for either of you. I've been in terrible battles, Maisy, and had officers I looked up to and those I didn't. But your father, although not a soldier, was born to lead. Had he been my commanding officer I would have followed him blindly.'

'Really?' she sobbed. 'You aren't just saying it to make me feel better about him?'

'Do I ever tell you things to make you feel better? I seem to remember calling you a halfwit one day!'

Maisy wiped her tears away and smiled. 'I knew you didn't really mean it.'

'Well, if you can be that sure of me, try trusting your dad too. I know the thing about your mother is distressing, but he handled that as well as anyone could. I think he would like to start again with you and Duncan, to be a real family. He spoke to me of selling your old house and moving somewhere you and Duncan would like better – Chelsea, or Chiswick. I suspect you'd like that, wouldn't you?'

Maisy nodded. 'It would be great to start again in a new home with none of the old memories. Why are you always so wise and reasonable? You ought to be grumpy and bitter, raging about the unfairness of it all. But instead you just glow with contentment.'

'I'm not a hundred percent contented. I get a bit lonely, and sometimes really irritated that I can't hop on a bus, weed the garden and a million other things. But I'm healthy, I've still got my sight and my brain, and I can sit here in the sunshine watching and listening to the birds. I don't feel bitter because I've seen men with far worse injuries than mine, and if I was grumpy I wouldn't get nice visitors like you.'

'I wish you didn't get lonely. It would be lovely if you found a nice lady like Janice, even if she was just a housekeeper and friend.'

He smiled. She got the feeling he thought she was being a little naïve.

'I agree, Janice or someone just as jolly and kind as her would be good. She's been along to visit lots of times and it's always a pleasure to see her. But I'm a realist, Maisy. Not many women would see me as much of a catch, and I'm never going to risk humiliation by touting for one.'

Maisy giggled. 'You do use some funny expressions. "Touting", that makes me see you holding up a banner saying "Be my friend".'

Dove laughed too. 'No point in "touting" in Burley. They all do that whispering behind their hands thing, no doubt saying, "Just look at that poor man."'

'With us they whisper, "Violet Mitcham is getting her comeuppance – one tragedy after another in that family."'

'As long as we can laugh about such things they can't hurt us,' Dove said.

'I'd better go now,' Maisy said. 'It's been good to laugh and to talk. When I get the plaster off my arm I'll come and spring-clean your kitchen.'

'I'll hold you to that,' he replied.

Back at Nightingales, Maisy told Janice a little bit about her conversation with Mr Dove.

'He's such a lovely man,' she sighed. 'I hate to think of him being lonely and struggling to do everything for himself.'

'If I was to lose my job here I'd gladly go and look after him,' Janice said, looking just a little dreamy eyed. 'That cottage needs some love and attention but it's a pretty little place, and like you said, he is a lovely man.'

'Oh ho ho!' Maisy pulled a silly face. 'You're a bit sweet on him, aren't you?'

'Don't be ridiculous,' Janice said stoutly. 'As if! I was only saying he'd be nice to work for, that's all. Now I need some things in Lyndhurst, so if you want to come too, we could go on the bus tomorrow.'

'Maybe I'll drop a letter to Linda at her house to ask when she'll be home again,' Maisy said. 'It would be nice to see her again.'

'And no doubt that boy you liked? I heard he was in the search party for you.'

'Where did you hear that?' Maisy asked. Janice hadn't said anything about it before.

'Surely you've realized by now that anything to do with Violet Mitcham's grandchildren is hot gossip?' Janice chuckled. 'At this very moment someone has probably been told you're having sausages for supper, and they're getting jealous.'

'Don't be silly, Janice.' Maisy pretended to put her nose in the air. 'But if you want to pass on some really hot gossip, you can say that I need to buy a new bra tomorrow in Lyndhurst.'

22

Mr Dove looked up from his books as Duncan came into his garden. 'Hullo! I didn't think you were ever going to come out of the forest again. It's been weeks.'

Duncan laughed. 'I do love it there, but sadly I know I've got to plan a career before long. Hence why I'm here. I want to pick your brains.'

'Well, pick away, my boy.' Dove smiled. 'But how about a cold drink, or a cup of tea first?'

'Some squash would be nice,' Duncan said. 'Shall I get it? And one for you too?'

'I do like visitors who wait on me. There's a bottle of orange on the draining board. Glasses on a tray, and, yes, I'd like one too, please.'

Once they were both settled with their drinks, Duncan asked Dove if he thought he had any chance of becoming a doctor.

'Well, you're certainly bright enough,' Dove said thoughtfully. 'You'd have to sit O and A levels and you'd probably need extra coaching to catch up, but I think you could do it easily. Perhaps it would be a good idea if I contacted a medical school to see exactly what qualifications you need to get in?'

'Would you mind doing that for me?' Duncan asked. 'I think Grandmother or my father would be happy to pay you to coach me.'

'That would mean you staying here in Burley. Is that what you'd like?'

Duncan looked thoughtful. 'Mostly it's the only place I want to be, but—' He broke off suddenly.

'You think it might be advisable to be somewhere with no bad memories?'

Duncan nodded. 'Did you find when you moved here that you stopped thinking about all the bad stuff you'd been through?'

'It wasn't moving here that stopped that. It was dealing with it, thinking it all through, laying it out and looking at it. People make a mistake in thinking moving away solves problems or bad memories. While it helps to have a new start, a new home, job or town, unless you can find a way of putting the bad stuff away, it will just rear its ugly head again. I suggested a while ago that you should write down what you went through, but I suspect you haven't done that?'

'No, I haven't.' Duncan hung his head. 'I tried once but the words looked so ugly, so I stopped. I started to tell Grace, but I found I couldn't tell a woman that sort of thing.'

Dove waited a few moments before speaking.

'But I think you could tell another man – me?'

He watched Duncan's face contorting, struggling with what he wanted to say, but not knowing where to start or even the right words.

'You could start by telling me how he picked you up,' Dove suggested gently. 'Your sandal broke, I think?'

'That's right, the buckle came off and my sandal wouldn't stay on my foot without it. I was looking in the grass beside the road for some string or something to tie it on to get me home, and Mr Grainger pulled up in his car. I was only a couple of miles out of Burley. He told me to hop in the car and he'd take me home. He put my bike in the boot. But then he said he just had to go somewhere first, and if I fancied an outing I could go with him. Well, I hadn't got anything else to do and I liked his company, so I agreed. He was so nice to me. He even stopped and bought me a drink and a sandwich. I was enjoying being with him.'

'But he took you somewhere and then you realized something was wrong?'

'Well, I started to worry a bit when he kept driving and driving past Southampton, because I was supposed to be home for supper. Then he turned off the main road on to a lane, and suddenly there were no more houses. We went through a big gateway, with huge, rusting iron gates, and at the end of the drive there was a big house, surrounded by tall trees.'

Duncan began to see that place again, reliving what it looked like and how he suddenly felt scared.

The house looked derelict, boards over the windows, weeds growing out of the steps up to the front door and out of drainpipes. 'I want to go home,' he said, but Grainger looked at him and laughed.

'Don't be silly, Duncan. I will be taking you home, but I've got to go in here first with some stuff. You'll like it, I promise you.'

Duncan opened the car door and got out cautiously as he had bare feet, having taken off the one good sandal. All at once Grainger was beside him, holding a large shopping bag. He put his arm around Duncan's shoulder and led him towards a much smaller door at the side of the house. He opened it with a key, but locked it again as soon as they were inside.

They were in a smallish, bare room. It smelled of mould and neglect, wallpaper peeling off the walls, and as they went through it into the hall, Grainger locked that door too.

At that point Duncan became really alarmed. The house felt sinister. He couldn't imagine what business Grainger could have here, and the locked doors suggested a prison of sorts.

'I keep it locked so my boys can have some privacy,' Grainger said, but he had a wolfish expression that made Duncan feel even more scared.

'What boys?' he asked. 'You mean there's some living here?'

'Yes, it's a regular holiday camp,' Grainger said, unlocking another door across a wide hall, and all at once they were in a very big, scruffy room, with several sofas and armchairs dotted around.

Four boys got to their feet as they came in; Duncan thought they were even younger than him. Grainger introduced them as Michael, James, Ian and Peter, but it was the strangest introduction Duncan had ever encountered because they all looked pale-faced and scared stiff. The room had no natural light since the windows were boarded up. Later Duncan was to discover it wasn't just the boards outside but steel shutters on the inside, operated from somewhere else in the house.

'Take the bag and put the food in the fridge, Michael,' Grainger said, and the boy leapt forward, grabbed the bag and scuttled out into an adjoining room.

'I want you boys to take care of Duncan. He'll be staying for a while,' Grainger said.

'I will not,' Duncan retorted, turning to Grainger in anger. 'What on earth do you think you're doing? What is this place?' He made for the door. 'Unlock this,' he demanded. 'Now!'

Grainger just gave him that wolfish smile again, and all at once Duncan knew this was some horrible kind of set-up and he was in danger. He ran at the man as if in a rugby tackle, intending to knock him down and take the keys.

Grainger caught hold of his shoulders and before Duncan could move to defend himself, the man punched him hard on the jaw, knocking him down on to the floor. 'You *will* stay here,' he said. 'I'm going now – my boys will explain what's expected of you.'

The shock of the punch and being delivered to some strange prison for no reason that he could understand was completely overwhelming. Grainger left the room quickly, locking the door behind him. Peter, a sweet-faced blond boy, came forward to help him up.

'We have to do what he says, or he punishes us,' he explained, and his eyes filled with tears. 'I've only been here three days, but Michael, James and Ian have been here for ages.'

Duncan rubbed his jaw. It really hurt, but the injury was the least of his worries. He just didn't understand what this was about. 'Why did he bring me here, and why are you all here?'

Michael, a dark-haired boy with freckles and mournful dark eyes, had just come back into the room from the kitchen.

'We're his slaves, we have to do what he tells us, whether that's sucking his cock, bending over so he can bugger us, or allowing ourselves to be cut.'

For a second Duncan thought that was a crude and unpleasant joke, but Michael pulled up a very grubby shirt to reveal lacerations across his chest. 'I got that on my first night here for trying to fight him off.'

All at once Duncan knew he had stumbled into something terrible. It was like the worst possible nightmare – but he wasn't going to wake up and find it wasn't real.

'All of you?' he asked, looking at each of the boys in turn.

They nodded, and now in the artificial, rather dim light he could see how listless, thin and drawn they all were. 'Have you tried to escape?' he asked. 'We must be able to if we all work together.'

'We've tried everything,' Ian, a small redhead, spoke up. 'He burned us all with cigarettes when he found we'd tried to smash the lock on the door.' He held out his arm to Duncan to show him ten or twelve small burns, some of them weeping and angry, looking as if they were infected.

James sat on the arm of one of the sofas. He was taller than the other boys, another blond but with a hard set to his features. 'I'd had all this from my stepfather, and when Don was kind to me and said he'd take me somewhere safe, I believed him. But he's even worse. Sometimes he brings a couple of mates here and they have their way with us too.'

That night Duncan learned about things he couldn't have even imagined possible, let alone happening to a group of boys aged thirteen to fifteen.

They called Grainger Don, and they all said how he had

seemed like a kindly stranger when he first spoke to them. In Michael's case he had asked him the way to a nearby road and Michael had got in to direct him as it was on his way home. He had stopped James, saying he was a doctor and he'd come to take him home as his mother was ill.

In all four cases the boys had been fooled into thinking he was a real gentleman, but once they had gone a little way in the car, he made an excuse and the next thing they knew he was putting something over their mouth and nose that made them pass out. When they came round they were here.

All that was alarming enough, but Michael said there had been two other boys when he first arrived, weeks ago. 'One was John Seeward from Portsmouth and the other was Eric Jones from Southampton. We think he took them out and killed them,' Michael said. 'It'll be me next, I've been here the longest.'

'Are you all right, Duncan?'

He heard the schoolmaster's voice from what seemed a long way away and came back to the present with a start.

'You don't have to go on telling me about it if you don't want to,' Dove said. 'I can imagine how much that took out of you.'

'I told you?' Duncan whispered. 'I thought I was just remembering.'

'Yes, you told me.' Dove's voice trembled, and when Duncan looked at him he had damp eyes.

'When the other boys told me what he'd been doing to them I couldn't believe it,' Duncan said, putting his hand over his eyes as if to shut it out. 'It's too nasty to describe,

327

worse than stuff we used to read about in those trashy books about Japanese POW camps. But those other boys weren't like me, sir. They hadn't come from good homes, or had enough education to know how wicked it was for anyone to do such things.

'Michael and James had become like animals. They grabbed the food in the kitchen, and they'd push anyone out of the way if they thought they'd gain anything by it. They sucked up to Grainger when he came, and played with his thing – you know what I mean? I think they thought that would make them special to him. But it didn't, I saw he despised them for being so willing. He was always hitting them and torturing them.

'Peter – that was the boy who was with me when we were rescued – he was a poor thing, weak, the kind of kid other boys pick on. He couldn't stand up for himself at all and Grainger loved to torture him. One time he visited he kept shoving things – a bottle, a corkscrew and other things – into his bottom. Peter screamed and screamed, he had blood pouring out of him, but the louder the screaming got the more Grainger seemed to enjoy it.'

'Couldn't you all have got together and overpowered him?' Dove asked.

'I suggested that, but the others were all so scared I knew they wouldn't back me up when the time came. When Grainger came he used to call out and tell two of the boys to go into the kitchen and close the door. They always did what he said. I stood behind the door one day and whacked him with one of the kitchen chairs as he came in, but my God he made me pay for that. He tied me up and made Michael do stuff to me while he watched.'

'You don't need to go on,' Dove said, reaching out and clasping Duncan's forearm, shocked by the pain in the boy's voice and the way he was hiding his face.

'I think I do,' Duncan said. 'He beat me black and blue after that. I didn't get any food for days either. He told Michael and James they could have my share. Peter tried to give me some of his, but they just snatched his as well. The worst thing of all was when Ian died. We thought he was just asleep at first, but then it dawned on us. We were there with his dead body for what must have been three days before Grainger came back and took him away. I don't know what killed him. I suppose once the police found his body, they would've found out.'

Dove knew, his friend Harry had told him. Ian had died of a broken neck, due to the force put on it while he was being raped. But he wasn't going to tell Duncan that; he already had enough terrifying pictures in his head.

'How long were you at that place?' he asked instead.

Duncan shrugged. 'It felt like forever, but when you're without sun or daylight you find yourself sleeping as much as you can. No one had a watch, so we didn't even know whether it was night or day. The only time we saw daylight for a few seconds was when Grainger came through the door.

'I didn't even want to talk to the others, not after the first few days anyway. I did talk to Peter but the others got nasty about that. The place was very dirty. Along with the main room there was a kitchen, a bathroom and another room with mattresses on the floor. I used to clean it up, more for something to do than anything. Grainger brought us food – just sandwiches, pork pies and stuff. We never had a hot meal except the times he brought us fish and chips. But days would go by when we had nothing. That was another of Grainger's ploys. It was like dog training – give you a treat and then you'll do tricks. But I never crept round him. I looked at him like he was a maggot, and oh, how he hated that!'

'Didn't it make him punish you more?'

'Yes, with beatings, swearing and belittling me, but he didn't do the sex thing to me as often as the others. I think he was afraid I'd bite his cock if he forced that into my mouth.'

Duncan stopped at that, tears running down his cheeks, sobbing like a small child.

'That's it now, stop,' Dove said. 'I think you've said enough, don't you?'

Duncan cried for some time, till eventually the tears turned to hiccuping gulps.

'I told Peter when we were in the last place that I'd never be able to talk about it if we got out, and I really thought I wouldn't be able to.'

'I think it was your courage in standing up to Grainger that saved you,' Dove said gently. 'So it was worth it.'

'Maybe. I fought him for Peter too. He was going to take him somewhere one time; I was sure it was to kill him as well, so I lashed out at him as it was only us left. Just after that he took us to the cellar where we were found. He never did anything further to us once we were in there, I think because we were too dirty. He just dropped food and the odd bottle of water down through the hatch. But he stopped coming for days on end, and when I saw how frail and ill Peter was getting I really regretted demanding he stayed with me.'

'Well, thanks to you and Maisy, Peter got to be rescued, he had food and medicine, and he wasn't strangled and put into a shallow grave.'

'Maybe,' Duncan sighed. 'But I'm not sure Peter was aware enough at the end to know he'd been saved. He might have fought harder to live if he had been.'

'You must stop reproaching yourself about Peter. You did the best you could.'

Duncan's eyes were filled with pain and sorrow.

'I can't really believe I've told you all that. Did you know men could do such things?'

'Not till I was a lot older than you, Duncan,' Dove said. 'I think the army attracts its share of bullies and men with perverted tastes. But you must always remember that men like that are a very small minority. When you get married and have children of your own you mustn't start thinking your sons and daughters are going to be attacked. Teach them how to keep safe – no going off with strangers and suchlike – but always try to remember there are more good and noble people in the world than there are bad.'

'Like you, Grace and Janice,' Peter said. 'All three of you are inspirational.'

Mr Dove smiled at the compliment. 'And you, Duncan, will get to be a doctor even if I have to rap you over the head with a biology book to keep you at your studies.'

At the end of May, a few days after Duncan had talked to Mr Dove, Maisy had the plaster taken off her arm.

'I bet it felt marvellous when they cut it off,' Janice said, taking Maisy's forearm in both her hands and rubbing it gently with a little cream because the skin looked so dry.

'It's liberation,' Maisy said. 'I might have learned to do most things with one arm, but I'm dying to submerge myself in a bath, to wash my hands properly, and to turn over in bed without it clonking on something and waking me.'

Janice smiled. 'I'm glad you won't be complaining about itches and asking me to poke knitting needles down it any more.'

'See how weak and sickly-looking it is compared to the other, suntanned one, though.' Maisy held up her arms together. 'I shall be known throughout the county as the girl with odd arms.'

'I could rub some gravy browning into it if you like,' Janice suggested. 'But I suppose you want to ride out to see Duncan now?'

'I thought I'd go tomorrow,' Maisy said thoughtfully. 'When he came over last week he seemed so much more relaxed, didn't he? And so suntanned. I got the feeling he wants to stay there forever.'

'Is he starting to come to terms with what happened to him, do you think?' Janice asked.

'I don't suppose he'll ever talk to me about it. He might be my brother but he's very like his father in many ways. Sweetly old-fashioned, believing ladies mustn't be told bad stuff.'

'I don't think you should know nasty things either,' Janice said. 'You've changed so much since the day Duncan disappeared. Most of it is good, but I worry about a few things.'

'Something like that makes you grow up fast,' Maisy said soberly. 'But what is it that worries you?'

'That maybe you need to step back and be a young girl

again, have foolish fun, go dancing, have a sweet romance. I sometimes feel you're like a lioness poised for danger. It isn't good for you to be so suspicious of everything and everyone.'

'I suppose as long as Grainger is out there free to attack another young boy, I can't help looking over my shoulder.'

'I'm convinced that wife of his has hidden him,' Janice said. 'Not necessarily round here, but he could have rung her and got her to meet him somewhere.'

Maisy shook her head. 'She'd have to be very stupid to do that. If she has helped him, she'll end up in prison. Besides, I can't believe any woman would condone what he's done.'

Deirdre Grainger was in despair. She had done absolutely nothing wrong, yet she was being treated as though she was a murderer.

She was completely trapped. She couldn't drive to the north of Scotland or somewhere far away because the police were watching and would follow her. The idea she'd had of taking her jewellery to London to sell wasn't a viable one either – she was sure if she attempted to get on a train she'd be arrested. Yet she felt if she stayed in here another day with the curtains drawn against prying eyes, she'd go mad.

She couldn't even go along to the grocery shop down the road for food because they had refused to serve her, so she had to get in her car and drive into Bournemouth or Southampton with a headscarf and sunglasses on, praying no one recognized her from the newspapers and television news. Even then the police followed her.

Did they really believe she would help Donald after what he'd done?

Her own family, her brother, two sisters and her mother, had disowned her. She had written to each of them, pleading for them to believe she was as much a victim as all the others. But they had hardened their hearts to her, and the worst of it was that they were never going to relent, not even when he was finally caught and hanged.

The days were endless, the nights even longer, and she had absolutely nothing to fill the time. She cleaned things, she tidied drawers, but she couldn't go into the garden because people threw things at her. They managed to attack her from the back of the house too, which they could reach from an alleyway. She'd had the fence set fire to, tins of paint thrown over the lawn, dog mess hurled at her windows, weedkiller put on her bushes and flowers.

In many ways the garden now mirrored what had happened to her life. Once it had been her pride and joy, almost a show garden with a manicured lawn, a fish pond and flower beds and not a weed in sight.

Now it was destroyed: plants dead and dying, and the pond full of rubbish and dead fish, because they'd been poisoned too. The lawn looked like a bit of waste ground now, with clumps of grass growing around the many broken bottles and cans that had been hurled on to it.

It was a similar story when she looked in the mirror. She saw a blotchy complexion, and her eyes, which had always been described as cornflower blue, were now dull and red-rimmed. Her auburn hair had lost all its shine and bounce. She'd even found several grey hairs. She was no longer the glamorous woman who used to turn heads.

She was thirty-seven, and Donald had not only laid waste to her life and her future; he had destroyed her will to even try to rebuild her life. She had married him because she loved him; richer or poorer was what she had vowed. If he'd lost all his money and they'd had to go and live in rented rooms because of some failed business venture, she could have lived with that.

But when she'd said those other words at the wedding, 'for better or worse', she never dreamed 'worse' could be this kind of hell. Night after night she'd lain awake thinking on what she knew he'd done. Not just killing those boys, but raping and beating them. The tragedy didn't stop with their deaths; it had ruined the lives of their parents, siblings, relatives and friends. If he was to walk in here now she would pick up the carving knife and thrust it through his black heart.

Of course he wouldn't walk in here. He would know that he could never look any decent person in the eye again, especially her.

She couldn't look anyone in the eye herself. Deep down she felt that he may have become like this because of her – something she did or didn't do.

Getting up off the sofa she went to the cupboard under the stairs and pulled out the hank of washing line he'd promised to put up over a year ago. When the police had searched the house they'd asked her about it. If it hadn't still had the pristine paper band around it, bearing the name of the local ironmonger, they would probably have taken it away as potential evidence.

Deirdre had learned to do many kinds of knots in the Girl Guides, and Donald had often complimented her on her slip knots when they needed to tie something to the roof rack. She intended to make this the best and final slip knot of her life.

An hour later she was ready, the rope secured round the balustrade on the upstairs landing, with just enough slack over the stairwell to achieve her aim.

She took off her slippers, placed a chair on the little bit of landing by the window and stood on it. There was a touch of irony in that when they'd come to see this house with a view to buying it, she'd loved this small space behind the balustrade, just big enough for a small bookcase and an easy chair. She thought it was rather grand but Donald had always said it was a waste of space. Since she'd become trapped in the house, she often sat here with a book, as it felt safer.

Picking up the noose she'd made, she tried sliding the knot up and down a few times to check it didn't stick. She then put it around her neck, stepped on to the balustrade, and jumped.

It was just after one in the afternoon when Grainger rode the BSA motorbike up the small, rutted lane into the forest.

He was feeling smug at finding a method of transportation which enabled him to travel cheaply, but also without being noticed. He had acquired it by a stroke of luck. After he abandoned the Rover 90, he stole an old Ford and drove it along the south coast in the direction of Eastbourne. He had no real plan about where he was going, but coastal resorts were safer with so many strangers coming and going for holidays.

It was six in the evening and raining when he turned off the main road to visit Seaford Head, a place where he'd often camped with the Scouts as a boy. He remembered an old coastguard's cottage there which he thought he might be able to get into to stay the night.

There were no cars parked below the steep walk up to the cliff top, and the whole area was deserted, not even a lone dog walker. But standing alone in the car park was the BSA motorbike.

For a brief period in his life he'd had the same motorbike, so he stopped to look at it. Then when he looked up, he saw the owner of the bike, a young man of about twenty wearing an old leather flying jacket which was too big for him and holding his crash helmet, coming down from the cliff top.

Grainger could see he was upset. He was mopping at his eyes, his shoulders hunched up.

'What's up, son?' Grainger asked the lad as he got nearer.

'Everything,' the man replied, sniffing. 'My girl told me to go and sell the bike – she's sick of getting cold and wet riding pillion. She said until I come back with a car to take her out, she don't want to see me.'

Grainger was pretty certain the lad must have gone up to the cliff top with the crazy idea of ending it all, but thought better of it once he was there. Grainger couldn't feel any sympathy with someone so feeble they'd even think of suicide because their girl didn't like motorbikes. But he did see an opportunity looming.

'I'm sorry, but if she means that much to you why don't you sell it?' he asked.

'I asked at a couple of garages, but they only offered me

'thirty quid for it, and the only cars you can get for that are clapped out.'

'You need a motorbike enthusiast,' Grainger said. 'Funnily enough, I'm one. I'd swop my car for that bike any old time.'

'Really?' The boy looked at the Ford, which was in good condition, back to the bike and then back to Grainger. 'You serious?'

Grainger hadn't been entirely serious, not because he didn't want the motorbike but because any sensible person would expect there to be a catch. But by the slow way the lad spoke, he wasn't too bright. It was like taking candy from a baby.

'Never more so,' he said. 'I used to ride a bike back when I was your age and I miss it. You say the word right now and I'll swop. I'll even take your jacket and you can have my raincoat. It's an Aquascutum, cost a small fortune.' He flapped it to show the checked lining and label. Not that the dim lad would know an expensive raincoat from a cheap one. 'You could drive to your girl's place right now. Think how impressed she'll be that you did it for her.

'Tell you what,' he went on. 'Write down your address and I'll pop the log book in the post to you when I get back to Hastings tonight. I'll give you mine so you can do the same thing.'

He took a card from his wallet belonging to Richard E. Wyatt, a businessman from Hastings who had approached him over a year ago about doing some legal work for him. His business was an engineering company. As it happened, Wyatt found someone else, but Grainger was quite happy to be Wyatt for now.

The lad stared at the address; clearly it was a good one. 'Well, if we're going to do this, let's make it now before we get soaked to the skin,' Grainger chivvied him, handing him the notebook.

The lad scribbled down his name and address, and Grainger smiled as he read it: the boy lived in a village just outside Eastbourne. 'Let's be having the leather jacket. Your girl is going to think you've won the pools when you turn up.'

And that was that. Grainger donned the flying jacket and the crash helmet, started up the bike and roared off. He didn't even look back to see what the chap looked like in his coat – all he cared about was that it would be in Eastbourne tonight. It might be weeks before the police found it; they usually only found stolen cars when they were abandoned. Jennings was so pleased with the exchange he'd be washing and polishing it weekly – he wasn't going to abandon it.

Since that night the weather had been good, and if it hadn't been for the fear that he might run into a road block, Grainger would have been really happy. He enjoyed taking back roads through little villages and loved the warmth of the sun on his face. He was even getting to like the challenge of finding a bed for the night – sometimes a caravan, sometimes a barn – and the further challenge of finding some money. A pound note left on a doorstep for the milkman, a charity box in a church – one day he even nipped into an open kitchen door and snatched up a purse lying in full view on the table. That was a real corker of a day as the purse contained nearly seven pounds.

But although he tried to convince himself that he was Jack the Lad, leading the police a merry dance, when the sun went down and he was cold and hungry, reality set in. He knew this couldn't go on forever. He was going to be caught eventually and hanged.

Again and again he thought what that would be like. He didn't want to carry on living if he had to exist like a tramp, and that was how it would always be without enough money to get out of the country and create a new identity. But he was scared of prison and the build-up before they finally put the noose round his neck. What would make it easier to contemplate, would be to plan to go out with a bang: to cheat the police by going back to the one place they assumed he'd never dare return to.

He had read in the newspapers that they watched his house constantly; foolishly imagining that he'd want to see Deirdre one last time. As if! All she'd been good for was cooking, cleaning and laundry; he called her Dreary Deirdre to himself because she was about as much fun as a dose of clap. He certainly didn't want to go to her. It was Burley and the forest that beckoned him.

He'd spent so much of his youth there – it was where he remembered having fun and adventures, and learning things. In fact his first tryst with a man with the same interests as him had been there, and others since.

As a successful solicitor he'd driven through it almost every day, wishing he lived there. From the first time he was asked to call on Violet Mitcham in a professional capacity, he began thinking about how he could manipulate her into leaving him Nightingales. He had thought he almost had it in the bag, all those months of pandering to her, listening to her vitriolic ramblings, charming her, taking her out for tea.

If it hadn't been for those damn twins, and that nosy parker of a mad woman, he might have succeeded. He'd even considered seducing the girl, so he could get his hands on her inheritance once the old girl died.

His biggest mistake was to take Duncan.

His other boys had always been life's rejects – not very bright, from bad families, the kind of boys who wanted to be loved. They were easy to dominate, eager to please.

But Duncan! It wasn't a bad idea just because he had a connection with the family, but because he was never his kind of boy. He was highly intelligent, well brought up, and with such strong principles that he'd have died rather than give in. He had to admire him for that, and for trying to protect that weakling Peter. Perhaps that was the reason he didn't kill him.

The old mad woman in the wood was his target now. He intended to make her death painful and drawn out. She was going to suffer, because she'd made him suffer. He was growing excited just thinking about it.

23

Grainger didn't know exactly where in the forest Grace Deville's shack was, but he had heard a few years ago that she kept a van at old Enoch's place, so it couldn't be far from there. It was June now, he'd been on the run since Easter back in April, and although he was sick and tired of being constantly vigilant and on the move, being back in the forest felt good.

He drove past Enoch's, remembering how he and his friends would knock on his door and run away. Enoch would come out shaking his fists, which they thought was very funny.

There was an old blue van parked up beside his cottage. It had to belong to Grace as Enoch didn't drive. He thought from what he knew about them, Grace and Enoch would make an ideal couple. Both recluses, as mad as hatters and cantankerous. The New Forest seemed to attract oddballs. He remembered that when he was a child, at least three women in the area had been reputed to be witches.

He quite liked it that he was likely to appear in New Forest history. He wondered what they would call him. The Slaying Solicitor, Gruesome Grainger, the Burley Beast? Maybe he'd even be depicted in Madame Tussauds in London.

Parking his motorbike just before Enoch's place, he

walked along on the forest side of the lane opposite Enoch's looking for trampled vegetation. He could only see animal tracks, but there was one place which looked as if a human had recently pushed their way through.

He was hot in the flying jacket, and it was cumbersome, so he went back towards his motorbike and pushed the jacket and his crash helmet into a nearby bush to hide them from thieves. No point in hiding the bike as no one knew he had it.

He smelled very ripe as he hadn't found anywhere to wash for the last two days. His beard was thick now, and it would have been a first-class disguise if the police hadn't recently given the press a mock-up picture of what he must look like now with a beard. He opened the pannier bag on his bike and took out the ropes, putting the long length around his shoulder and chest and securing the shorter lengths to his belt, along with his hunting knife.

Walking carefully, making as little noise as possible so as not to alert the old girl's dog, his progress was slow. But he could smell smoke so he was fairly certain he was going in the right direction. About fifteen minutes further on, the shrubs and trees began to thin out. Peering through a bush he saw a glade ahead and assumed this was the right place.

He moved himself into a position where he could see more and crouched down, pulling back a branch to peer through.

A hundred yards or so ahead, to his surprise and delight, was Duncan, digging up a piece of rough ground. He looked good, wearing only shorts and boots, his naked torso tanned a deep golden brown.

As he watched, Grace Deville came into view. She was wearing a navy blue baggy shirt, equally baggy trousers and a straw hat. She appeared to be showing Duncan a piece of paper. He stuck his spade into the ground and pushed his blond hair back off his face as he listened to what she was saying. He looked more mature and stronger than Grainger remembered, and he felt his cock unexpectedly responding.

He thought the paper she was showing the boy must be a shopping list, because she had a string shopping bag in her hand and as she walked away, she put two fingers between her lips and whistled. At that the black-and-white collie dog came bounding over to her.

She disappeared into the bushes on the far side of the glade, the dog going with her, and Duncan picked up his spade again and continued to dig.

Finding Duncan here was like winning the pools. He'd daydreamed of killing him to hurt both his father and his sister, but thought he was unlikely ever to find him alone. But here he was, in the middle of the forest, a sitting target.

Getting himself into a more comfortable position, Grainger mulled over his options. He needed to think about how he should tackle Duncan, and also to check out the whole area.

He couldn't strike now while the boy was out in the middle of the clearing. To get the element of surprise he needed to be hiding in a place where the boy had to go.

As far as he could see there were only three places: the stream to get a drink or wash his hands, the privy, or the shack the old girl lived in. He ruled out the stream as there wasn't enough cover, and he didn't think he could get into the shack without being seen. But the privy would be good – big enough to hide behind while Duncan went in, then jump on him as he came out.

Grainger decided he would get into position right away, but if he crept around in the bushes close to the glade, Duncan was likely to hear him. So he retraced his steps back towards the road, then once he felt he was well out of earshot, he made his way diagonally through bushes and brambles in the direction of the privy on the other side of the shack.

It was hard going, almost impossible to get through in parts, but he persevered. All the while he could hear the sound of Duncan's digging, so he knew he wasn't making him suspicious.

Once he reached the privy and was well hidden by a bush, he sat down to make himself comfortable and thought how he was going to kill the boy. He had a knife and rope, so it could easily be stabbing or strangulation.

But neither of those deaths hit the right spot for him. They were too quick; he wanted to be able to relish the boy's pain.

Then it came to him.

Burning alive. Even by his standards it was brutal, but if this was to be his swan song, he might as well make it one that would be talked about for years.

Capture the boy, gag him, tie him to a tree or a post, then light a fire under him. Just the thought of it made his heart beat faster, and his cock twitch again.

Better still, what if he tied the boy to the tree, then waited for the old girl to come back and tied her up too, where they could easily see one another? That way, they would not only feel themselves burning, but see the other one burning as well.

He peeped out from his hiding place and saw the ideal trees. One was behind where Duncan was digging now, the other fifty yards in front of him, close to the way Grace had gone. Two strong, mature trees. Perfect.

When Grace got back she'd rush to Duncan to untie him, assuming that someone had robbed the shack. Then Grainger would step out from behind the bushes, seize her and tie her up.

The dog was the only problem. Grainger had heard the noise the beast made when it attacked Hugo, and he didn't want that happening to him. The newspaper said Hugo's face was disfigured. Perhaps he could bargain with Grace, tell her that he wouldn't hurt her and he'd let Duncan go as long as she tied the dog up for the time being. Would she do that?

Somehow he didn't think so, so he'd have to be prepared to kill it.

An hour passed and still Duncan kept on working. He was hauling out tree roots and big stones with a pickaxe, then breaking up the soil with a fork, making a very thorough job of it. He looked hot, and at one point he went over to the stream and drank greedily from his cupped hands, then splashed his face and under his arms with water, but he still didn't come over to the privy.

It was nearly three in the afternoon now, and Grainger was getting anxious. Not only was he very hungry but also the chances were the old girl would be back soon, and he'd have to abandon his plan for the day. Or come back when it was dark and set fire to the shack with them in it.

As he was mulling this over, Duncan suddenly speared

the ground with his fork and began walking over towards Grainger.

He stood up silently, almost holding his breath, heard the door of the privy open, and then heard pissing. At that he crept around the privy, standing where the door would be when it opened, a length of the rope in his hands and his knife ready in his belt.

The door opened, and out came the lad. Grainger leapt forward, swinging the rope around his throat and pulling back on it firmly.

Duncan yelled, bucked and writhed, waving his arms and kicking out with his legs, trying desperately to get free,

'Hold still,' Grainger warned him. 'I've got a knife and I won't hesitate to use it.' He pricked the boy's back to ensure he knew he really had one. 'Now just walk calmly back to where you were digging. No heroics, I don't want to hurt you, only to get some answers.'

He thought maybe Duncan was too shocked to speak or even struggle because he walked back across the garden quite calmly; he'd even stopped flapping his arms around. But he knew the boy was smart, so there was a strong possibility he was working on a plan.

'To that tree and put your back against it.' Grainger nudged him towards it. All at once Duncan began to fight him again, catching hold of Grainger's shirt with one hand and smashing his fist into his side.

The blow really hurt – the boy was stronger than he had expected – but then Grainger had a better position, standing behind Duncan with the rope around his neck and the end tightly wrapped around his own left hand. He pulled it even tighter so Duncan could do nothing but slump back against the tree, his fingers clawing at the rope to loosen it. 'Hands down,' Grainger ordered him, showing him the knife. 'Or you get this in your guts.'

He drew the blade across the boy's flat belly just hard enough to lightly pierce the skin. Bright red beads of blood popped out. 'Now, hands behind the tree trunk or I'll get your cock out and cut that too.'

Duncan obeyed. Grainger pulled one of the short pieces of rope from his belt to tie his hands together behind the tree, then another around his ankles to secure them.

'There, that wasn't too bad,' he said, coming round to the front of the tree to jeer at his prisoner. 'If only you hadn't been so prudish back at the big house. Things could've been so different. But I've cracked up now, you probably realize that. I'm officially a psychopath – I read that in *The Times*, so it must be true – and I don't care what happens to me. But I want one last bit of fun first.'

He pulled a lump of rag from his pocket and forced it into Duncan's mouth so hard it made him gag.

'That's better. You can't try to reason with me. I'll just sit and wait for the old hag to get back.'

It was only half an hour before she appeared. Grainger heard her in the distance, singing to herself, giving him enough time to hide behind a tree. Then he heard a rustle in the bushes and the dog came rushing out, going straight over to Duncan and jumping up at him joyfully.

That was a far better outcome than Grainger had expected. He went over to the dog, who was still intent on getting Duncan to stroke him, and quickly slipped a length of rope through his collar and hauled him away, bucking, barking and writhing, behind a bush.

It took just one thrust of the knife, straight into the top of the dog's head, and he fell to the ground.

Then, hiding himself again, Grainger waited for Grace Deville.

She came out of the bushes carrying a shopping bag. She saw Duncan immediately and dropped the bag and ran over to him.

'Who did this?' she shouted out. Grainger heard the faint mumblings of the boy trying to warn her, but it was too late. He leapt out from behind the bush and grabbed her wrists, pulling them back behind her and securing them. Like Duncan, she tried to fight, kicking out and even headbutting and spitting, but she was no match for him. He soon had her tied to the tree opposite the boy, with a rag in her mouth.

Grainger was so excited now that he felt he might burst. He went to the woodshed and filled a box with kindling, then made two piles, one in front of each of his captives. When he brought logs over he made a great show of slowly arranging them neatly on top of the kindling. 'I love fires,' he said, grinning at both of them. 'Did you know human flesh smells like roast pork as it burns?'

The old girl looked so terrified he thought she might have a heart attack. Her eyes were almost popping out of her head, her nostrils flaring, reminding him of a cow he once watched being led into an abattoir to be killed. She'd known that it was the end for her. He was fairly certain if he took the rag out of Grace's mouth she would bellow just the way that cow did.

Duncan's reaction was disappointing. He was remarkably calm, not struggling at all, just looking at the old hag as if trying to send her a silent message that someone would rescue them.

To make their misery greater and their fear sharper, he got the dead dog and laid it down between them.

That got a reaction from Duncan: his eyes widened and it looked as if a tear was running down his cheek. As for the old hag, she looked as though she'd like to skin her torturer alive.

Finally Grainger sat down on a bench to watch them. This was the best he'd ever known, two people tightly secured, scared out of their wits, and he could take his time now and savour their distress. Later when he poured paraffin on the logs and set fire to them he knew it would be like the biggest and best orgasm ever. But for now it was enough to just sit, watch and anticipate.

Maisy rode her bike to Enoch's cottage because that way was easier going, and not so far to walk to Grace's.

She had brought with her a jam and buttercream Victoria sandwich she'd made herself that morning, and a bottle of elderflower wine made by Janice.

Leaving her bike propped up against a tree, she noticed the motorbike parked by the bushes and was immediately suspicious. She had never before seen a motorcyclist come into the forest. There were plenty on the roads, and parked outside the tea shops, but somehow she didn't see men who rode motorbikes as being people who went for walks. It just didn't fit.

Besides, if the owner of the motorbike had been calling on Enoch he would have left it by Grace's van. Suppose it belonged to some lout who'd heard the rumours about

Grace being eccentric and possibly rich, and had come to try and rob her?

Although Maisy didn't think Grace could come to much harm with Duncan there, she still took care to be stealthy along the overgrown path. Within a couple of minutes she realized it was very quiet – too quiet, she thought – no barking from Toby, no shouts from Duncan, or even the sounds of digging, chopping or hoeing. Her heart started to beat faster.

The path came out very close to the shack, but she stopped further back to peer through a bush to see what was going on. What she really hoped to see was both Duncan and Grace fast asleep on the grass, and she even thought if they were she'd give them a scare by banging on the old tin bath hanging on the side of the shack.

But what met her eyes was a man with a bushy dark beard sitting on the bench. It was a second or two before she recognized him, and only then because he was looking intently at something to his right. Grace, tied to a tree.

A cold shiver ran up Maisy's spine. Grainger! And what had he done with Duncan?

Moving slightly, she spotted her brother tied to another tree, and what made it even more terrifying was that there were piles of firewood in front of both of them. And Grainger had a paraffin can next to him.

Placed an equal distance between Grace and Duncan was Toby, clearly dead, the white parts on his face and coat stained with blood.

For a second or two Maisy thought she was going to faint with shock. She bent over so her blood would travel to her head again, and then turned to go and get help. But she had only taken a couple of steps when it occurred to her that Grainger could strike a match at any time. It would take at least ten minutes to get to a phone, and heaven only knew how long for the police to get here.

She had to act herself. But what could she do alone? He could easily overpower her.

Then, like a flash of lightning in her head, she remembered Grace had a shotgun.

It was fixed in a rack just inside the front door of the shack. She had told Maisy she always kept it loaded just in case anyone did try to come and hurt or rob her.

There was no question of getting into the shack by the front door. Grainger would see her immediately. But there was a window at the back.

Creeping on tiptoe so she didn't even step on a stick or rustle a bush, she got round the back. The window was about five feet up, and there were no toeholds, so she had to get big stones and pile them up.

Her heart was hammering. If she delayed or he heard her, they could be burned alive. After all, he had nothing more to lose now. Finally she was able to reach the window, prise it open, then climb in.

Grace's bed was just below the window. She had hung a curtain round it since Duncan arrived, and he slept on a mattress the other side of it.

After the bright sunshine outside it was gloomy inside, and very warm, because Grace always kept a fire going to cook on. Maisy made her way across the room to the shotgun, offering up a quick prayer that she could do this.

She had never held a gun in her life, much less fired one. But Grace had talked to her about shooting once, so she hoped she knew enough. The main thing was that she had to shoot straight and kill Grainger. A minor injury wouldn't do. It was all or nothing.

Glancing out through the small side window she saw Grainger hadn't moved. His back was to her, and he was looking from Duncan back to Grace, taunting them with the paraffin can. To see Toby lying on the grass between them, and to know he'd killed that beautiful, clever dog was just too much.

It was all she could do not to rush out of the door screaming in rage at him. But she took a deep breath and brought the gun up to her shoulder, then held it firmly and looked down the sights.

'You have to squeeze the trigger,' Grace had said. 'Take your time to line up your target then gently squeeze.'

'Guide me, Grace,' Maisy murmured as she made her way out of the door and on to the veranda. She stopped there, gun to her shoulder, and looked down the sights till she had Grainger's back right in the middle.

Slowly, she went down the three steps on to the grass, and still keeping him in her sights, she walked closer.

She didn't dare look towards Duncan or Grace but she felt they had seen her, and she tried to breathe in their spirit to strengthen her own.

When she knew she was close enough she stopped dead.

'Prepare to die, you bastard,' she screamed out, and as he spun on his seat to face her she squeezed the trigger. The recoil of the gun on her shoulder almost knocked her over, but not before she saw Grainger fall to the ground.

24

Maisy crumbled and fell to the ground, so shocked by what she'd done that she couldn't stand. But a second or two on the ground, blood racing back to her head, brought her out of it and she got to her feet again.

She checked first that Grainger was really dead, although she had no real knowledge of how you did this. He had a hole in his chest and blood was gradually soaking the whole of his shirt front. He certainly wasn't breathing and his open eyes looked glassy and sightless. Maisy ran first to Grace, snatching the gag out of her mouth.

'Oh Grace, how long had you been there?' She tried to untie her, but her hands were shaking so much she couldn't do it.

'He had a knife,' Grace said. 'Get that for the ropes.'

Maisy ran and took Duncan's gag out, then back to Grainger to find his knife. It was beside his body. For a second or two Maisy stared at the hole in his chest and the blood slowly turning his shirt raspberry red, and wondered how she had been able to do it.

The questions and praise came the second both Grace and Duncan were released.

'You were magnificent,' Duncan said, tears streaming down his cheeks. 'You never wavered. I watched you walk down from the shack and my heart was in my mouth in case you missed when you fired. I can't even find the words to tell you how brave you were.'

'I can,' Grace said, coming towards Maisy with her arms wide open. 'The bravest, cleverest and most cool-headed person I've ever seen.'

Maisy let herself fall into Grace's sweaty embrace and began to cry with shock.

'There's stuff we have to do,' Duncan warned them. 'First, call the police. If you two are OK to be left I'll go and ring them. Grace, you make yourself and Maisy a cup of tea. I'll just cover Toby up before I leave.'

'I'll do that,' Grace said, her lips quivering with emotion. 'My beloved Toby, he was such a loyal and devoted dog. I'm going to miss him so much.'

'It's so sad, and I'm terribly sorry for you, Grace, I know how much you loved him,' Duncan said. 'We'll bury him tonight. But I must go now. Maisy, is your bike by Enoch's? I'll take that.'

A short while later Grace and Maisy were sitting on the bench by the shack, with a mug of tea each. Maisy was still trembling with shock. Grace had covered Toby with his own blanket but she had refused to cover Grainger.

'Let the flies lay eggs on him, it's no more than he deserves,' she said. 'You know, Maisy, I thought I heard someone coming through from Enoch's. I prayed it wasn't you, and then I heard nothing more and I thought I'd imagined it.

'I was looking at Duncan and saw him looking towards here, so I looked too and there you were with my gun. I was with you when you shouted, I swear I guided that bullet. But did the recoil hurt your shoulder?'

'A bit,' Maisy said, rubbing it. 'I expect I'll have a fine bruise tomorrow. But let's talk quickly before Duncan comes back, because we know this is likely to shake everything up. Has he told you anything yet?'

'A little, but I think he told your Mr Dove more. If the police leave him here with me, I think he will tell the rest now. He's a great lad, and he's going to grow into a remarkable man. I've loved having him here.'

Maisy slid her hand through Grace's arm and nestled closer to her. 'We both love having you in our lives too,' she said. 'Who would have thought it? Remember that first time we came crashing through the bushes and you shouted at us?'

Grace leaned nearer to Maisy and kissed her forehead. 'I had a feeling that night I hadn't seen the last of you. As much as I hate what that animal of a man lying there has done, I can't be sorry he brought us three together.'

'You are an honorary mum now,' Maisy laughed. 'I think we may start bullying you into going to live somewhere safer, warmer in winter and with a few modern conveniences.'

'Maybe I'm even ready for that now.' Grace sighed. 'I don't think I'll like being here so much now, not without Toby and after all of this.'

Maisy didn't suggest she got another dog. She sensed that would be tactless right now. In truth she felt that, at this moment, nothing mattered for any of them: what to do with their lives, where to live, who to see. She had no doubt this feeling was partly due to shock. They'd lived under the Grainger cloud for a long time, and they had to put all that to bed now.

She also had to come to terms with killing a man. Right now it didn't seem real, as though it had happened in a film. But for the rest of her life she would know what she was capable of. And that was a little scary.

'I'm staying here with Miss Deville,' Duncan repeated a little more forcefully to Sergeant Williams.

It was seven in the evening now. Several lots of policemen had come, including a police doctor to verify Grainger's death, and afterwards his body was photographed from every possible angle, along with pictures of poor dead Toby and the piles of wood by the trees where Grainger had intended to burn them alive. Finally he was carted off to the mortuary, the shotgun taken as evidence, and both Grace and Duncan made statements about what had happened earlier.

Maisy hadn't made an official statement yet. She would do that in the morning at the police station.

Sergeant Williams had been trying to force Duncan for the last half-hour to go home with Maisy to Nightingales.

'I need to bury Toby and look after Grace,' Duncan said, in a tone that suggested the policeman ought to keep his nose out. 'Ideally I'd like Maisy to stay with us too, but that's up to her.'

'I would like to stay,' Maisy said, looking defiantly at the policeman. She had never wanted to be with her brother more. 'You can pop in to see our grandmother and tell her. I think she'll understand, and anyway we're old enough to make our own decisions.'

'This is all very irregular,' he grumbled. 'When I telephoned Mrs Mitcham to tell her what had happened she said you were to hurry home.'

'That's what you say to children coming out of school,' Maisy snapped at him. 'Grandmother has got Janice and no doubt she'll spend the evening on the telephone to our father. She's not a victim; us three are and we need to stay together.'

The policeman looked at Grace questioningly. She shrugged. 'You heard her. I wouldn't argue with a girl who can shoot that well!'

Duncan sniggered at Grace's joke and Maisy looked away so the policeman wouldn't see her struggling not to laugh. She could see the funny side of this whole investigation. The police had done little to catch Grainger – it seemed they'd hounded his wife more than him. She and Grace had done most of the work, and in view of that she didn't know how they had the cheek to try and tell them what to do now.

'You do understand, Miss Mitcham, that you could be charged with the unlawful killing of Mr Grainger?'

Grace stepped forward, her face flushed with anger.

'Are you mad, insensitive or just very dim?' she snarled at him. 'Yes, legally I expect charges will have to be made. But right now you've got a couple of kids who have been astoundingly brave, and done *your* work for you. They need to stick together, so bugger off right now and tell their grandmother.'

Sergeant Williams and the other men left the glade a

few minutes later and the twins burst into laughter. 'You were marvellous, Grace,' Duncan said. 'I can't really believe you told him to bugger off!'

Grace laughed, but there was real sadness in her eyes. The twins knew she was devastated by Toby's death. He had been her only friend and companion for a long time, and she was going to find life hard without him.

'I'm going to dig Toby's final resting place, Grace,' Duncan said gently. 'Will you come and show me where you'd like that to be?'

'He liked a spot over there,' she said, pointing to a slightly raised area close to the bushes which surrounded her glade. 'It gets the early morning sun and he liked to bask in it. But he was always back there on warm afternoons for the shade. He'd lie with his head on his paws and look down on me working in the garden.'

'Then that's where we'll put him,' Duncan said. 'You go on in while I'm digging. I'll come and get you when I'm ready to put him to rest.'

At ten that night, Grace lit some candles and a tilley lamp. They had buried Toby earlier with his ball and his blanket, and all three of them cried at his graveside.

They'd had sausages with potatoes baked in the fire for their supper, and they'd polished off the bottle of elder-flower wine Maisy had brought with her that afternoon. A large slice of Victoria sponge afterward went down very well, while they had a post-mortem on the events of the afternoon.

'Did you really think he was going to kill you?' Maisy asked. 'Or did you think someone might save you?'

'There was no doubt he really was going to set fire to

that wood,' Duncan said. 'You should've seen his face, he was really savouring how it would be. I couldn't think of anyone who might come by. We'd seen Enoch in the morning, and he told me he was going to Southampton on the bus. He wouldn't come over here anyway, and even if I'd thought you might turn up, I certainly wouldn't have imagined you could save us.'

'It's weird the thoughts that go through your head when you're scared. I thought of the dirty clothes by my bed that someone would come in and find,' Grace said. 'I was embarrassed about it. Imagine that!'

Maisy smiled fondly at the older woman. 'It's silly thoughts like that, that make us human,' she said. 'An animal has no sense of embarrassment.'

'I think his death has freed me,' Duncan said quietly. 'I feel lighter tonight, like something heavy has been taken from my shoulders. While he had me locked up, especially at first with the other boys, I felt he'd picked me because he knew I was weak and an outsider. The other boys were like that, you see. He would do terrible things to one of them, and make someone else watch. It was doubly horrible for the watcher because he knew the situation would be reversed in a day or two. Then it would be his turn.'

Grace and Maisy just listened, both sensing that this was his time to talk, and they didn't need to ask questions or pass comment.

'But even though I thought I was like the other boys, I would not accept it. So I fought him. Not punching him or anything, I hadn't got the energy or strength for that. But I didn't cooperate at all, not the way the others did, hoping

360

to gain favour. I let my revulsion show. I can't tell you what he made us do, to him, or each other, it's not something you can tell women. But I can tell you that it was my unwilling attitude that saved my life. I saw him take Michael and James out of that place, three weeks, maybe a month apart – I don't know exactly as it was hard to keep track of time – and I knew he was going to kill them. We all did, and we all thought next it would be us.'

He stopped, taking deep breaths as if trying to fight back nausea. Grace and Maisy waited.

'He had a real thing for me. It excited him hoping I'd get so desperate that I'd become willing. But sometimes he'd get drunk and talk to me, and at those times I almost felt sorry for him. He told me he'd had a thing for our dad. But Dad called him a reptile. He didn't say any more about that, but I got the idea that when he was young he'd been just like the other boys in there, weak, unattractive, kids that didn't fit in, so he punished them because he'd been punished. Does that make sense?'

Grace and Maisy were so surprised to be asked their opinion that they didn't answer for a moment.

'Yes, it does make sense,' Grace said after a couple of seconds. 'I've heard these things go on in a never-ending circle, the damaged child damages his or her own child, and so on.'

'I think you are kind that you try to find an excuse for him,' Maisy said.

'Not kind, I wanted to kill him. God, I hated him. But he was so messed up. I don't think he really fancied boys, even though he did that stuff. He was depraved, but it was all about having power over us. That's what really thrilled him. He was the same this afternoon. He could have lit the fires straight away, but he didn't because he wanted to enjoy seeing our fear and misery.

'Back in that place with the other boys I knew that the only chance of survival I had was to challenge him, be mean to him, to show I wasn't going to lie down and take it. I got more beatings than I want to remember, but I tried to pretend I was in one of those Japanese prisoner of war camps, like in *Bridge on the River Kwai*, that I had to hold it together and survive so I could escape.'

'Why did he move you to the cottage where we found you?' Grace asked.

'The other boys were all gone; Peter was really sick and would almost certainly die before long. I think he moved us there intending to leave us to die, but he couldn't quite do it. He came back now and then with some food and water – never enough, but it was something. I don't think he could actually bring himself to kill me. Not with his own hands.'

'Yet he was going to burn you alive today,' Maisy said.

'He said he had cracked, and I think he had. He said he was going to become a Legend of the New Forest.'

The three of them lapsed into silence, staring at the fire and sipping the wine.

After about five minutes, Grace spoke. 'As of tomorrow, you two must pick up your lives again,' she said, looking first at Maisy and then at Duncan. 'I think you need to go back to your grandmother's, Duncan, with Maisy.'

'But you'll be alone, without Toby,' Duncan said. 'Come home with us. I know Grandmother will give you a room.'

'I couldn't live in someone else's home now.' She smiled. 'Maybe I do have to find a safer, more modern home. I might go and ask Enoch tomorrow if he knows of anywhere. But you two have your whole lives ahead of you, and you must live them.'

25

July

Alan stepped right in front of Maisy, his face a picture of delight at seeing her.

'Hullo, Maisy. Gosh, it's good to see you!'

Maisy blushed. It was almost two years since they'd first met in Bournemouth, and a year and a half since he told her it was over after the Christmas dance. He was a bit taller now, his face had lost its boyish plumpness, and although she'd sworn a thousand times to herself that she would never feel the way she used to about him, she experienced that well-remembered lurch in her stomach.

She had hoped she might run into him in Lyndhurst – Linda had said he'd come home for the summer from university. She'd wanted to be able to confirm she really was over him. But perhaps she wasn't.

'It's good to see you too,' she replied. 'How's life in Bristol?'

'Come and have some tea with me and I'll tell you,' he said. 'Now I've actually caught up with you again, I don't want to let you go.'

It would have been an ideal time to say she was too busy, or even that she couldn't think of anything worse than having tea with him, but neither was true.

'Tea would be nice,' she said. 'I was going to pop round to see Linda later, but she isn't expecting me till four.'

He took her to the Copper Kettle further along the High Street. 'They do the most marvellous chocolate eclairs here,' he said as they took a table by the window. 'I dream of them while I'm in Bristol.'

She laughed. 'I'm sure your dreams are a bit more exciting than chocolate eclairs. But I like the cream slices here. Messy to eat, but yummy.'

'So tell me all, Annie Oakley,' he said once the waitress had taken their order for tea and cakes.

'Don't!' she said, holding up a hand like a stop signal. 'That's been said too often.' She wasn't really cross. One of the newspapers had called her the New Forest Annie Oakley and many people had used the name since. At times she even found it funny.

'OK, tactless, I suppose, but I was well impressed at what you did. As was everyone I know.'

'I need to live it down now,' she said. 'I was finally cleared of any charges. They decided self-defence and defence of another is a complete defence in law.'

'There would've been a public outcry if you'd actually been made to stand trial,' he said. 'I heard his wife topped herself. My parents knew the Graingers slightly, only casually at social things, but Mum said she doubted the woman knew anything about what he was up to.'

'It was awful that they didn't find her till three weeks after,' Maisy said. 'Right up till he was dead, the police were watching the house, by all accounts tailing her every move, yet they didn't find it odd that they didn't see her, or that there were no lights on in the evenings.'

'You should join the police,' Alan said with a wide smile. 'You seem to be a much more able detective than any on the local force. But what are you going to do now?'

'I'm not sure. My dad's coming down from London tonight, I think he wants to talk to Duncan and me about the future. You know I was an au pair in Brighton? I went back there recently to see the children, and Mrs Ripley, their mum, got me a two-day catch-up course for my shorthand and typing. I did the final exam too. I wasn't brilliant – good marks for accuracy, but lower for speeds – but I still passed. So I might get a secretarial job if I go back to London.'

'Do you want to do that?' he asked.

'Not really, but I think secretarial experience will be good for almost any career. Also it would be good to get away from everyone here treating me like an exhibit in a freak show.'

'Well, it was impressive what you did. And people are only admiring, not being nasty. Even Grace Deville has stopped being seen as the local mad woman. How is she?'

Maisy grinned. 'That's the best thing to come out of it all. She's bought a tiny cottage very close to Nightingales. It's just got one bedroom up in the eaves, and downstairs a living room, kitchen and a bathroom – a really sweet little cottage. It's called "Robins", which is such a nice name.'

'Gosh, a real change from the forest, then. How was she persuaded to move?'

'I think it was all really because of Toby, her collie, being killed. I suspect she's secretly thrilled to have a bathroom and a proper sink and gas cooker, but it was the garden that swung it. It's huge – part orchard, a large vegetable patch and then lawns and flower beds, with lots of mature trees. She intends to keep bees, and of course her chickens. Also the garden backs on to the forest, so she's got all the advantages of her old home, with none of the disadvantages.'

'You are such a kind girl, Maisy,' he said, and his expression confirmed he was sincere. 'Taking such pleasure in Grace's new life, and I've no doubt you'll be helping her move in too.'

'It's not kindness, but gratitude and love. No one will ever know what she has done for me and my brother,' Maisy said. 'Duncan wouldn't be the happy boy he is now if she hadn't been there. We mightn't even be alive. We've come to think of her as family. And she us, I think.'

She and Duncan were astounded to find Grace had enough money tucked away in a bank to buy the cottage, but they were also very excited for her. This week they had been helping her paint and paper throughout the cottage, and Duncan had cut the grass, which had grown very long since Mrs Merriot, the old lady who used to live there, died.

Grandmother had given her some furniture she'd been storing in one of the spare rooms for years, and a lovely traditional red and gold Axminster rug with fringes. But the biggest surprise for Grace would come from Alastair the following Monday, as he'd bought her a refrigerator as a thank you for all she'd done for his children.

Maisy couldn't imagine what Grace would make of it – a fridge was a bit of modern life which had passed her by.

The waitress brought the tea and cakes, and they talked of more general things: books they'd read and films they'd seen, and Alan told her he'd taken up rock climbing.

'Why?' she laughed. 'What is the point of it?'

'To get to the top, of course,' he laughed back. 'It's great – exciting, scary, and you have to keep fit to be any good at it. I'm going up to Scotland in September to try a couple of mountains there.'

'Do you still do any dancing?'

He grinned. 'Only the odd drunken stagger round the dance floor at university dances and balls. Mostly everyone jives now, no one does quicksteps. I only ever went to a few lessons at uni because of you anyway.'

'Did you really?'

'Yes, it's true. I suppose I thought I'd see you again and by then my parents would've forgotten. I still can't believe I let them make me drop you. It must've been so hurtful to you.'

'It was, very, but my mind was really on what had happened to Duncan. It was a horrible time.'

'I wonder if we could try again now?' he said very quietly, reaching across the table and caressing her cheek. 'That is if you can forgive me?'

Just the touch of his fingers on her cheeks made her feel shaky.

'I forgave you a long time ago,' she said.

'Well, come to the dance at the village hall on Saturday with me?' he asked, looking right into her eyes. 'I'll even try to remember how to waltz if it will please you.'

'Can you ring me at home tomorrow?' she asked. She knew she would go, but she wanted to make him think he had to try harder. 'I think Duncan might like to go too, maybe even with Linda. He likes her.'

'She likes him too. So I think it will be a definite date. But I'll phone you anyway.'

*

Alastair arrived in time for supper that evening. He looked tired, and he said the traffic coming out of London had been appalling. But he hugged both Maisy and Duncan, something he'd never done back in the old days. He was different in so many ways now. He often took Grandmother to task for being so chilly and such a snob, pointing out she'd have more company if she wasn't so unpleasant to people. He was really interested in his twins now; they both felt he was trying hard to catch up on all he'd missed. He also told them funny stories about his work colleagues and even reminisced about his work in Europe at the end of the war.

After supper he said he wanted to talk to them, giving his mother a sharp look which suggested he didn't require her there. She didn't like that and flounced off to the sitting room, leaving them in the dining room.

'After all you two have been through it isn't easy for me to tell you this,' he began. 'But I want to take you to see your mother tomorrow.'

'Why now, Dad?' Duncan asked.

'Because she hasn't got much longer to live. The tumour has grown, and she has secondary ones in her lungs and in her lymph glands.'

Maisy gasped. 'That's awful.'

'For her it might prove a blessing,' Alastair admitted. 'She has no quality of life. She doesn't know people any more, and she's on constant medication for the pain. But I think you do need to see her, so that you don't feel cheated or feel bad that you hadn't visited while she was alive.'

'We would've gone before if you'd let us,' Duncan said a little sharply.

'I know, son, but believe me I was only trying to spare you something of an ordeal. She isn't the mother you remember from your early childhood any more; she can be frightening, violent sometimes. The chances are she won't know you either – she always thinks I'm a doctor when I visit.'

'What time do you want to leave tomorrow?' Duncan asked. That was his way of turning the conversation to something he felt more comfortable with.

'I thought about ten, we can have some lunch on the way. I've got to go and talk to your grandmother now – is that all right with you? We can talk more tomorrow in the car.'

'I wonder what he wants to talk to Grandmother about,' Duncan said as he and Maisy went upstairs. 'I thought he was being a bit cloak and dagger, didn't you?'

'No, your imagination is getting the better of you. I expect it's about us – whether to get us to go back to London with him, or to see if she wants us to stay.'

'In all this time we've been here, I'm still not sure she really likes us,' Duncan said thoughtfully, going into Maisy's room and flopping on to her bed.

'I think she likes us better than anyone else,' Maisy laughed. 'That's something. She hates almost everyone.'

'Does she really, though? Or could it just be an act, like she thought it was clever when she was young to be cold and aloof and she just stayed that way? How come our grandfather loved her if she was always like that?'

'Maybe she was a sensational kisser?' Maisy joked. 'Now get off my bed, I want to get into it. Tomorrow might be a bit harrowing.'

Duncan got up. 'I expect it will be, but I'm really glad we're getting to see her at last. Whatever she's like.'

Down in the sitting room Violet glared at her son. 'How dare you ask to see my will? It's private.'

'Grainger was your solicitor, we know now he couldn't be trusted with anything. What sort of son would I be not to check what he'd done with your estate?'

'I checked it,' she said stubbornly. 'It is exactly how I wanted it.'

'He would've given you a copy, but how do you know he hasn't altered the original, which he would hold for you?'

'If that's the case you won't find out anything by looking at my copy,' she said.

'Mother, I don't give a damn who you've left your estate to – that's your decision to make – but I'd be happier if you made a new will now, with another firm of solicitors. Surely you don't wish to have anything more to do with his firm?'

'No, of course not. All right, you can see it, but you won't like it.' She got up and crossed the room to her bureau, pulled down the flap and took out an envelope from one of the pigeon-holes.

Alastair opened it and read it.

'Now you're going to sulk because I left everything to Duncan,' she said peevishly. 'It was only so you wouldn't fritter it all away on that place you've got Lily in.'

'That is so uncharitable,' he said in exasperation. 'Lily is my wife, and as such I have a duty to care for her. It isn't her fault she got a brain tumour. If you'd had one would you have liked my father to stick you in some rat-infested loony bin because he didn't want to pay for you to have comfort?'

'Well, I didn't have one, so that's immaterial,' she said with pursed lips.

'But you're growing old now. How about me putting you in somewhere horrible when you're too feeble-minded to protest?'

'You wouldn't do that.'

'No, I wouldn't, because you're my mother, and I wouldn't do it to Lily either. But as for squandering your money on her, I couldn't even if I had wanted to, because she is dying.'

'Oh!'

'Well you might say "oh", and for the record, Mother dearest, I've never minded paying for Lily's care. I don't give a damn what you do with your estate, that's your business. But please call another solicitor to write a new will for you, and burn every single bit of correspondence you've had with that monster.'

'I will do that. I'm very sorry that I ever let him come into my life and meet the twins. But you always had it in for him, even when he was small. Why? Were you jealous?'

Alastair laughed. 'Jealous! God no, I felt sorry for him when he was small. I knew he'd been beaten a lot, and in the light of recent events, I suspect much worse. No, the reason I despised him was his cruelty. I caught him burning a cat one day. He'd put paraffin on it and then set it alight. It died before I could put out the fire. Then there was the interfering with little girls. Three times I caught him doing inappropriate things. He wasn't even twelve then.'

'But he joined up and did well in the RAF,' she said. 'He was something of a hero.'

Alastair shook his head. 'All rubbish. If it hadn't been for the war he'd have been thrown out. Remember, Mother, I have a lot of contact with the armed forces. He was never a fighter pilot as he claimed, he was in the stores, and there was evidence he was running a food racket there. He used the war to line his own pockets and I have no doubt he used some of the proceeds to persuade boys, and girls too, into nasty practices.'

Violet looked appalled, and her eyes were welling up. 'Why didn't you tell me all this before? I would never have let him near the twins if I'd known.'

'If you remember back when Father died, Grainger came to the house, smarming his way into your affections. I warned you then, Mother. I said he was a reptile that had no morals, that he had no interest in you personally, only for your money and the property. I said he would work on you until you thought of him as another son, a kinder, more thoughtful one than I was. But you accused me of jealousy, and said it was because he was handsome, bright and articulate, all things I wasn't.'

'I didn't say that!' she exclaimed.

'You did, Mother, and you were right about him being handsome – he was. But you mistook his smooth talking for kindness and generosity. He only used his sharp mind for devious plans. I am, and have always been, far more intelligent than that piece of human garbage. I may not offer flowery speeches, but I tell the truth. I'm also loyal, which clearly I did not inherit from you.'

'Oh Alastair, how can you say such a thing?' she bleated.

'I'm an old woman and you are my only child. Why are you turning on me?'

'I'm not turning on you, I just want you to admit your failings. For some extraordinary reason which I cannot really fathom, my children have grown fond of you. Somehow, despite Lily being ill for most of their lives, and me being an absentee, and undemonstrative father, they have turned out to be brave, honest, kind-hearted and generous young people. I am so proud of them, and my only regret is that I had no hand in it. So leave them your estate with my blessing. Just get a new solicitor and write a new will.'

He got up to leave the room, but weakened when he saw how crushed she looked.

'Duncan and Maisy do love you,' he said, putting his hand on her shoulder. 'Maybe your sarcasm and sheer bloody-mindedness has added a bit of grit to their personalities. I often see a bit of you in Maisy. But let's try to pull together as a family from now on. We all need one another.'

26

Hambledon Hall was not as Maisy had expected. She had imagined a Victorian red-brick hospital kind of place, with the interior painted dark green and cream, and that it would smell unpleasant.

But it wasn't like that. It was a big Georgian country house, set in large grounds with a long, tree-lined drive.

'It was used as a hospital during the war,' their father said as they approached the front entrance which had steps up to an impressive portico. There were tubs of geraniums everywhere, dispelling all ideas that they were going to witness some horrible sights. 'The families that once lived in homes like this back at the turn of the century floundered during the Great War. So many of their workers left to fight and never returned, and many of the women found they could earn more in munitions factories. Most people think it was a great shame, but personally I take the view that it was wrong for just a few people to hold all the riches, while the masses had nothing. The war at least began the process of making life fairer, giving opportunities to those who fifty years earlier would have had none.'

'Does Mother know what a nice place it is?' Maisy asked in a small voice. She was scared, of what she was going to see, and of losing all her good memories of her mother.

'She did at first,' Alastair said. 'If she was having a good day we used to sit out in the garden when I visited. But sadly the bad days came more and more frequently. The last time I brought her outside was spring of last year. There were millions of daffodils on both sides of the drive. It looked beautiful. That day she remembered taking you to Hyde Park, I think you must have been three or four. She said you wanted to pick the daffodils there.'

Maisy had a feeling that was the last time her mother had remembered she had children, because she saw how sad her father looked.

They had come straight to Kent, only stopping to buy some flowers on the way. Their father said he thought it would be better if they ate on the way back, as it wouldn't be so rushed.

The spacious entrance hall was all painted cream, a thick red patterned rug on the black-and-white tiled floor and a large, highly polished chiffonier to one side holding a huge vase of flowers.

'Good morning, Mr Mitcham.' An attractive, dark-haired lady in a blue uniform dress came towards them. 'And these must be the twins. Maisy and Duncan, I believe?'

'Yes, here they are, a little apprehensive. How is my wife today?' Alastair asked.

'Don't be nervous,' the lady said to the twins. 'Your mother is having one of her better days today. Her nurse told her you were coming. But I'd advise you not to stay long; she does get agitated if there is any change in her usual routine.'

She led them up to the first floor and along a wide corridor past many rooms, to the one at the far end. 'I'll just go in first to see everything is as it should be,' she said. She opened the door with a key and went in.

The twins got only a glimpse of a hospital-type bed

with a screen partially round it, but they didn't have to wait long before the door opened again and she beckoned them in.

'Nurse Franklin will let you out when you're ready,' she said, then as they went in she closed the door behind them and they heard her locking it.

Alastair led the way, putting the flowers they'd bought on a chest of drawers by the sink.

'Hullo, Lily,' he said. 'The twins have come to see you.'

The person lying in the bed looked nothing like the mother Maisy remembered. Her face was skeletal, her eyes sunken in and her hair nearly all gone, just wisps of it between bald patches. But the most alarming thing was that there was no recognition on her face or in her eyes. It was as if she couldn't see them.

'Hullo, Mummy.' Duncan moved first and took the bony, claw-like hand on the sheets in his hands. 'Are you going to tell me how tall I've grown? That's what everyone says.'

Maisy felt a bit bolder with Duncan making the first move, so she went round the other side of the bed and took her other hand. Just the touch of it made Maisy feel nervous, so dry and bony like the legs of a chicken. 'I'm Maisy,' she said. 'This is a lovely hospital. What a super view you have.'

The room had windows on two sides so the light flooded in. There were shutters folded back, and Maisy got the idea these would be shut and locked over the windows if her mother was having a bad day. The room was a bit bleak, with just a couple of landscapes placed high on the wall, clearly so they couldn't be reached, and everything else was just like a hospital room. But on the locker beside her bed there was a photograph taken seven or so years ago, of Lily and Alastair with Maisy and Duncan sitting in front of them. Maisy remembered it being taken in a studio in Shepherd's Bush. Her mother had made a scene that day, she recalled, something about putting on the wrong cardigan. They'd had to go straight home after the photo was taken.

The claw-like fingers gripped Maisy's, and the sunken, washed out blue eyes turned to her. 'Yes, it's Maisy,' Maisy said. 'I'm so pleased to see you, Mummy.'

'You are too old.' Her mother's voice was so weak that Maisy had to bend her head to hear her. 'You aren't my Maisy.'

'Of course she is,' Duncan said firmly from the other side of the bed. 'You just haven't seen us for a while. I'm Duncan, we're twins.'

Their mother's eyes went from Maisy's to Duncan's and back again. 'My beautiful babies,' she said. 'I didn't expect two.'

'You always used to say that,' Alastair chipped in. 'Every time I came home you'd say, "I didn't expect two." I used to say it was good, as you wouldn't have to bother again.'

'My Ally,' Mother said, and her mouth tried to smile. 'You came back.'

'Of course I came back,' he said. 'I've been coming every week since you first moved in here.'

All at once her eyes began to fill with tears and she squeezed Maisy's hand so tight it hurt. 'God save me,' she exclaimed. 'The devil is in my head again.'

'I think you'd better go now,' Nurse Franklin said.

'When she mentions the devil it's always the start of an episode.'

Maisy retracted her hand and kissed her mother's cheek. 'Bye, Mummy. I love you.'

Nurse Franklin took hold of Maisy's arm and made it quite clear they had to go now. She practically pushed them out the door and locked it again, then as they stood there, a trifle stunned at the hasty exit, they heard a roar.

It didn't sound human, more like the sound cows made when their calves were first taken away, only louder.

'Come on,' their father said. 'There's nothing we can do. They'll give her something to calm her down.'

They were outside back in the car before Maisy spoke. 'Did she make that noise because we'd been taken from her?'

She was in the passenger seat, Duncan behind. Alastair took her face in his hands and kissed her nose. 'No, sweetheart. It was the pain coming back. That's how it is now, a few short minutes of calm and recognition, then the storm comes, and each time it's stronger and lasts longer.'

'Isn't there anything they can do?' Duncan's voice was shaky.

'No, son, sadly they've tried everything. It's just a matter of time now, and it will be a blessed release for her.'

The twins barely spoke on the way home. They stopped near Arundel for some lunch in a pub, but they just ate the food mechanically, not even tasting it.

'I'm sorry I put you both through that,' Alastair said suddenly when they were nearly home. 'I thought you ought to see her, but now I wish I hadn't taken you.'

'Don't think that,' Duncan said. 'She knew who we were, even if it was just fleetingly. But I think the most

379

important thing to come out of today was for us to know you never abandoned her.'

Maisy turned to her brother, so glad he'd been able to put into words what she had thought, but couldn't say.

'Yes, Dad. Duncan's right. We were guilty of thinking that.'

Alastair shook his head and smiled sadly. 'I've been my own worst enemy, haven't I? Never talking about things like this to you. Never asking you what you thought. But let me tell you now, I married your mum because I loved her, whatever nasty little ideas my mother might have put in your head. And you two came out of that love. Never doubt that.'

Maisy spent all of Saturday afternoon getting ready for the dance. She had a leisurely bath and washed her hair, then set it on the new big rollers she'd spotted in the chemist's. Her new blue dress had a dropped waist, with a pleated skirt. The lady in the dress shop said it was the 'Twist dress' and she'd seen girls on television wearing ones just like it.

As she waited for her hair to dry under the plastic cap attachment to her hair dryer, she painted her toe- and fingernails baby pink.

Duncan had looked in from time to time, laughing at her preparations. 'Do all girls do this for a date?' he asked.

'Yes, well, I think so,' she said.

'You mean Linda might be polishing herself up too?'

'She's bound to be, so make sure you are equally well groomed,' Maisy replied. 'Let me look at those fingernails.'

He had scrubbed them, and by the smell of Attar of

Roses soap, he'd scrubbed his whole body too. 'You'll do,' she said.

Their father was going to drive them to Linda's house, and Alan would join them there. When they came down the stairs at six thirty, ready to go, Alastair whistled.

'Take a look at this handsome pair!' he said to Janice. 'All grown up and far too attractive for their own good.'

'You look so pretty,' Janice said to Maisy. The blue dress brought out the colour of her eyes, her blond hair was shiny and falling into loose curls on her shoulders. She thought Maisy looked like a beauty queen, and if that boy Alan didn't fall in love with her tonight there was something wrong with him.

Duncan looked like a matinee idol, tanned, broad shouldered and so handsome in his navy suit. No girl would be able to resist him.

'Outside for a photograph,' Alastair said. 'I've had my camera in the car for weeks, meaning to get a really good picture of you both. Now's the moment.'

He took several pictures in various places around the garden, and when his mother came out to see what was going on, he took some of her and Janice too.

'Let Janice take one of you, me and Duncan too,' Maisy said. 'We need family ones for when we're very old and our children ask about their grandfather.'

'I must say, you two look splendid,' Grandmother said when they were finally leaving. 'You have a wonderful time at the dance. Your father will be back to get you at twelve thirty. I'm sure that gives you enough time for a spot of canoodling.'

*

'Canoodling!' Maisy whispered to her brother as their father drove off from Nightingales. 'Is that the same as snogging?'

'I think so, and it's a nicer word,' Duncan said. 'I do hope I get to do some.'

Maisy squeezed his hand. She guessed that if he could say he hoped to kiss someone he really was on the mend.

As they walked into the hall, together with Linda and Alan, Maisy was swept back to that first dance here. It seemed like a lifetime ago, and so much had happened since then. But there were changes. Although the decorations were much the same, the music was coming from a young four-piece group who played Neil Sedaka, Bobby Vee, Elvis Presley and Ricky Nelson. There were far fewer older people here too, perhaps because ballroom dancing was now out.

But the feeling when Alan held her in his arms was the same: shivers down her spine, wanting to press closer to him, and yet sheer happiness at being out on a warm summer's night, with everything to look forward to.

When she glanced at Duncan and Linda they seemed to be having a ball too, laughing as they clowned and sang along with the song by Clarence 'Frogman' Henry: 'I Don't Know Why I Love You But I Do'.

Alan was surprisingly good at jiving, for someone who claimed he couldn't dance, and not bad at the Twist either.

It was almost the end of the evening when the band played 'My Kind of Girl' by Matt Monro. Alan held her tightly and sang the words to her as they danced. Maisy shivered with pleasure and wished the night could go on and on.

Alan promised he'd walk Linda home after Maisy and Duncan had been picked up by their father, but they had half an hour, and they spent it in the churchyard kissing.

Maisy heard her brother and Linda laughing; they seemed to be clowning around on the gravestones. She wondered fleetingly if Duncan was a bit scared or shy; after all, he'd never had a girlfriend before.

But being kissed by Alan put such thoughts out of her head. Sweet, tender kisses that made her feel she was fizzing inside like shaken up lemonade. Somehow she knew this was a romance that would stay the course; everything about it felt right.

All too soon Duncan was calling to her saying they must get back to the hall for their lift home.

As they walked back down the High Street, Duncan paused by a board outside the newsagent's where people advertised things they had for sale.

'Look, sis,' he called out. 'Collie puppies for sale.'

'You really need a collie puppy right now,' Alan joked.

But Maisy knew what her brother was thinking, and looked at the card.

'It's the farm that used to be Brady's, where she worked during the war,' she exclaimed. 'Well, that's it, Dunc, we have to go and see them tomorrow.'

'Who worked where during the war?' Alan asked.

'Grace.' Maisy grinned. 'And it's the most perfect housewarming present we could buy her.'

'I love the way a puppy wipes out our lovely evening together,' he said, with a mock mournful face.

Maisy leaned in to kiss him. 'It doesn't, it's been the best night ever. But we've got the rest of the summer hols to have more fun together.'

'But no more tonight, because there's your dad,' he said gloomily.

'Ring me tomorrow,' she said, and looking round for Duncan she saw he was kissing Linda as if his life depended on it.

'Was it a good evening?' their father asked.

'The best,' they said in unison, then started to giggle.

'Mine was fun too,' he said. 'Your grandmother insisted on me going through a box of old photographs to write on the back who was in each of them. This was for your benefit.'

'Thanks, Dad, wonderful,' Duncan said.

'Sarcasm is the lowest form of wit,' he retorted, and all three of them laughed.

'Do we take the puppy there before or after the fridge arrives?' Duncan said on Monday morning.

The previous day they had gone to the farm and found there were just two boy puppies left, both adorable. But one had all black ears and a white bib, and they decided he was the one. They paid the farmer's wife and asked that she keep him till the next day because they knew Grandmother would complain about a puppy in her house, however small.

Janice looked round from washing up at the sink. 'I've just seen the van from Tinkers Electricals go down the lane, so it will be delivered by now. You ought to whizz round there and show her she has to plug it in. When your dad left this morning he was a bit worried about that. Then you can get the puppy to her later. I just hope her heart can stand so much excitement in one day!'

Maisy and Duncan did as Janice had suggested – just as well, since Grace was looking quite perplexed when they got to the cottage.

'I don't know anything about refrigerators,' she said. 'The man that delivered it said to put it in the kitchen, but surely something that keeps things cool doesn't like being by a cooker?'

They assured her both things were well insulated, but anyway there was a better place to put it, opposite the sink, and a power plug there ready for it. They heaved it into position and plugged it in. Grace peered into it as if she expected something to happen.

'You put your milk, butter, meat and anything else that goes off in it,' Maisy explained. 'Let's do that now. It's warm today and that pantry isn't very cool at all.'

Grace didn't have that much to put into it. She was so used to planning and eating meals in one day, it was going to take a while before she saw the advantages.

'I used to give all the leftovers to Toby,' she said. 'But just this morning I had to throw out some ham cos it had gone off.'

She had made a start on arranging her new home, but she looked hurt when they said they had to go. 'I thought you would help me put down the rug, and things,' she said.

'We will later in the week,' Duncan said, trying not to laugh at her expression.

'That was mean,' Maisy said as they cycled away. They planned to put the puppy in the basket in front of Maisy's bike, and tuck a cloth over it to keep him safe. Duncan had found an old picnic rug of Grandmother's for him to sleep on, and the farmer's wife had said she would give them enough food for the next couple of days.

*

'Back already? Got nothing better to do with yourselves after all,' Grace said churlishly when they appeared at her door again.

'We have a special delivery for you,' Duncan said. 'You'll have to come outside.'

'Not some other new-fangled gadget?' she said. 'You know what they say about not being able to teach old dogs new tricks.'

'Just come with us.' Duncan took her hand and led her back to where the bike was in the front garden. 'How do you feel about teaching new dogs old tricks?' he said as he whisked off the cloth.

The puppy jumped up so its front paws were on the edge of the basket, his ears like little egg cosies trying to stand up too. But the twins barely looked at the puppy, only at Grace's face.

It was lit up, eyes wide with astonishment and a smile like a slice of water melon.

The puppy whimpered.

'Pick up your new baby,' Maisy said. 'He needs to get to know his new mum.'

'He's for me?' she asked, her voice going all squeaky.

'He certainly is, a token of our affection for you and a huge thank you for everything.'

She picked the puppy out of the basket and buried her face in his fur. She began to cry, but at the same time was laughing with joy.

'I don't know what to say. Thank you doesn't seem enough.'

'You might not say that when he's peed all over your new house,' Duncan said.

'We've brought an old blanket and enough food to tide him over till you get organized,' Maisy said.

Holding the puppy over one arm and stroking him with the other hand, Grace smiled at the twins. She suddenly looked ten years younger, her eyes bright, her skin glowing.

'It was the best day's work I ever did when I let you two into my life,' she said.

The new novel by
LESLEY PEARSE

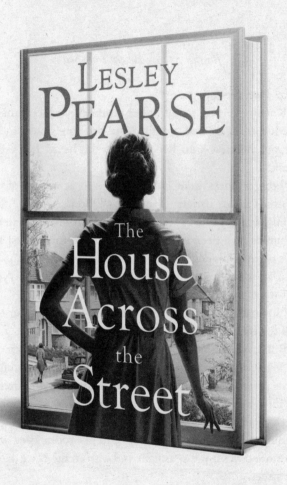

Read on for an extract . . .

I

'Fire! Fire! Get up, get up!'

Katy woke with a start at her mother's shrill command. She leapt out of bed, grabbed her dressing gown and as she put her feet into her slippers, she heard her father speak.

'For goodness' sake, Hilda. The fire is across the street, we aren't in any danger. Leave the children in peace.'

His plea was one of weariness and Katy's heart went out to him as he'd been in the office until late for the last few days because his engineering company was having an audit.

'You wouldn't think to jump into water even if your feet were on fire,' Hilda retorted. 'Lazy oaf!'

Normally such nasty remarks were like a red rag to a bull for Katy, but she just wanted to see the fire.

Rob emerged from his room as Katy passed his door.

'What on earth is going on?' he said grumpily, clutching at his pyjama bottoms as if afraid they would fall down.

'Fire, but Mum's probably over reacting,' she replied. 'Let's go and see.'

But as they stepped in their parents room they were astounded to see it was as light as day from the blaze across the street.

'Oh my goodness!' Katy exclaimed, her mouth dropping open at the scene outside the window. Vivid scarlet and yellow flames were licking up the front of the house and illuminating the whole street. Set against the night sky, it made a terrifying picture. This wasn't some little kitchen fire, but a real inferno.

'I can't believe it,' Katy burst out, her voice shaking with emotion. 'Poor Mrs Reynolds, I just hope she isn't still in there. Did someone call the fire brigade?'

'Of course I did,' their father said, pulling his trousers on over his pyjamas. 'I may be an oaf, but I can manage to dial 999. And now I'm going to check on whether she did get out, and if she has, I'll be inviting her and the neighbours either side back here.' Katy heard the steel in his voice and turned back from the window to look at him.

'Good for you Dad, can I help in any way?'

'No, you and Rob stay here in the warm with your mother,' he said, glancing at his wife, who had got back into bed as if nothing unusual had happened. 'It looks like it's freezing out there.'

He was right, away from the blaze the pavements sparkled with frost.

'Please God. Tell me she got out,' Katy felt faint at the thought of what might have happened. There were a few neighbours out there looking at the blaze, but she couldn't see Mrs Reynolds amongst them. She turned towards her mother. 'She's not out there Mum! Did you spot her when you first saw the fire?'

'No, but it was already blazing away when I woke, so she probably ran to someone's house.'

Katy nodded. She hoped that was the case. 'Usually on a Saturday night she goes to her daughters. Let's just hope she did this time.'

'Since when did you get to know that woman well enough to find out her movements?' Hilda asked, her voice sharp and disapproving.

Katy looked at her brother and rolled her eyes. It was typical of their mother that she would be more concerned with how her daughter knew someone, rather than expressing sympathy for their plight.

'Seeing as her shop is only two doors away from the office it would be very rude if I never spoke to her,' Katy said curtly. 'I like her, she's very interesting to chat to, and she's got two daughters, one's twenty-three like me. But it's the older one who she goes to on Saturdays. She lives in St Leonards.'

The bell on the fire engine drowned any response from her mother, and Katy turned back to the window to see more people arriving at the burning house. A police car came right behind the second fire engine. Two policemen jumped out to move the crowd further down Collington Avenue.

The blaze was so fierce now Katy could feel the heat even through the windowpane. As the firemen unrolled their hoses, she saw her father talking to old Mr and Mrs Harding. The pensioners lived in the house attached to the burning one. They were looking fearfully at the blaze, huddled together with coats over their night clothes, clearly afraid their house would soon be consumed by it too. She guessed her father was urging them to come over the road and wait in the warm.

Rob came over to stand beside Katy at the window and squeezed her forearm, his silent way of communicating his disapproval that their mother hadn't gone out there, too, to try and help in some way.

'I'll go and put the kettle on,' Katy said. She needed to do something, as just standing watching a house burning down seemed awful. 'Dad might bring people back, so maybe I should make some sandwiches too. Would you like something, Mum?' she asked.

'Some cocoa would be nice and a slice of that fruit cake I made this afternoon.'

Katy merely nodded confirmation she'd heard and made her way downstairs. She didn't understand why her mother was taking the fire so calmly. Even if she didn't approve of Mrs Reynolds, surely she would care whether she was alive or burned to death? As for the Hardings, they'd lived here for about fifteen years before Katy was born, and she and Rob had often gone to their house after school for tea. In fact, they thought of them as almost stand-in grandparents. At their age it must be awful to think their house and all its treasured contents might burn down too.

As she filled the kettle Rob came down. 'Sometimes I wish I was still five,' he said sadly, his mouth downturned. 'Back then I didn't know that other mothers cared about others, sang, danced, or chased their kids round the garden. I can't believe she hasn't gone out there with Dad to see if she can help. What's up with her Sis? She must have

393

a heart of stone. Was she born that way or did something happen to her?'

'I don't know, Rob,' Katy sighed. 'I used to pray at Sunday school that she'd change. The worst of it is that I almost don't notice how cold and hard she is any more. It's only because this is something so dramatic, so serious and so damaging for everyone affected that it's reminded me just how peculiar she is.'

'I'm definitely not coming back for the holidays any more,' Rob said. He was in his first year of studying for his Masters at Nottingham University. 'Each time I come back it's like a punishment, not a joyful homecoming. I'll miss you and Dad of course, but I can't deal with her any longer. She snipes at me, as if she resents my life. I don't think she's ever asked about my friends, or how I find the work, or even what my digs are like. All she does is clean and polish.'

Katy saw her brother was close to tears and she embraced him. He was just a year younger than her and they'd always been close. They were not allowed to go and play in other children's homes when they were little, so they believed all mothers were like theirs. Later when they were allowed to play outside and they learned that wasn't so, they found their own ways of compensating for a difficult mother who rarely showed any affection.

Rob was clever, he could make things: soap box carts, bows for archery, stilts and many other ingenious toys out of next to nothing, which made him popular. Katy found her niche by being daring, climbing trees, knocking on doors and running away and acting the clown to make the other kids laugh. Although very different in temperament, Rob being shy while Katy was outgoing, they made a good team, supporting each other and sharing their resources.

'I've been considering moving to London,' Katy admitted. 'Funnily enough it was Mrs Reynolds who put the idea in my head. She said Bexhill is the dullest town in England and I ought to be whooping it up in a big city. She was right; Bexhill is dull. Dancing at the De La Warr Pavilion on a Saturday night is as good as it gets. The only boys I ever meet are the ones I went to school with, and half of them are married now with a couple of kids.'

'I'd suggest you come up to Nottingham, as I'd love you to be there, but I don't think it's a very good place unless you are at the university. London is where everything is happening now, so I'm told.'

Katy smiled at her brother. 'I wouldn't want to cramp your style. And anyway, if I go to London you can come and stay with me.'

As Katy buttered some bread for sandwiches, she thought about her parents. Katy had once got a sneaky peek at their wedding certificate. They were married in May of 1941, and she was born five months later. As she understood it that wasn't unusual then: they said people lived for the moment and many brides were pregnant. But it was very hard to imagine her mother having ever being swept away by passion. She was so totally disapproving of pre-marital sex. When she'd tried to explain about the birds and bees to Katy, she looked and sounded like she was almost choking at the thought of such things.

So why her dad had ever been attracted enough to Hilda to even speak to her, let alone sleep with her, was unfathomable. Albert was almost the exact opposite to her mum: kind, caring, softly spoken. He was a tall, handsome man with thick dark hair, good teeth and a ready smile.

She longed to ask her mother about those days and her romance with Albert, but Hilda wasn't the kind to confide in anyone, and she found personal questions an affront, even if they were from her own children.

It was mainly the problems with her mother that made Katy want to leave home. But she also longed for the hustle and bustle of London. Here she felt she was under a microscope. If it wasn't her mother cross-examining her, it was friends and neighbours constantly watching her.

Bexhill wasn't just dull, it was quiet too. A story had gone around that the police had once pulled the vicar in for questioning because he was out after nine on a winter's evening. They were convinced he was a burglar, and refused to believe he was visiting a sick old lady until he took off his scarf and showed his dog collar.

That story had always amused Katy, but despite the town's shortcomings she had affection for it. Aside from the sea it had wide tree-lined roads, at least where she lived, and more lively towns like Hastings or Brighton were only bus rides away.

Rob had left the kitchen to take their mother her cocoa and cake, and as he came back in Katy was brought back to the present.

'Looks like the fire is coming under control now,' he said. 'But no one in there could've survived.'

Katy ran into the sitting room and looked out the window. Rob was right, the flames were no longer licking as vigorously up the front of the house, and the blaze in the front room appeared to have lowered. A lump came up in her throat, even if Mrs Reynolds was safely at her daughter's, losing her home and all her personal possessions was terrible. But much worse was the possibility that such a lovely woman had died in the fire. That was too tragic to even think on.

Rob came up behind her. 'Mr and Mrs Harding won't be able to go back in their house,' he said thoughtfully. 'It might not be burned as such, but the smoke will have damaged everything. They are old and frail and I don't think they've got any family to go to.'

Katy could think of nothing to say to that, so she pointed out she had sandwiches to make.

'Are you going to tell Mum and Dad you won't come home for the holidays again?' she asked her brother when they'd gone back in the kitchen. Rob was stoking up the Rayburn stove, as she made the sandwiches. 'Or just make excuses each time?'

Rob looked sheepish. 'I think the excuses route. I'm not as brave as you.'

'I think it's more diplomatic actually. I mean it won't make Dad so sad will it? I don't like the thought of walking away from him, but I suppose parents do expect their kids to leave at some time.'

'Maybe Mum will be nicer to Dad once they are alone?' Rob suggested.

Almost as if he'd heard his name mentioned the back door opened and Albert came in on a blast of icy cold air. 'Brrr, it's freezing out there,' he said, rubbing his hands together. 'Mr and Mrs Harding are going along to the Brady's down the road. They play Bridge with them, so it's better for them than here.'

'What about the Suttons?' Rob asked. They were the couple who lived on the other side of number 26.

'Well, as their house isn't attached to number 26 it hasn't burned. They went in with fireman to check it. They said it stinks of smoke but it's okay. Anyway, they are going to their daughters until it clears. She's on her way.'

'Did the firemen find out if Mrs Reynolds was in there?' Katy asked.

Albert frowned. 'They don't know yet. Mrs Harding said she was in earlier in the evening as she had heard her television. As it went off later, hopefully that means she went out. But the firemen can't get in there just yet to check, so we'll have to cross our fingers that she's safe somewhere else.'

'Do they have any idea of how the fire started?' Rob asked.

'I heard one of the policemen say they suspected arson. But they won't be able to confirm, or rule that out, until the fire is properly out and the house has cooled down,' he paused, his dark eyes glinting with what looked like emotional tears. 'If it was set deliberately and Mrs Reynolds died in there, I would want to personally burn the person that did that to her.'

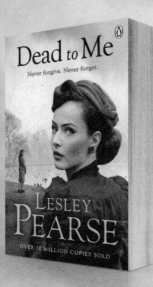

Dead to Me
Ruby and Verity become firm friends, despite coming from different worlds. However, fortunes are not set in stone and soon the girls find their situations reversed.

Without a Trace
On Coronation Day, 1953, Molly discovers that her friend is dead and her six-year-old daughter Petal has vanished. Molly is prepared to give up everything in finding Petal. But is she also risking her life?

Forgive Me

Eva's mother never told her the truth about her childhood. Now it is too late and she must retrace her mother's footsteps to look for answers. Will she ever discover the story of her birth?

Belle

(Belle book 1)

London, 1910, and the beautiful and innocent Belle Reilly is cruelly snatched from her home and sold to a brothel in New Orleans where she begins her life as a courtesan. Can Belle ever find her way home?

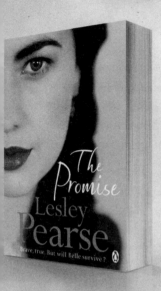

The Promise
(Belle book 2)
When Belle's husband heads for the trenches of northern France, she volunteers as a Red Cross ambulance driver. There, she is brought face to face with a man from her past who she'd never quite forgotten.

Survivor
(Belle book 3)
Eighteen-year-old Mari is defiant, selfish and has given up everything in favour of glamorous parties in the West End. But, without warning, the Blitz blows her new life apart. Can Mari learn from her mistakes before it's too late?

Stolen
A beautiful young woman is discovered half-drowned on a Sussex beach. Where has she come from? Why can't she remember who she is — or what happened?

Gypsy
Liverpool, 1893, and after tragedy strikes the Bolton family, Beth and her brother Sam embark on a dangerous journey to find their fortune in America.

Faith
Scotland, 1995, and Laura Brannigan is in prison for a murder she claims she didn't commit.

Hope
Somerset, 1836, and baby Hope is cast out from a world of privilege as proof of her mother's adultery.

A Lesser Evil
Bristol, the 1960s, and young Fifi
Brown defies her parents to marry
a man they think is beneath her.

Secrets
Adele Talbot escapes a children's
home to find her grandmother —
but soon her unhappy mother is
on her trail . . .

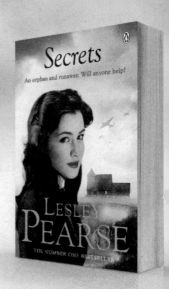

Remember Me
Mary Broad is transported to Australia as a convict and encounters both cruelty and passion. Can she make a life for herself so far from home?

Till We Meet Again
Susan and Beth were childhood friends. Now Susan is accused of murder, and Beth finds she must defend her.

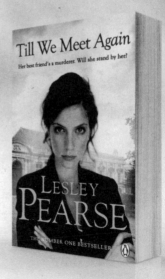

Father Unknown
Daisy Buchan is left a scrapbook with details about her real mother But should she go and find her?

Trust Me
Dulcie Taylor and her sister are sent to an orphanage and then to Australia. Is their love strong enough to keep them together?

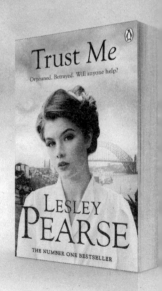

Never Look Back
An act of charity sends flower girl Matilda on a trip to the New World and a new life . . .

Charlie
Charlie helplessly watches her mother being senselessly attacked. What secrets have her parents kept from her?

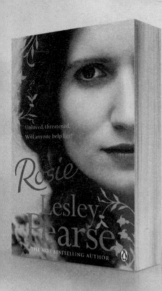

Rosie
Rosie is a girl without a mother, with a past full of trouble. But could the man who ruined her family also save Rosie?

Camellia
Orphaned Camellia discovers that the past she has always been so sure of has been built on lies. Can she bear to uncover the truth about herself?

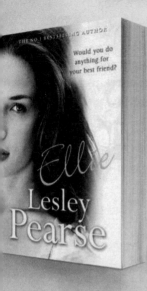

Ellie
Eastender Ellie and spoilt Bonny set off to make a living on the stage. Can their friendship survive sacrifice and ambition?

Charity
Charity Stratton's bleak life is changed for ever when her parents die in a fire. Alone and pregnant, she runs away to London . . .

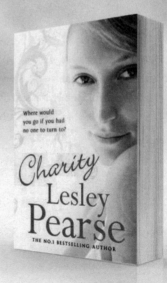

Tara
Anne changes her name to Tara to forget her shocking past — but can she really become someone else?

Georgia
Raped by her foster-father, fifteen-year-old Georgia runs away from home to the seedy back streets of Soho . . .

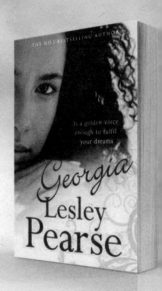